STATE OF EMERGENCY

FLOYD SALAS

Arte Público Press
Houston, Texas
1996

This volume is made possible through grants from the National Endowment for the Arts (a federal agency) and the Andrew W. Mellon Foundation.

Recovering the past, creating the future

Arte Público Press
University of Houston
Houston, Texas 77204-2090

Cover illustration and design by Robert Vega

Salas, Floyd, 1931-
    State of emergency / by Floyd Salas.
       p.   cm.
    ISBN 1-55885-093-7
    1. Americans—Travel—Europe—Fiction. 2. Novelists, American—Fiction. 3. Narcotic habit—Fiction. 4. Paranoia—Fiction. I. Title.
PS3569.A459S73   1996
813'.54—dc20   95-45264
                                   CIP

For Claire Ortalda

STATE OF EMERGENCY

Episode One

LONDON

1

Bent over under their backpacks, they walked out of the big house and down onto the wet sidewalk, hurrying in the misty rain. Penny had a knit cap pulled down tight on her head. Her long, reddish hair fanned out over her shoulders. Hatless, Roger's dark curly hair glistened with dampness.

Besides the pack on his back, Roger carried a big leather briefcase in one hand and a portable typewriter in the other. He turned his upper body around as he walked with his backpack as if checking to see if he was being tailed, and Leary stepped back on the porch across the street before Roger turned his way. He waited a few seconds, then peeked out with only one eye as they reached the corner.

They were about the same size: five and a half feet. Roger was a little taller, muscular but slim and wiry, too. Both were dressed in green Levis, though Roger had on a brown corduroy coat with a wool collar in the wet September London weather and Penny a blue navy peacoat.

Roger and Penny were on their way to Spain, and George Leary was going with them. Wherever they went, Leary was going. Whatever they did, Leary would know.

On the tube, underground, he got into the next car, and when they came out onto Charing Cross station and went to catch the train to Southampton, he stayed back in the crowd, not letting them see him at all yet. There were so many people in the big cavernous station—built of white-painted bricks a hundred years ago at least, with a hollow, reverberating echo—it was easy to follow them without being seen.

From back in the crowd, Leary watched them go to the ticket booth, buy their tickets, then hurry across the platform to the train, step into a car, take their backpacks off, put them on the opposite seat and sit down. Then Roger twisted around in his seat and looked over the whole car. Leary stayed back in the crowd, on the platform, until Roger faced forward again, then bought his ticket and got into the next car.

It was interesting to see how self-engrossed they were, as if they weren't leaving because they were unhappy in England. The bug in their bed-sitting room had told Leary everything. Roger knew the Company wanted to stop his book. Scotland Yard had been helpful to a member of the Company, had talked to the landlady and put the bug in the very first day, as soon as Roger and Penny went out to eat. And the Brigada de Investigación Social, the secret security force in Spain, was waiting right now, ready to move. Palma de Mallorca and Ibiza in the Balearic Islands were already cabled and waiting, too, because Roger had said he wanted to go there when he left San Francisco.

The trip down through the green, wet English countryside was uneventful. Leary got off at Southampton before they did to get a taxi. The train was running late and they might miss the ship across the channel, if they didn't hurry. He had to help them make it; doing them a favor was a good way to reintroduce himself to Roger.

They took their time getting out of their seats and putting their backpacks on, barely getting out the door onto the train platform before it closed. Leary hurried out to the street and waved down a big black cab, then got in the back and said, "There's a couple coming out now. Wait for them." He gave the driver a pound note. The guy didn't even turn around, just nodded and waited. All Leary could see of him was the back of his sandy hair.

Roger came out first and headed straight for the cab right in front of the station. It was almost dark already, and all the station lights were lit, too, so it was easy to see him come rushing out, Penny following, hurrying to keep up, bent over from the big backpack.

Leary threw open the back door of the cab and said, "Hey! Good to see you! Jump in!"

Roger stopped and stared, looked surprised, and said, "Are you going to Bilbao?"

"Yes! Get in, if you want to make it!"

Leary slid over, and Roger put his typewriter and briefcase down on the wide floor of the back seat, slid out of his pack and dumped it next to them. He then helped Penny out of hers, slid it in next to his, and let her get in first.

"The wharf and the ship to Spain," Leary said, and the driver put the car in gear and moved out into the traffic.

"You going to Spain, too, huh?" Roger said, settling back, putting his arm around Penny as if to let Leary know she was his.

"Sure! I would have told you that if you hadn't run off so quickly at the bed and breakfast place."

"Where to in Spain?" Roger said, ignoring the breakfast reference.

"Anywhere! Down into the sun! I'm taking my time. How about you?" Leary asked, putting it right back on Roger.

Roger looked over at him from the corners of his green eyes, dark in the soft darkness of the cab. "We're doing the same thing. Though we may try to go to my father's village in León."

"Your family came from there?"

"Yeah, this one branch of it. My father's grandfather on his father's side—my great-grandfather. It's a small village outside the city of Leon, near the Atlantic Coast. The other branches have supposedly been in the United States since Ponce de León came."

"Interesting," Leary said, knowing who else he had to contact now. This could get good.

"Where you from?" Roger asked.

"Family came from Ireland in the nineteenth century, potato-famine immigrants," Leary said. "Your girlfriend? Penny's her name, I think."

"British Isles on both sides," she said, and she looked English with her pale, slightly freckled skin.

The streetlights flashed on Roger's face, and Leary could see him staring at him from the dark corner of the cab.

2

On board, Leary stayed to himself. Better this way. Follow Roger without bothering him. That night, his leather coat collar up around his neck, Leary watched him through the glass doors from the deck outside the dining room, where the band was playing. Some middle-aged Spaniards danced it up. One bald man with a pale, glistening skull really enjoyed himself. He kept watching Roger and Penny jitterbug to swing music. Roger was very graceful and Penny was good, too. They took synchronized steps, bouncing and swaying in perfect time to the music on the swaying ship.

Leary had read in the report that Roger was an exceptional dancer, which gave Leary something else to use on him. Still, he did like watching them. Roger could really dance, with an athlete's easy, rhythmical movements. The band was mediocre, all gray-haired old pros. But the music helped put Roger in a good mood—he'd be approachable. Leary was waiting to greet Roger when he came out on the deck about eleven, leading Penny by the hand.

"You boogied pretty good there," Leary said.

Roger smiled, showing his even teeth. Then, as if trying to be friendly, he asked, "How's the weather looking? Is it going to get warmer in Spain?"

"According to a radio report, it'll be choppy all across the channel to Spain," Leary said. He didn't add that the weather report had also said storm.

"Too bad," Roger said. "We left London to get away from the wet weather. We need to get someplace where it's warm and friendly, and I can write in peace."

He smiled at Leary, who smiled and stepped back to let them go on their way.

3

The next day it got bad. The ship pitched and dipped and people threw up slippery, messy breakfasts all over the deck. Leary saw Roger alone on deck and later alone in the bar having a beer. He guessed that Penny was seasick, but he stayed away, content to follow Roger without bothering him. Roger wasn't going any place Leary wasn't going, and there was plenty of time to talk to him. They wouldn't dock in Bilbao until the next day, and they'd get off together. He wondered where Roger smoked the hashish he bought from Robey O'Brian in London, since the men and the women were separated on board and Roger shared his cabin with three other men just down the hall from Leary. It must have been somewhere on deck or in a public restroom. The Brigada Investigación would want to know that, and, from what he knew of them, they didn't mess around. Franco kept a firm hand.

4

Roger didn't get sick and Leary didn't either because he had sail-boated all over Puget Sound as a kid with his father. He had his sea legs, and Roger had a sound body. He ran four miles a day, the report had said. The guy was deep into his thirties but stayed in shape. That could cause problems, too.

Leary got off with Roger and Penny in wet Bilbao, although the rain had let up for a while. But when Roger complained at the wharf about having to wait for the bus for the five-mile-or-so drive into town, Leary said, "Let's take a taxi." And they were back together in a taxi again, in the most natural way.

"I don't like this wet weather. I didn't come all the way from San Francisco to sniffle in the damn cold," Roger said as they rode in the old cab toward the city.

"If your great-grandfather's village is in the mountains anywhere in Northern Spain, the weather's not going to be very good until next spring," Leary said. "Why don't you head south? The Mediterranean's warm until December, and pretty warm even then."

"That's an idea!" Roger said, and touched Penny's arm. She was wearing her blue peacoat, and her round cheeks were rosy in the cold weather. Long lashes hung over her big green eyes. She didn't look a day over nineteen. A cute little thing.

"I don't like the cold weather, either, Roger, but you said you wanted to go to your great-grandfather's village. If you go south, you won't do it," she said.

"Maybe next year, if you're still going to be around," Leary said.

Roger nodded and said, "I sure don't like the wet weather."

Leary nodded now to encourage him, but Penny said, "What are you doing, Leary?"

"I'm heading south. Enjoy your company, if you come along," he said, not pushing them.

"When does the train leave for Madrid?" Roger asked.

"In a half-hour, and it's not raining up in the Pyrenees, away from the coast," Leary answered.

"I'm going, then. You wanna go, Penny?"

"Sure," she said, taking a deep breath, then looked up at Leary as if searching his eyes.

He looked away, out the window at the old dark buildings of Bilbao and said, "The train station's pretty close now."

5

Leary was walking with them in the big depot to their train when they passed a couple of hundred pale-skinned young Spaniards, all in civilian clothes, lined up next to a coach car to go to military training camp. Penny had on her bell-bottomed blue jeans and was carrying her backpack. When the Spaniards saw her, they started whistling. Then all of them joined in and their whistles exploded in the station with a huge, piercing, prolonged shriek.

Leary looked over at her, and so did Roger who frowned as Penny's face turned bright red.

They sat in a compartment together and Leary started reading a book on the radical student personality. He saw Roger glance at the cover, but didn't say anything. Leary didn't either, but it still might provoke a good, informative conversation later on. About a half-hour after they had left the depot and were passing through the Pyrenees Mountains, Roger got up, stepped out of the compartment and walked down the corridor. Leary waited a couple of minutes, then closed his book, got up and asked, "Which way are the lavatories, you know?"

Penny just pointed in the direction Roger had taken and looked out the window again.

Leary walked down the narrow corridor outside the compartments until he got to the lavatory. He tried the door. It was locked. He leaned against the wall and waited. It took Roger a long time, and when he finally came out, the toilet was still flushing. Roger looked up at him with pale, greenish eyes, but didn't say anything. The smell of burnt matches was strong in the lavatory, and Leary knew what Roger had been doing. Investigation was the name of the game.

Roger didn't talk to him when he got back, and Leary put his nose in his book and only closed it when they rode high into the mountains and stopped at a village. Roger and Penny opened their windows to buy sandwiches of *salchichón*, a type of salami, on crunchy rolls from a vendor. Leary bought one, too. Still, Roger didn't start any conversations, and Leary figured Roger suspected he had purposely followed him to the lavatory. Leary kept reading over the Pyrenees and down into the wide plain to Madrid, well into the late afternoon, when he decided he'd better let Roger and Penny go their own way.

There'd be a surveillance team waiting anyway. They knew what Leary looked like, and they knew what Roger and Penny looked like, so there'd be no problem. He could pick him up later on the trip. Roger'd go to Mallorca and Ibiza. He'd been talking about that since he first got his plane tickets last spring with his State College friends, Ruth and Craig, according to the report. Ruth and Craig were cooperating. They had called Leary as soon as Roger called Craig a punk in London.

He shouldn't have followed Roger to the toilet, but it was too late now. Roger was taking off with Penny and away from his surveillance. Leary had to get Roger away from Penny and completely alone, then get a woman agent in bed with him. Then Leary would have control. That was the plan. And if that didn't work, he'd try to get Penny to cooperate. But that was very touchy. She loved Roger. She had been a virgin when she met him as a student in the creative writing class he taught, and they had lived together since June, '67, over a year now. But Roger had said once during a quarrel that he didn't trust her. That was enough to work on if Leary had to.

Outside the depot, a fair-haired cabby talked to them in German at first, as if he guessed they were German students, then in English, telling them he'd take them to a nice pension that was cheap.

"I'm going to go look for a friend who might put me up. Mind if I don't come along?" Leary asked, leaving it up to Roger whether or not he went with them. Roger just looked up with his green eyes and nodded.

6

The Company office in Madrid was ready. Debono—his olive Italian-American skin wrinkling up behind his rimless glasses—got up to meet Leary and shook his hand hard. Leary could see past him, out the window, down onto the busy Madrid street, a typical, crowded European scene. Well-dressed men and women passed each other on the sidewalk.

"I've already made contacts with Spanish Security here, in Barcelona, and Mallorca," Debono said. "That middle-aged, bald-headed man who danced his heart out on the ship was their first ploy. To make him think the Spanish people were happy and outgoing like him, to make him feel at home."

"Coopt him, then?" Leary said, tilting back his head and looking down on the shorter man with his pale-green eyes.

"The usual procedure," Debono said. "But he's different; that's why you were chosen. With your literary education, you can talk books to him, and your Irish Catholic background fits right in with the Irish strain on his mother's side.

"Use his Catholic idealism, you mean?"

"Yes. Anything you can. But stop him from writing that book. That's the point. It could really endanger some people pretty high up among the student radicals, the older commies and the liberal pinko professors in San Francisco who cooperate with us. But most of all, it might blow the cover on some of our own men and how we work. Some of those student radicals might try to kill them. They'll do anything to stop the war in Viet Nam." Debono rocked his head a little. "You know what I mean."

"Sure, I know," Leary said, noticing how the patches of window light on the surface of Debono's glasses hid the wrinkles around his dark-brown eyes. "It's a worldwide revolt that's spreading from the American colleges. And a book like this could help fan the flames. I'll stop it."

"How else we gonna handle the bastards," Debono said, "when they cut every corner they can, and use the constitution against us? We've got a hard enough battle with the communist infiltrators in the Spanish labor unions and the liberal members of the Spanish press, who fight America while pretending just to be against Franco. Now we have to mess around with some misguided idealist from America who could maybe fall in with the Basque terrorists and cause some real trouble, not to mention bad publicity for us with his lousy book. It's a pain in the ass," Debono said, shaking his head. His high forehead rippled with lines up into the thinning, graying hair.

"I'll handle it, I said," Leary said.

"You'll have lots of help. Spanish Security is right now on his tail. The cabdriver took him right to the *pensión* where the Senora has already worked with us. Wherever he goes, he'll be followed by different surveillance teams until he settles down and you can arrange to have our agents start to work. Mallorca's ready to go, and Robey O'Brian's going to Ibiza. All you have to do is get there and run the show. Lots of help. Lots. But stop that book, or get him to change it."

"There's no Company office in Mallorca?"

Debono looked up, little puffy sacks under his eyes.

"No, only Madrid, Barcelona and Bilbao, but you've got lots of help. Lots of help."

"Where's he going next?"

"According to the bug in the *pensión*, Valencia, and from there to Palma de Mallorca," Debono said.

"I better get going then, and make contacts with Spanish Security in Mallorca. See what they've got cooked up. But the main thing should be to break him away from Penny Lawson, if he persists on that book."

"Work on it. Mallorca and Ibiza are full of women."

"He's supposed to really like the women," Leary said, frowning, trying to think of how he could do it.

"That should make it easy," Debono said, smiling again, the whole length of his long brown face rippled with wrinkles. Leary smiled, too.

7

Dumb, that's what Roger was. So smart and yet so dumb. Idealistic and naive. A dupe of a worldwide Communist conspiracy. Those commies will use him and all those spoiled college kids to bring down America, if they can. He'll play right into the hands of the commies, but not if George Leary can help it. Because what America had was the best there was—

even if wasn't perfect—then the thing to do was to keep it that way, and that was Leary's job as a security agent: to keep things secure; to keep guys like Roger, who thought they were so pure, from messing things up.

George Leary had read all those books on liberation, too. People wanting to be free is how America came to be, and that's how it was going to stay without bringing down the free enterprise system. Keep democracy even if it took a little deceit, a little twisting of the knot around the throat sometimes, to bring people to their senses. But that's the way life was. It'd be silly not to do it. Silly not to have an intelligence force capable of holding off the forces of Communism all over the world that were fighting to control the land mass, and through that, the economy of the world. No matter what idealists like Roger wrote, the world was tough, and death was the order of the day if you didn't have your two fists up.

Leary was a cop. He might be educated and wear plainclothes, but he was still a cop, like his father. Cops and priests, that's what came out of his family, and so he was a step up from his father who was only a patrolman for twenty years and didn't get to be a sergeant until he got gray hair. He, himself, could have gone to a seminary like his uncle and studied for the priesthood like his mother had wanted him to after he got his degree. It was that close between the Church and the Company for him. Both gave him a sense of security. Both kept society in order—one spiritual, one law enforcement—but both watchdogs. A watchdog, that's what he was, and watch Roger he would, stop Roger he would. Roger would be stopped.

8

The camera was pointed right at him. He saw it at the girl's waist, her dark head bent over it, saw her thumb go up and down on it just as he stepped through a puddle on the asphalt landing field, the whole field the color and wetness of the English sky. His hazel eyes, gray now in the drizzly light, quickened with the fluttering in his chest, but he toughed it out, didn't falter a step, kept walking straight toward her and the tall man next to her in the dark suit, white shirt and tie, who reminded him, when he first saw him on the plane, of the cop who had been tailing him in San Francisco. The girl turned away through the big, open door of Heathrow Airport without looking at him, but he recognized her blue suit and thick legs as the one who sat with the man behind Craig and Ruth on the State College charter plane to London. He then turned to see if Penny had been caught in the picture.

She stepped gracefully through the wide puddle, only a couple of steps behind, her shapely legs showing clear to the thighs in her miniskirt, but her large green eyes narrowed as if she had seen the camera. She knew how much that bothered him and hurried to catch up, then took his arm and stepped with him into the large customs room filled with student tourists from San Francisco State College. Most of the young men and women, except for a few like the guy with the girl, were dressed in hip clothing—leather vests and jackets with long buckskin fringes, bell-bottomed trousers, blue jeans and miniskirts. They crowded into long lines in front of the customs inspectors, the room buzzing with chatter. That's why the girl, who looked like she had on a Catholic school uniform, and the man in his white shirt and tie, had been so noticeable.

"Get in line and keep a place for us while I go get the bags, Penny," he said, without mentioning the camera, not wanting to trouble her. Her mouth twitched in a smile, and she squeezed his arm as he turned away, making him feel a little better.

He walked toward the baggage trailers parked in a line against the wall at one end of the large room, looking for the man and the girl as he worked his way through the crowd, hoping he wouldn't see them, sick of all that secret-agent stuff going on back in America. He wished right now he'd never got involved in the student strike and hadn't hit that cop who tried to club Penny at the administration building, that he had not got himself clubbed and arrested. The next day, his picture was in the paper, under the headline: WRITER LEADS STUDENT CHARGE. They started following him from the jail that very morning, as soon as Penny bailed him out. There was no way out. He was already involved and he was going to write that book about it, too—all about the dirty tricks of the FBI and the CIA, like the girl and her camera, trying to suppress democracy on the campus, just to keep the war machine going. It was going to be a blockbuster of a book, too—exciting, thrilling, moving.

Craig's sandy hair and plastic-rimmed glasses stood out above the heads around him. Preoccupied as usual, he didn't see Roger. Though he didn't seem to be worried about the ounce of hashish he was smuggling into the country with him. His wife, Ruth, her blue eyes striking with her pale skin and long, black wavy hair, had made a big show of offering Roger a grass cookie on the plane, with a smile that had too many teeth showing for him, especially with that man and girl sitting right behind her staring at him. He had hesitated in mid-reach, glancing at them, and didn't take the cookie until they both looked out the window.

Roger kept looking for them now, to see if they were still watching him as Craig picked up two bags and moved slowly through the crowd to Ruth, who stood in the line next to Penny. The girls hadn't been too friendly with each other since Roger had written that poem about Ruth last spring, when they all lived together. It had been a moment of illumination, inspired by Ruth's beauty by candlelight at dinner, and everybody praised it, even Penny, though she got tears in her eyes. Ruth had started coming on to him then, spreading her legs, rubbing up against him, kissing his neck, giving him the blue eyes, smiling. Penny had left him and come back. Ruth was married and it was now past.

Roger picked up his and Penny's briefcases and backpacks and hurried through the crowd to Penny. Ruth smiled again. He shook his curly head and walked away, remembering how Ruth had turned tiger when he didn't return her advances after the poem.

Roger and Penny reached their customs inspector just after Craig and Ruth reached theirs. But Craig's inspector just stamped both their passports and let them through, while Roger's inspector studied his passport for several moments, then looked up and, staring through rimless glasses, asked, "How long do you plaun to stay in England?"

"I don't know," Roger said, shrugging the shoulders of his green, bell-bottomed corduroy suit, beginning to worry they might not let him in. "Maybe two months? Depending on what happens."

"Oh, we could be here six months," Penny said.

"And we could leave right away, too," Roger said, raising his voice so she'd stay out of it.

"How much money do you hauve?" the customs man asked, rimless glasses glimmering with light. Roger stared at him, trying to outguess the guy. His short black wavy hair was combed straight back and in perfect order. His square face was perfectly symmetrical, and precise and direct as his speech; Roger couldn't read it.

"About...three-thousand dollars."

"Show it to me," the customs man said.

Roger's cheeks reddened with anger, but he reached into the inner pocket of his suit coat, pulled out his book of travelers checks and handed it to the customs man. The inspector ruffled quickly through them to the last check. He stared at the number on it as if multiplying in his head, then handed them back, and asked, "Are there any 'matings' that you plaun to attend while here?"

"'Matings?'" Roger asked, but the customs man just stared at him through his glasses, and Roger turned to Penny.

"Meetings," she said.

"Oh, none," Roger said, turning back to the man, seeing that the man didn't even look at Penny and was searching for something that would decide whether he let him in or not.

"No dates at all that you plaun to keep?" the man persisted. The guy in the white shirt and tie on the plane and the camera now seemed even more significant. They suspected Roger of something, yet they didn't seem to know anything at all about his planned book yet.

"None at all," Roger answered in a low, weary voice. Then he suddenly remembered there was supposed to be a big "Demo" in London in October that a young Trotskyite leader had told him to attend. But he was leaving the U. S. to get away from all that: agents all over the rioting campus, funny noises on the phone, guys following him.

The inspector opened Roger's backpack and began to search through the clothes, squeezing the socks folded into balls; sticking his fingers into the hiking boots, as if looking for lids of grass; examining each piece of toiletry, from the shaving cream to the case with the razor in it.

Roger sighed, lips parting, his enthusiasm at coming to England seeping out of him. More suspicion and paranoia, fear of getting busted. Sadness over the killing of King and

Kennedy. Everything he had hoped to leave behind in America and write about without fear in Europe. He felt like a simpleton for thinking they'd leave him be after all the publicity he'd gotten for fighting both the secret police and the student party leaders in an attempt to keep the strike democratic. WRITER LEADS STUDENT CHARGE.

The inspector finally finished going through the backpack and opened Roger's briefcase, shifting quickly through it. He then took out a large manila envelope with the word BROTHERS hand-printed on it. It held the novel Roger had gotten an advance on, but didn't want to write now.

The inspector put it back and picked up the manila envelope with BODY also hand-printed on it, and a pulse of fear shot through Roger. It had all his notes for a novel on radical campus politics, one he wanted to write on the workings of the secret police, the collaboration with them of some student leaders and old Stalinist reds, and how this tied in with his own persecution and the murders of the Kennedys. The envelope could cause problems, maybe keep him out of the country, and get him sent right back to the political mess he was trying to leave so he could write his book in peace. The inspector would think he came to join the Demo if he looked at those notes.

Roger breathed again when the man put the envelope back in the briefcase and flipped through a leather-bound manuscript of poems called PRAYERS OF HERESY. They were about the modern rebel messiah shunned and stoned by the people he was trying to save. The inspector put the manuscript back in the briefcase, too, without once glancing at Roger. He then merely opened Penny's backpack, glanced inside, closed it, did the same with her briefcase and the typewriter, then stamped both their passports and waved them through. Roger stepped past him with a big sigh of relief.

9

"Glad we get to go into London together," Craig said when Roger put his backpack on the baggage truck without even mentioning the hassle the guy had just put Roger through.

Without answering, Roger stepped out onto the platform to wait for the train and get away from the phony face.

The view touched him. The sun had come out from the clouds just before it set over the wet, green English countryside, streaking the smoky sky with orange and tinting the shiny tracks that stretched off into the distance a burnished gold. Only tiny red lights showed in the far darkness, and a sad, sweet kind of melancholy came over him.

"Don't worry," Penny said, slipping her arms around his waist and pressing herself against his back. "Everything's going to be all right. Your second book's coming out in January, and we're going to find a place where you can work on your book about the student strike without being bothered by the police anymore."

He cupped his hands over hers and pressed them against him, then, still in her arms, twisted around, put his arms around her, pulled her small, shapely waist hard against his, and kissed her.

10

Craig pulled two stainless steel bolts out of his shirt pocket and screwed each one to the end of the threaded inch-long connecting stem. He fitted them together into a hashish pipe, then glanced out the window at the wet night sky and said, "Let's have a hit before we go get something to eat, Roger. I need something to perk me up. This jet lag's got me sleepy."

Roger nodded from his cot, the last in the row in the long room they had taken together in the only bed-and-breakfast house that had a vacancy. He still couldn't forget the trouble he'd had getting into the country and he watched Craig, who'd had no trouble at all, closely. The lamp light was so dim that Craig's eyes looked as colorless as water through his rimless glasses. The whole room was shadowy.

"I'm hungry now," Ruth said from her cot near Craig.

"It'll just take a minute, honey," Craig said, and reached into a folded-over cigarette package, bringing out a cube of dark hashish. He cut some off with his pocketknife, stuffed it into the bolt with a well in it, then lit a match and puffed through the hole on the other bolt. The cube glowed red in the dim light.

"What are your plans, Roger?" he asked with a tight mouth, holding the smoke down, handing the pipe to Ruth, who rushed it to her mouth trying to keep the ember lit.

Roger waited to see if the ember glowed and the hash kept burning, giving himself time to think, afraid Craig was up to something. "I need to find a place right away so I can start writing a novel on the student strike at State," he finally answered.

Craig blew a cloud of smoke and said, "Student strike! I thought you were going to write that book about you and your brother called BROTHERS. I thought you had a contract on it?"

His eyes looked as big and accusing as his glasses.

"I do have a contract on it, but..." He paused, then only said, "I'm not excited about it like I am about the idea of doing a book on the student strike."

Ruth handed the pipe to Penny, who puffed on it, barely keeping it lit. She handed it to Roger, who sucked on it, but couldn't keep the ember smoldering. He beckoned to Craig for the matchbook.

Craig held it in his hand but, instead of throwing it, said, "You ought to fulfill the contract; that's the only proper thing to do."

"What'a you mean?" Roger asked, and beckoned again.

"Well," Craig said, still not throwing the matches to him. "They were pretty nice to give you the contract and you already substituted *Kilo* for it, so it seems you ought to fulfill the terms of the contract, sometime, at least." His mouth was tight as if talking to an irresponsible child.

"Throw me the matchbook, man, and, besides, I've already filled the contract by giving them *Kilo*. Throw it!"

Craig flipped the matchbook over the cots. Roger dropped one hand over the edge of his cot and caught it. He lit a match and sucked in a big enough blast of smoke to hurt his lungs and make sure he'd get high off the hit. He held it down, chest puffing up, aching, determined not to tell his real reasons for wanting to write the book on the strike. He held the smoke until he couldn't hold it any longer, then blew it out in a big stream toward Craig. Then, in spite of himself, he said, "Do you think the students would be striking if we had a working democracy? The strike was more than just to stop the Vietnam War. It was against the military-industrial complex, against the collusion between the corporations, the politicians and the police—including the FBI and the CIA—against everybody who keeps the country in a state of war in order to make profits."

"I thought you had enough of all that stuff? That you left the country to get away from all that?" Craig said, shaking his head.

Both Penny and Ruth wouldn't look at Roger, as if he were causing trouble.

Roger held the pipe up to his mouth, then remembered that it was Craig's turn and passed it to Penny with the matches. She then handed it to Ruth, who gave it to Craig. But he didn't light it, as if waiting for Roger to answer first.

"I did have enough of it, and that's why I did leave the country, but the same police mentality that made an outlaw out of me for smoking pot killed Bobby Kennedy and Martin Luther King, and keeps the war going now," Roger said, starting to get irritated, feeling himself being sucked in.

Craig lit the pipe again and sucked furiously at it, a crease between his brows. He then held the smoke in, staring at Roger through his glasses, his eyes hard and brittle. Finally, he blew the smoke out and said again, "I thought you had enough of that, Roger. I thought you said you had signed a separate peace and didn't want trouble with the police anymore. I thought you said that you had paid so many dues being persecuted by the police over smoking pot that you were never going to fight them again?"

"They never stopped persecuting me!" Roger said, feeling like he was losing it. "They just allowed me to live a little. That's all. The hunt still goes on. Why shouldn't I fight back?"

Craig held up the pipe and stared at it as if to see if it were lit, but Roger knew he was ignoring his comment.

"Because you're not being an artist. You're being a politician. You should be writing about your brother and you and make literature out of that instead," he finally said. But when Roger sat up to answer him, he focused his eyes on the pipe again, as if it took all his attention.

Penny straightened up, too. Roger, seeing the worried look on her sweet, round face, said, "My motive as an artist is to write about the great experiences of my life, of my time."

Penny's face smoothed somewhat, though she still watched him closely.

"So what's the point? What's that got to do with the strike?" Craig said through a tight mouth, holding the smoke in again.

"I'll tell you what the point is," Roger said, raising his voice. "I'm going to write a book that tries to stop the Vietnamese War, that tells of all the dirty tricks the secret police, like the FBI and CIA, played during the strike, how they corrupted the movement and got the old reds and young students to spy on each other for them."

Craig's colorless eyes met Roger's just for a moment, then switched away when he lit another match and held it to the pipe without lighting it. "Why don't you just write your book about you and your brother? That's controversial enough, and you won't cause so much trouble for yourself."

"Trouble for myself?" Roger shouted. "I had trouble getting in here! Remember? I got my picture taken! I got held up at customs, while you were holding hash, and yet you walked right in! They're already messing with me! They've never stopped! We live in a democracy in America, remember? Where I have human rights and the right to object when I'm not treated fairly or disagree! And I mean object in a big way, with a book!"

Craig looked over the pipe at him as he sucked on the chrome nut. Finally, he blew his breath out and his words seemed to smoke as he spoke. "You're going to cause a lot of trouble, Roger, and it's going to backfire on you."

A hot flash of anger burned Roger's cheeks and he jumped off the cot.

"What is it? Don't you want me to tell on you?" he said. "The other students didn't trust you at the strike and they finally did trust me. You were so conservative, they thought you were a police informer, remember? Remember that? Maybe you just don't want me to tell on you? Maybe that's your real reason, huh?"

Craig's full cheeks darkened with a blush, then he set the pipe down and said, "You're really looking for trouble, Roger. And you'll probably get it."

11

"You can buy dope in all the big cities, if you want to risk yourself," the American said, and looked at Roger. "But the governments look down on it, of course, and you're taking a chance on getting busted."

The guy was sitting with Craig in the breakfast room in the basement of their building late in the morning.

Roger looked him over, suddenly cautious. He was a big American in his late twenties or early thirties who looked like someone Roger knew. Then he realized the guy had the thick wavy dark hair, the handsome bevel-shaped face, and the bright green eyes of Teddy Kennedy. And the cops knew he liked the Kennedys! They could have brought the guy to him for that reason!

The radio was playing swing music out of the forties. The rest of the room had that forties look, too, like the English spy movies made in World War II. The radio was a table model with cloth over the speaker and antique rococo wood trim. Starched, ruffled curtains with big yellow bows on them hung over the high, street-level windows, and the old-fashioned sofas around the room were a worn brown color in arabesque print.

The American shrugged and cut a piece of sausage with his fork. "Some people don't think it's worth it—the chance of ruining their vacations, or whatever." He put sausage in his mouth and chewed.

Craig said, "Roger's not here on vacation. He's here to write a book. And he claims it's his right as a writer to smoke pot."

He looked across the table at Roger with what seemed a superior glint in his eyes, a smile like a thin line below the frosty surface of his glasses. But Craig sounded as if he were still annoyed over Roger saying the students thought he was a police informer, and Roger didn't want to get sucked into talking about dope in public with a stranger, even if he did look like Teddy Kennedy.

When the big guy looked at him with his bright magnetic green eyes, Roger said, "Well, 'right' might be too strong a word. Who are you?"

"George Leary, by way of Boston," the guy said, and stuck out his hand.

"What do you do?" Roger said, taking the guy's hand, but still asking the questions. Leary had a solid grip.

"Graduate Comparative Lit major from Harvard," he said, and smiled, his eyes penetrating. "I got a BA in accounting though, English minor."

"Why did you switch to Lit?" Roger asked, still trying to make Leary reveal himself, remembering Craig's warning threat that he was asking for trouble and would probably get it.

"It's what I love, but I've got to earn a decent living, too. I don't want to live on a teacher's salary, so I'll earn a decent living doing accounting and enjoy the pursuit of literature as a hobby," Leary said.

"That makes sense, if you don't want to write yourself," Roger said.

Leary smiled. ""But you write, I gather?"

"He wrote *Every Mutha's Son*," Craig said, but he didn't smile. "It won some awards."

Leary raised an eyebrow, but his green eyes looked opaque. "Because you won awards for a book you wrote high? Is that why you think smoking pot is your right?"

"Lots of the great writers used drugs. Even Goethe drank a bottle of wine in the evenings before he began to write," Roger said. He sat up and leaned his chest against the table, holding up one hand to gesture, and saw Leary and Craig glance at each other. "Nietzsche took a tablespoon of chloral hydrate every day, which is sleeping medicine, and it drove him crazy. Baudelaire, the greatest poet of them all, and Edgar Allan Poe, both took hashish and opium. So did Rimbaud and Verlaine."

"Well, but Poe was pretty weird," Leary said, grinning, "and Verlaine shot Rimbaud for leaving him." He pointed at Roger. "And you just said the chloral hydrate drove Nietzsche nuts. So you can't say drugs helped them out, in the long run."

Craig smiled at Roger with smug, thin lips.

Although Roger sensed that it could be a trap and he should shut up, he said, "In the long run, they all produced great art." He held up both hands. "And how about Coleridge then? And De Quincy? Both from right here, from England. And Maulraux from France? They all used drugs and weren't destroyed. Maulraux is the minister of culture right now! Coleridge wrote his masterpiece, "Kubla Kahn," while experiencing an opium dream. Maulraux smuggled a kilo of hashish out of Cambodia as a young man before he wrote his classic novels!"

"So some didn't get destroyed," Leary said, grinning again, a lump of sausage in his cheek. He chewed and swallowed. "Why don't you just admit you like to get high like the rest of us? Why elevate it to the level of an artistic rite?"

"I didn't bring up the subject," Roger said, pointing at Leary now. "You said we could buy dope in all the big cities here in Europe."

"Because he asked me if there was any around London, that's why," Leary said, sticking his chin up at Craig. Craig nodded.

No longer suspicious, Roger said, "Smoking pot wasn't against the law in America until 1936, after Anslinger was put out of a job by the repeal of prohibition and went around the country preaching against marijuana so he could get another job suppressing people and curtailing their liberty."

"That's funny," Leary said "I like that. Making a drug illegal so cops can have jobs." He smiled at Craig.

Roger slid his chair back and said, "Listen, man, that's a fact. But I don't want to argue about who made it against the law. The real fact is that you went to jail for drinking in the Roaring Twenties, and you go to jail for smoking pot now. That's the point! Think of all the great writers in America in this century who were lushes and broke the law during Prohibition! Fitzgerald! Wolfe! Steinbeck! Faulkner! The artist has a right to use drugs if they help him create."

Leary shook his head. "Look, anyone who knows me knows I like to get a little buzz on myself, but you tell me how pot, or alcohol for that matter, helps an artist create. I mean, why can't you admit you just like the high?"

Roger slid onto the edge of his chair, leaned against the table again, and looked the guy right in the eye. He sensed that maybe he was being led on, but he wanted to explain. It was important. "This is how it works," he said, raising one finger. "All drugs put the brain to sleep. That's why if you drink too much, you'll pass out."

"So?" Leary said.

"So, if you use the drug sparingly, you can put your brain to sleep just a little bit."

"So?"

"So you can have the best of both minds simultaneously. You can daydream on paper without having to struggle to invent, like Poe did in his short stories, like Coleridge did with "Kubla Kahn", and Faulkner with the retarded mind of Benjie in his novel, "The Sound and the Fury". He wrote it on white lightning booze when it was against the law."

"So you're equating yourself with Faulkner?" Leary said, glancing at Craig, whose glasses frosted with the bright light.

Roger shook his head and almost shut up, sure now that he was being pumped. But he'd already spoken out and he wasn't stopping out of fear.

"I'm an artist, too, and I have the right to use a mild, outlawed drug, pot, if Faulkner had the right to use an outlawed drug, booze, to create a masterpiece."

Craig smirked and Leary asked, "Are you saying that you have the right to break the law if you can create masterpieces?"

Roger felt his face get hot. "Yes."

"Are you saying that you can create masterpieces?"

Roger blushed again, then said, "Don't try to drag me into that! I'm saying that I have a right to use a drug if I don't commit evil with it. I have a right to practice my art in any way I choose, if I don't interfere with the happiness of others."

"Well, like I said," Leary said, holding up his fork, "I like to get high, too, every once in a while, but I certainly don't put myself above the law."

"I'm NOT putting myself above the law. I'm saying we should change the law, like we did with Prohibition. We should make pot legal like it was before Anslinger and 1936. It's the mildest drug known to man. It's beneficial. Pot will pacify man, not excite him to violence like booze. It's the drug of this Love Generation, remember? Pot will help create a world without war by making man more passive and loving."

"And then he'll get destroyed," Leary said. "Man has got to have a killer instinct. Booze is good in that way."

"I'll still work with my art to change the law, so I can smoke pot legally. Like Shelley said, 'Writers are the unacknowledged legislators of the world!' I'm going to preach the

religion of humanity with my art. The artist as priest and pot
as a ritual tool, a political and religious right."

"The religion of humanity sounds to this Catholic boy like
buzzwords for the kind of humanism that rejects Christianity," Leary said, not smiling now. He dropped his knife and
fork with a clatter into the center of his egg-streaked plate
and pushed it away from him toward Roger.

"I don't reject Christianity. Not the humanity of it," Roger
said, looking at the dirty plate, then raising his eyes to Leary.
"I want to live like a true Christian through my art, the closest thing to immortality I believe I can realistically reach! And
I can make that attempt now while I live, and pot is one of my
ritual tools, my rite, r-i-t-e, my right!" He suddenly realized
that he was standing up.

"How are you going to carry it in Europe then, Roger?"
Craig asked.

"In a natural way," Roger said without thinking, lifting
one hand and opening the palm in an explanatory gesture, as
if there were no problem. He suddenly saw Leary's green eyes
fixed on him, and he stopped with his hand still in the air,
feeling like a fool for being taken when he'd guessed it was a
trap all the time.

"Let's get out of here, Craig. You've already got your
room. How about showing us how to find one?" he said with an
angry snap to his voice.

12

Craig rang the bell of the neat brick building, looked
down at Roger and said, "His name is Robey. He's got a wild
natural. He's really a hippy. He said he might have some dope
for sale. Then you can start writing your book about the
strike."

When Roger just nodded without answering, Craig smiled
and said, "I'm sure glad you got a bed-sitter room so fast and
so close to us. We can have a lot of fun together, especially
after we get the dope."

Roger nodded again, thinking Craig was trying to make
up for exposing him in front of that guy at breakfast, but willing to accept the offer for the sake of friendship and the

chance to get some dope on his own, since Craig hadn't offered to share his hash stash with him. He looked up quickly when the door opened and saw a skinny hippy with wild, curly blond hair teased out a foot long around his bony face standing there.

"Come in," the guy said. His thin mouth with its crooked, brown-stained teeth under his long, pointed nose and tiny chin made him look like a witch. He was dressed like a rock musician in bell-bottomed trousers and a flowery shirt with billowing sleeves. He led them into a bed-sitter room that was so clean and well polished with a good rug on the floor, a pretty spread on the bed, a nice couch by the windows, which were covered with pretty curtains and overlooked a garden, that Roger's bed-sitting room looked like a dump next to it. The soft rock sound of the Beatles singing "All those lonely people/ where do they all come from?" came out of a stereo in one corner and set a nice, pleasant mood, but Roger was still on guard.

"What do you hauve in mind?" Robey asked, turning to face them in the middle of the room, his hands on his narrow hips.

"Do you have any grass?" Roger asked.

"Grawss?" Robey repeated. "No grawss in England, only hash."

"Hash, then," Roger said. "How much for an ounce?"

"Ten pounds."

"That's about twenty-five dollars?"

"About."

"You got it with you?"

"Sure. I'll light up some and let you try it," Robey said, and pulled a small slab of hashish wrapped in tinfoil out of his pocket. He cut some off with a little pocketknife, crushed it with his bony fingers, and put it at one end of some cigarette papers with a small filter of rolled cardboard at the other end. Then after sprinkling tobacco in the middle, he started to roll it up.

"Say! I don't smoke and that nicotine will get me sick," Roger said.

"Oh, I say, I don't think so. Why don't you just try it? It's only at the end, you know."

"All right," Roger said, but he didn't like the idea. He admired, though, the way Robey had made a filter out of the little piece of cardboard.

But his lungs ached with the first deep toke, and when he hit on it for three more tokes his head seemed to swell with dizziness and a quick nausea gripped him. He gagged and ran to the sink, vomited and broke out in a hot sweat. He remembered to run water in the sink and clean it, but he was so weak and dizzy he had to lie down on the rug.

"Say! I'm sorry, you know," Robey said. "I'll roll some straight hash cigs in a moment without the tobacco and we'll smoke them. You want an ounce, right?"

"Right," Roger said from the rug, his head beginning to clear, Robey's face coming into focus.

"Here it is then," Robey said, and pulled another small tinfoil packet out of his pocket and handed it down to Roger.

Roger opened it, turned it around, sniffed at it, balanced it in his palm and said, "Looks good to me. I can feel it in my head already, even though the rush from the tobacco has gone."

He sat up, put the hash in his pocket, then stood up on wobbly legs. He stepped to the sink, rinsed his mouth out, then looked in the mirror. His face was pale even under the summer tan. It looked gray and his eyes were watery and bloodshot. But he turned around and reached into his pocket, pulled out a ten-pound note and handed it to Robey.

Robey took the note, glanced into the sink to see if it was clean, then suddenly asked, "Are you evading the drawft?"

A tingle of apprehension hit Roger, both fear and sudden understanding. He was being set up! He had been turned on, hurt and punished by the tobacco for smoking hash and was now being interrogated! But when Craig smiled as if amused that Robey thought Roger was still draft age at thirty-seven, Roger wondered if the hash was making him paranoid.

"No, I'm too old to be drafted, but I'm not too old to care about other guys having to go fight some war and kill innocent people for corporate profits," he said.

"So you think draft-age lads should evade the draft?" Robey asked. Roger just shook his head, knowing he shouldn't say anything again, but explained: "The thing to do is not evade the draft and make yourself an outlaw, but fight it in the courts and prove it's an immoral and illegal war. The system has to be tested so that it's not immoral and unpatriotic to oppose a war like Vietnam. The whole mess in Nam was started by the CIA in 1954 when they disrupted the free elections set up by the United Nations by bombing the polling stations."

"How do you know it was the CIA?" Robey said, his blue eyes pale as water. "I never heard that before."

Roger caught himself and, turning to Craig, said, "We better get back, man. The girls are waiting for us." He went right to the door, opened it, said, "Thanks for the hash, man," and stepped out into the hall and out the front door. He didn't turn around until he had reached the street, where he waited for Craig to catch up.

He didn't speak as they walked back to Craig's bed-sitter room in a steady mist, along rows of big, peaked Victorian houses and leafy trees, under a sky heavy with dark clouds. Behind them, a big man in a black raincoat, who reminded him of Leary, walked down the deserted sidewalk, turning every corner they turned, crossing every street they crossed, slowing down behind them at every corner they stopped for traffic, then hurrying to catch up, but always staying the same distance behind them. Roger could tell he was a cop. But he didn't know whether or not it was Leary or what he might know, if he were or weren't Leary, and whether he was concerned with politics or dope or both. Roger knew he must be careful, though, and he wondered whether it had been wise to try and escape from the political police in America. There, he at least had the rights of a citizen, whereas here in England, he had no rights at all. Maybe he should have stayed home to write his book.

13

The American, the one he'd met at the bed and breakfast house, Leary, was on the subway, too. Roger nodded hello and looked away, but Leary kept smiling and staring at Roger from across the aisle as if he were trying to make up to Roger. It was as if he knew Roger was suspicious of him over the pot talk and the way he'd gotten Roger to expose himself over both using and carrying it. But Roger, on his way to an English publisher where he was going to try and get both his first and second novels published, wasn't going to let the guy ingratiate himself or distract him in any way, and turned so that hi sface looked out the rain-streaked window.

But when the car dropped underground and he couldn't see anything but the concrete wall rushing by, he turned and saw the guy still smiling at him, still trying to play him. It got him so angry, he stared so hard and unbrokenly into the green eyes that the guy finally turned away, then turned his whole body around toward the front of the car to avoid Roger's stare. But Roger kept staring and made him pay for following him. He examined his face so closely that he could have drawn a profile of the man's face: the big head, with thick, brown, wavy hair, the big, wide jaw. The way the bottom lip jutted out, as if set forward. The thick paunch that showed even under the leather jacket buttoned over it.

14

The luxurious white foyer of the publishing house with its thick carpet, padded chairs, bright, abstract paintings, and display cases filled with black and white picture spreads of Norman Mailer's last book, *The Armies of the Night*, stopped Roger when he stepped in. He grinned at Penny, then said, "Anthony Brown, please," to a ginger-haired secretary. Turning to a display case, he stared at a glossy photo of Mailer's handsome face, the dark eyes, curly gray hair and the long, straight nose.

"Look, Penny," he said. "Mailer's fighting the military-industrial complex, without being destroyed! I *should* think positive, like you said. I'm not going to let any little harassment deter me. Mailer attacks the Pentagon and gets published. That's not selling out!"

She smiled and looked at the picture.

"This looks too good to let those guys who seem to be tailing and pestering me bring me down and depress me so I blow this chance," Roger said, and, following the secretary's finger, added, "Thanks," leading Penny into the next office.

A slender man about forty, with gray starting to streak his dark, wavy hair, looked up at him.

"Roger Leon," Roger said, holding out his hand. "And this is Penny Lawson. I've brought a paperback copy of my first novel, *Every Mutha's Son*, and the manuscript of my second novel, *Kilo*, which'll be published in January in America."

"Anthony Brown," the man said, shaking hands, then taking the large manila envelope and the book from Roger.

Roger sat down, but when he leaned back, the shiny black receiver of one phone turned crosswise on the base caught his eye. It didn't fit the slot, as if someone not in the office were listening.

"I like your spread on Mailer's last book," Roger said.

"I'll get you a copy," Anthony Brown said, smiling, his brown eyes wrinkling at the corners. "Your first novel was a social protest book, too. Was it not? A crime book of some kind?"

"Sort of. A boy goes to a reform school for a streetfight, and in a couple of months, ends up a murderer. They deformed him instead of *reformed* him. I wrote it out of a great sense of injustice."

Roger pointed down at the large brown envelope and ignored the phone next to it. "That second book is about three young hippies run to the ground and destroyed by the Mexican police for smoking pot in order to protect the big American power interests like the liquor industry and the police lobby."

Little lines appeared at the corners of Anthony Brown's mouth.

"And the novel I'm writing now is on the same theme as Mailer's *Armies of the Night*, a battle against the Pentagon and the CIA. It's how the secret police in America infiltrate and corrupt the student revolutionaries who have seized a college administration building and do the radical writer-hero in for knowing what they're up to."

"So, the book you plan to write now is strictly political?" Anthony Brown asked. "I thought you had a contract with Forest Press to do a book on boxers?"

Roger sighed, glanced at the phone, which seemed a subtle warning that he'd be tailed until he did what he was told. He wasn't a Mailer. He was barely known.

"I do. That's *Brothers*. But I satisfied that contract with *Kilo*. So, I'm free to write on any book I want."

"Oh!" Anthony Brown said, his mouth shaping a perfect O. He turned sidewards, facing the phone turned crosswise on

the desk, then leaned back, studied Roger through narrowed
eyes and said, "It's best to finish the book the publisher is
expecting if a young writer wants to get published."

"You think so?" Roger asked, thinking of how his picture
could be up on the wall with Mailer's, if he did what he was
told. *Every Mutha's Son* had been a dual selection of the Forest Book Club with Mailer's *Why Are We in Vietnam?* The
shiny black receiver turned crosswise on the phone now saddened him. He was never going to escape harassment unless
he quit fighting the police. He was no Mailer.

"Even *Brothers* is about cops, you know. The boxer brothers become bunco men and get arrested. Some of the cops beat
them up in jail. It's like all my books: man against the police
state."

Anthony Brown nodded as if he heard all right, but didn't
like what he'd heard. Roger, trying to save some chance of getting his books published in England, smiled and said, "You
know that Forest Press is avant-garde. They look for controversial books—even books about smoking pot. You smoke pot
yourself, right? My editor told me about that time you were
visiting Arizona and you didn't know what an American Indian writer meant by grass and thought he was going to smoke
real grass."

"He told you that?" Anthony Brown said. He sat up,
smiled. "That was quite confusing. You smoke grass, do you?"

"I did in America," Roger said, thinking of his picture in
the display case again, if he didn't talk too much and tell on
himself. Yet, he answered truthfully: "But you can only get
hash in England. You don't know where I can buy a hash pipe,
do you? I've got this ounce of hash I just bought and no way to
smoke it."

"Oh, say, I think I might know someone who might,"
Anthony Brown said, and picked up a phone receiver on the
opposite side of the desk from the criss-crossed one. He quickly dialed a number.

"I have an American novelist here who would like to buy
a pipe."

He glanced over at Roger, who then glanced at Penny.

"Not that kind. For hashish. Yes. All right."

He put the receiver down and said, "He said to try the
Soho District. There are a lot of East Indian stores around
there, and you can probably pick one up."

"Thank you," Roger said, glancing at Penny again, then waited for Anthony Brown to say something.

Brown leaned back in his chair and said, "Mailer's in town, you know," then squinted his eye as if he thought Roger, who was supposed to be a big rebel, might attack Mailer. When Roger didn't say anything, Brown smiled, leaned over the desk and said, "Why don't you come over to the house tonight? We're having a little party for him."

He squinted his eye again, then said, "Take it easy on him, though, will you? He's been working hard this past week to publicize the book and needs to relax a little bit."

"Don't worry. I won't be antagonistic," Roger said, wondering now if Mailer might be listening on the other end of that line.

15

The whole room was dark when Roger lifted his head off the pillow, then saw the luminous hands of the clock pointed at eleven. He guessed he'd blown his chance of getting dressed in time to catch the last subway train to Mailer's reception. He felt red-eyed and puffy-faced from drinking two half-pints in a Soho pub, where he'd gone after failing to find a small-bowled hash pipe.

"Fuck Mailer," he said, dropping his head back on the pillow and trying to fall asleep again. But he knew he was throwing away a chance to meet one of his heroes and said, "Let's go, Penny!"

She jumped up, and they rushed around in circles getting dressed, then ran down the stairs of their house and trotted three blocks to the tube. They ran down several long flights of stairs to the deepest subway level to catch the last train going their way, only to discover when it pulled up that it was the wrong last train.

Roger grabbed Penny's hand and ran back up the stairs, where he asked a man in a trench coat where the train to Rochester stopped.

"Up two flights! You've still got a chance!"

Roger grabbed her hand again and they ran up the stairs and reached the subway platform just as the train to Rochester pulled up with a roar. They rushed on board, Roger sweating from the frenzied run.

"I've always wanted to meet him," Roger said. "I guess I'm just not used to drinking two beers in the middle of the afternoon."

She smiled. "I'm glad you woke up," she said. "This is fun."

He smiled, but it was a long, slow, frustrating, forty-five minute journey, with fewer and fewer people on the yellow-lighted train, the monotonous clip, clip, clip, clip of the wheels on the tracks, and the rattle and the roar and the occasional swaying of the car. At last they reached their station and came up out of the underground depot onto a darkened street.

Finding the correct address, a very narrow brick house on a dark, curving street, he rang the doorbell, afraid it was too late.

"Yes?" asked the slender, fortiesh woman with the red hair who opened the door.

"I'm Roger Leon and this is Penny Lawson. Are you Mrs. Brown?" he asked.

"Yes, yes, I am," Mrs. Brown said, her mouth twitching in a tight smile, as if peeved at how late he was.

"I'm sorry I'm late. Is Mailer here?" he asked, and she stepped back to let them in.

"Oh, yes, he's upstairs," she said, closing the door, turning her narrow, freckled face toward him. "But he has this horrible awkcent and no one can understand him. Go right up. It is late."

She pointed to the stairs.

"Thank you," Roger said, and led Penny up to the second floor. He looked quickly around the long, attic room, fashioned into a small hall, at the women in high heels and men in suits and ties scattered around it with drinks in their hands. He spotted a small group crowded around a stocky, gray-haired man in a blue suit, recognized him as Mailer, and thought, "So there's the great man."

He was aware that he had never used that term in reference to Mailer before, always reserving it for Faulkner and Hemingway when he thought of great American novelists. But he believed it once he thought it. Mailer had influenced not just his writing, but his very thought as a radical and an existentialist. He liked the rugged man behind the work, too.

He crossed the room and stood with Penny slightly behind the man and watched him. He saw Mailer eyeball him from the corner of one eye, eyeball him again, then suddenly turn towards him and say, "You're Roger Leon, aren't you?"

"How did you know?" Roger asked.

"I recognized you from the cover of your book," Mailer said, and reached out and shook his hand. "I should have written to you when our books were chosen for the book club together. But I don't have any class. I'm from New Jersey and full of shit up to here."

He held his free hand over his eyebrows, throwing the finely shaped eyes and the classically narrow nose into shadow, reminding Roger of pictures he'd seen of him in his youth when he was beautiful. He saw that even now in middle-age, with an alcoholic puffiness to his face, he was handsome.

"I always wanted to be published with you. I wrote my first story after I read the section about the southern sergeant, the part that says, 'Crack that whip! Crack that whip!' in *The Naked and the Dead.*

Mailer smiled and said, "I first began to write after I read Farrel's *Studs Lonigan.*"

The blue eyes met Roger's, and in a soft voice, feeling a bit self-conscious with all the eyes of the small crowd on him, Roger said, "You showed a lot of class in that poem you wrote about Jesus and the sweet bitch of success. The one in which you said you had to remind yourself that 'that guy died for me.' It was really an honest poem. It really made me respect you."

Penny touched Roger's arm and he turned to her, knowing she liked his words. Her pink face was sweet and smiling.

"Who's this? Your girlfriend?" Mailer asked, smiling.

"Yes. Penny Lawson."

"Cute," Mailer said, nodding at her, then he stared at Roger, kinky gray hair frizzing up on top like a modified natural. He turned to Roger and said, "This is a tough game. If you think that fighting game you were in is tough, you'll find that this game is a lot, lot tougher."

Then, his mouth twitching in a hint of a smile, he added, "Awww, you were probably cute in there anyway, without a punch."

"Oh, yeah!" Roger said. He dropped into a fighting stance, fists up, and jabbed Mailer in the stomach with the tips of his left fingers. He felt the thick belly tighten a little. "Pretty solid," he said, and watched the older man smile. He then straightened up and, dropping his hands to his sides, said, "I'm cute all right, a Fancy Dan. But I can stop a guy with one punch of either hand."

"Small men, though."

"Any size," Roger said. "I rarely take a backward step. Had over a hundred fights and never lost one. Won most by knockout, too."

"You're kidding," Mailer said, eying Roger over his highball glass.

"I'm not talking about ring bouts. I've only had four amateur fights altogether," Roger said, seeing the mistrust, and Mailer looked away as if Roger had now exposed himself. He guessed that the publishers had pushed him as an ex-pro when he had only an aborted college boxing career.

"I'm talking about street fights, like from the age of eight up," he said, holding his hand down low to signify how small he meant.

Mailer's eyes widened, and Roger remembered Mailer's essay on how he envied men who had to fight street battles as little kids because it made real men of them.

"You're going to have to fight a lot tougher battles now, though," Mailer said. "Much tougher than you ever fought in that street."

"I know. I know," Roger answered, thinking of what had just happened in Anthony Brown's office that day.

Mailer squinted at him, sighting with one eye over the rim of the highball glass, his gray face below the rim telescoped and blurred by the drink. He lowered the glass and said, "You've got to become an entertainer in America, if you want to make it. You've got to make up your mind that no matter what you write, you've got to help sell it or you're going to become a bitter man. That's the fate in store for every serious writer in America who doesn't learn how to play the game."

Roger's eyebrow popped up on his forehead. He stared at Mailer for a long time. Mailer, who had written those anti-fascist novels about persecuted communists in the fifties, who had declared himself a socialist and brought the conservative

critics of the Eisenhower years down on himself. Critics who
finally convinced him and the public he couldn't write novels
anymore. Mailer, who then turned to journalism and reaped
fame and all the monetary rewards a capitalistic society could
give him. Mailer, his hero, who had just written another book,
even if not a novel, on fighting the Pentagon, the very enemy
Roger had been fighting since Martin Luther King got killed
just six months earlier.

"I...I..." Roger caught himself. "You...I don't mind going
on T.V. I'd like to be on T.V. It's fun. But why do I have to
choose between success or my writing? Why can't I have values and still succeed like you?" He stopped and took a breath.
"I want to write books that are socially important like yours.
I've written two already which are about the suppression of
individuals by the police, though they have different locales.
My next book's going to be about the coup d'etat that took
place in America only three months ago with the killing of
Bobby Kennedy. I'm going to write a novel about a guy who
fights the subversion of his country by the CIA and the FBI
and all the radical rats and establishment writers who go
along with it. I'm going to write about how the secret police
sucks the lifeblood of liberty from the land in a secret network
that will eventually crush all true political dissent, all true
democracy! Somebody killed our president and Bobby
Kennedy and Malcolm X and Martin Luther King! And Nixon
and the military industrial complex were the winners in all
cases!"

His voice rang throughout the attic. Everyone stopped
talking and stared at him.

"I'm going to tell the truth as I see it, not like the FBI and
J. Edgar Hoover and Rockefeller and Nixon want us to see it.
I'm going to fight for my country and democracy! I'm going to
write about the young who love their country! I'm going to
help bring in the Age of Aquarius, of cooperation instead of
competition, like you, man. I want to be like you!"

He stopped with his fist in the air. His voice was
high-pitched, and his face was flushed with blood. He was
close to screaming. Mailer was watching him with all the fine
lines around his eyes magnified. He shook his leonine head
very slowly, almost sadly, and said, "It's going to be a hard
road, Roger." He then turned and walked across the room, but

he stopped at the top of the staircase and said, "You come to see me when you get to New York."

"Will you remember?" Roger asked, feeling like he'd really blown it.

"Call me and remind me," Mailer said, and stepped down the stairs, his gray head slipping out of sight. Then Roger noticed Anthony Brown staring at him and slowly shaking his gray-streaked head back and forth, too, and Roger guessed that he'd just lost all chance of being published in England.

16

Streams of rain drumming on the tall windowpanes, streaking them with rivulets, woke Roger up to the gloomy gray light of a late morning. It barely penetrated the open drapes of the long, dark, high-ceilinged room and the shadows at the far end of his bed.

Roger looked over at Penny in the next bed and saw her looking at him. She reached out with one arm from under her covers when their eyes met and touched his shoulder. She kept her hand there and stared at him with dark green eyes without speaking or smiling, as if waiting to see how he felt first. Then she frowned and asked, "What's wrong?"

"Just Mailer," he said, and got out of bed. Later, as he soaked in an old-fashioned bathtub and shaved, every bit of dialogue at the party between himself and Mailer ran through his mind and seemed to hang in the steamy air around him. He blushed at the memory of how Mailer left him standing there like a soapbox orator deserted by his audience. Mailer's last words kept resounding in his head as he dressed and went down to the basement for a breakfast of cold toast and strong tea that tasted rank as piss. He was still hearing Mailer's words when he was about to close the door to his room and a woman's voice called: "Sir! Oh, sir! The rent is due today!"

The landlady's freckles gave her words an urgency, somewhat like exclamation points as she stepped down the hall to him. He didn't like the tight expression on the round Irish face she pushed into the doorway either, though he had thought her personable before.

"But we paid the rent broker for a week only two days ago!"

"Well, I say the rent is due today for a week. We pay on every Wednesday week here, you know," she said, nodding her head as if talking to a child.

"Well, I paid two days ago for one week. And my week is still five full days away yet, counting today," he said.

She puckered her mouth and he closed the door and listened to her feet stomp off down the hall and then down the stairs to the main floor, where she lived.

"Did you hear that?"

"Yes," Penny said, still lying in bed, with a funny look on her face as if she had been sucking her thumb, which she did sometimes when she was unhappy. She was showing signs of strain, too.

"This is a game concocted by the police for the things I said to Mailer last night," he said. "They want to make sure I keep my mouth shut."

"You mean they told the landlady to cheat us?"

"Yes."

"To punish you for shouting about the CIA and the assassinations last night?"

"Yes."

"I don't believe it," she said, and dropped back down on her bed, letting her head smack against the pillow as if she were sick of it all.

"You don't believe it, huh?" he said, then spun around and walked down the faded gray carpet to the tall windows with the rusty-colored drapes. He looked out at the tall trees up and down the block and the tall houses with all the little sports cars parked along the curbs in front of them and the leaves scattered all over the wet pavement. It had stopped raining, and he could see a green leaf splattered on the sidewalk below, which glistened like an alligator skin. This touched him because all the other leaves around it were brown and dead, and the rain had evidently knocked it off the tree before it was supposed to fall.

"That's what's happening to me. I mean that every bit of my life is being manipulated here, just like it was in California, where I'm probably the only guy in America who ever got two passports in the mail! Just the right thing to get me in trouble! Somebody else gets a hold of one of them and runs around committing crimes, using my name!"

"What's that got to do with here?" Penny said.

"It's the same thing! There was a phone off its base in Anthony Brown's office, and either a cop or Mailer was on the other end of the line listening to every word I said to Brown. And what I said last night to Mailer about choosing truth over success was listened to and a decision made to punish me for it!"

"I don't believe that," she said, and sat up in bed in pale-green nylon pajamas.

"And they took my picture as soon as I got off the plane, too, by that girl who was sitting with that man with the tie, the cop behind Ruth and Craig on the charter plane. And Craig and me were followed back from Robey's by some guy in a black raincoat, who looked like Leary, that American guy from breakfast, who just happened to be on the tube with us yesterday, and stared at me until I got angry and stared him down. And look at the way Ruth comes on with me! Trying to make me go for her in front of you, so you'll get jealous and it will cause trouble between us, maybe drive you away."

"You like Ruth smiling at you," Penny said, getting out of bed, pajamas hanging loosely on her slender body. "You have to take some responsibility for girls coming on to you! You can't blame all your personal problems on the police, on Big Brother. How about you? What's your share in it? I'm getting sick of you always blaming your troubles on something else outside of you, like the women coming on to you."

She crossed the long room toward him and shivered in the damp air when she got close. She looked pink like an Easter bunny. She always looked cute in the morning.

"I only want what I can't get: a woman who's totally true to me. What's wrong with that, Penny?" he said, wanting to hug her, but keeping his arms down at his sides.

"You don't trust me, do you?" she said. "It doesn't make any difference how loyal I am to you, you still won't trust me and I'll waste my life for nothing!"

"What do you want me to do?" he shouted. "Prove in court what's happening to me? Don't you understand that I was a campus leader of the New Left in the early sixties? One of its leaders who was driven off the campus more than once? That you and I, yes, you, too, were participating in activities the

CIA and the FBI like to call subversive? Demonstrations! Civil disobedience! Campus sit-ins! That they're probably following anybody who played any kind of a prominent role in the campus strike last spring? And that now they don't want anybody writing about it? Especially about how they infiltrated the movement and corrupted student and black and communist party leaders? And how they corrupted my family, got them to cooperate with them against me?"

Her eyes were a sad blue-green in the gray light, and so, hurt and unwavering, he said in a lower voice: "I don't want revenge, Penny. I want to capture the idealism of the students who joined the Peace Corp under President Kennedy to save third-world nations, but are now fighting just to save their own democracy. I want to do good, Penny. But don't you see that any serious writer is important, especially if he wants to tell the truth as he sees it, not just cater to some party line, capitalistic or communist? Don't you see that our lives are bound up with international politics? Can't you see that?"

She stood facing him for several moments with a frown on her face. Then she said, "I see you don't really trust me, and it's hopeless. There's nothing I can do about it, nothing. You'll just keep being bitter and I'll just keep wasting my life."

He watched her turn and walk away, leaving him by the window, wanting to scream.

17

Head bent over the keys and sitting right next to the window to get as much of the dull light as possible, Roger punched the keys of the portable typewriter hard. He was trying to describe the crowd scene in the hallway of the state college administration building, trying to catch the noise and the movement, the constant turning of the people on the outskirts of the crowd, the T.V. lights and the students squatted down in front of the president's door, listening to speeches by student revolutionaries in blue Levis.

He heard Penny come into the room and leave again, then come back, lie down on her bed and start to read by the weak lamp. He wanted to say something and make her feel better, but he was too busy. He had to keep writing when it was going good. When he finally looked over at her an hour or so later, she was lying on her stomach, the book face down on the floor next to her. She seemed to be asleep. Soon, it grew so dark he took the lamp and set it up near him and kept writing until he heard a heavy footstep in the hall and a hard knock on the door. His stomach tightened with apprehension. He noticed her stir when he walked by. When he opened the door, a short well-built man, obviously a worker of some kind, stared into his eyes and said, "The rent is due today."

Roger shifted his position so that his left foot was forward and his right foot back, his left hand on the door and his right hand down by his side, ready to punch or protect himself from the powerful-looking man. The guy was his height, but at least twenty pounds heavier than his own hundred and twenty-five pounds and none of it fat.

"I talked to a barrister friend today," Roger lied. "And he said that I don't have to pay the rent until my week is up."

"The rent is due today!" the man said, and squared his shoulders. His jaw was set and his eyes unwavering.

Ready to shoot out a straight left or a right hand, whichever was handy, if the guy moved on him, Roger said, "You'll have to talk to my barrister."

The man faced him for a few seconds, as if looking for some sign of fear or a lie, then turned, and Roger watched his wide shoulders move off down the dark hall before he closed the door and locked it.

"I feel like getting out of this town," Roger said before he even finished turning around. "It rains all the time. Hell! There's a lot better weather in San Francisco right now. They follow me everywhere I go! Phones are left off the hook! Nobody wants me to talk about the assassinations! Or about the secret police! Especially the secret police! Anthony Brown just about threatened me that I was going to stay unpublished if I dared to write about politics. Mailer warns me I'm going down a hard road. We don't have any friends here. The landlord tries to rip us off for rent in one of the baldest bunco games I ever heard of. No good crook would be that dumb! Somebody put them up to it! We might as well leave if we're going to spend all our time on a bummer!"

"Yesh," she said, and sat up on the bed and looked with saggy-lidded eyes at him.

"What's wrong? Your voice sounds funny. Are you sick?"
he asked, frowning, leaning down to look at her more closely
in the faint light, thinking that she looked pale. But she didn't
answer and he stepped to the cot and touched her shoulder
and asked, "What's wrong with your eyes? They're just slits."

Her eyes suddenly brimmed with tears and she covered
her face with her hands and hunched over.

"What's wrong, Penny?" he asked, and kneeled on the
bed, putting his arms around her.

Her body shook with sobs, her face and hands covered by
the long, fine strands of her hair. Finally her slurred voice
came through her fingers.

"You, you don' trush me."

He pulled away from her and stared at her hunched body,
wanting to console her, but wanting her to believe him, too.

"But what's wrong with your voice? Why are you slurring?
And why are your eyes so saggy?"

She lowered her hands and looked up with wet, sagging
eyelids.

"I took some ashpirinsh."

"Is that all? Are you sure?"

"I took shix," she said, and sobbed again but kept her
hands in her lap.

"Six! Why six?"

"I wanted to die," she said.

"Just because I tried to convince you of what's happening
to us? Because you said I didn't trust you? And six can't kill
you, Penny!"

"Thash not all. Thash not it," she said, slurring still. "Ish
the girls. Thash the part that bothersh me. I can believe all
thoshe other thingsh, if you want me to. But I shee the way
you get attracted to pretty girlsh ash if I washn't around.
There'll alwaysh be shomebody like Ruth around. I took them
ash much becaush of Ruth, more becaush of her. Becaushe
you alwaysh go for it. Becaush she actsh ash if you were her
boyfriend, ash if you like her not me. Thash why!"

She looked so pink and soft and vulnerable, he hugged
her, then leaned back and looked in her sagging eyes again.

"I know I go for it. But I go for anybody who shows affection for me, who's willing to be my friend. Guys, too! I treat
'em like buddies, if they're at all friendly. I'm starved for any
kind of affection after being ostracized all those years. But I

don't want you to suffer like this. I love you too much for that! We'll go! We'll go away from here by ourselves. This is the capper to everything. Though it might interfere with selling the book. But the publisher shook his head at me when Mailer left as if I was all through with him anyway. I don't think he'll even contact me about my books. Let's go! You want to go, don't you?"

"Yesh," she said. "But what about Craig and Ruth?"

"The way they've been acting since I said I was going to write my strike book! And Craig bringing that suspicious guy around? Besides, he made it a point to tell me they were going to travel by themselves."

"I'm willing to go right now," Penny said, her speech suddenly clear as if the very idea of leaving made her better already. "You should know that. You know what I think about Ruth. You know I..."

She stopped in midsentence with a shout from outside. Craig's voice.

"There they are now," Penny said, lowering her voice near a whisper. "Maybe they're bored."

Roger walked across the long room to the tall center window and slid it up.

"How about having dinner with us? We haven't been together in a couple of days! Let's have a smoke!" Craig called out from the wet sidewalk below. Ruth was standing in a thick jacket and Levis next to him. Their faces were a blur in the darkness.

Suddenly, all the problems came to a boil with a flash: Craig, who played the game all the way. Who was probably watching him for the police. Who got him to tell how he'd carry his dope in front of a stranger who looked like Teddy Kennedy, one of his heroes. Craig who was going to think of himself from now on. Craig who wanted to smoke with him now that he felt like it.

Just barely able to keep from cursing, Roger leaned out the window and shouted down, "We don't want to! You guys go your way and we'll go ours! We're going to leave tomorrow, anyway! You're a punk, Craig! It'll be all right with us if we don't see either of you again!"

He slammed the window down and turned to Penny, who had gotten off her cot and stepped up to hug him.

"Well, at least we know where we are!" he said. "At least, we're choosing this together! Everything's up front now!" He squeezed her tightly. "Well, baby, we're on our own now! We might as well get out of here! You can forget all about Ruth and any other girls, you're the only one for me. And I'm going to go find someplace where I can write my book in peace!"

Episode Two

MALLORCA

1

Black and white sea gulls, *Gallinas del Mar*, Chickens of the Sea, wheeled in white-flecked currents of wind in the bright blue sky, rose and fell in slow-moving clouds above the bright white plastered houses, then settled slowly over the green olive trees on the hillside below, curving and swaying over and about like a current in the swelling sea. The wooded hills went right down to the sea, and the last hill line faded into the last sea line, far out, where the sea was a deep blue, flat and meaningless, and the edge of the world disappeared in a mist.

"It couldn't be prettier, could it?" Roger said, glancing over at Penny who was slipping into a summer minidress, one knee up, balanced on one leg, as poised and pretty as a ballerina in her pink panties and bra.

"Nor you," he added, and looked long at her.

She looked up and smiled, then put her foot down and pulled her dress up under her shoulders with a wiggle of her hips, slid her rosy arms into the short sleeves and straightened her back. Her lifted face and long neck caught the light from the wide windows, and he said it again: "Nor you."

She smiled again, then her face suddenly tightened and, looking at him with solemn green eyes, said, "I hope we'll be happy here. I hope you can write your book without somebody bothering us."

2

The thin, pale-skinned waiter with the bony face and the light-brown hair handed them each a menu, glanced at Penny, then rushed off to wait on another table. The light from the waves of the pool just outside the open patio doors flickered like pale flames on her face, lighting up the smile she gave him. He thought she looked pretty, even without makeup, and,

as always, even in her minidress, modest. Only her breastbone
showed above the bodice. Yet, he noticed how the waiter
stared at her with hard, green, bulbous eyes when he came
back and how harshly his voice sounded when he asked, "Sí?"

His knobby hands clutched the pencil clumsily and wrote
their orders down in a jerky, angry way, as if he could barely
control his hatred of her. Yet, Roger smiled when he said,
"Cervezas, dos," and tried to withhold judgment, not wanting
to misinterpret something and ruin their beautiful feelings.
He had even shaved his long sideburns off to help him get
along with the conventional Spaniards. He wanted to be
happy here. He liked the hotel and all the sun-browned
tourists chattering away at the other tables. He wanted to
keep out of trouble so he could work on his book.

The waiter returned with the beers and set them down
with a cold face, hiding his eyes from them. Roger wanted to
do his best to get along with the Spanish people, but he was
going to watch and protect Penny. Then when the waiter
returned with the plates and glanced down at Penny's bodice.
He scowled, his upper lip lifting on one side, as if she were
dirt. Penny blushed, Roger had to keep himself from saying
something sharp to the man. Was it because she had no wedding band? he wondered. But he kept quiet and reached out
and squeezed her hand.

3

Clasping hands, Roger and Penny walked down the steep
stairs on the hillside outside the hotel which led down to the
boulevard and the buses, intending to catch one into town to
mail the manuscript she carried in her straw bag. But when
they turned down the stairs that led past the kitchen, he saw
the thin waiter standing in the doorway smoking a cigarette.

A scowl came over the waiter's face when he saw Penny,
his upper lip curled so that Roger could see his teeth. He kept
scowling at her as they approached him, and an angry rush of
blood filled Roger's head. He glared at the man and flexed his
torso, spread his shoulders and the wings under them like a
cobra, ready to fight. The waiter blanched when they reached
the bottom stair and stepped back, out of the doorway.

"I hope he isn't any indication of the way things are going to be here," Roger said as they turned down the last long flight of stairs to the boulevard. "It would be a shame to waste all this," he added, and swung his arm out at the sight before him: the blue sea and the blue sky and the small hotels with the thin but steady trickle of cars and suntanned people in bright, casual, summer clothes moving up and down the street.

"I hope not," she said. "Why do you think he was so nasty?"

"It could be he sees no wedding ring on your finger and considers you a whore by hypocritical Spanish male standards. Or he doesn't like the way you dress. Or we're back where we started from again. Maybe they've been waiting for us. We let that cabby on the pier bring us right here from the boat, remember? Maybe this is some kind of harassment. We might have wasted our time leaving England. But let's not give up. Let's see what we can do. We'll go mail this manuscript of *Brothers* back." He pointed down at the manuscript in her bag, carefully sealed and tied with strong cord.

4

The gun turrets in the big redstone fortress overlooking the blue harbor with its thousands of sailboats gave Roger a sense of Spain when it was the greatest power on earth. He loved the blue sky, the hot weather, the fair-skinned, good-looking people, and, especially, the giant trees that shaded the main thoroughfare, the tile promenade, and the trill of thousands of birds fluttering in them like leaves. But he also noticed the silence.

Everyone was very quiet. The children were well-dressed and well-loved, but everyone was subdued. No one attracted attention to themselves. Shopkeepers were thin-lipped and impatient. One reached down and slapped Penny's hand when she touched an orange she wanted to buy. She jerked her hand back. Roger kept his temper. Later when he stopped to ask a tall cop where he could find the post office, the man stood stiff as a board before him in his white breastband and belt and gray tropic helmet, and, with his chin up, pointed at a big building a block away and said, "*¡Allá!* Over there." Then he stared through slanted lids at Roger in his green Levis and black, silken T-shirt, sandals and dark glasses, and didn't smile, as if Roger were somehow suspect.

5

"*¿Es bastante?* Is it enough?" Roger repeated in English, afraid his Spanish wasn't good enough to be understood by the woman in the post office. Her lightly tanned face was just starting to get bony, with lots of hollows and highlights on it, though it was still pretty within the frame of her fluffed blonde hair. She was taller than he in her high heels, but smug, sarcastic, he thought.

He turned to Penny. Her face with its round cheeks and small mouth and long-lashed eyes was completely calm, as if she thought nothing in particular about the low price of the postage. He had already mailed back pictures and clothing to the States and knew it should cost a lot of money to mail a heavy manuscript.

"*¿Es bastante?*" he asked one more time.

"*Sí,*" the clerk said, and stared him in the eye. "*¡Es bastante para usted!*"

Roger flinched when he realized she meant, "Yes. It's enough for you!" But he turned and walked with Penny across the cool marble building with the high, high ceiling and outside into the heat.

They were crossing the wide marble porch and starting down the wide stairs to the sidewalk when he noticed a group of men standing near the foot of the stairs. All were dressed in suits and ties except one handsome army officer with a dark mustache. None of the other men appeared to notice them, but the army officer smiled. Roger's first reaction was to smile back. But then the man's smile grew into a toothy leer, as if he were ogling a whore. Roger tried to ignore the leer. But the officer kept leering and even nudged a man in civilian clothes next to him when Roger and Penny were only a few feet from them.

Roger turned and stared directly at the mustachioed man, his own face set, his jaw rigid, his dark glasses hard and impenetrable. Determined not to take another insult, he tensed himself to fight the officer and the three other men, too, no matter what the cost.

When Roger stepped close to him, the officer's wide mouth snapped tight like a rubber band and vanished under the thin line of his mustache. Penny grabbed Roger's arm with both hands in a tight, desperate way, and he wondered how he could ever suspect her.

6

"Mesero!" Roger called from his deck chair to the thin, white-jacketed waiter who was bending over, placing a drink before a brown-skinned woman who was lying on her side, propped up by an elbow. She was so suntanned, the skin on her shoulders glowed red.

The bulbous eyes of the waiter who had scorned Penny glanced over at him, then back down to the bill in the woman's brown hand. The waiter took it, dropped change on the tray, straightened up and spun around. Then, carrying the tray flat as if he still had drinks on it, he moved quickly along the pool's edge into the shade of an awning over the bar at the far end, and then up to the counter at the waiter's station without once looking back.

"We know where we stand with him, don't we?" Roger said, letting his glance skim over the twenty or so people sitting around the pool. Nearly all were Scandinavians, judging by their big bodies and the many blonds among them. Only a handful were slim and had tans. The rest were pale and fleshy.

"Let's not pay any attention to him or any Spanish men," Penny said. "Come on, let's get wet and have some fun."

She got off her chair and led him past the brown-skinned woman to the pool. Penny grabbed the chrome ladder and reached down. She stuck one toe in the water, wiggled it, turned and smiled and said, "It feels just right." Then, backing down into the water, holding on to both sides of the chrome ladder, still smiling at him, she suddenly stared past him. He turned and saw the brown-skinned woman, incredibly striking with her black, fluffed hair and brown tan, looking at him with deep blue eyes. Transfixed for a moment, he then remembered Penny and turned back to see her down to her shoulders in the water, watching him.

He walked around the corner of the pool to the diving board and stepped up onto it, conscious of the woman's blue eyes staring at him. He wondered if his hair would look too thin when he came up all wet after the dive. He took two steps forward and jumped into the air anyway, came down on his toes at the end of the board and sprang high in the air. At the top of the dive, he spread his arms and arched his back. He pointed his toes, then pointed his arms at the water and cut into it. He felt the cool rush of the water as he curved down with his eyes closed, then opened them and frog-kicked down to the end of the pool through the bubbles, as if suspended in air and free for a few leisurely moments. He came up where he could stand and snapped his head to clear the hair from his face. Penny was smiling at him from the foot of the chrome ladder. The woman's face was directly above hers, and the blue eyes were still on him.

He pushed off toward Penny, swimming with overhand strokes, catching a glimpse of the blue eyes every time he turned his head up for air, seeing them even when Penny swam to meet him and, splashing water, tried to dunk him. She then put her arms around him and let him pull her through the water, pressing her face against his when he reached shallow water and turned to face her. The woman was still looking at him.

"What's with her?" Penny said. She climbed out at the shallow end and walked over to her deck chair without passing by the woman, Roger following.

"You got me," he said, drying himself off as he watched the woman stand up and walk in her black one-piece bathing suit, her shapely ass swaying, down the pool to the shallow end they had just left.

"Hot babe, huh?" Penny said, and Roger had to smile.

He stopped smiling, though, when he noticed the tall young Scandinavian with dark hair, big cheekbones and hairless cheeks staring at Penny from a table on the other side of the pool. He sat in the shade of the awning and was the only person wearing street clothes in a group of several men. All the rest were in bathing suits and were heavy, blond, and big-boned. He was as large in body build as the others, but was spare and dark-haired and seemed younger.

"Looks like you've got an admirer, too," Roger said.

"What?" Penny asked.

"That guy over there with all the clothes on is eyeballing you."

"Yes, I saw him," she said, and laid her head back against the webbed chair, letting the sun shine down full on her face.

Roger looked back at the guy, who looked away.

7

Roger again caught the young guy staring at Penny when they walked into the restaurant at dusk. He was sitting with his group of friends at a table near the door. Following the maitre d' to a table in the very center of the crowded room, then sitting down to study the menu, Roger looked up to find himself facing the deeply tanned woman at the next table.

She was dressed in a black cocktail dress with a low bodice that showed the swells of her bronzed breasts. Up close, the absolute black color of her fluffed hair was in perfect harmony with her dark complexion. Her lips were full and heart-shaped, and the bridge of her nose was thin and delicate like the stem of a cocktail glass. But it was her black eyebrows and black eyelashes that struck him. They seemed to set off the deep blue color of her luminous eyes. When he looked up at Penny, the woman was still staring at him, and he finally turned his chair so he wouldn't have to meet her eyes every time he looked up.

Penny noticed. "She hangs around, doesn't she?"

For that moment, with the clatter of dishes and silverware amid the chatter of the diners around them, her comment brought everything out in the open between them, and he reached across the table and clasped her hand, feeling really close to her.

8

"Very good dive," the young Scandinavian said when Roger climbed out of the water on the chrome ladder and stepped onto the tile deck.

"Thanks," Roger said, and met the eyes of the beautiful dark woman who was sitting next to the guy on a separate deck chair. She smiled and Roger smiled back, but quickly walked past them and over to Penny, wondering what the two were doing together.

"Looks like our friends are getting friendly all around," he said to Penny, who was sitting in a deck chair facing the sun.

"Good," Penny said. "That was a nice dive, Roger."

"Why?" he asked, drying himself off, as much interested in perfecting his dive as in wanting to know if the young man was trying to flatter him.

"Oh, you had your legs straight together and your body was straight when you cut the water."

She lay back to get the full force of the hot sun on her stomach and face, and Roger saw the young guy smiling at him again. He smiled back this time, but wondered why the guy was talking to him when he had the woman.

9

At dinner, the tall young Scandinavian and the beautiful woman, talking and laughing, drank champagne together at the very next table. It took Roger a few moments to find the young man's friends at a table by themselves on the other side of the room.

"It sure looks normal on the surface," Roger said to Penny.

She glanced over at the couple. "I hope it stays that way," she said. "Takes care of two pests at once."

Roger touched his lips with his finger to hush her when the couple broke into a laugh. The young man poured their glasses full of champagne again, and the woman suddenly leaned over and, putting her hand on Penny's arm, asked, "Why don't you two join us? We could have fun together."

Penny looked at Roger, who answered, "We appreciate it, but we have to eat dinner."

"Well, after dinner then?" the woman said, and smiled with an even row of white teeth.

"What do you think, Penny?" he asked.

Penny scanned his face as if looking for certain signs in it, but he was totally relaxed, prepared to accept her decision. "Sure, why not?" she said.

The woman smiled and the young man said, "We'll have a good chat together."

Roger noticed how surprisingly mature his voice sounded and wondered if he was making a mistake, then pushed it out of his mind, thinking, "I don't have to be afraid of them."

10

"Well, who's going to win the election in November?" Ingrid asked, twisting on her stool to face Roger and resting her arm on the counter of the poolside bar. Light shimmered off the water at her side and shivered on her face and on her bare brown shoulders as if she glistened with starlight: a shifting, evanescent pattern constantly playing over her, giving her a glamorous, ethereal look, and it took him a moment to react to her question.

"I don't really care," Roger said. "The war machine keeps rolling either way."

She blinked, then glanced at Jan standing next to her. His wide, hooded eyes concealed his thoughts. His broad forehead was perfectly smooth.

"Don't you think that Nixon will win, though?" she asked, her eyeballs perfectly white around the deep-blue retinas.

He had to make himself stop looking before he could answer, yet felt his senses quiver in him, a hint that he was being baited. "He might win the election, but he'll never be my president. I don't care how long he stays in office."

"Why?" Jan said, and Roger wondered just how old he really was. He seemed so much more mature and sure of himself up close. The shy, gangly kid seemed to disappear, although his skinny angular arms still stuck out of the short-sleeved sportshirt.

"Because he'll only get there over the dead bodies of two Kennedys and Martin Luther King, that's why."

"What proof do you have of that?" Ingrid asked. She was so tall on the bar stool that the low-cut bodice of her black cocktail dress was just below Roger's eye level, and he couldn't help but see the upper mounds of her breasts even as he met her eyes. They seemed to be watching him closely.

"Because John F. Kennedy beat Nixon and was assassinated two years later, just three weeks before he was going to bring the troops back from Vietnam!"

He heard his voice rising and stopped. He didn't want another scene like the one in London with Mailer, and he lowered his voice but still spoke loudly, and his voice started rising again.

"Kennedy had refused to allow the CIA to fly air power in the Bay of Pigs invasion, and Oswald, who was a CIA man, who learned how to speak Russian in an army camp in Japan and had only right-wing Russian aristocrats for friends in America, who ran with the Bay of Pigs exiles who hated Castro, shot him down in Texas so the military industrial complex could then put in Johnson, who, though he campaigned to stop the war, sent all the troops to Vietnam the complex could want!"

Roger couldn't keep his voice from ringing with anger.

"But the students ran him out with their constitutional right to demonstrate, and the complex had to run Nixon against another Kennedy. But Martin Luther King got in the way and warned of a right-wing coup d'etat in America by 1970 and was killed three days later. Bobby Kennedy was assassinated only a month after that, the very night he won the California primary."

He stopped to take a deep breath.

"I worked really hard for the peace candidate, McCarthy, so there'd be a strong peace plank in the Democratic platform. But that's a long story. The coup took place in 1968 instead of 1970. So no matter who wins this election, the right wing will take over the country because Humphrey, like Johnson, plays the Pentagon power game."

"But the Kennedys were separate incidents," Jan said.

"Yeah! Quite a coincidence that two Kennedys were murdered! One who had beat Nixon for the presidency and the other who was going to beat Nixon for the presidency! Quite a coincidence all right!"

Roger's face twisted with the irony.

"And all the rats get ready to cash in and go along. All the so-called patriots! All the punks interested in their bank accounts!"

He stopped and took a swallow of his beer. His mouth was dry, and he still wore only his silken black T-shirt and black cords, it was so warm, though it had to be nine at night. "What you say about the murder of Bobby Kennedy as part of a coup d'etat is hard to believe. All of it's hard to believe. But it's thought-provoking," Ingrid said. "Yet, the way you say it makes me want to argue with you."

Roger hesitated, thinking of London. He didn't want to bring everything down on himself all over again, and he looked at Penny for support. She sat on a high bar stool between him and Jan, her hands on her lap. Her small, tiny-chinned face and round cheeks looked childlike and pure next to the glamorous beauty of Ingrid.

"Don't talk about it anymore then," Penny said. "Let's have fun, Roger."

"All right," he said, and sipped from his glass.

"What?" Jan said, leaning over to catch Roger's word.

"Drink up!" Roger said. "Everybody have a drink on me!"

11

As Roger listened to the music from the bar, a soft, mellow blur came over everything, as if a sheer veil had dropped over the world covering its harshness. Yet it was so transparent, he could see everything around him in all its beauty. Even the bartender behind the counter in his white jacket, with the bar lights on him and the dark wall of bottles behind him, seemed a half-real image on a screen. It was like living a movie. Roger lost track of time. He told himself it was only the effects of hashish and alcohol. But as he watched the lights of the pool flicker on the awning and over the faces of the two women, he was torn between a desire for the beauty of Ingrid, which was new and glamorous to him, smooth and sophisticated and knowing, almost corrupt, and Penny and her sweet, young loveliness.

When she saw him look at her, Penny reached out from the stool and rested her hand on his shoulder, leaned close to him, then put her arm around his waist and pressed her cheek against his. He squeezed her to him, but pulled away when Jan said, "Say! I've got a guitar. Why don't we go up on the hillside with a bottle and sing? I've got some vodka in my room, too."

"That would be fun," Ingrid said, and Roger turned to Penny, who slid off her stool and said, "Let's go."

"Down with Nixon! Down with Nixon!" Roger shouted when they walked out the swimming pool gate and started up the dark stairs past the hotel to the dirt road at the top of the hill where all the cars parked.

His cry echoed over the pool, and Jan said, "Shhh, be quiet. You don't know Spain. They won't let you shout like that." He shook his finger at Roger and led them up the stairs to the wide patio in front of the main entrance.

"Wait here while I go get my guitar and the bottle," Jan said. He opened the big wooden door of the hotel, built like a chalet on the steep hillside, then stepped inside.

The slight hum of traffic from the street below was the only sound as they stood quietly in the patio light waiting for Jan to return, until Penny said, "I have to go to the bathroom. Be right back." She stepped around Roger, pushed past the door, and left him, somewhat surprised, with Ingrid.

He turned to her at his side, her beautiful eyes glowing in the faint patio light, and he knew, he just knew, that she had been planted on him, though there was no possible way to prove it.

"You're very passionate, aren't you?" she said, and when he didn't answer, she leaned against him and put her hand on his chest.

He pulled her to him, crushed her breast with one hand and tried to kiss her.

"No, no," she whispered, and writhed in his arms as if trying to get away, but kept her mouth next to his and pressed his hand tighter against her breast. Then, she suddenly moaned and pressed her lips to his, stuck her tongue in his mouth, curled it around his tongue, and tried to cling to him even when he heard the hotel door open and he tried to pull free from her.

Penny stepped outside, squinting, stepped away from the door, saw how close Ingrid was standing to Roger, and said, "Looks like you two are getting mighty chummy, fast."

Roger didn't say anything, but stood there kicking himself for going for the bait, for letting a woman who had probably been put up to it, come between Penny and him.

"Can't we go inside? I don't feel like partying anymore," Penny said, and he stepped toward her, trying to make amends.

12

"What's wrong?" Roger asked when she pulled back from sucking him and sat up on her knees. Her nude torso glowed in the faint light from the window.

"Nothing," she said. "I just got turned off."

"Ingrid?" he asked.

She didn't answer and he reached up and pulled her down on the bed next to him and kissed her. He then fondled her breasts, trying to make her feel better. Then he slid between her legs and fitted his penis in her.

She finally started working at it. She got herself up to a rhythmic state where she pumped back and forth to meet him, but the long, passionate kisses, the whimpering and the whipping of her head back and forth with little cries never came.

13

The doorknob turned very, very slowly, then stopped, and the door creaked and gave a little with pressure from the outside, but held because it was locked. Roger shot his hand out, twisted the knob and jerked the door open on Jan, who was still standing with his hand out, his face bloodless and his hooded eyes round with fright.

"What's up, man?" Roger asked, and Jan blushed bright pink and turned and jumped up the short flight of stairs to the first door at the top, then stepped in without looking back.

"Did you see that?" Roger asked Penny, who was standing right behind him. "I can't figure it out," Roger said, locking the door behind him. "All he had to do was knock. We know who he is."

"What do you mean?" Penny asked, zigzagging down the carpeted stairs with him to the main lobby on the middle floor of the hotel.

"He's a freak, a sex pervert, a thief or a cop," Roger said, lowering his voice when he saw the young, fair-haired woman at the desk glance up at him. He squinted his eyes at the bright morning sunlight, put his dark glasses on and started down the terraced hillside to the dining room.

"If he was a cop, wouldn't he wait until we had gone out?" Penny asked.

"That makes sense. Only an amateur would make that mistake," Roger said. "Unless it was done on purpose to throw me off the track, make it seem like he's hot after you. They can always get in there when we're gone. But people do make mistakes, even cops. He could be just an informer working for the cops and getting carried away. That's a possibility."

"Oh, let's not talk about it," she said. "It's too confusing. It ruins all the fun—people pestering all the time."

"He could be both is all I want to say," Roger said.

"And he could just be a horny guy, too," Penny said, putting her finger to her lips before he could answer, for they had reached the outside entrance to the dining room and Ingrid was standing in the foyer.

She smiled at Roger when he stepped in after Penny, and she turned to walk with them into the dining room without even saying good morning, as if her joining them was taken for granted. Roger took Penny's hand and said, "We're going to have breakfast now, Ingrid," and left her standing there with the smile still frozen on her face.

14

Bare-breasted, her pink nipples velvety soft, Penny walked across the room in only her panties, but her face was long and sad, and she turned away when she saw Roger looking over his typewriter at her. He had slid the clothes bureau into the light from the picture window and stood before it typing.

"Why don't you go swimming?" he suggested. "I'm rolling too good to stop now. I'll go down later."

"I don't want to," she said.

"Afraid you'll see Jan down there?"

"Partly," she said, but still didn't look at him. She stood with her face in shadow, her body in the sun near the window, where he could just see the gun turrets of the red stone fortress in the bright blue sky behind her.

"Ingrid, too?"

"Partly."

"Why don't you go shopping then? You said you wanted to buy some more summer things for this hot weather. I'm getting bumkicked seeing you moping around."

"I don't want to."

"Why not?"

"I just don't feel like it."

"Why not?"

She finally looked at him.

"I don't know how to say the Spanish words. It's just too hard to make them understand me."

He picked up the Spanish-English dictionary from the top of the clothes bureau top, and stepping across the room, slammed it down on the coffee table. "Decide what you need, write it out in English, then write out a translation next to it and go to a store and buy it."

"I don't want to," she said.

"Why not?"

"I don't know."

"Are you afraid guys will bother you on the street?"

"Yes."

"Even in this neighborhood?"

She stared at him, but didn't answer, and he shouted, "Goddamnit! You've got to go do something or you'll stop my writing!"

She stomped barefooted across the floor to the closet and jerked a dress off a hanger. He felt for her, but he had to make her do it, if nothing more than to force her out of her depression. He could see that she was still vulnerable because of Ruth. He couldn't forget the way her mouth quivered when he read the poem about Ruth's beauty. It was a deep hurt that showed on her face. He hurt when she hurt. He wanted to be with her. She loved him and he loved her. But he knew that it was Ingrid who was making her withdraw now, even though he put Ingrid down at breakfast.

He looked up from the typewriter when she closed the door and guessed that someone was trying to break them up. She was suddenly getting bothered by a lot of men in Spain. And women were still pestering him. But he did like the attention, he admitted to himself.

He shook his head and tried to concentrate on the page in the typewriter, focusing his eyes through the horn-rimmed glasses. But the words blurred out. There was fear underlying his desire to love and live with Penny forever, the fear that she would betray him eventually, not to another man but to the state. That, like his wife, she'd cooperate with the police against him. He shook his head again.

"This is what keeps me from totally believing in her," he said to himself. "This is what prompts me to keep my eye out for other girls. The belief deep in me that it doesn't make any difference. That they'll take her away when they want to to anyway, and another girl will do the same thing. I don't have a chance for true love. I'm fatalistic about it, too. This is what eats at the love between us."

He tried to type again and had barely got back into it when he heard her key in the door.

"Did you really try to shop?" he asked as she stepped back into the room.

"Yes," she said in a tiny voice, hiding her eyes from him.

He stepped away from the typewriter on the clothes bureau and asked, "What's really wrong, Penny?"

"I don't know," she said.

"Do you want to go home, goddamnit!"

"I don't knoooow," she said, and turned away from him. With her hair pulled back in a ponytail, her cheeks were flushed and round as apples. She kept her eyes turned down toward the rug.

"Are you going to punish me for letting that girl come on?"

When she shook her head, he asked, "Are you still hurting over that poem I wrote about Ruth, then?"

He was trying to control his voice, trying to keep the anger out of it. But it was loud and accusing, and he could almost see her wither under the sound, as if a blast of heat had come out his mouth.

"I don't...don't knoooooow," she said, and turned away toward the wall.

He stepped toward her, threw his arms around her, pulled her to him, pressed her close, and patted her back.

"We'll try to do something about it. I'll try to make it up to you somehow, by being loyal and good to you, by giving you back that trust you once had, that faith that I would always be there to take care of you, to love you."

He wondered, just for a moment, why she had left him alone with Ingrid, but he added: "I'll try. We'll try. This place is deadening to you. We'll get away. We'll try someplace else. We'll go to where there are lots of young, hip people, so you'll have some kind of social life. So you won't have to wait around all day for me to finish writing because you're afraid to go outside by yourself or afraid some woman will be there to make trouble when we go out together."

She lifted her face.

"I don't trust Ingrid or Jan," he said. "The CIA might be behind the whole thing, trying to break us up."

She looked down again.

"We'll go to Ibiza and then, maybe, the Canary Islands. We'll go where it's warm and keep ourselves footloose. As long as we have our own room, I'll be able to write, I'm sure. Come on, let's go someplace else. We've got the money. To hell with this place. Let's go live and love each other."

He pressed her against him, pried her chin up and kissed her on the mouth. She gave herself to him. But there was a certain tightness to her lips and the way she squinted her eyes instead of merely closing them, the almost desperate way she squeezed her body to his.

Episode Three

FORMENTERA

1

Bent over by his heavy pack, with a typewriter in one hand and his briefcase in the other, Roger stepped out of the airport shuttle bus in his hiking boots and stepped across the asphalt toward the Ibiza bus terminal door. His short-sleeved green T-shirt dark and damp on his chest and under his arms from sweating in the hot weather, he turned his whole body around so he could see how Penny was doing behind him.

Bent over from her backpack in the hot sunlight, too, long hair falling over her face, briefcase and straw bag in her hands, she stepped down from the bus with steady steps, then saw him looking at her and smiled.

Roger wanted to hug her, but turned and pushed through the swinging glass door into the small, one-room terminal. He stopped at the sight of Robey squatted down on his haunches as if waiting for him to arrive, his wild natural glinting gold in the sunlight. With the sun shining through the wide storefront windows, it was hot as a greenhouse inside.

"What are you doing here, man?" Roger asked, stepping aside for Penny and putting his typewriter and briefcase down.

"Just tripping. I've been here a week already. I decided I needed more sunshine. That London weather's just too nausty for comfort," Robey said, grinning, standing up and reaching out to take Roger's hand. "I've been here before, you know. I stayed here six months laust year."

"Why don't you help us get a place, then?" Roger said, picking up his briefcase and typewriter again. "This is Penny."

"Pleased to meet you," Robey said, showing his gray teeth. "Follow me."

He pushed open the glass door and led them down a cobblestoned street that ran along the wharf. "What hauve you got in mind? How long do you plaun to stay?"

"It all depends. We wanted to get some place with our own kind of people—hip, you know—so we could feel more at home," Roger answered. "And..." He glanced at Penny. "...So she could have something to do. I need to score some dope, too. A lot this time, so I'll have enough to finish the book I'm writing without having to worry about running out."

"How much?"

"A pound," Roger said, then added, "This is nice."

He looked over the colorful waterfront with the wooden wharf to his left. Small boats were tied up to it, and the blue water which lapped at their hulls stretched off flatly to the horizon. Casually dressed young people sat at open air tables under the awnings and umbrellas of outdoor cafes to his right. A half mile of white medieval buildings and winding, cobblestoned streets lined a steep hill with an old brown fortress at its peak. Gun turrets and old, rusted cannons faced out over the cliff edge to protect the natural harbor. Penny returned his smile, and he sensed they could be happy here.

"You want hash?" Robey asked.

"Yes, but how about a drink now? I'm hot."

"How about here?" Robey asked, and they sat down at a table only a half block from the bus terminal, among other tables filled with mostly long-haired young men and women.

"Three beers," Robey said to the waiter, glancing at Roger to see if he agreed, and, at his nod, said, "There's going to be a full-moon party on Formentera, a little island near here, tomorrow night. That's the place to score some quantity."

"Let's go then," Roger said, wondering if Robey had planned the party for him. Still, he didn't have much fear and had to take a chance if he wanted to smoke. He'd learned that since his so-called rehabilitation in the nuthouse: the cops had given him personal freedom but not political freedom. They seemed to be willing to let him smoke as much dope as he wanted as long as he stayed out of radical politics.

"Can we go right away? There's no use looking for a room here when we'll only have to move tomorrow," Penny said.

"There's a ferry at eight tonight. We can take that," Robey said. "We can eat here first, if you like, and have something to do until then."

"What about these bags?" Roger asked.

"We can leave them behind the bar here, with a tip!" Robey said, and grinned.

Roger relaxed a little at his interest in money. It meant he wanted a cut for copping the pound for him, that he might not be working for the man.

2

Holding hands, Roger and Penny stepped out of the front door of the two-story, box-shaped green stucco building into the bright morning sunshine of Formentera. They started across the rutted dirt road to the restaurant on the bottom floor of the pension on the opposite side. Roger was in his black T-shirt, light summer Levis, and sandals. Penny wore cut-off Levi shorts, a green halter tied in back, and thongs.

There was a small row of shops down the sidewalk on their side, which formed the main block of the small village, three or four stucco buildings on each side of the only intersection in town at the opposite end of their block, and two dozen stuccoed houses scattered around the adjoining fields. The land was low and flat and surrounded by the sea. Peasant women in long, black dresses, black kerchiefs and white aprons moved around the houses doing chores.

Roger returned Penny's hand squeeze, pleased by the whole scene, really expecting to be happy in the quaint village, when the horn of a cab parked first in a row of four honked and grinning teeth showed behind the shiny glass windshield. Still holding onto Penny's hand, he walked straight across the road toward the restaurant when another horn honked, then another and another, straight down the row of cabs. He gripped Penny's hand tightly and picked his way over the ruts while the horns beeped all the way across the street.

They no sooner reached the restaurant and stepped inside when another foreign woman in a miniskirt that showed everything but her buttocks, stepped past them with long, golden tanned legs. She walked out into the street, heading for the *pensión*, and Roger turned around to watch and wait for the horns. But not one honked, not one time the whole time it took her to cross the street. The horns were only aimed at him.

3

Standing next to a faded drape by a second-floor window of an empty dining hall which overlooked an empty swimming pool coated with dry green scum, Roger toked on his briar pipe. He had fitted a thimble poked full of holes in the bowl and now filled his lungs with the sweet-smelling smoke from the burning black nugget he had cut off the end of his checker-sized ounce slab of hash.

He looked out over the fields of flat farm country at the little island surrounded by the flat sea, at the women in toe-length, full-skirted black peasant dresses. Below him, a little crippled child in a red bathing suit walked on all fours like a monkey just over the fence from the patio, cluttered with old furniture and rusted chairs with bent legs.

A vague, mellow mood came over him. A sudden glimpse of his hero standing on a trash bin at the edge of a crowd in the administration building appeared in his head, and he turned and sat down at his typewriter and began to type.

He tried to capture a scene in which the hero, trying to help the student sit-in from the outside, made a pronouncement for the professors and got attacked by the young hippy speaker, who shouted "Go tell the professors to run their sit-in and we'll run ours!" and was wildly applauded. Roger worked hard. He concentrated. The keys clattered. The picture began to take shape on the page. He hurried so he could get it all before it got away: the mood of anxiety, of fear, then of humiliation. He had it going. The hero was beginning to speak, frightened at drawing so much attention to himself, when Roger noticed a young man in a brown sport shirt come into the dining room and sit at the opposite end of the table right next to his.

He glanced over, but didn't want to lose his train of thought. He saw the man staring at him, but kept on writing. He showed the professor looking up at the hero, asking him to make the announcement, and was trying to capture the rugged build of the man when he heard a loud rasp from the next table. Roger raised his head to see the man in brown scraping the flint of his cigarette lighter over the table as if trying to make it light.

The guy so resembled Teddy Kennedy that Roger was astonished. Then he thought it might be Leary from London. But it wasn't, although it was such an obvious attempt to interrupt him that he looked down again, reread the last paragraph and started typing once more. He focused his eyes on the page and started hitting the keys hard, kept hitting them, forced himself to keep typing even when he heard the rasping sound of the flint on the table again, then again. He kept typing until he finished the scene, never allowing himself to look up even once.

Then, after he had finished three long pages, he stopped, leaned back and looked over to see that the guy had turned his chair and now was watching him full face. The guy then reached out and scratched the flint over the table again. Roger turned and gazed out the window at the flat farmland and the bright blue sky, annoyed, but pleased that he had kept writing under the guy's pressure. Still, saddened a little by the harassment, he clipped his pages together, put his typewriter back into its case, picked it up and, without looking at the guy, walked past him out of the dining room and down the bare hall to his room.

Penny sat by the window reading. She looked up and smiled at him, then stood up and reached out for him.

"A guy pestered me out there," he said, slipping his arms around her. "He looked a lot like that guy Leary from London. I kept writing, though, and, don't worry, I'm going to write this book, no matter what they do."

"It's too bad, though. It's really too bad. I hope he doesn't chase us away from here. I think I could like it here. It's so unpretentious. I hope, I really hope we can make it here, Roger," she said, and hugged him.

4

The moon was high and bright. It shone like a spotlight on the sea. They waited in the warm darkness for the dealer to appear at the party. A single weak bulb hung from the thatched ceiling of the wall-less hut. But the lights in the house across the yard, the light from the fire in the middle of the yard, and the full moon beginning to rise over the dark island made it easy for Roger to see everyone around him. He liked the cosmopolitan atmosphere of the place. There were different types of young Europeans: blond Swedes, curly-haired Spaniards, a young black American, several other Americans, some English guys and girls.

"What kind of stuff has the guy got?" Roger asked Robey.

"Some powerful shit. Kif pollen," Robey answered.

"Is it as good as hash?" Roger asked.

A beautiful blonde girl with a golden tan in white hot pants looked up at him and smiled, as if amused at his naivete. He had to smile himself. A stream of light from the open door of the house touched her long blonde hair, and it glowed white in the darkness. He guessed she was English. She was about as big as Penny and very beautiful. She smiled at him again, and he smiled back and caught Penny frowning at him. He turned away and saw how the flame bristling from a big fire in the middle of the yard reflected on the shiny black wood of a big conga drum. He looked around to see if anyone claimed it, then went over to it, sat down on a log near the fire, pulled it between his legs and started pounding a deep bass beat.

Penny got up, picked up a flute, walked over and started playing variations of trills to accompany him. Then a curly-haired Spaniard picked up some bongos, another hippy came over with a conga drum, and both joined in.

The beat was loud and deep, with a throbbing pulse to it. Roger could feel it in his arms, as if they were separate from him. They seemed to move by themselves without effort or strain. The beat carried him along. People started coming out of the house to crowd around the fire. Soon, they made a thick circle around them and the blonde in the hot pants started dancing in a wide space between him and the flames. Some other willowy girls joined in, then some guys. He kept up the pounding beat while the bongo drum pop-popped in counterpoint and Penny's flute trill floated over the whole sound in a loose, spontaneous, shifting melody which seemed to roll on and on.

"Dance, baby, dance!" Roger shouted, getting into it. But when the beautiful blonde swaying back and forth before him, twisting and gyrating, smiled his way, the tone of the flute dropped low and mournful. Penny was staring with a long face at the blonde. He dropped his head and tried to lose himself in the beat, but his arms got tight and tired, and his hands began to sting. He kept pounding though, until his hands turned numb and his arms finally relaxed. He felt himself start to float as he played, always conscious of the beautiful blonde with the bare brown midriff and the white hot pants swaying back and forth before him. More flutes joined the sweet sound of Penny's flute, and although he couldn't escape the sadness on her face, the flame bristled, the yard glowed white in the moonlight, and the air throbbed with musical sound. People danced and smoked hashish, and he began to feel as if he were finally finding a place for himself in Europe.

He started double-timing a fast beat in the spurt of joy that gripped him when a slender, handsome Spaniard with brown, curly hair tapped him on the shoulder and said, "Hey! That's my drum, man!"

"Okay," Roger said. He kept drumming, not letting the beat go, feeling his hands fan the air, still deep in the sound.

"Hey! That's my drum, man!" the guy said again.

"Well, can't I use it, man?"

"I want to," the guy said, and in the flickering light from the flames, Roger had the eerie feeling that the guy looked just like him: the same widely spaced eyes, sloping down at the corners, the wide jaw and pointed chin, the high cheekbones and narrow cheeks. It could be his own face.

"Let me finish this piece, at least," Roger finally said.

"I'll be right back," the guy said, and left, but returned within a minute or two stripped down to a white loin cloth so that all the muscles on his slender, tanned body rippled in the glow of the flames.

"Now!" the guy said. Roger stopped pounding and shoved the drum at him, then stood up and walked around the big circle of people, not bothering to even glance back.

He stepped into the front room with the dirt floor and poured himself a glass of wine. There were only a few people in the room. He thought of lighting up some hash, anything to relieve his anger, when the blonde came in and joined him by the table.

"I'm Anne Marie," she said. "What's your name?"

"Roger," he said, and poured her a glass of wine, too.

"The beat's not as good now," she said, sipping from her glass.

"I agree," Roger said, and laughed. He noticed that she was standing only a foot away from him. He was still sweating from the drumming and could see how her tanned skin glistened with moisture from dancing. Her light-brown eyes stared into his, her lush pink lips were slightly open, and the desire to kiss her fluttered with fear in him. Drums pounded. High excited cries, laughter. "Dance! Dance!" someone yelled.

She kept staring at him, without speaking, and he put his glass of wine down and turned to face her again. Penny came hurrying through the doorway with a worried crease between her brows. Fear filled him as if he'd been caught kissing the girl. "This is Anne Marie, Penny," he said.

"Let's go," Penny said, not once looking at Anne Marie.

"So soon? It's still early," he said.

"Look at all the people crashed," she said, pointing at the stoned people lying around on the dirt floor in a dark, adjoining room, as if the strong hashish and alcohol had already taken its toll.

"Okay," he said. "But we have to walk back and find our own way, and it's dark on those narrow roads."

"I don't care," Penny said.

"I'll go with you," Anne Marie said. "I know the way. I'm tired of this party, too."

Penny slanted her eyes at her, suspicion giving her face a sly appearance. Her eyes sparked green. Her small mouth looked thick and sullen.

"Well, maybe..." he said, shocked by Penny's ferocity, not knowing what to do.

Robey came in the door and said, "I say, Roger, I've found what you're looking for."

"Here?" Roger asked, trying not to talk in front of the girl.

"Not quite. It's out back a ways, in another house."

"Come on," Roger said, glad to get away.

But Anne Marie stepped behind Robey and, slipping her arms around him, leaned her face over his shoulder and pressed her cheek against his, asking, "Can I come, Robey?"

"Charming," Robey said, grinning. "But it's up to Roger. I certainly don't mind. What say, Roger?"

Anne Marie smiled at him.

"Okay, let's go," he said, although he didn't want people to know his business and he knew Penny didn't want her around.

5

His hands felt as if they were melting together with the hash pipe—finger to knuckle to pipe stem to mouth tip to rim—and even the smoke curling mysteriously up from it looked like the flute trill he could hear from the full-moon party in the distance. A heightened sense of being came over him. He could feel it in his head, way up high at the top of his brain where a dizziness came over him, swept over his body, seemed to shorten his breathing, making him nauseous, separate him from his body, from his hands now holding the pipe far below him, from his knees and feet, too, so close yet so far away, as if under another light. The earthen floor at his feet was like a faded print in some impressionistic painting. The slight rises and hollows had a floating quality, like vaporous cloudy hills hovering over some rural landscape, medieval almost, in which he was walking for a great distance. He was like a giant, making his way slowly, carefully, arms slightly spread for balance, towards the door of the adobe house, to get outside into the fresh air.

He seemed to drop a yard before he touched the hard-packed earth outside and had to brace one arm against the door jamb to stay up, then take deep breaths to keep the nausea down. He tried to stop the dizziness by focusing his eyes on the deep-blue Mediterranean Sea under the moon, the ink-blue sea. He could see the sea in the other direction, too, between two low buildings, with pale clothes on the roofs, the fences before them like iron bars. He could see the moon glimmering like a silky ribbon on the sea.

The moon was phosphorescent, a low molten fire. Even the flat fields of the low island were silvered by it.

A coolness came over the farmland, darkened by a cloud passing over the moon, creating hollows like rolling hills. Moonbeams passed through the shadow of darkness and quivered on his chest like leaves. A lighthouse blinked every other second or so on the dark sea beyond. He could hear dawn coming with a hum. It was a quiet *shhhh* in his head. He could hear water run: *shhhhhhhh*. He stood there tingling, pipe still in hand. He hadn't moved one muscle since he had stepped outside. He heard voices from the party and some girl's name ending with a soft *awww*. He could hear his own voice, coming from some place away from him. He could hear it speak, and the tones were urgent but calm: "I've got to keep a clear head or I'll get busted. I've got to be able to see everything coming down around me: every gesture, every flicker of an eyelash, every cross of an expression on a face. I've got to stay on top of it. Anne Marie is probably a plant. How could she dig me so much so soon? Robey could be playing some kind of game. I've got to stay on top of it! I've got to keep sharp and stay free and alive to finish this book! I've got to!"

6

"Satisfied?" the little Englishman asked from the mat on the dirt floor, rocking back and forth with his arms crossed over his chest. He peered up at Roger from under a lock of short red hair. Anne Marie was just behind him, staring at Roger from her slightly hooded, light-brown eyes, widely spaced like his own. For some reason, she reminded him of his younger sister, though he wasn't sure why. He liked her tiny mouth, with the slightly puffy lips and the slender, slightly bony nose, like some girl from Texas or Oklahoma with just a touch of Indian blood in her.

"Totally!" Roger said, and kneeled down to look into the big clay urn. He ran his fingers through the pale-green pollen. The soft, fluffy substance was soft as flour to his touch. It was like stirring smoke through his fingers—green smoke, magic smoke. He stirred so long, he lost track of time, then finally noticed everyone looking at him when the little Englishman asked, "How do you want to carry it then? What kind of shape?"

"Very considerate of you," Roger said, lifting his hand out of the urn. He'd already been touched by the delicate way the guy brought the pale-green kif pollen in from the other room of the primitive, dirt-floored hut in a giant urn, then let the soft powder fluff through his fingers.

"Dig your pipes in," the guy'd said, handing out long clay pipes and then circling around lighting the pipes, making sure the powder caught before removing the match, firing everyone up like a perfect host.

"I like buying this dope from you because you're not a hard-ass street dude," Roger said. Both the Englishman and his old lady smiled.

"Thank you, very much," she said. She knelt next to the Englishman, as freckle-faced and tall and slender as he, but pretty, with curly hair and a faded orange summer minidress that showed her lightly tanned, freckled legs from her thighs to her toes.

"Two hundred for a pound, right?" Roger asked. He saw doubt in Penny's light eyes, in the low glow of the candle. He noticed how lightly freckled and lightly tanned she was next to the English girl.

The Englishman nodded.

"Then I'd like to carry it in my briefcase, among my papers."

"Good enough," the Englishman said. He dipped a cup into the urn and poured it into a small clay bowl, then did it again, stared at it, put a half cup more in and asked, "Is that fair?"

"No scales, huh?" Roger said, and when the Englishman shook his red head, added, "Looks about the size of a pound of coffee. What do you think, Penny?"

"It looks like a pound, Roger," she said.

"Fine, then," Roger said as he watched the Englishman take large sheets of coarse gray paper, fit them together, pour the powder on them, fold the sheets close to an 8½-by-11 sheet of paper, sprinkle water on the package, and then lay hot bricks from his fire hearth in a corner of the hut on it to flatten it down. He then let them steam the package into shape until they cooled off, replaced them with some newly hot bricks, and kept repeating the process with slow, careful motions which fascinated Roger.

"I sure love the sight of that," Roger said, watching the steam curl up from the bricks. "It makes me feel transcendental. I..." He stopped, aware that Anne Marie was smiling at him. He felt self-conscious, but he reached into his back pocket, pulled out his notebook and pen, leaned in next to the fire for light, laid the notebook on the mat, hunched over, and started to write. He wrote quickly to capture the feeling before it escaped, oblivious to everything around him.

IN THAT LIGHT

I keep hearing my voice now that I'm high
and my mind is floating
a sense of oneself in the third person
like an insane man
or an artistic genius
at the height of his inspiration

I
under the hazy veil of hash
view myself by accident
suddenly hear my words
all the I's &
what I did &
I do
feeling very satisfied with myself
idling the time away
a calm in the storm
of what's usually happening with me

until my voice reaches
the mind inside
where the light is &
the way to truth
if followed
&
in that light
how small and yet
how fine
to hear
oneself

"Hey! Do you guys want to hear a poem?" he asked.

"Yes," Anne Marie said, and everyone nodded but Penny. She watched him silently from a mat against the wall.

"I just wrote it," Roger said. "So expect flaws. I mean I haven't edited it. I don't know what's there myself."

"Read it," Robey said, and Roger read it in a slow, almost halting manner, wanting every word to sink into everybody's mind. When he finished, he lowered the notebook and looked around.

"Beautiful!" Anne Marie said, and smiled, lips puffy and sensual. "It was a religious experience, Roger."

"Oh, thank you!" Roger said.

"It was very deep!" she said, and slid over next to him on the mat. Roger wondered if she was putting him on, but she looked right into his eyes. "I really like it."

"It was quite on, quite appropriate," Robey said. "I liked the spontaneity, the way it came out of your high."

"Quite good," the Englishman said, and his old lady smiled at Roger and asked, "You're a novelist, too, aren't you?"

"Yes," Roger said, feeling as if he had finally found a place in Europe where he'd be accepted. But when Anne Marie leaned slightly closer to him and Penny crawled over from the wall and sat on the other side of him, her mouth hanging down at the corners, he suddenly found himself sandwiched between the two girls and very aware of the competition between them.

7

The narrow lane wound silvery and silent between the high stone fences before them. He could make out the houses in the village now. Their footsteps made hardly any noise and no one spoke. The package was still warm in Roger's hand. He wanted to reach out with the other and take Penny's hand, to console her for Anne Marie's coming along. But still hurt by her indifference to his poem, he kept his free hand down at his side.

Anne Marie had called out, "Roger! Oh, Roger!" and ran to catch up with them, explaining that she could show them the way back.

"Isn't it a beautiful night?" she said now.

"Really, it is," Roger said, and gazed up at the full moon, which had reached the very center of the sky, then fixed his eyes on the gauzy strip of the milky way, clear as poured milk curling into a hot cup of coffee.

"All the days have been like this, this summer," Anne Marie said.

"It must have been a real pleasure," Roger said, trying to be congenial, but too conscious of Penny's silence to volunteer much. He watched his footing and stepped over a deep rut in the road, grateful for the bright moonlight.

"I'll have to go back to England pretty soon," Anne Marie said. "I've had three months of fun now and I'll have to work through the winter. I sure wish I could find a job in Spain so I could stay. Why don't you come and see me in London? I can give you my address."

She touched Roger's bare arm, then, leaning to see around him, said, "And you, Penny!"

Penny didn't answer, her face white and sullen in the moonlight. There was only the sound of their footsteps in a tight silence until the stone fences finally ended. The village lay white and quiet before them. Anne Marie stopped at the first house and said, "I live right here, you know. Nice to have you around. I'll see you tomorrow."

"See you," Roger said. He walked quietly with Penny until they turned up the wide, rutted main road of the small settlement, with every window dark, then asked, "Why didn't you like my poem?"

"Because she made such a fuss over it," Penny said.

"You don't think much of my art then," Roger said, stepping up his pace, wishing he could get away from her.

"Try to understand, Roger," she said.

"Understand what? That you're so jealous you shut yourself off to my spirit—the best part of me?"

She skipped to catch up with him and grabbed his hand.

"She liked you so much. She paid so much attention to you that she ruined something both you and I would have shared. It wasn't that I shut myself to your spiritual beauty at all! It was that I couldn't get past her petting you and complimenting you every chance she got. And the way you liked it!"

"Goddamn, Penny! I'm only human!" he said, and jerked his hand free and crossed onto the left side of the road as they drew near their box-shaped, two-story *pensión*.

"Wait a minute, Roger!" she said, and ran after him, grabbed his hand again and said, "Stop! Listen to me!"

He stopped but stared straight ahead down the dark road.

"It's no fun seeing some girl fall all over you. We might as well have stayed with Ruth and Craig. Can't you see that? Would you like to see some guy pawing me all over? Now would you?"

Her face was shaped like a cat's, with slightly uptilted corners to her eyes and long, curling lashes, but it was so serious now it touched him.

"No," he said. "I wouldn't like it."

"Can't you see how I feel then?"

"Yes," he said. "I can see it."

"Don't you see that if we stay here with her around, I'm going to have to be on guard all the time?"

"I could see that," he said.

"Can't we go, then? Can't we leave here and try some place else? We don't have any strings. We're free to go."

She gripped both his arms and looked into his face, and a wave of feeling for her swept over him.

"She's probably a plant anyway," Roger said. "She saw the whole dope deal come down and even walked it home. She couldn't have been in a better position if she was working with the cops. Yes, we can go. I've got some great dope and plenty of it. My book's rolling, even though we're on the move. Yes. We can go. Maybe we can still find some place we won't be messed with. Sure! Let's go! Let's get out of here!"

Episode Four

LAS PALMAS

1

Turning to see who'd bumped into him in the steamship ticket line in Barcelona, Roger saw the big, glistening front teeth of a smiling black man behind him, then the immaculate white collar of the turtleneck sweater and the shiny black skin of the face.

"I just can't understand it. My fiancee sold three cars of mine in Sierra Leone but hasn't mailed the money to me."

He lifted his hands and showed the orange palms to Roger, as if asking him to explain it. Roger just shrugged his shoulders, then turned to face the ticket booth and Penny again. The problem was much too personal for him, and it involved money, which put him off. He sensed something.

"Well, she probably has taken the money and spent it all on a good time for herself, anyway," the black man said, and snorted, making Roger glance back at him again and then smile with Penny at the guy's tight grin.

The black man was about thirty with a healthy round look to his face, obviously well-fed and educated, broad-shouldered and very neat and clean, with just the slightest hint of an African accent, which was more in his choice of words than in the pronunciation.

"Definitely, I'm in trouble though," he said in a low, mournful tone. "There's no question about it. I, Abdulla, am definitely in trouble."

Roger turned to face the ticket booth again, wishing the three people in front of him would hurry up, thinking the guy was either a con man or an agent playing con man. The second involved the first here, but either way it would cost money and blood, his money and blood. Roger kept his back to Abdulla until he finished buying his ticket to the Canary Islands, a warm place he could go to without having to cross any international border lines with his pound of kif pollen. He only returned the black man's smile when he was walking away.

"Looks like he's up to something, doesn't it?" Penny said when they walked out of the tall building onto the sidewalk of the waterfront district.

"Don't worry," Roger said. "We probably won't ever see him again."

"I hope not," she said. "We've got enough problems."

2

"Uh-oh! Guess who's here!" Roger said, looking past Penny, who was sitting next to him at the long bar. The door was open wide, and he could see the black man stepping in off the wet cobblestones of the little Barcelona street. A bleached blonde in a tailored suit with bright makeup on her face and long false eyelashes, standing just outside the door, smiled at him as he stepped by.

"Who?" Penny asked.

"Abdulla, the black guy from the ticket line."

"Oh, no! Where?" Penny asked, and leaned out from the dark bar on her stool to see where Roger was pointing.

"Better lean back or he'll see us," Roger said. Penny fell back against the bar right away so that she was hidden by the man sitting on the other side of her.

Ornate mirrors lined the wall behind the bar. The whole atmosphere was dark and secluded. Abdulla walked straight down the line of people and occasional empty stools right down to the end of the bar where he spotted Roger. He broke into a wide grin and said, "Oh, how delightful! I knew...I just knew I would see some friends out tonight!"

Roger looked over Abdulla's new sportscoat, his creased slacks, and his white turtleneck sweater. He then glanced at his bright teeth and thought how handsome they were. "Have a drink," he said.

"Cognac," Abdulla said to the thin bartender with the pale skin and narrow black mustache.

As soon as he got his glass, Abdulla raised it and said, "Your health." Then he set it down and asked, "What made you come in here?"

"A cloudburst. We took the first spot we could find to get out of the rain."

"Well, if you bring your girl in here, you know what the Spaniards will think, don't you?" Abdulla's eyes slanted nearly closed as if he knew something mysterious.

"What?" Roger asked.

"They'll think she's a whore," Abdulla said.

"Why?" Penny asked.

"Because the women on this street are whores," Abdulla said, then grinned.

"I don't think she looks like a whore by anybody's stretch of the imagination," Roger said, raising one eyebrow.

"Oh, don't misunderstand me. Ha-ha-ha-ha!" Abdulla laughed and rocked back on his stool, showing the whole upper row of his teeth. "I did not mean that the lady looked like a whore at all. I did not mean that. I just meant the way the Spaniards think, that's all. Ha-ha-ha-ha!"

3

"I wonder what his story is?" Roger said when Penny put her arms around him in the big, soft bed. The shades were up. Lightning flashed through the rain-streaked glass panes, making the room look like a large aquarium, lighting up the stark white face of the gentleman in the top hat on the faded wooden hotel sign outside their window.

"I don't know, but I don't trust him," she said, huddling closer to him when she heard the distant boom of thunder that followed a moment after the flash. "I hope we never see him again."

"He just might show up on that boat tomorrow, though," Roger said.

"I hope not. I really hope not. It's first one thing, then another. Aren't we ever going to be able to just lead our own lives?" she asked, and he squeezed her to him with another shimmering flash of lightning and the long, rumbling burst of thunder which followed.

4

They stood facing north and backwards on the main deck of the passenger liner headed south. It looked like a toy tin steamship with its molded lines and bright orange colors. The Spanish coastline was a low green line to the west on their left. They watched sea gulls, hovering with stiff-chevroned wings in the wake of the ship. Buffeted by invisible currents, they glided along an unseen wind at fifty knots an hour, keeling off to break and dive at times into the pale-green foam for garbage. The tinfoil glimmer of the waves curled toward them under an overcast sky like molten lead cooling off. "Isn't it beautiful?" Roger said.

"Yes," Penny said. "When you aren't bothered by anybody."

"You mean Abdulla?" he asked.

"Yes," she said, frowning. "Look."

Abdulla stepped out of a glass door onto the deck near them. Dressed very fashionably in a rust-colored turtleneck sweater, brown sportscoat and shiny brown slacks, he said, "How are my friends today?"

"We were just going inside," Penny said, and stepped past him to pull open the door, then held it open for Roger. They both stepped into the swaying lounge of the ship, hurried down a carpeted hallway to the first-class lounge, and moved down it to the darkest corner. Roger ordered two Heinekens from the white-jacketed bartender. "You sure let him know you didn't want him around," he said to Penny.

"Unless he's stupid," she answered.

"Or persistent," he said, paid the bartender, then clicked glasses with her.

They both turned to face the bar. Roger studied the mediocre landscape painting of turreted buildings on top of a rocky hillside that sat over the bar. He guessed that the landscape was put there to steady dizzy sea travelers like himself. Even now he was so totally overwhelmed by the sight and movement of waves, he could see the wavy lines of the sea on the green slopes and terraced hills of the painting. He turned around to refocus his eyes on the distant horizon when he saw Abdulla only a couple of steps away.

"Let me buy you a drink," Abdulla said.

Roger had to smile, it was such an insincere offer. "Since I've already got one and so does Penny, I'll buy you one. What'll you have?" Roger said.

"Cognac," Abdulla said to the bartender. As the bartender poured it for him, he asked, "How do you like sailing?"

"Except for the wobbly feeling and getting dizzy when I try to read, beautiful," Roger said.

"Beautiful? Why is it that Americans always choose the word *beautiful*" Abdulla asked, taking a sip of cognac without smiling once. "What does it mean, really? They always tell you if they like something by saying *beautiful*! They should be more specific, I think."

"That makes sense," Roger said. "I'd have to go along with that."

"And it's like the dogs. Americans always like the dogs. They think the dogs are so wonderful. They are always saying how beautiful the dogs are. All I know is that the dogs eat shit and bark at the moon!"

Even Penny laughed with Roger, but Roger added, "Americans like dogs because they live in mostly urban areas, and dogs are about the only natural things they get to associate with that like them, too. America's not like Africa, where you've got nature all around you."

"Oh, yes. I can see that. Yes, yes, I can," Abdulla said. Then he turned his attention to the mural, which he seemed to study for quite a while, stealing glances at Penny but not saying even one word. Roger and Penny finally stared at each other and then, as if with mutual consent, both finished their beers, got off their stools, and left. Only Roger said, "See you."

"That was really strange the way he suddenly got quiet, wasn't it?" Penny said when they started down the hallway to their cabin.

"He's a strange bird, all right," Roger said.

"And the way he kept glancing at me as if I was one of the whores in Barcelona last night," she said.

"He seemed to have his eye on you, that's for sure," Roger said when she took out her key to open their cabin door. "But I feel like writing right now. Maybe it's the beer, but I feel inspired. I'll see you in a while."

He walked away and, wanting to look out at the sea but not go out into the strong wind again, found himself a warm spot in the first window he saw, sat on its ledge, which was the size of a short bench, put his feet up on it, leaned his shoulder against the glass and pulled the drapes closed behind him.

He sat enjoying the slow rise and fall of the ship, the cushiony sway, listening to the creaking of bunks, the gurgling noises and splitting groans from inside the ship as if it was being torn apart. He guessed that the noises must have whispered in the ears of sailors as they slept in their old sailing ships, and he was sure he had discovered one of the reasons they believed in ghosts. But in his cubbyhole of privacy and warmth, he looked out at the scales of sunlight on the leaden sea out by the horizon, feeling a mood of ecstasy coming over him. He pulled his notebook and pen out of his back pocket, opened the notebook on his knee and poised his pen over the paper to write, when the drapes suddenly ruffled at his side, and he looked up to see Abdulla's round face smiling at him.

"Aw ha! So, here's where you've been hiding," he said. Roger sighed as the ecstatic feeling slipped out of him.

5

"Do you know what the Captain said to me?" Erica said. She was sitting between Roger and Abdulla who had come over with her and sat down at Roger and Penny's table as if they were old friends, without even asking them. She was a Dutch girl with short blonde hair cut off just below the ears exposing her plump white neck. The dining room was enclosed in glass, and Roger could see the sun with only a slim cloud trailing across it down low near the horizon in a clear blue sky.

"What?" Roger asked, noticing how high-bridged and thick her nose was, her long nostrils giving her the appearance of a shark.

"He asked me if I wanted to earn a little money when I got to Las Palmas."

"What do you think he meant?" Roger asked.

"What do you think?" she said, staring at him with big gray eyes, and Abdulla snorted and grinned and looked at Penny.

Roger picked up his menu without answering Erica and said, "I think I'll have some oysters."

"I will, too," Penny said, smiling at Roger as if she were pleased he hadn't gone for the girl's bait.

"And so will I!" Abdulla said. "You, too, Erica?"

"Mmmmm, yes," she said, and Roger gave the order to the waiter who had the features and thick, black, wavy hair of his cousin, Julian. Roger felt as if he had been manipulated into being host of the dinner party. He was sure of it when Abdulla said, "How kind everyone is. Somebody always comes through when another person is in need. Like twenty dollars at the right time can save a person's life sometimes."

Erica kept staring at him as they ate, and he wondered if she wanted some money to screw him, or if she just wanted to screw him, or if she was just trying to cause friction between him and Penny, who ate her meal quickly and said, "We've finished eating, Roger. Why don't we go out on deck and watch the sun go down? It's warm out this evening."

"Sure," he said, and motioned to the waiter, who came over and gave him his check. But by the time he had come back with the change, Abdulla and Erica had finished eating, too, and they both stood up when he and Penny stood as if they intended on joining them.

"I hate that corny music they play in there," Penny said when they all stepped out on deck.

Roger nodded as if he agreed, although he thought he knew the real reason she wanted to get away from the table. But he liked it much better outside himself. The setting was warm. The sea was so smooth now, and there was just a light flutter of wind to cool him off.

"I don't like the music either. It's so old-fashioned. Why don't you and I go in and see the captain and ask him to play some more modern music, more suitable to our generation?" Erica said, and took Penny's hand and turned as if to walk inside with her. But Penny jerked her hand loose, her eyes slanted nearly closed with the wounded suspicious look she gave Anne Marie at the full-moon party, and said, "I don't want to!"

"No offense," Erica said, standing stiffly next to her.

Roger was embarrassed for her, thinking Penny reacted a little too strongly. Still, he admired Penny for fighting back what she considered a subterfuge. "Don't do anything you don't want to do," he said, killed his beer and heaved the glass so far off the ship that it made a long, falling arch before splashing into the waves.

Erica watched where it disappeared for a few moments, then turned to Roger and said, "I wish I were that free," in a wistful manner that touched him. "I think I'll go to my cabin," she added, and turned and stepped back into the dining room.

Roger felt a little sorry for her then, even insulted for her, when Abdulla said, "I screwed her three times this afternoon. Three times! All afternoon we were in bed."

"I don't want to hear that," Penny said, and, glaring at Abdulla, turned and stepped inside, too. Roger waved to Abdulla and stepped inside after her.

6

Roger had just dropped his backpack on the bed of the *pensión* when there was a knock at the door.

"Yeah?" he asked, glancing out the fifth-story window at the gray water of the Las Palmas harbor.

"Why don't you come down and see the view from the sun porch?" Abdulla's voice said, and Roger glanced at Penny, whose green eyes had a flat expression in them.

"You can see most of the old section of town from there. It's nothing like those fancy buildings we saw when we left the ship."

Penny looked out the high window as if she hadn't heard Abdulla, and Roger hesitated. She'd been icily silent since Abdulla suddenly stepped next to them at the foot of the gangplank in a shiny dark gray suit, carrying expensive bags in his hands, and got into the cab with them, sitting down with his briefcase in his lap. Roger had guessed that he'd be the one to end up paying the cabbie, not Abdulla. He was sure of it when Abdulla said he knew where a nice cheap hotel was in the older section of the city, then told the driver where to go without waiting for an answer. But Roger let him lead, since he didn't have any idea of where to go himself.

"All right, Abdulla, we'll join you," Roger said. "Come on, Penny." He motioned to Penny and opened the door to walk down the hall with Abdulla.

"Nice view!" Abdulla said, pointing out the hills with a scattering of houses near the top, maybe three or four miles from them. Then he leaned over the edge of the porch and pointed down at the narrow street, crowded with people and cars. "There's a nice cafe down there, too. Mmmmmmmmmm-mm, smell the hamburgers! You can even smell the hamburgers from up here. Perfect time for a hamburger!"

"I'm not interested," Penny said, and turned and walked back down the long, dark hall toward their room. Roger waved as he left Abdulla out on the sun porch and followed her into their room.

"What's the matter?" he asked.

"I'm tired of him hanging around, that's all. I don't want to go have a hamburger with him, at all. I don't want to go anywhere with him. He's sleazy."

Penny shook her head in exasperation, then turned away and looked out the window when there was a knock at the door.

"Yes?" Roger asked.

"It's me, Abdulla!"

"We're talking right now, Abdulla," Roger said, glancing back at Penny.

"I just thought it would be nice to go to the Russian Circus. Why don't we go tonight?"

"I don't know, Abdulla," Roger said, expecting Penny to say something. But she kept her back to him, staring out the window. He stepped next to her and stared down at the small, red-striped circus tent, five stories down and a block away.

"Cute, huh?" he said.

Penny glanced down at the tent but didn't speak, not even when Abdulla called out, "What do you say?"

"What time does it start?" Roger asked.

"The *patrón* says seven."

Still, Penny didn't say anything, just stared down at the circus with soft, long-lashed green eyes. Her pink lips were pert but sensitive, without any hardness, and Roger, trying to compromise, said, "We'll meet you there."

"Out in front!" Abdulla said.

Roger had to smile, but when his footsteps moved off down the wooden floor of the hall, Penny said, "We're not going to pay his way."

7

The Cossack marching sound floated in the window from the striped circus tent. Flags fluttered from the poles. A line of people filed in, but Roger couldn't see well enough to make out Abdulla. The sky over the African coast, fifty miles to the east, was already turning dark. "People are going in now!" he called. He wanted to go to the circus, and Abdulla was entertaining and full of energy, even if there was the daily hit for food and money and the sexual innuendos.

"I'm almost done," Penny called back from the bathroom, but she'd already taken an awful long time and he hoped Abdulla didn't get offended.

8

"Would you like to go have a drink?" Roger asked after the show. Abdulla stood with his back to the canvas flap of the tent exit and appeared to be looking down the now darkened street behind their hotel. Roger guessed Abdulla was annoyed because they hadn't met him and paid his way in.

The circus was fun, though the only thing Russian about it was some of the music and the costumes of the performers. Roger had finally seen him sitting in the second row near the entrance to the tent after they had gotten seated. But Abdulla kept his black face turned away even though they had to pass in front of his section to get to their seats.

Without saying hello first, Abdulla looked down at his jeweled gold watch, studied it for a moment, then said, "Hmm-mmmmm, yes, I've got time."

9

"I'm having trouble getting my boat fare home to Sierra Leone," Abdulla said, leaning over the counter of the curved bar, his elbow next to the inner shelf, lined with cooked meats, fish and poultry, and different kinds of bread.

"Why?" Penny asked, sitting up straight at the bar so she could see him better, not even looking at Roger, all her attention focused on Abdulla's round, black face.

"I stayed in school in Italy one semester longer than I planned, and now my reserves are all gone. I'm just in trouble."

"Why don't you wire home then?" Penny said.

"Like I told you in Barcelona, my fiancee has not wired me the money. I can't understand it."

"What about your family?" she asked.

"Oh, I have no family. I'm an orphan now," Abdulla said, and shrugged his shoulders like life was very tough.

But it was too much to ask, and Roger wasn't going for it. "What will you do when you get back?" he asked, taking it in another direction.

Abdulla stared at him for a moment, then straightened up on the stool, his eyes bright and black, and said, "I'll make my education pay off! I'll become a big man!" Then, he suddenly grinned and said, "Maybe a consul!"

10

"He does look like a black consul though, in some tropical port or other, with his shiny gray suit, polished black shoes, briefcase and expensive bags," Roger said, glancing around at the bare room they lived in: yellow plaster walls, unpolished wooden floor, yellow light from a single unshaded bulb hanging from a wire in the ceiling. The bed was rough, unpolished wood, too, and so was the bed stand and clothes bureau and two chairs. There was no desk or table, though it was one of the best rooms on the fifth floor, with its own bathroom and shower.

"What do you think he's up to?" Penny asked with a tone that implied she had no doubt Abdulla was up to something.

Roger smiled because it meant she admitted that something was up and that it could be the police, if Roger said so. "He's not just a con man. I don't believe that. He has ability. He's very clever, and he's obviously educated. It requires not just money, but smarts and guts to study."

He watched her step out of her purple minidress, then slide her panties off in one continuous motion and stand slender, curvy and nude before him, a small triangle of dark brown bush at her crotch.

"So, he's not a bum, not by a long shot. He could become a consul, possibly, with the right connections in Sierra Leone, since educated men are rare and important in an under-developed country."

"Why's he so cheap then?" she asked, pulling his old pajama pants up around her waist, pinning them in front.

"That could be a con; I mean, a cover, a front. He could be playing that way for several reasons. First of all, it could be a smoke screen for his real job of watching and manipulating us."

"What do you mean by that?" she asked, turning to face him, her bare breasts masked by a band of white from her bathing suit top.

"If a guy gets you giving to him, he makes you responsible for him, which gives him power over you and also allows him to be around you all the time to watch you."

"It's a pretty negative way to go about it, making you resent him," she said, her upper lip lifting with her contempt.

"Not if we'd gone for the bait. We'd feel sorry for him then, and he'd have worked his way into our hearts. He'd have a grip on our emotions. A pretty strong place to be."

She slipped the buttonless pajama top over her head as he talked, but he could tell she was listening.

"That's the way some women rule their men, with their weakness. They can't order them around since they're not strong enough, but they can control them by making them feel compassion for their female weakness. It's pretty clever. And the police know I have this thing for black people. It could have worked."

"You think he's an agent then," she said, her body covered now, but the nylon material clinging to her curves.

"Mainly," he said, leaning back on the bed, propping himself up by his elbows.

"Then why does he come on so sexual at times? Another way to turn us off on him."

"He might be trying to break us up, too, to get to me, get between me and somebody I trust, trust as much as..."

"...You trust anybody," she finished for him, and sat down on the edge of the bed and stared down at the floor with a far-away stare in her eyes.

He rolled over and, with his left elbow still holding him up, put his right arm around her and pulled her back down on the bed next to him.

She lay still with her mouth closed and her eyes open, staring up past him at the ceiling.

"First, there was always somebody messing with me, and now there's always somebody messing with you," he said. "I can see how he gets you annoyed, and I don't dig it either. The way he always appears around us, finds us in a tiny bar in a side street in Barcelona, and gets off the boat with us after we freeze on him on board."

"Why can't you just tell him to split then?" she said.

"Then they'll just bring in somebody else, and I'll have to go through the whole thing over again with them. This way I know who it is and how to deal with him. He's not going to get to me."

"He's getting to me," she said, then lay still.

He felt sorry for her for being involved with him.

"I still believe he's just a leech though, that you could tell him off, and we'd have some peace. You probably go along with me just because you don't want to have to start all over with another girl, because you already know how to deal with me. Is that it?"

"I care for you," he said, without denying her words. "And I'll continue to treat him as a cop. That's my way of surviving under this kind of constant pressure."

She turned her face and stared right into his eyes. Her eyes were so close that his eyes strained to adjust.

"Why do they keep putting this pressure on you then? Why don't they just kill you like they killed the Kennedys and King?"

He rolled back away from her, thought a moment, then swung his legs over hers and sat up on the edge of the bed, still not answering. Then he stood up and began to undress, taking off his pale-green cardigan sweater, his dark-blue turtleneck shirt and his black T-shirt, which he hung on the wall hook above his backpack. "Probably because my family's involved too deeply already," he said, turning to face her.

"They've cooperated too completely already and would know if I died mysteriously."

"They could get away with it. They could pretend you committed suicide or got killed in an accident."

"Yeah, they could," he said, and sat down and untied his hiking boots, pulled them off one by one, stuffed his socks into them, then stood up and pulled his green Levis off and hung them on the hook, too. He didn't speak again until he was standing nude before her with his green nylon pajamas in his hand. "Maybe there are still cops who believe in trying to be human. Whatever it is, they've ruined my life with or without killing me! They ruin my life now. They've almost driven me to suicide before. They still might!"

He put the trousers of his pajamas on.

"They won't have guilty consciences, even if that's still possible in a cop. But we're still a partial democracy, not a total corporate fascist state yet!"

He slipped into his pajama top, reached up and turned off the light, then slid in under the blankets next to her. "They could be charged with murder, too. Maybe they'll open a can of worms that will grow into monsters they can't control, if they do. Maybe if they started killing the writers like Hitler did, they'd have to kill too many other people. And they might get killed! Maybe we haven't reached that state of fascism yet. I honestly don't know."

"In the meantime"—her voice was right next to his ear in the darkness—"every person that comes around with sex or money on their mind, man or woman, you think they're cops and won't chase them away, because you figure somebody else will just turn up and you'll still be in the same boat," Penny said.

"Yes," he said, turning toward her, but barely able to make her face out in the dark.

"And you go along, not trusting anybody because anybody might be a cop or an agent for the cops, including me, right?"

He watched her face, which was in profile to him, facing up toward the ceiling, rather than at him, talking up into the darkness.

"Yes," he said, and put his arm around her. But she didn't move or look at him. He slid his hand down to her crotch, touched the mat under the nylon cloth and cupped his fingers over it, feeling the soft slit. He kissed her on the neck. She didn't move, so he took her hand, slid it down to his crotch and placed it on his dick, but she just let it lay there. He then leaned over and kissed her on the lips, but she just stared at the ceiling. He could see the glow in her eyes from the faint light of the window.

He leaned back and rolled over on his stomach, let one arm hang down over the bed for a long time before he began to get sleepy, aching inside, feeling that she was being unfair to him. They had talked about this in London already. He felt she should try to understand, take as much love as he could give her and try to help him build on this. But he didn't tell her, just kept it inside where it hurt.

11

A knock on the door woke him. Gray clouds filled the window, but he saw her still in his mind staring up at the dark ceiling, a faint glow in her eyes, saying, "You go along not trusting anybody, including me," and his belly tightened with sadness as he fell asleep.

He lifted his head at another knock. "Who is it?"

Nobody answered, so he let his head sink back down on the bed, glad to be able to fall back to sleep, but another knock cracked through the fog in his mind.

"Who is it?" he asked again, and again there was no answer. He threw the blankets back and slid out of bed, stepped across the cold floor to the door and opened it on Abdulla standing in the dark hall.

"Good morning! Would you like to have breakfast with me?" he asked, smiling, looking all teeth and dark shadow in the dark hall.

"What time is it, Abdulla?" he asked, his voice rising with his right eyebrow.

"Ohhh," Abdulla looked down at his gold watch, "about eight."

"Don't you think it's a little early to come knocking on a man's door?" Roger asked, wild curls sticking out all over his head, trying to keep his patience.

"Oh, I can wait for you," Abdulla said, showing the whites of his eyes.

Roger snorted and shook his head with a grudging smile
on his lips. "You're incorrigible, man. All right, wait out on the
sun porch. But it'll take me a few minutes."

"Certainly. Certainly. No trouble at all," Abdulla said,
and turned and walked off down the hall, passing under a skylight. Roger saw a new blue sportscoat and gray flannel slacks
he hadn't seen before.

Penny was staring at him from her pillow when he closed
the door.

"It's time to get up anyway," he said, assuming she heard
everything. "It's almost eight."

She turned her head away and faced the wall. Her long
hair fell in a wide wave over the pillow behind her. She shud-
dered and the blanket jerked.

"What's wrong?" he asked, and dropped to his knees on
the mattress, stomach fluttering, leaning over to see her face,
sure he'd hurt her badly last night.

"I can't breathe. It's too humid in here," she said, a green
eye glancing at him over her shoulder, but still not letting him
see her face.

But at least she wasn't crying, and Roger, feeling better,
touched her forehead with the palm of his hand, letting it lie
there a moment.

"You've got a little fever, I think. Your forehead's warm.
Do you want to see a doctor?"

She turned her face toward him and studied him for a
moment, green eyes intent, then said, "No. It'll pass. I just feel
icky, that's all. I'd better not get up."

"Are you sure? I don't want you to get sick."

"Yes, I'm sure," she said.

"Should I get you something to eat? Should I bring something up to you?"

Her eyes had that intense green stare in them again, as if
she were studying him.

"Tea! I'll bring you up some tea," he said, but she said,
"No, nothing now." Then, still staring at him with those deep
green eyes, she said, "You go on down and have breakfast. I'll
sleep in. I might feel better later."

"All right," he said, then quickly showered and shaved
and dressed and walked out on his toes to keep from waking
her. But he was unsure now if she was really sick or didn't

want to be with Abdulla or was hurt because he said he didn't trust her either.

Abdulla wasn't on the sun porch. The sky was overcast with pale gray clouds and there was a heavy warmth in the air, almost sticky. So she could really be allergic to the dampness. She'd been sickly as a child, like him, and did have several allergies. He stepped back off the checkered black and white tile floor and walked down the long hall to Abdulla's door and knocked, then knocked again, staring at the dark wood and the number 7 on it. When there was still no answer, he walked a few steps down the hall to the men's room, where he looked around and glanced into the stalls, saw no one, and hurried down the long flight of stairs to the street and down to the cafe. There, he asked for tea for his sick wife, "*¿Es posible comprar té para mi esposa enferma? ¿Para llevar arriba?*"

"*Sí,*" the fat *patrón* said, and poured Roger a pot of hot water, put two tea bags in it and placed it on a tray.

"*Bueno, bueno, gracias,*" Roger said as he paid him and hurried back down the sidewalk and up the five flights to the top floor. He strode down the dark hall to his door, and, holding the tray in one hand, unlocked the door with the other. He put the tray on the chair.

"Here's some tea for you!"

Penny's green eyes studied him again. Then she said, "Thank you," wheezed twice and asked, "You going back down?"

He shook his head. "I'll stay here and drink the tea with you."

"What about Abdulla?"

"He was gone by the time I got dressed," he said.

"Good," she said.

"I really can't figure the dude myself, not all the little things. Maybe they know he's a leech and just want to use him, since he's passing through and convenient to use." Roger saw her stare at him with that intent look again, and, not wanting to bring up the subject again, he didn't tell her that he hoped Abdulla would go so they could try and make it.

She looked down at her pillow, punched it into shape behind her, slung one arm over it and poured some tea into her cup with the other hand. Then she poured it back into the pot without looking at him.

12

Her tiny heart-shaped lips popped open with a wheezing intake of breath, then closed as she blew it out, like some fish on dry land on the bed next to him in the soft light of the dark room. A glow wavered on the ceiling from the circus lights below. Abdulla had disappeared without saying a word of goodbye to them, but Penny hadn't acted any happier at all.

"I don't know what else to do," she said. "It looks like we're going to be bothered as long as we live. And it's not worth it to me if you don't really love me and don't really trust me. I might as well go home."

Roger turned over on his side so he could see her face better. "How can I really trust you when you won't admit that Abdulla's following us and making trouble for political reasons? You keep insisting that all the problems we have are just coincidences. You hate him being around more than I do. Yet you won't admit *why* he's always around!"

She turned to face him, too. It was a small bed, he saw, but they both fit.

"He's lecherous!" she said. "He has sex on his mind all the time."

"Not true. Not just sex, but food!"

"And money!" she said.

"He's a total mooch," he said. "He never mentions politics, but he's from a conservative black African state! His behavior is greedy like a conservative!"

She touched his hand. "Neither of us like him, really, though me less than you."

She shook her head very slowly, and he could see the light from down below shift in her eyes then stop and glow like tiny dots. "If you only trusted me," she said, "then I could bear it. All of it! But I feel like I'm dying now! He's always a pest to me, and there's always some girl around who wants you!"

He reached up and touched her face. "They put them on me."

She pushed his hand away. "You don't believe in women at all, do you?" she said, her upper lip peaked at the cleft. "We haven't been happy in a long time. It's not just Abdulla or Anne Marie or Ingrid or even Ruth!"

"Right!" he said. "It's politics! We haven't been happy since Martin Luther King got killed and I got back into radical politics!"

Her mouth softened. The accusation went out of her face. He pressed his advantage. "Since I started writing articles on the Black Revolution and student unrest! Since I joined the student strike at State! And hit that cop when he swung that club at you! Since then!"

Her eyes stared straight at him. She knew he had saved her. He had gotten in trouble for her! On a deal, he had pleaded guilty to the lesser charge of disturbing the peace and paid a fine for *her!*

"Remember all the trouble we started having then? The funny phone calls in the middle of the night! Girls wanting to lay down everywhere I went! You remember! All the cops and all the student leaders were down on me! They kept me from using the mike even! Because I wouldn't play politics! Because I wanted to keep the strike democratic! They're still following me!"

He heard his own voice sharp in his ears, but he couldn't stop, and he sat up. "Do I have to go through everything that's happened to us in Europe to prove it? They don't want me to write about what I know about their underhanded ways! Do you understand? It pulls the covers on them! Then they can't keep playing dirty games on everybody!"

She waited until he stopped, then sat up and said, "Tell me one reason why you don't trust me! That's what I want to know!" Her face was as defiant as his, with her chin up and her tiny mouth puffed and birdlike.

"Because you went up to the bathroom and left me with that beautiful chick, Ingrid, in Mallorca when you knew she was after me. Then put me down for being tempted! Tell me what your reasons were for that!"

"I had to go to the bathroom!" she shouted, then dropped on her back again and stared up at the ceiling.

Below him, her eyes were like soft half-moons and so sad he suddenly felt sorry for her and reached out to stroke her round cheek. "Don't you see that they're trying to break us up?"

"Why?" she said.

"Maybe because you love me too much, and they want to get me with someone who doesn't, so they can use her to manipulate me?"

She looked up at him again, and her eyes rode her lower lids like half-moons, as if she wanted to see if he really believed what he was saying and trusted her.

"Maybe because no matter how carefully they try to set things up, a person like you, who wants to be happy, has to like, even love, the person they're with. So you can't help but be loyal to that person, and are, therefore, in the way of the cops! Who can't manipulate you and, through you, me!"

She kept staring at him, but he couldn't tell by the soft web of her lashes whether she liked what he said or not until she said, "You could say that, and yet say you don't trust me?"

Her mouth was so hurt he couldn't answer at first, then he said, "I have to think of everything. I have to write my book!"

"Oh, Roger," she said, and reached up and touched his cheek. "I don't want to leave you, but I don't know what else to do. I feel like I'm dying! I feel like I'm going to die here away from home without anybody, even you, to help me. I feel alone, totally alone."

He grabbed her hand and, as the romantic melody of "I Could Have Danced All Night" flowed from the circus into the room, pressed it to his lips, hard. Then when she looked up past him toward the window, he fell on her and squeezed her to him, aching with love for her, wanting to tell her that he did trust her. The music was so sweet and lonely that tears came into his eyes, and he stared through them at the blurry reflection of the circus lights on the ceiling, afraid he was going to lose her for sure.

13

There was a dark cover of clouds through the long window and streaks of rain dotted the pane when he sat up in the chair after tying his hiking boots. The thought of being in this overcast place without Penny saddened him, and he glanced over at her lying in bed, staring at him.

"You better get up. I'm already ready," he said.

"I'm not going down, Roger."

Long brown lashes veiled her eyes. She wouldn't look at him.

"How will you get breakfast then? I don't want to bring it all the way up those stairs again! If I don't have to!"

"You don't have to. I just don't want to go down. I don't feel well," she said.

"You've got to eat, Penny," he said.

Her pink mouth trembled, and her eyes looked right into his. "I will later. Right now, I'm going to write a letter to my parents and ask them for my plane fare home."

"You're going to leave then?" he asked, a slight tremor in his voice.

"Yes," she said.

"All right," he said, and, belly tight as a fist, he stood up, turned away and looked out the window at the gray sky again. He took down his corduroy jacket and slipped it on, picked up the bottle of honey and the small plastic bag of wheat germ, and stepped out the door without looking at her.

He walked down the long dark hall, stomach still tight, and waved to the skinny *patrón's* daughter, who nodded and smiled without speaking. In her black dress, with her black hair combed so severely down close to her head, and one thick braid in back, she looked older than her thirty-odd years. She was curt with Penny for not being married to him, he supposed. And because Penny was young and pretty, too, he thought. As he started down the steep stairs, he missed her badly again. He stopped at the next landing and looked over the banister. There was room for a body to drop straight down to the white tile floor of the foyer. It would be quick and easy. Just a few seconds of fear and one good swan dive. That's all. Then falling, knowing it was too late. The gaping hole had a magnetic pull, like a promise that would end all his troubles. He had to push himself away from the banister and make himself turn to start down the stairs again.

The tension had gotten to her. She couldn't stand the tension. They turned the tension on and took her away.

He stopped on the next landing and looked over the banister again. It was still a long drop, but a guy might live and be crippled for life. He shook his head. Any drop would have to be from the top floor so there'd be no question of living.

He started down the next flight of stairs and peeked in through the open door of a room where several young women, pale-faced from no sun, sat and sewed all day, every day. No unions to protect them since Franco overthrew the socialist government and killed the poet Lorca while he was at it. Spain didn't worry about killing poets or prisoners.

At the bottom floor, he walked down the wide sidewalk a few doors to the cafe. There, sipping at his tea, he listened to the low, melancholy flamenco moan of the waiter and wondered, what next? He felt helpless. The moan was like a solitary man's cry, his own cry about the incomprehensible force that swept everything before it, which he could do nothing about. Like Fate or God or The State or The Cops! Nothing was untouched, everything destroyed, even a man's love for his woman.

He took a deep breath and covered his eyes with his hands as the waiter cried out in a high, yelping moan and tried to fight the fatalistic feeling that filled him. He loved her. She loved him. He knew that. There was that in spite of everything. He could go up and try and talk her into staying with him. They could move again. Nothing was keeping them. He shook his head. Who was he kidding? He sat until he drained the last drops of his lukewarm tea from the bottom of the white porcelain cup.

He pushed outside, stopped in the middle of the wide walk and stared at the gray city scene before him. Old gray brick and stone buildings built at the turn of the century stood like canyon walls above him, with iron balconies and iron fire escapes criss-crossing them up into the dirty, dark, rumbling clouds. A stream of cars flowed toward him on the narrow black asphalt street on one side of him and, on the other, a crowd of housewives in black, balancing themselves with shopping bags, older businessmen in narrow-lapeled, pinstriped suits and younger men in long mod haircuts and bellbottom pants moved past. Female manikins stood in the shop windows in high heels and dresses. Just like home, he thought, and remembered that it was November twenty-second, nineteen-sixty-eight! Five years after John Kennedy had died! And he had cried!

14

"I don't know if it's worse to drag it out like this," Penny said. Her long hair was pulled back from her face to the back of her head, where it tumbled down in a ponytail and cascaded over one shoulder like a stream of water.

"You made the plane reservations for Monday, right?" Roger asked. His large forehead was pale in the low bar lights, his eyes large and dark and sloping. Where the pointed tips of his widow's peak and eyebrows and his long dark sideburns gave his face a sharpness, her small face was round and soft but as sad as his.

"I wish I could have gotten them for today," she said. "It could be over with."

He let go of his beer glass and put his hand over hers. "I'd rather have the three days with you," he said, and she glanced up from under her long lashes at him.

The soft lights and the slow, romantic music suited the sweet sadness of their last weekend together. The thought hurt so much he turned away from her sad face and saw the door of the nightclub open, then a guy walked in followed by a girl who looked familiar. He looked at the guy again, then said, "Look who just came in! Unbelievable!"

Penny looked up, then stood up and waved when Roger called, "Craig! Over here!"

The couple turned to look his way, squinting, trying to see in the low lights of the club, and he stood up, too, to let them see him. Yet, as he watched them walk across the floor toward him, an undercurrent of disbelief swelled in him. He was surprised at his own feelings of pleasure at seeing them. "What are you doing here, man? How could you possibly appear here in this bar in the Canary Islands?"

"We were just traveling with the sun, that's all," Craig said, and seemed thicker to Roger, and older, too, with a short, light-brown beard.

"Sit down and have a drink," Roger said, and kissed Ruth on the lips, still filled with a sense of disbelief, barely able to keep from asking the question again.

Dressed in Levis and a sweat shirt, Ruth looked dark and pretty, and Roger suddenly said, "I'm sorry I said that in London. I could go into reasons, but I'd rather not talk about it."

All four of them stood around the table for a moment. Their last meetings seemed as recent as just yesterday to Roger, who, aching with the loss of friendship between them, suddenly felt self-conscious and sat down.

"Are you staying in Las Palmas long?" Craig asked, then sat down, too, pulling a chair back for Ruth.

Roger hesitated, and Penny said, "I'm going back to San Francisco alone on Monday."

When neither Craig nor Ruth said anything, Roger said, "This is our last weekend together. We're pretty sad. Why don't you join us? Why not help us party this final time?"

"Say, that's an idea," Craig said in a soft, feathery voice, not asking why they were separating. "We heard about a village a hundred kilometers down the coast, called Arguiniguin, where a lot of hippies from all over the world live. Why not go down there?"

15

When he stepped out of the jitney in the little fishing village of Arguiniguin, Roger turned and touched Penny's hand, pointing at the sight before them: A street light hung from an oar on the dark corner of the building by the sea and cast a halo on the white plaster wall of the inn. A rowboat was turned upside down on the rocky beach of the little cove just next to the wall. A Spaniard stood by it with a shortened shadow, a beret and a hot-tipped cigarette in his mouth, which glowed with the slow rumbling sound of the small breakers.

Penny's eyes creased at the corners with the slow smile that spread over her face. She took his hand and stood watching with him for a few moments, then finally turned when he did to pick up their bags.

"How many rooms?" the landlady asked. She seemed to be scowling at them from tiny black eyes under heavy black brows and a short, wrinkled forehead. Coarse piglike hair was pulled down flat against her skull, with two braids hanging down her back.

"*Dos*," Roger said, holding up two fingers, then stepped inside so she could see that there were two couples.

"*Doscientas pesetas cada uno.* Two hun'red," she said, thin-lipped mouth closing to a knife edge, thin mustache on her upper lip, thick nose drooping down at the tip.

"*Está bien*," Roger said, and gave her two one-hundred-peseta notes, then stepped back and spun his backpack up and onto his back with one practiced motion, picked up his typewriter and briefcase and waited for Craig to pay for himself and Ruth.

Roger got excited at the sight of all the people in the bar just across the dirt passageway. He peeked in through the door, trying to see who was playing the flamenco guitar, then followed the landlady's broad back and wide buttocks in her ankle-length dress down the passageway through the inn and into the dark backyard where two rows of rooms sat like monk cells at either side.

His room had a dirt floor, a single three-quarter-sized bed, a bed stand of weathered wood, a single chair, a high, tiny window and a bare, flickering light bulb hanging from a cord in the ceiling. He smiled and Penny giggled when the landlady pushed out past Roger, brushing her big boobs against him, without giving him a chance to get out of the way with his backpack.

"Let's have lots of fun, Roger," Penny said, and put her arms around him. With his backpack still on, he slipped his arms around her and pulled her close to him, pressed her against him and kissed her long and warmly, prolonging the pleasure. He didn't pull away until he heard a knock on the wall and Ruth say, "Are you guys ready?"

"Sure," he said, pecking Penny's lips once more before he slipped his backpack off onto the earthen floor. Taking Penny's hand, he led her out, locked the door and walked with Craig and Ruth back down the open passageway in the center of the inn to the saloon. Penny reached for his hand when they sat down at a table in the bar. A plump, bespectacled pale-skinned Spaniard with dark wavy hair strolled to their table, stopped, bowed and picked the strings of his flamenco guitar for them.

Most of the people in the crowded place were Spaniards dressed in casual clothing. The few foreign men had fairly long hair that covered their ears in the mod style, but wore conventional clothes. None had the really long hair of the American hippies, who were supposed to be in the village.

There were a couple of pretty girls with long straight hair at the bar who looked English. Expatriates all, Roger thought, feeling like Hemingway. He was so pleased by the intricate, soothing melody the guitar played for them that he squeezed Penny's fingers and leaned over and pecked her on the lips, then stood up, dug his hand in his pocket and handed the man a one-hundred-peseta note. The plump man reached out and snatched the note, then stopped playing, turned around and sat down at a table. Roger and Penny looked at each other, then at Craig and Ruth, and they all laughed.

"That sure didn't get the desired results, did it?" Craig said.

"The way I feel now, I don't care," Roger said, and Penny scooted her chair over next to him and laid her hand on his thigh.

Roger put his arm around her as another middle-aged man in shabby clothing and a gray hat began to play a folksong on his guitar. Then a pretty little man with the slight build and the full, wavy brown hair of a boy stood up and began to sing an accompaniment.

For the first time, Roger could see a resemblance between Spanish and Mexican music. The Spanish folk songs sounded like the *ranchero* songs of Mexico, with the same bouncy fast pace and yodeling, light-hearted melodies. He liked the little man so much that he began to clap in time to the guitar. When Penny and Ruth joined him, the little man got so excited that he stopped singing and skipped across the dance floor to them, smiling all the while. The wrinkles on his face showed when he got close to Penny, grabbed her hand, pulled her out of her seat, and danced a one-step all around the cafe for several minutes. Everybody clapped and cheered when the song ended.

Penny sat down, smiling, her eyes flickering, then slipped her arm around Roger, put her lips to his ear and whispered, "I'm so happy! I love you, Roger!"

Roger turned his head to whisper back in her ear when Ruth, in a high, piping voice, said, "I admire you, Penny. I really admire you for having the courage to go home and lead your own life! Lots of women talk about it, but not many women do it." She nodded her head as she spoke, her blue eyes hard and serious, and she suddenly made Roger conscious that Penny was leaving again. He looked right into

Ruth's hard blue eyes and guessed that she was prodding Penny to leave. So he pressed his lips to Penny's ear anyway and said, "And I love you!"

16

Squinting his eyes even through his dark glasses at the brightness the hotel roof reflected, Roger looked down at Penny, Ruth and Craig lying on the roof sun porch and thought "It's all so ephemeral, so fleeting." Just looking at Penny, who lay on her back next to him in a red bikini, eyes closed, body a rosy tan color, with light freckles over her chest and shoulders, made his chest ache. They had made happy love the night before, then slept until eleven in the morning. It hurt that they could only make great love when she was leaving. Ruth lay on the other side of Penny, a deep-brown color to her back. Larger than Penny, her wide shoulders tapered down to a narrow waist, where her hips belled out in the bikini. Craig had a little inner tube of fat around his hips, even while lying on his back, and Roger wondered if he'd gotten a little heavier himself.

He pinched the crease of skin on his stomach. It was sticky with sweat. But he always carried a crease, even when in top shape. It was the thickness of the crease that decided if he were fat or not. You fed the body until it finally died. Then there was nothing. That's all there was to it. The only thing that made it worthwhile was to be in love. And his love was leaving. This was Saturday, and since tomorrow was Sunday, there was only one day left.

He stood up and walked over to the edge of the hotel roof and leaned his arms on the wall, then looked around at the other roofs of the town, which were all lower than his. Many people were moving around on them, and he suddenly realized there were two Arguiniguins: the one of the dirt streets, the bars and cafes, the tiny stores and houses, and the one on the rooftops of the mainly one-story buildings. People were alone up there, puttering with flowers, women hanging clothes, little girls in curlers, children getting baths in big, portable tubs. He wished he could share all their lives, and he wished they could all live forever. He, too, with Penny.

Every part of the town seemed precious. He could see that
the main part of the village formed a rough half-circle around
a small bay with a rocky beach, beginning with the inn where
he stood. Most of the houses were of brick and gray tile. The
opposite side of the little bay was a quarter of a mile away, a
finger of land that stuck out like a short peninsula. There
were some more tile and brick buildings on that side, too,
although most of the houses were tarpaper and plywood
shacks. It was where the fishermen lived, and the foreigners
called it Shantytown. A lightly traveled highway formed an
inland boundary between the town and the small, dry, tree-
less hills behind it.

At the far end of another, bigger bay, which stretched
from the other side of Shantytown for a mile or so to what
looked like a dock for loading ships with gravel, lay a small
settlement of houses and cafes. In the deepest part of the
half-moon made by the other bay was a grove of tall eucalyptus trees dotted with the tents, lean-tos and grass huts of the
hippy camp. Just behind it, past a block or so of bamboo fields,
was a banana plantation with a high brick wall around it.

The two little bays and the village were hemmed in by
hills on all land sides. It seemed to be cut out of space, like a
separate plane of existence, a touching little hamlet out in the
middle of the ocean, a tiny little spot of sputtering life, lost in
space and time. This was all there was. It made him sense his
own mortality, the futility of his own existence. He turned to
look again at the others and felt a sense of sadness at the fragile nature of their beings, their relationship, even their pitiful
love, his love for Penny.

Penny opened her eyes and looked up past her nose as if
she were above him, then lifted her head and shaded her eyes
with her hand, caught his eyes with hers and smiled. Even
her smile filled him with pain, and he glanced away, over the
edge of the roof at the pebble beach of the cove below where
the rocks rattled like marbles in the rocky surf as the last
wave drew back to be sucked under by the next wave, which
broke like a small explosion, then rumbled away like an echo
of a departing train in the London tube.

He saw the whole town spread out around him again: the
small, delicate cedar trees which lined the road that curved
around the cove, the translucent glimmer of the tail feathers
of a proud male cock scratching in the dust, and heard the

mournful wail of a maid singing two roofs down. A breeze touched his face, and he looked up to see a crow hovering in midair at a wavering standstill in the strong wind up there, as if balanced on a high wire. Then he looked down at Penny, who was still smiling up at him. She made it all worthwhile, and he wanted to reach out and touch her, make sure that it was all real, that she really was with him this one last time. He couldn't make himself do it, it hurt so much just to be alive. But when Penny reached up for him with her slender arm and held out her hand and tried to touch him with her fingers, he wondered how he could be so lucky to be alive and with her these last few moments together.

17

Penny stood next to Roger with her arm around his waist and her shoulder under his, her body as close to his as she could get without embracing him face to face as they watched the swarthy fishermen dig their feet into the pebbles, slant their bodies at a steep, straight angle, and push their boats up on the beach. Their powerful arms glistened golden in the last rays of the sun, their curly red, blond and brown hair frizzing kinky at the ends. Others stacked fifteen-to-twenty-pound tunas into flat boxes and carried them up to the scale of a yellow, stucco icehouse to weigh them, then carried them up some stairs and inside.

He wanted to share everything with her. They had walked through the town holding each other close. They moved from street to street of the little village of small one-story buildings, past the generator plant, which put out weak electricity until midnight, then shut off. They walked past the cedar trees of their little cove and across the half-mile thumb of land covered with shacks and small boats. They walked right up to the cliff edges on the eastern edge of town and the larger bay protected from the afternoon west wind by the cliffs, where they could see the hippy camp in the grove of eucalyptus trees and the gravel dock a little further beyond.

The slight breeze ruffled the fine hair on Penny's head and strands of it tickled his chin. He noticed how Craig and

Ruth stood separately from each other beside them. It made him appreciate how close Penny and he were now, and he felt an urgent need to capture this moment, to sustain it as long as possible and drain it of every possible emotion. When Penny said, "I'll really be sorry to leave you, Roger. I want you to know that," he squeezed her hand and said, "Well, let's have a lot of fun, then."

And when she squeezed his hands back and said, "Yes, let's!" he said, "Hey! Why don't we give a big party tonight in the hippy camp? I'll pay for it! Let's spend some of that fifty dollars your father sent you, too, Penny! We'll buy a lot of tuna fish and bottles of wine and get it on for one last big blowout! Let's do it! Whatta ya say?"

"Yeah, let's!" Penny said.

"I'm for it!" Craig said, and Ruth added, "Oh, good!"

"Come on then," Roger said, and, pulling Penny along, headed for the hippy camp, making Craig and Ruth hurry to keep up. As he walked he wanted to be happy, and he was happy, walking across the half mile of open field on the flat next to the ocean. When they reached a small stream just outside the grove of eucalyptus, he skipped across the rocks and strode up the road through the natural fence of bamboo and bushes that encircled the grove of giant trees. Then they strode between the two big eucalyptus trees that stood like giant gate posts into the camp. Bamboo huts and tents and lean-tos were scattered around below the trees like Indian hogans.

Roger led the way toward a campfire built at the base of a big tree in a clearing in the center of the camp. Three cars and a couple of campers were parked in the clearing, and a small crowd of young people in shorts and bathing suits and Levis clustered around. They all turned when Roger stepped up and said, "We're all from San Francisco and want to have a party our last weekend together. Who wants to help carry the wine and tuna?"

A rosy-cheeked guy stood up, his light-brown hair curling in bangs over pale-brown eyes, and said in the clipped tones of an Englishman, "I'll help." Then a muscular young man with a deep tan, a short, red-haired Englishman about twenty years old, and two other guys, all said, "Sounds good." Some girls said they'd help, also. Soon Roger was leading them back along the path under the trees and through the bamboo, across the field and up to the scale, where he bought ten tunas.

The fisherman weighed the flat empty box and pointed at the scale so Roger could see how much it weighed. He didn't care, although he looked at it, and when the man pointed at the scale above the box with five big tunas in it, again he didn't look close, just paid so the English guys could pick up both boxes by the rope handles and head back to camp.

He followed the first guy, Tim, around the cliff and onto the flat land of the road up to a shack of old, weathered wood in the center of Shantytown, where the fishermen lived. They stepped up from the dirt into a kitchen-size room with a bar down one side where they bought twenty bottles of wine. Back at the camp, they found the long-legged English girls cutting the fish up into plate-size portions and placing them on a wire grill over the fire. Somebody else had set up a phonograph and a speaker on top a Volkswagen van. The Beatles' "Revolver" album was playing, "She's leaving home, bye-bye!"

"Oh, Roger," Penny said, and slipped her arm around his waist while he unscrewed a cork from a wine bottle with his boy scout knife. "This is so much fun! So much fun!"

He grinned to show he heard her, then took one long, chug-a-lug and handed her the bottle. He got such a quick rush, and got so happy, the whole scene looked surreal to him. Bottles were opened and passed around, and people kept tipping them up to their mouths as darkness swept slowly over the camp. The flames of the fire were soon the only flickering light. He noticed that for a so-called hippy camp, no one had broken out any dope, in the open at least, and that most guys had fairly short hair.

Penny kissed him with the taste of wine on her lips, and he cushioned his mouth on hers, then let go of her and looked up to see a light-haired Spaniard stand up from a crouch at the edge of the clearing to stare at him. Tanned and good-looking, he stood off by himself, and Roger knew he'd keep his dope in his pocket. They were always there. They were watching him now.

Soon it was dark. The sizzling tuna steaks were passed around on plates, and everybody drank and ate and laughed and talked. Roger and Penny both ate lightly, then danced in the dirt clearing by the fire. Everyone watched, but Roger didn't care. He hugged Penny and kissed her each time a tune ended, then leaned back and stared at her in the flickering light, thinking how beautiful she looked.

She seemed to read his thoughts and took his hand and lifted it up to her lips and kissed it. Roger pressed her to his chest, aching sweetly for her, then saw a big boat sailing by their little camp by the bay, with tiny bobbing lights at each end. Suddenly he shouted, "Hey, you guys, look!"

He pointed out at the yacht and said, "This is one of the most beautiful moments of my life! See that yacht out there! Cruising so slowly by in the moonlight on the sea there between the bamboo! See! A sailor told me it cost nine-hundred dollars a week to charter a boat like that. Some corporation lawyer probably took it out on his expense account and, sailing by out there, sees our campfire and all the people around it and wonders, mysteriously, who we are!"

A murmur went up from the lighted faces around the fire, several nodded their heads. Penny squeezed him with both arms and said, "That's beautiful, Roger! That's a poem! I never want to leave you as long as I live. I want to be with you always, if I can."

"You do?" he said, wanting to make sure he understood her. But when she nodded her head and smiled, he jerked her tight against him and rocked back and forth with her, saying, "Penny, Penny, Penny," until he saw Ruth staring at them, the flames from the fire throwing big, weaving, distorted shadows on her face.

Episode Five

ARGUINIGUIN

1

Roger sucked air between his lips and, his bare feet balanced by his toes on the edge of the seat of the only chair in the dark room, stripped to the waist, dropped down between his elbows the foot and a half to the floor, just let his chest tap the pale-green tile between his hands, shoulder muscles bunching like thick fingers, then pushed up again for the twentieth time. He felt good and strong, hadn't touched a beer in four weeks, was in love and full of energy and enthusiasm, and his novel was going full blast. He and Penny had moved from the inn by the cove to this *pensión*, without a dining room or bar, run by a tall Arab with a spare tire of flab around his waist. His room on the second floor above the Arab's little store was twice the size of the last room, with an almost private patio surrounded by ten-foot walls. Since the Arab wouldn't let anyone come up to their room, Ruth and Craig couldn't come to visit. They were cool to him when he saw them in the late afternoons and evenings at the cafes.

"Thirty-one, thirty-two," he said to himself, not wanting to lose track, which was so easy to do when he daydreamed during exercises. He strained a little bit more now, using more effort to lift himself, but still strong, keeping up the rhythm, strengthening himself with the thought that he'd been able to resist all temptation to flirt with Ruth. Nothing had been the same since London. He didn't like her that much anymore. She seemed more self-centered and calculating now, though the line where she acted in her own self-interest and maybe in the police's interest blurred together. He couldn't really trust them. He couldn't forget Leary in London staring at him at the breakfast table when Craig asked him how he was going to carry his dope.

Craig and Ruth were cruel to Penny when he wasn't around, she told him. They wouldn't talk to her when they saw her at the beach, not even to say hello. They might make her want to go home again. He had to remember to pay more attention to her. But he was going to work on his book. That was the most important thing. That's what he had to do or die; that's what he existed for. Without that, even with Penny, his life was meaningless. But he had to remember to pay attention to her and keep her from getting sad. He had to remember to think of her, not just the book. He could sacrifice himself, but he didn't want to sacrifice her.

"Forty-eight... Forty-nine!" he said, pushing himself slowly and painfully up, pausing at the top to get his strength back, re-gripping the chair edge with his toes, then dropping slowly down again with a deep intake of air, staying a long time down on the bottom this next to last time, and finally pushing himself slowly up again, said, "Fifty!" He exhaled, then creaked back down again, touched his bare chest to the cool tile, exhaled while down there, then inhaled again and pushed back up again, one elbow almost caving in. He straightened it and pushed all the way up, saying, "Fifty-one!" with a big rush of air, his face bright red. He placed his feet down on the cool tile one at a time and stood, feeling a warm glow in his face as the blood rushed out of it.

He checked to see if Penny had heard his gasping and the slight creaking of the chair, but she slept soundly, her small face so touching, so innocent that his heart turned with love for her. He wanted to keep her with him, but just as having her and not writing the book was useless, so writing the book and not having her was sadness.

He picked his towel off a nail and unlocked the door to the short, dark hall with two closed doors at one end and a tall rectangle of light at the other. He went out to the patio, surrounded by high, pink walls, stepped over the blurred glass skylight above the store below, then entered a door and sat on the toilet. A swarm of flies rose up when he pulled the chain. Then he stepped out and into the next door, slipped off his pajamas, hung them on a clothes hook with his towel and turned on the shower. There was no hot water, but his body was warm from the push-ups and the water felt cool and refreshing. He began to think of his novel, the novel he was paying so many dues for. What happened next when his hero charged over to the mike and there were police provocateurs posing as students at the strike?

As he daydreamed, he soaped himself down, getting every part of his body. Then he rinsed off, turned the water off, dried himself with a big pink towel, slipped back into his pajama bottoms and draped the damp towel over a clothesline in front of the alcove. He then recrossed the patio, slipped into his green Levis and his sandals, and hurried downstairs to the store where the sundry goods were stacked in monumental disorder.

"*Buenos dias*," Roger said to the quiet Arabian landlady with the long hooked nose. Her whole brown body was wrapped in a long dress and shawl. He put fifteen pesetas down on the counter and picked up the bowl of *café con leche* she had quickly mixed for him. He then hurried up to his room again, poured wheat germ into the bowl until it made a large heap which settled gradually into the thick, creamy liquid, and stirred it with his camper spoon.

He sat down at the table by the room's only window, screened and overlooking the patio, then slipped on his glasses and began to reread the pages he had written the day before. He edited with a ballpoint pen as he moved along, while scooping up wheat germ and coffee with his spoon. He finished the coffee at the same time as he finished editing, then reread his notes, made a couple more and put a sheet of paper in the typewriter. Then he zipped open a leather pouch, pulled out his small hash pipe and a small matchbox of green kif pollen, filled the pipe, lit it, and sucked it quickly down and out with three deep hits. He then tapped the ashes out of the pipe, blew out the last of the smoke, grabbed his toothbrush and toothpaste and stepped outside to the sink in the patio.

He quickly brushed his teeth and put the toothbrush and paste down on the sink edge. He then stood in one corner, head bowed, an arm against each wall, small, light freckles on his tanned shoulders. The sun beating down on his whole body, his shadow spread-eagled crookedly against the two walls and the tile floor beneath him, his mind churning, churning, he waited for the swarm of details to drop into place.

Finally, he turned and sat down on a rough, wooden bench, rested his elbows on his thighs, clasped his hands and bowed his dark, curly head to the sun. He let the warmth soak in through his skin and into his whole body, thinking, dreaming, all the blurred pictures of the crowd scene mingling

together. Then, suddenly, he saw a redheaded girl stand up
and shout, "You're the fink! You're the stool pigeon! You're the
cop!" and he stood up, hurried across the patio and down the
hall to his room.

He let the door shut behind him, sat down at his chair,
put his hands on the typewriter keys and began to type, to try
and transfer the picture in his mind to the white sheet of
paper in the machine, barely conscious of the shifting of the
blankets on the bed to his left as Penny stirred to begin her
day.

2

At siesta time, the wind whined through the village, rattled the palms, and blew dust in Roger's eyes. He squinted
behind his dark glasses as he hurried to find Penny and make
up for not being with her the whole day. Now that the writing
was over for the day, he wanted to be with her, to show her he
loved her. He kept his head up, his face to the hot sun, his
eyes on the pale-green stucco building called La Rubia's,
meaning "The Blond One," which was built down the cliffside
of the cove a quarter of a mile away in the center of a row of
pastel-colored shacks in Shantytown. Its bottom windows
looked out on the exposed rocks of low tide, flat and cratered
like the moon.

A girl splashed water on the dirt street to keep the dust
down and a black cat scurried out of the way and rushed past
a peasant woman in a black dress and kerchief hanging
clothes on a cobblestone patio. Just inside a concrete and brick
wall, where a workman slept in the shade with a hard hat
over his face, another cat slept at eye level on top of a stone
fence behind him.

Roger had lived internally for six hours already, his eyes
seeing but his mind not really registering Penny's figure as it
moved about the room, then reading on the bed, finally kissing him on the cheek and saying, "I'm going out to Mama
Rubia's and maybe the beach."

He saw it all in brief and widely separated fragments as
he wrote, but his mind was crawling with pictures of a crowd
scene and he couldn't come back from it to respond. He regret-

ted it now as he hurried to find Penny, to see her and tell her he loved her. He had sat at the table with his horn-rimmed glasses on, his eyes dreamy and glazed, looking within, bare-chested all day in the deep shade of the room; it had been so warm with no breeze coming in from the window. He some-times looked up from the page to stare at the wall or out through the screen at the sun-bright patio to dream, then drifted back to the page, picking up the next word or words and beginning to type again. He had finished at three o'clock by his wristwatch, then stood up, stretched, yawned, and went out to shave. Then he remembered: Penny! He had to find Penny!

Roger entered La Rubia's from the top of the little cliff where the rooms for rent were and walked down the narrow stone steps to the dining room on the bottom floor. A row of windows overlooked the now exposed shelf of crater-like rocks at low tide. He stopped at the foot of the stairs to look around, noticing how grimy the windows, the tables, and the floor looked in daylight.

Mama Rubia held a pan top in one hand and a large dip-per in the other as she stood back from the kitchen table because of her fat belly and big breasts. She looked up and said, "*¡Buenas tardes!*" Lucy, her twelve-year-old niece, a dirty white apron covering her flat breasts, turned around behind her, and, her hair pulled back in a ponytail, smiled at him. But Juan, Mama Rubia's husband, kept his head bent over the large stove in the corner where he was cooking something. He never said hello, and Roger wasn't surprised to see his gray, grizzly head turned away from him. Juan wasn't unpleasant, merely uncommunicative. Roger was surprised to see, though, that no one was in the dining room or in the nar-row extension of it. Guessing that nobody had come back from the beach yet, he turned to trot back up the stairs when he heard a girl's voice call, "Roger!"

He had to walk back down into the main dining room to see who had called out to him. He stopped in surprise. It was Anne Marie, the beautiful blonde from Formentera, waving to him from the very last table.

He looked at her, then looked down, then looked up again, stunned by how beautiful she looked with the sunlight shim-mering on her hair, her brown shoulder giving off a golden glow and her heavy-lidded dark eyes focused on him.

"Come and sit with me," she said as she motioned for him to join her.

Roger stepped up into the long room and walked down to her table, trying to keep his pleasure at seeing her under control, trying to keep from staring at her.

"How are you, Roger?" she asked, and pointed at a chair next to the window opposite her.

"How did you get here?" he asked, suspicious again.

She looked deeply at him with her soft brown eyes, and said, "There was a big police drive on Ibiza and Formentera to get rid of the hippies. We remembered that you had said you were going to the Canary Islands, so we hitched a ride in a friend's van through Spain and Morroco to Agadir. There we caught a fishing boat straight across to Las Palmas for only eighty pesetas. The whole trip didn't cost us much at all."

"Who's us?" Roger asked, still suspicious, afraid it was a guy and annoyed at his own feelings.

"Robey," she said, and when a tremor of surprise ran over his face, she quickly added, "But I really like men like you." She smiled, showing her slightly crooked front teeth.

"What do you mean?" he asked, afraid of being flattered now.

"Because you're not like the Spanish men who bother me on the street so much and think it's dashing to pester a girl in front of their friends."

"I still don't understand. Lots of Americans and Englishmen aren't that way."

"Because you're so shy," she said. "The way you hide your eyes when you see me, as if by looking right at me you'll show how much you like me."

He had to smile, but he looked away, out the window at the rocky shelf just below the window.

"You don't have to hide your eyes, Roger. I like you, too. A lot. Why don't you come out to the beach and see me?"

"You mean Pata La Vaca?" he asked, thinking of the beach between the cliffs a kilometer and a half beyond the village where a big hotel was being built. Tourists were already occupying it, and the young hippies from the camp and town spent nearly every day sunbathing in front of it on the stretch of moon-like rocks above the sand. Penny might be there right now, he reminded himself.

"Yes. We moved into a cave inland from the cliffs three days ago. Some friends of Robey turned us on to it. You haven't been to the beach since we've been there. We asked about you, and everybody knew you and told us you didn't come out in the daytime much."

"I'm working on a novel," he said. "It takes up most of the day."

"Will it for long?"

"I don't know. This is just a first draft. It might take a couple more months. Then I'll take a break before starting the second draft."

"Oh, too bad!" she said, and stuck her bottom lip out in a mock pout.

"Why?"

"We're running out of money and we'll have to leave soon... unless one of us get's a job or Robey figures out a way to make money playing his guitar. Why don't you come and see me in London? I'll give you my number."

Before he could stop himself, he asked, "When you get back to London, are you still going to make it with Robey?"

She stared at him for a moment, then said, "Heavens, no! His family lives in East End. I never go there. Here!" She pulled a notepad and pen out of her purse and started writing her name and address down. As he watched her write in her very neat script, he thought of how much she looked like his younger sister, Belle. Then he thought of how many people he'd seen in Europe who looked like other people he knew in America. That was perhaps the most mind-boggling thing that had happened to him on the Continent. On the first ship crossing the English Channel from Southampton to Bilbao, the captain looked like his father. The same slightly tanned complexion, the hook at the end of the nose and the thin lips. Roger was so amazed that the first Spaniard he'd seen looked like his father that he gave him his ticket and said, "You... You look like my father!" Then repeated it in Spanish: "*¡Se parece a mi papá!*" The captain smiled, but tried to move Roger away from the gate so the sailors could close it and the ship could get underway.

Then on board, one of his cabin mates looked like the old, former best friend he'd modeled a character after in his first novel. Robey himself could have been the younger brother of a poet friend in San Francisco.

Roger had saved himself in the past by remembering the faces of cops who had tried to bust him for smoking pot. He wondered if the law was planting these people on him to convince him that he didn't really remember people all that well, so he wouldn't trust his memory when he saw the faces of plainclothes cops and finks who had come into his life before.

"Here," she said. "Don't lose it, now."

He nodded and was reaching around to slip it into his notebook when the town cop came into the main dining room in his blue uniform and cap. He was a thin, mustachioed, fair-skinned man who smiled and lifted his hand in greeting. Roger just nodded back.

"He's a nice guy. He told me he'd like to talk to you about *arte*. Why don't you talk to him?" Anne Marie said.

Roger felt a quiver of fear. He remembered how he had suspected her when he left Formentera. He wondered if they had brought her around because he wasn't going for Ruth's bait and might let her distract him from his book. This guy was a cop, after all, and no matter how nice, he was on the other side of the fence from Roger.

"Not now. I've got to go find Penny," Roger said. Anne Marie's eyebrows drew together in a frown as he stood up.

3

The bare steel supports and the empty concrete floors of the giant shell of the luxury hotel under construction at Pata La Vaca beach loomed up against the ocean when Roger came around the bend in the winding road at the top of the cliffs. He was still thinking of Anne Marie and that cop who wanted to talk about art. He really wanted to find Penny now more than ever, not just for her sake but for his, for reassurance. Anne Marie was pretty, though, no denying it, he thought as he walked past the end of the building. The hotel tourists who were already staying in the hotel sat out on the sun porches and down in the hotel cafe just above the beach: big Scandanavian women in floppy hats and wide-skirted sundresses, tall men with pale, puffy bellies.

Anne Marie still bothered him, pretty or not, as he picked his way down the canyon alongside the hotel, through a rugged, sloping field of broken rock, wheelbarrows, pipes, jackhammers, stacks of lumber, trucks and workmen in hard yellow hats moving back and forth to the sand. He stopped at the block-long crescent of yellow beach below the hotel to see if he could spot Penny. He thought he saw her red bikini down at the opposite end in a crowd of young people sitting on towels outside the beach cafe on a small hillock of volcanic rock. He hurried toward her, happy again.

As he walked up the sloping volcanic hillock toward the pipe rails that fenced the deck of the cafe, he noticed big Leary squatting down on the rock with Craig, Ruth, and Penny. His sideburns grew down his cheeks now, like a hippy. Something was up. When Roger reached them, Penny, the only one wearing a bathing suit, stood up in her red bikini and kissed him. Ruth glanced up at him but didn't smile or even say hello, though Craig said, "Remember Leary, Roger?"

Roger reached down to shake hands with the big man in his T-shirt and khakis, and was struck again by his resemblance to Teddy Kennedy, with the same powerful forehead, wavy brown hair, and pale-green eyes. Roger also remembered how, when he was smoking hash in the toilet on the train to Madrid, he'd seen the door handle turn and found Leary standing outside.

"We were talking about the presidential elections," Craig said.

"You mean the coup d'etat," Roger said.

"Coup d'etat," Leary said, grinning and shaking his head. "This guy kills me."

"Right," Roger said. "Killing. That's what I'm talking about." Leary sat up, resting his hands on his big thighs, his belly bunching.

Penny nudged Roger with her arm, but he went on. "Like when Bobby Kennedy, the shoo-in winner, was murdered. Two Kennedys had to be killed to make Nixon president of the United States. That's what I mean."

"Roger," Penny said in a soft voice. "Let's go swimming."

"Are you saying the election was fixed?" Leary said, and glanced at Craig who shook his head, laid back down on his towel again, and closed his eyes behind his glasses.

Roger scanned Penny's frowning face, but answered, "I'm saying that Bobby Kennedy was killed so that no matter who won the election—Humphrey or Nixon—the coup d'etat would take place and the military-industrial complex would stay in power. That's what I'm saying."

"Come on, Roger," Leary said, "give us a break! Everything's not a big conspiracy, you know. The people voted. That's it. And it was shown, proven, that Sirhan Sirhan and Oswald acted separately and alone."

"Not a damn thing was proven. Seventeen people...you can count them...seventeen witnesses to the JFK assassination were killed within two years of his murder. Most under strange circumstances. Tell me that's a coincidence."

"Roger, get real, for once, will you?" Leary said, rubbing his eyes with the heels of his hands.

"Real? Even the John Birch Society, the most far right group outside the military, said the CIA planned the killings."

"Okay, okay," Leary said, dropping his hands and staring at Roger. "Suppose you were right. What are you going to do about it?"

Roger brushed Penny's hand from his arm and said slowly, "If there's a revolution in our country, the military-industrial complex which committed the murders and robbed the people—not only of our country but the world—will be the cause, not people who see things the way I do."

Leary squinted his green eyes at Roger. "So, you think there'll be a revolution?"

"There's already been a revolution, a right-wing revolution with the murder of the two Kennedys. Something like there was here in Spain in '36." He swung his arm out. "These people can't do anything about that. But there'll be a people's revolution in our country when the Nixon administration makes things so bad for the majority of Americans, and I mean the middle class, that they'll finally start fighting back. Then, and only then, will the truth come out. Then Nixon will be up against the wall and we'll see who the patriots are."

"Roger, let's go swimming. Come on," Penny said, and pulled on his arm.

Roger stepped back and started to unbuckle his belt when Leary said, "So, you feel, then, it's your job as a writer to expose this coup d'etat?"

"Yes!" Roger said, and pointed at Leary, one eyebrow raised. "Shelley said it, like I told you already: 'Writers are the unacknowledged legislators of the world.' And the Bible, too: 'The pen is mightier than the sword.' That's my role, to write for liberty, to fight for liberty with my pen. Like the romantic poets, Keats and Byron and Wordsworth, too. What good is writing unless it does good in the world? This world! The one we live in, the one the writer lives in now!"

Penny touched his shoulder, but he couldn't tell if she was just agreeing with him or pleading with him to go.

"I thought Roger the writer was just going to smoke pot and create?" Leary said, his face all big bones, his mouth twisted in a grin. "I didn't know you had all these other lofty plans to change the world."

Roger had to smile, too, but though the ploy was transparent, he said, "Even the so-called dope fiends like Baudelaire and Rimbaud fought for the people against the totalitarian state. Baudelaire ran with the communards fighting against Napoleon the Third, and even tried to shoot his father, a general. Rimbaud ran away and joined the freedom fighters in Paris, too, and fought on the barricades."

Leary nodded his head as if agreeing. Then he said slowly, "So, you'd fight in a revolution, too?"

"Yes, if I thought it was genuinely against a fascist system!"

"How would you fight?"

"Are you serious?" Roger asked, squinting, the sun blurring across his tinted glasses. He realized he was being pumped, but was too aroused to care.

"Yes, I am. All this talk about revolution. What would you actually do, say, in a town like this? If there were a true uprising?"

Roger looked at him, knowing it was a loaded question, that Leary was leading him into a trap. He stalled by pulling his T-shirt over his head, then dropped it on Penny's towel, thinking that Leary won if he talked and won if he didn't. But he'd be intimidated by fascism if he kept silent. "You mean as a writer?"

"Yeah. If there was a revolution, there'd be no time to talk. What would you do? Would you really fight like Baudelaire? I don't believe it."

Roger could see he was conning him. He was making him risk all or shut up. "I'd take the mayor captive first. That would be the first and most important step. In any city, that would be the first thing to do, capture the head of local government and try to do the same thing on a national level."

"Roger!" Penny said, her voice snapping with anger, her face spotted with angry freckles. "Come on in!"

He slid his belt out of the buckle, stepped out of his Levis to his swimsuit underneath, slipped off his sandals and tip-toed down the lava rock behind Penny to the soft sand of the beach. She grabbed his hand and jerked it, then started running down toward the water, pulling him with her.

"Won't you ever learn to protect yourself?" she said when they reached the waves.

"It was a setup, wasn't it?" he said, then suddenly grinned and asked, "Did you see his face when I said that thing about taking the major hostage?"

"I sure did," she said, and had to smile, too.

4

The mayor's pink face snapped up behind the tile counter when Roger first stepped in from the dark street. His puffy cheeks turned pale, then his whole face flushed red all the way from the gray roots of his thin blond hair down to the stiff white collar around his flabby neck. Roger knew Leary had told him what he had said.

Leary was sitting at the counter on the other side of the mayor and waved at him. "How's the revolutionary?" he asked when Roger and Penny stepped next to him.

"Good," Roger said, on guard, but not afraid, knowing Leary was trying to get him to talk in front of the mayor. He felt Penny touch his back and felt secure.

"Two Heinekens," Roger said, and the mayor took two green cans out of the red Coca-Cola box and slid them across the counter. He then took Roger's bill, gave him change and stayed near them, washing glasses.

Roger guessed the mayor was eavesdropping, but couldn't help staring at his pink, puffy hands. He was a gentleman, the richest man in the village. He was always in dress clothes to distinguish himself from the poor fishermen and the construction workers who were helping build the hotel.

"What would a revolutionary like yourself do with the church in case of a revolution in Spain?" Leary asked, peering over his beer can.

"Well, I'm not a revolutionary. I'm a writer, an artist. Let's get that straight," Roger said and looked right into Leary's green eyes.

"You're the one who talked about great writers joining the revolutions of the past. It's your hypothesis," Leary said.

"Okay. As long as it's an hypothesis, I'll consider it. In the interests of education and the dissemination of knowledge, Mr. Fuzz."

"Mr. Fuzz?"

"You have the same values as a cop," Roger answered.

"All right. I'll accept that," Leary said. "You call me Fuzz, if you like, but answer to the hypothesis."

Roger had to smile again, the second time over this guy. He couldn't help but respect him. "Okay," he answered. "I won't let fear shut me up either. Why should a revolutionary have to do anything with the church?"

"Well, your revolution will be communist, right? And communists are against the church, right?"

Roger felt the steady pressure of Penny's hand in the middle of his back and thought a moment, looked at the mayor, who was obviously listening, just on the other side of the counter in the brightly lit room, noticed his soft, pink flesh and pale-green eyes, the long pink nose and heavy pink lips.

"First of all," Roger said, "my revolution is artistic." But in any revolution, who says it has to be communist? And what makes you think a communist can't believe in God? What makes you think religion and politics are the same thing? There are Catholic Marxists in France. There can be Catholic Marxists here. God and politics are two different things. Don't you remember what Jesus said when the Pharisees tried to trick him into exposing himself as an enemy of the Roman state, not just as a religious heretic, 'Give unto Caesar what is Caesar's and unto God what is God's!'"

Penny slipped her arms around him and pressed herself against his back, and he knew that she liked his answer. The mayor even flushed a little, and there were slight smile lines around Leary's eyes.

"You express yourself well," he said.

"But that's not my point," Roger said. "I'm an artist.
That's my revolution, like the artists of the early twentieth
century who, though they had an artistic revolution, also
fought political battles. Gide, Sartre, Koestler and Camus in
our time had to choose politically, and though they all joined
in the battle for economic good, they all chose liberty in the
end. That's what they were about—the rise above nationalism
or ideology."

He stopped, pointed at Leary and said, "You're of Irish
descent. James Joyce was an Irish revolutionary against all
oppressors through his art. In his books, he attacked British
imperialism, Irish nationalism, and the spiritual domination
of the Catholic Church. After leaving Ireland at twenty-six, he
never lived there again and only went back once, when his
father died. And he refused to join the Irish literary union
that Yeats started."

Penny's face was next to his. He could tell by her soft look
that she liked what he was saying. He went on: "Gide came
back from Russia and wrote a book on his disappointment
with Russian Communism and told other leftists that even in
the case of a communist revolution in France there would
have to be a special place for an eccentric and artistic and
political revolutionary like Joyce. And Koestler wrote *Darkness at Noon* as his realization of what a dictatorship of the
proletariat could lead to: disappointment, disillusion and
death!"

He jabbed his finger at Leary again. "So don't be telling
me about some communist revolution. The revolutionary students in France fought the communist unions this year! The
same so-called revolutionary unions who backed the bour-
geoise government against the student rebels! Local control!
Democracy! Not slavery in some old-fashioned ideological way.
That's what a student revolution would be about, not old-fashioned communism!"

Leary's eyes were fixed on him.

"Look at Camus' *The Rebel*! He chooses freedom, not slavery! Sartre himself could never fit into some society that
demanded he obey. He wrote about a great writer like Jean
Genet and said, 'You can tell how unfree a man is by how
much he identifies with a group, whether a union man or doctor or lawyer!' So don't tell me about some communist revolution where all the writers do what they're told, Mr. Fuzz! I'm a

writer. I'm for freedom! I don't care what the economic state
is! And I mean that!"

When Leary didn't answer, just kept watching him, he
explained, "There are two things to consider. A political system is separate from an economic system. An economic system, whether communist or capitalist, can be either a
politacal dictatorship or a political democracy! I don't care
what the propaganda says about the 'Free World,' meaning
anything capitalistic, and 'Totalitarian,' meaning anything
communistic. I don't care what the economic system is, I want
the political system to be free! And I'll fight for that! So, don't
try to suck me into acting like some stereotype you've got in
your academic, authoritarian head, Mr. Fuzz!"

Penny squeezed his chest from behind him, leaned her
chin on his shoulder and pressed her cheek against his.

5

"Well, look at this, will you? ¡Buenas noches!" Leary said
as a big, very dark-skinned cop in a blue uniform stepped
through the doorway into the light of the cafe. A young boy
about twelve or thirteen, who looked like a miniature of him,
followed him in.

"Who's this? I've never seen him before. What happened
to the other cop?" Roger asked.

"He's been transferred. This is the town cop now," Leary
said.

"I just saw the other cop today," Roger said, thinking how
he wouldn't talk to him.

"Yes, I did, too. How would you know that?" Penny asked,
squinting suspiciously at Leary.

"I talked with him last night," Leary said.

Penny kept looking at him with her head cocked slightly
to one side, long hair hanging down over one shoulder, but
Leary turned to the cop and invited him to a drink, "¿Quiere
una copa?"

The cop stepped up to the counter, stared at Roger from
small black eyes and said, "Buenaaasss," with thick purple
lips as if he were drunk. "This your amigo?" he asked Leary,
round cheeks wobbling as he spoke.

He was a very dark man, like Roger's Arabian landlord, as tall but huskier, at least six feet two and over two hundred and fifty pounds, with a belly, a huge chest and shoulders. He was imposing, and Roger felt a hint of fear inside when Leary said, "We were talking about your...uh...theories, and wondering how would you fight in a town like this, even if it were for liberty, like you say."

Roger just looked from Leary back to the cop and didn't say anything. Penny let go of him and stood next to him, looking at the cop, too.

"I mean, in some demonstration, like in Paris, where you didn't have guns," Leary said. "Like the strikes back in the colleges in America."

The cop kept his small black eyes on Roger.

"You mean a demonstration?" Roger asked.

"Yeah, if the cops charged you en masse with clubs here in the village."

The big cop kept his eyes on Roger, who could also see the mayor watching him out of the corner of his eye while he pretended to look off over the small cafe.

"That beach is full of rocks, if I had to fight back," Roger said.

"You couldn't do more than pester them a little. You couldn't stop a charge with those rocks," Leary said.

Roger felt like answering that he could if he were throwing at him, when Penny said, "Oh, yes, he could. Last week he hit a big dog in the ribs when it was chasing a chicken, from about fifty feet, too."

"Is that true?" Leary asked.

Roger nodded his head, sorry that Penny had been dragged into it. "I've got a good eye and those rocks are well-rounded by the waves and easy to throw."

He looked at the cop again, who stared back at him as if he didn't understand. Roger picked up his beer can and took a deep swallow, but lowered it when Anne Marie stepped through the door behind the cop. She looked golden, stepping into the light from the rectangle of darkness with Robey behind her.

"How did you get here?" Penny asked, her voice ringing with hostility.

"Didn't Roger tell you?" Anne Marie asked, her puffy lips spreading in a sensuous smile.

"No, he didn't," Penny said, and looked at Roger.

"I saw her today at La Rubia's before I came to the beach. She told me they got kicked off Ibiza." Roger felt silly trying to keep Penny from being jealous when he didn't really want them around either.

"Do you plan to stay long?" Penny asked.

"If we cawn," Robey said, and, smiling with crooked teeth, reached out and grabbed Roger's thumb in a handshake.

"What does that mean?" Penny asked.

"Money," Robey said. "How are you, Penny?"

She hesitated, then answered, "All right," but didn't smile.

"Like a drink?" Roger asked, turning his back on the cop and Leary.

"Sure," Robey said, smiling again, his wild blond hair frizzing into kinkiness at the ends.

Anne Marie nodded, meeting Roger's eyes, and he raised his arm at the mayor and asked, "*Refrescos, por favor.*"

"How are you, Leary?" Anne Marie said, and Roger asked, "Do you three know each other?"

"Oh, yes, we met at the beach," Anne Marie said.

Roger felt a wave of suspicion sweep over him, and he looked down at Penny and sympathized with the sad frown on her face.

The cop picked up his beer and knocked his gray cloth glove off the counter. Roger started to bend down to pick it up when the cop blocked him with a powerful forearm and slurred, "*Momentito,*" then stepped back and waited with narrowed eyes.

Roger didn't understand what he meant and glanced at Penny when the cop's plump, dark son, as tall as Roger, bent down and picked up the glove, placed it neatly on top of the other gray glove on the counter, stepped back at attention with his hands at his sides and his feet together, and then nodded his head in just the smallest bow to his father, who nodded back.

The sight of the bestial cop with his thick, hanging lips, and his thick pig-like neck made a chill run over Roger's scalp, as if every hair on his head were rising with his horror.

6

Penny was like a shadow around him all day. He sensed her, but couldn't see her, his mind was so full. Yet, she didn't go out to the beach or even to La Rubia's. She laid out on the patio on her towel and read all afternoon. He saw her out of the corner of his eye. He wondered why she didn't go out, but didn't ponder it. He caught a glimpse of her with her towel in her hand and her bikini bathing suit on in one corner of the window, down near the side of the screen, out of the corner of his eye. Once he heard the toilet flush and some footsteps cross the tile, but he didn't really look at her all day while he was writing. Whatever had happened the day before was not going to be part of his mind-set the next morning, or he'd never get any writing done. So, he dismissed it. He'd worry about it when he had time.

He knew that Anne Marie had bothered Penny and Leary had bothered him. But that was all. Tonight, that's when he'd worry about that. Yet, Penny was on his mind. He tried but couldn't forget her presence: that rosy tan body in that rosy-colored bathing suit. She seemed to hang around without getting in the way, but he looked up when he heard a patter of footsteps and saw her step through the open doorway from the dark hall into the cool room. She stepped past his bare chest, then sat on the bed near him and asked, "Do you love me?"

"Yes," he said, turning his head to look at her.

"How come you don't kiss me a lot anymore, then?"

"I kiss you," he said, glancing back down at the page to see where he was, then glancing back up when she said, "Only when I kiss you."

Her blue-green eyes, set and dark with big black pupils, accused him. Suddenly he saw Anne Marie's face and understood.

"I've been working hard on this book. That's probably the reason. I think about you, Penny. I want you to be happy. I appreciate us being together like this in Arguiniguin. I hurried to the beach yesterday when you weren't at La Rubia's." He looked full into her eyes with his green eyes, trying to let her see that he was honest and meant it.

Her gaze softened, she got off the bed stepped next to him, pressed her nearly bare hip against his bare shoulder, and said, "I feel like you don't want me around sometimes."

Her eyes looked all long lashes and soft green irises, like flowers with petals. He smiled, but turned away to pull his page out of the typewriter with a quick swish, then picked up a paper clip and clipped the page behind the other pages he'd written.

"Do I irritate you?" she asked.

"I didn't say that!" he said. "I'm just busy and preoccupied with the book."

He put the paper-clipped pages on the clipboard, then pressed the spring down and slid them under it, letting it down with a tiny snap.

"You act it."

"No..." He stopped, then stalled and evened the pages on the clipboard again, let the clip down again, and said, "But you're making me irritated now."

"You've been thinking about Anne Marie, haven't you?" she said. Roger straightened on the chair, ready to shout, but almost bumped heads with her because she hadn't moved back and was leaning over so that her eyes were steady and level and searching and only a foot from his.

"Not the way you think," he said in a low voice.

"Why didn't you tell me you'd seen her yesterday, then?"

"I probably would have if Leary hadn't been at the beach. He got me off on the assassinations and I completely forgot about her."

"Is that true?" she asked, and though her eyes were still searching his, her voice was soft as if she already believed him.

"Yes!" he said. "Why shouldn't I tell you? If she came to meet me, it's not going to happen. Why should I ask for trouble? She might be a cop! They might have brought her around because I won't go for Ruth! I'm going to keep writing my novel! Nothing's going to stop me!"

Penny blinked, stared at him for a moment, then, with a tight mouth, asked, "Would you like to make love to her?"

"That's not a fair question, Penny. Any man would like to make love to a pretty woman, any pretty woman."

"Do you think about making love to her, then?" she asked, but in a softer voice.

"No," he said, and she smiled, straightened up and put her hands on his shoulders and, leaning against him, pressed the sun-warmed skin of her stomach against his shoulder.

"Why don't you make love to me then?"

"I do," he said.

"I mean now," she said, inviting him with her eyes, too.

He stared up into them for a moment, his own eyes large and dark and penetrating. Her head was tilted slightly, and he saw that she needed reassurance over Anne Marie. That's why she hadn't left the room all day. He pushed his chair back and stood up. He realized that she stood there in front of him, wanting him, weeks after she was supposed to leave. He was lucky, after all, to have her, and he pulled her to him and kissed her long and soft, tonguing her mouth, feeling her bare body fit into all the contours of his own nearly bare body, and then felt the hump of her groin press up against his crotch. He pushed her back against the side of the bed as they kissed, and just as he fell on top of her, a glimpse of Anne Marie in the sunlight by the window in La Rubia's, all tan and golden, flashed in his mind.

Penny cried "Oh!" as she hit on the bed and pulled him to her, then opened her mouth wide and kissed him hard, cushioning the force with her soft lips, tightening her arms around his neck. A surge of love for her filled him as they kissed, and never parting to take a breath, he began to pump slowly on her. She spread her legs wide under him and he pushed his body into the middle of her and met her thrusts with his thrusts, and he found himself wanting only her, his love who loved him!

Then he slid next to her and, still kissing her, slipped his finger under the crotch of her bikini bottom and started stroking the soft cleft between the bristly hairs. He slid his finger in and felt her body tighten, then relax as he began to pump it back and forth. He could have come right then.

When she began to squirm and twist and pump hard, he couldn't wait anymore and pulled his finger out. Then, still kissing her, he lifted his body over her leg and slid her bikini bottom down until she could kick it off. He then moved his body back between her legs again, and still kissing her, unbuckled his Levis and pushed them down over his hips. He guided his tool into her, pinching the soft flesh over the head of it until he placed it next to her opening. He then pushed into the snug fit, feeling the foreskin act as a sleeve until he was joined body to body with her, pubic zone to pubic zone, flesh to flesh.

He began to pump back and forth in her, feeling her body rock with his, pushing her further and further up on the bed, still kissing her, feeling her breath snort out of her nose on his cheek and her tongue twist and twist around his. Then she lifted her legs up and hooked them around his legs and her hips began to pump fast and sharp against him, faster and faster and faster as he snapped it into her, snap, snap, snap, snap, snap, her bottom rising up under him, lifting him, finally, above her, until the breathing and pumping got so hard and fast that she twisted her mouth off his and started panting and moaning and thrashing her head around, pumping faster and faster and faster and faster until she broke out into little cries, "Oh! Oh! Oh! Ooooooooooooh!" and his whole body froze as his penis exploded in her with an excruciating shiver that ran down his spine.

He pushed it as far in as he could, so that the soft skin of her inner loins seared his whole crotch area, and held it there while it throbbed in her until the thrill finally stopped. He then fell to the side of her, still joined to her with his lower body, still caught between her legs. Slowly his eyes closed and he drifted off into a deep-breathing, prolonged, daydreaming state, happy, pleased that she'd thrashed in such passion with him and that he'd had such a thrill himself, too, feeling like they were really lovers still, when a loud knock on the door made him jump.

"Yes!" he asked, expecting to hear the landlord's deep voice.

"It's Anne Marie and Robey," Ann Marie said.

"Wait a minute," Roger said, and separated himself from Penny and stood up, grimacing when the bed squeaked. He then grabbed a towel from a nail, wiped himself with it, gave it to Penny, then pulled up his Levis, slid into his green T-shirt and buckled his belt as she hurriedly wiped herself and slipped her bikini bottom back on again.

"How did you guys get in?" Roger asked when he opened the door.

"We just came up," Anne Marie said, and stepped quickly into the room, allowing Robey to step in right behind her.

Robey stared at Roger as he stepped by him, wild strands
of his curly hair hanging like blond cobwebs in front of his
eyes, then stared at Penny and walked across the room
toward her.

Penny, who was running a comb through her hair, bent
her head with the pull of her arm and shielded her eyes
behind her elbow from him.

He stopped by the table, glanced at the typewriter, then
turned and stood with his back to it and looked at Penny. His
long-sleeved brown turtleneck clung loosely to his skinny
body, his legs like pipe stems in his bell-bottom pants, a
day-old brown stubble on his cheeks.

"What's up?" Roger asked.

Robey just crossed his arms over his chest, and Anne
Marie said, "Just dropping by on our way to Las Palmas."

"So late?" Penny asked, putting the comb down, facing
Anne Marie.

"We can get a ride with Fuzz," Robey said. "He has a van."

"Who's Fuzz?" Roger asked, thinking of Leary, the nick-
name for cop alerting him.

"Leary. You know George."

"You call him Fuzz now?" Roger asked, cocking his head.

"Yes," Robey said, but, without explaining, let his eye
drift over to Penny again.

"Would you two like to go with us?" Anne Marie asked.
She still hadn't moved, and stood with her back to the now
closed door, the soft light and shadow in the room making her
skin look flawless. Below her miniskirt, her tanned thighs
glowed with light from the open window. She spoke directly to
Roger but didn't smile, as if afraid to offend Penny, he
guessed.

"When you coming back?"

"Tomorrow."

"We can't then. I've got to write in the morning."

Anne Marie frowned, then said, "Oh, all right. Let's go,
Robey," and stepped right back out the door, moving off down
the hall. Robey waved and grinned as he closed the door
behind him, as if he knew he had caught them with their
clothes off.

When Roger could no longer hear their footsteps running
down the stone stairs, he said, "I didn't like that."

"I didn't either," Penny said.

"They came in here like they knew we'd been fucking. And he acted like he wanted to get in on it."

"I know."

"That means the room's bugged," Roger said.

"Not necessarily," she said.

"Whatta ya mean, 'not necessarily?' They rushed in here like they wanted to switch, and what would we have done in Las Palmas tonight? All slept in the van, that's what! And probably nude! And Leary's name is now Fuzz! Meaning, they know I suspect him of being an agent and want to still play him on me."

When Penny cocked her head and looked at him from one eye, he said, "Anne Marie and Robey have probably been put up to it, too! He looked you over like you were a piece of meat. And that's probably why I haven't gotten any word on my second novel being published next month like Forest Press promised! They're all attempts to stop this book I'm writing."

"All of it, Roger? That's far-fetched," she said, her head still cocked.

"Yes!" he said. "Craig and Ruth acting all hurt because I'm working on my book! They've lived with us before. They know I write every day of the year when I'm not traveling. They were with us when I wrote *Kilo*. Shit! I read the chapters to them as I finished each one. It's all a game to keep me from writing a controversial book about the subversive secret police! That's what!"

"You're jumping to too many conclusions!" she shouted, dropping down on the edge of the bed and striking her fists against her thighs. "None of the things you say might be true! They could all be coincidences! She's following you around because she knows you like her!"

"All of them coincidences?"

"All of them!" she screamed. "You use the agent bit, the bait thing, as an excuse for liking her and for her coming around over it. You use that to cover up that you want to make it with her!"

"Is that right?" he said, bending over from the waist and pointing a finger at her. "Then tell me why you didn't want me to talk politics with Leary, Fuzz, or whatever you want to call him? On the beach and in the Bar Nuevo? In front of the mayor, no less. And what about the way the cop came in when I should have been deep into another political explanation of my views, prompted by Mr. Fuzz himself? If I hadn't shut up Fuzz right away? Tell me about that!" he said in a high-pitched voice.

She was silent for a moment, staring at him, then lowered her eyes and looked away.

"Answer that series of coincidences! Pattern is a better word! Answer that!"

"I don't have to! I don't have to answer anything! I don't have to answer!" she screamed, and struck both fists against her thighs again.

"And that's why I can't trust you in the end," he said in a low voice, his eyes dark green. She turned her back on him and stared at the wall for a long time.

When she didn't turn around, he turned and grabbed his dark glasses from the table and jerked open the door, stepped out and slammed the door behind him.

7

Roger put his hand over his sunglasses to shield his eyes and see how far he had to go in the hot sun. The empty pavement of the highway stretched in a wavy-heat haze straight through the bare, dry desert land, up into the cliffs next to the ocean a half kilometer more at least ahead of him. He was walking to Pata La Vaca beach just as he would have done if Penny were with him! He was still boiling inside.

"Fuck!" he said, and let his hand slap down against his thigh. There seemed to be no way he could ever get her to admit that the police were after him and behind almost everything that happened! She wouldn't take the final step and call it what it was, and this could cause them to fight and break up!

"Shit!" he said, wishing he'd brought his kif along so he could light up, but by the time he got to the high cliffs, the village was so far back, he was glad he hadn't gone back to get it.

When he walked down on the sand, he was surprised to see Anne Marie standing in her pink bikini on the cratered rocks by the concession stand. Her body was petite and golden-tanned and so perfectly shaped he couldn't resist staring at it.

"I thought you were going to Las Palmas?" he asked.

"It wouldn't have been any fun," she answered, and looked directly at him with her pale, golden-brown eyes.

He felt so down on Penny, the urge was strong to say, "Let's go now!" But they had fought over Anne Marie and what he thought about her motives. The irony of the idea of going with her after fighting over her made him turn away and take off his T-shirt, then lie down on the large rock, propped up by his elbows.

Anne Marie sat down on it next to him. Her golden thighs stretched out right next to his. Then, when she leaned back, supporting herself by her arms, he could see the fine crease of her stomach where her body bent and the hump of her pubic zone under the patch of pink cloth that barely covered it, and felt desire rise in him. To get the urge out of his mind, he looked off at the small beach that stretched for a hundred yards between the high cliffs, then glanced out at the gray-blue sea, wishing Penny were with him,

Anne Marie said something and he turned toward her, but made himself not meet the look in her golden eyes. Still wanting to be polite, he asked, "Want a Coke?"

She shook her head, staring at him, trying to get him to meet her glance. But the fight with Penny was still too strong in him. He kept quiet and looked off at the sea again, and she did, too. They sat there a long time without speaking, until the longing to see Penny again built up in his chest. When he couldn't take it any longer, he said, "I've got to get back," and stood up to a stiff-mouthed pout on Anne Marie's face. He didn't want to hurt her feelings, but he loved Penny. Anne Marie didn't speak when he walked off.

After he came around the last bend in the road and started down the last long stretch that led right to the village, he wanted to tell Penny that they shouldn't let the argument over the cops get in the way of what they felt for each other, that they couldn't let Anne Marie break them up now when Ruth couldn't.

When he reached the flatland of the cove where the village was and started down between the buildings of the main street, a warm feeling flowed through him. He was going to tell Penny how much he loved her and that's all that counted. He was touched with tenderness for her when he ran up the dark stairway, seeing her respond in his mind with a soft mouth and sweeping-lashed green eyes. But when he tried to open the door, it wouldn't open. Fear ran through him as he rattled the knob.

"Penny!" he said, and knocked, then knocked again. When there was still no sound, he pulled out his key and stuck it in the lock, fear turning in him again with the key.

He scanned the room when he stepped in, and his heart quickened when he saw the note under the small, brown pine cone on his desk. He snatched at the paper and his heart pounded as he read.

"Goodbye, Roger. I love you. I want you to know that. But I'm going away. I should have gone back like I planned. It was a mistake to stay. When you left today, I went down the stairs to the street and sat down on the porch and looked at the bay through the cedar trees and wrote my name in the dirt next to the veranda. I don't know why. But I realized I didn't know who I was. Today was the first time that I've come with you in a couple of weeks. That means something. Then our argument over what's been happening, what's *always* happening, took it all away. Living with you is in a way like living with some abstract force. You've got your mission, and you submerge yourself in it, and anything that doesn't fit in with it you suspect of being the fault of the police. Maybe that's true sometimes. But I feel as alienated from America as you do sometimes. I feel the pressures you do indirectly through you. It involves and hurts *me*. But what hurts the most is that you *don't trust me in the end*, your own words. I've got to build a life for myself. I can't always live through you. I exist in my own right. I want to be treated as a worthy, whole person. It costs too much to stay with you. So, I'm going away. Don't worry. I'll be okay. Love, Penny."

He dropped his hand and let the page slap against his thigh. His throat was so tight he had to swallow to keep a sob down.

8

The waves were crashing in a flurry of foam against the rocky beach at full tide as Roger hurried down the dirt road in the dark before dawn to catch the bus in front of the inn for

Las Palmas. The rattle of the rocks when the waves drew back sounded ominous to him, and he began to have doubts about the bus, which left at six-thirty in the morning. Would it get him to the post office in the old section of Las Palmas when it opened at eight in the morning, where he hoped to catch Penny?

She wasn't in bed with him when he woke up, an absence that filled the early morning darkness of the room with sadness. It was as if she had just died, and he appreciated her more now that she was gone than when she was with him. That empty spot in him still filled him with regret when he saw the bus lights go on. He began to run, his body, with his brown corduroy jacket on, heating up immediately.

There was no one else on the bus but the driver with his hat pulled down low over his bony face. Roger jumped in, and the driver closed the door with a big sigh of air brakes, gunned the motor and pulled right away, turned the corner of the inn and headed for the highway and the hundred-kilometer ride to Las Palmas.

Through the bus window, Roger watched the sun come up over the eastern edge of the ocean: the horizon a luminous wash of red and blue, with gold and purple shadings that made him ache at its beauty. He kept glancing at his watch, trying to judge whether they'd make it or not, thinking when they passed one landmark that they would and then, when they passed another, that they wouldn't, then with the third, again that he would. He knew he was cutting it close, but he hadn't found anyone with a car willing to give him a ride the night before. Fuzz was nowhere to be seen, and he didn't want him to know anyway. Craig and Ruth kept telling him to have a drink, relax a little, have some fun and not worry about it.

He looked at his watch again as he had done every five or ten minutes since he started. It was already ten to eight and they still had twenty-five kilometers to go. He couldn't possibly be there when it opened. He could only hope that she wouldn't get there at exactly eight, and that he'd have a chance to catch her and talk to her and maybe bring her back with him.

"*¿Qué hora es?*" he asked the bus driver when he got off the bus, hoping his own watch was fast. But he saw that it wasn't when the driver answered, "*Las ocho y media.*"

Roger started trotting, trying to cover the mile to the post office fast. The morning streets had a cold, fresh cleanliness, but by the second block he began to sweat anyway, and, still running, he took off his corduroy coat, then increased his pace by stretching his legs longer and getting a bigger bite with each step. He kept to his faster speed even up the sloping hill the last six blocks, looking at his watch every little while. He finally reached the "Lista de Correos" window by eight-forty, and panting, asked, "*¿Una señorita, Penélope Lawson, recibio sus cartas esta manana?*"

"¿Penélope Lawson?" the young man repeated.

"*Sí, por favor.*"

The clerk turned and went back to the wall of slots, shuffled through some letters, then stepped to the window and said, "*Sí. Ahora recuerdo. Esta mañana. Temprano.*"

"*Gracias,*" Roger said, and turned and walked out without asking if he had any mail himself. He drifted down the narrow sidewalk, carrying his jacket over an arm, trying to figure out what to do next, afraid now that she'd picked up her mail, he'd never find her. For the first time, he was afraid that she really didn't want to be with him. This scared him. He hadn't really thought of that because she'd said she loved him in the letter. Now, he had to really think of the future without her, he alone standing in front of a blank, frightening screen or looking off some mountain top at a huge, wide, gray distance. It really scared him. He saw the selfishness in his need, but he did need her.

Then he remembered that his old *pensión* was only about six blocks away. He picked up his pace and started walking with a bouncy stride toward it, his hopes up again. He ran up the five flights of stairs, past the open door where the Spanish girls sat and sewed, and up to the *pensión* door. He knocked, nervous, his senses alive with anticipation.

"*Perdonéme, senorita,*" he said to the bony and very dark daughter of the landlord, whose black dress hung past her knees. He asked her if the girl he had lived with had rented a room.

"No," she said, and he remembered how curt she had been with Penny for living, unmarried, with a man, and for being only nineteen when she was around thirty and still unmarried. "*No está aqui.*"

He asked her to tell Penny, if she came by, that he wanted to talk to her, spacing his words, exasperated by his clum-
siness. But when her black eyes first widened with
understanding, then slightly wrinkled as if she were about to
smile as she closed the door, he regretted giving her such obviously satisfying information. He walked with a sagging body
down to the boulevard and caught the first bus to town, truly
convinced now that Penny really was trying to get away from
him. Again, he saw himself alone, facing a great, gray void. He
saw how insignificant he was and how important her love
really was to him. But she didn't know that he knew this.
Somewhere, wherever she was, she didn't know this, and she
didn't want to be with him.

Still, he stared out the windows and searched the sidewalks for her, spotting young women in the crowd, on a bus
passing in the opposite direction, in the window of a restaurant, scanning each of them quickly for familiar signs, his
heart quickening inside him when he saw a girl about her size
in blue jeans with long brown hair. But it wasn't Penny, and
he felt depressed by the time the bus reached Parque Santa
Catalina, the main landmark on the boulevard just on the
other side of the street from the port with its wharves, ware-
houses, and docked ships. He stepped down from the bus to
the curb with sweaty hands and without much hope that he'd
find her.

He walked slowly around the block-sized park, carrying
his coat, crossing through the southern end where the main
walk was lined with artists' booths. The poorly done paintings
depressed him even more, but he was alert and searching all
the time. When he turned up the western edge of the park
next to the restaurants and buildings which formed a solid
wall to the end of the block, he scanned every table under
every umbrella at every outdoor cafe, looking closely at every
group of people, whether standing or sitting. The small spark
of hope still flickered with apprehension inside him, ready to
shoot into flame at the first sight of her.

But he reached the other side street at the end of the park
with no sign at all of her. He then walked along the northern
edge and stared through the windows of an ice cream shop
where he and Penny used to stop when they lived in Las Palmas. He had an urge to go ask the pretty girl who worked
there if she'd seen Penny, but he didn't.

He walked instead down the long, eastern edge of the park next to the busy boulevard which stretched from where he stood a hundred and fifty winding kilometers south to the tip of the island. He kept glancing on the other side of the boulevard at the port buildings, at the docks, hoping he'd see her, but he didn't.

He walked along a long row of palm trees that served as a wide-picket fence to the park, until he got to the very center of the park where concession stands of souvenirs, photos and candy stood. He turned, stopping next to a round concrete bench in the middle of a small plaza that served as a giant flower pot for bushes and ferns. From there he could rest and still see in every direction.

He sat in the shade on the bench for two hours, his mind turning over and over with darker and darker thoughts about how fragile their relationship was and how susceptible to any kind of outside pressure. As soon as Anne Marie showed up it broke. And now Fuzz, too! It was politics and girls. The politics were destroying his life. She left him not just because Anne Marie upset her, but because he didn't trust her. Now the politics would take her away from him. There seemed to be no hope.

He watched the leaves on a thin branch near him flutter with a faint breeze, and the shadow of the branch sway back and forth on the smooth white tile at his feet. He turned to look up in all directions at intervals to make sure that he didn't miss her. He wondered if she was walking by the outdoor cafe tables when he was looking toward the artists' booths or if she was walking by the artists' booths when he was looking at the tables. He got up every once in a while to check the booths, the outdoor tables, the boulevard, the ice cream shop. He began to think that maybe he should cross the tourist section, which stretched a mile from the park and was composed of small hotels, cafes, shops and nightclubs, to the mile-long, crescent-shaped beach where the luxury hotels were.

But as he stood there listening to the low undertone of chattering voices and street traffic to the sigh of bus brakes, he knew that his best chance to find her or make contact with her was in the park, because everybody they knew came here when in town. He could tell them he was looking for her, even if he didn't catch her himself. So, he sat back down on the bench and looked at his watch.

It was only five past eleven, but he hadn't much hope that she would come around. He was sure she was really trying to escape from him. He was thinking of leaving, of going back to the village, when he saw Fuzz and Robey appear on the other side of the tiled plaza in the center of the park.

"Hey, Robey! Fuzz!" he shouted, and jumped up.

They both stopped and looked over at him, and when Robey waved, Roger hurried over to them.

"You haven't seen Penny, have you?" he asked.

"No. You lose each other?" Robey asked, then grinned, the beard stubble shaved off his now clean, pointed chin.

"Sort of," Roger said, then added, "She left me yesterday and I'm looking for her."

"Yeah, you were supposed to be writing today, right?" Fuzz said.

"That's right," Roger answered, not liking the sarcasm or the reminder that he wasn't writing. "If you see her, would you tell her that I'm looking for her and want her to come back?"

Both of them stared at him as if surprised he'd expose himself so openly, but Roger could almost guess they already knew. Then he noticed that Fuzz now had a growth on his chin trimmed in the shape of a goatee, but it was only a couple of days old and hard to see. Roger wondered if Fuzz would let his hair grow now, too, so he'd look even less straight. Still, neither of them said anything, and he asked, "Where's Anne Marie?"

"You got me," Robey said.

"Didn't she come with you?"

"You might say that, but she's not with me now," Robey said, and turned away with a wave of his hand, then walked off with Fuzz.

A little hurt that they didn't ask him to go with them or stay around and talk, Roger went back to the bench and sat down in the shade again, wondering what Robey meant by that last remark. If Penny was gone and Robey was gone, wouldn't it be neat if Anne Marie came around? But he rejected the thought. He looked at his watch. It was noon already, and here he was wasting a day of writing looking for somebody who didn't want to be with him! A bitter feeling curled in his chest. Maybe he was weak looking for her? He stood up. He'd go home. He'd try to make a new life without her. He'd respect her wishes, if that's what she wanted, and leave her alone. He'd be strong. But he looked around once more, still hoping he'd see her. He didn't and, sensing that this was it, started down the plaza toward the boulevard. He'd only gone a few feet when he heard his name called in a woman's voice: "Roger!" He spun around, hopes high, searching for Penny, only to see Anne Marie come hurrying across the plaza toward him.

"I just saw Robey," he said, walking back to meet her.

"I don't care," she said.

"Didn't you come with him?"

"I did, but I'm not going back with him," she said, and looked closely at him with her pale-brown eyes. It was the smooth, heavy lids, he realized, that made them look so beautiful: heavy and long and curving at the outer corners with the long, so long lashes.

"Looks like I'm not going back with Penny, either, though I didn't come with her."

"What happened?" she asked, an opaque glaze to her eyes. But when he tried to look into them, she lowered her heavy lids.

"She split on me when I was at the beach talking to you, over you, in a way," he said. "She's jealous of you."

"Oh, she doesn't have any reason to be," she said, glancing up, her brown eyes conveying exactly the opposite meaning to him. "Well, if you're alone and Robey and I aren't talking, why don't we stay together?"

"I was going to hitchhike back to the village now. Do you want to join me?" he asked, jumping at the chance for some companionship.

"I'd love to, but do we have to go back right away? The afternoon bus leaves at four, and we could catch it if we don't go now."

"You mean stay here in the park? I don't want to hang around here. It depresses me. And it might take a long time to get a ride, even with a girl, so we should start now, if we're going to hitchhike."

"Okay, let's go," she said, but he could tell by the way she turned away that she really didn't want to leave yet.

9

When the truckdriver's eyes switched to the side of his head, staring at Anne Marie, as he passed them, Roger, with his thumb out behind her, saw it, as he had been seeing it from almost every man in every car that passed. After the truck rumbled by, tailgate rattling, they both dropped their thumbs and turned around and started walking down the edge of the street again, just next to the parked cars, through the downtown district, past small shops and stores and busy sidewalks.

Guys on the sidewalk stared at her, too. Roger looked at her himself, scanned her slender shape, saw how the brown sweater clung to her petite body, the nice swellings of her breasts, and her golden and shapely legs under her brown miniskirt.

When they heard more cars coming and turned around to stick out their thumbs together, she saw him staring at her and looked back at him. He noticed how creamy and golden her high cheekbones were, and how golden her natural blonde hair glowed in the sun. She was striking from a distance, but up close she was gorgeous. The sensual puff of her lips so close to his made him want to kiss them. And the sloe-eyed slope of her long, heavy-lidded brown eyes was so sensual it struck him like some miracle of life that she, this exotic animal, so beautiful and almost untouchable, was now not only looking out at him, but knew him and wanted to be with him. All he had to do was reach out and touch her.

Then, as if reading everything he thought through his dark glasses, she smiled and stepped closer to him, stood with her hip and shoulder pressed against him, her head so near that he could see the part in her hair and the thick, golden strands growing out of it.

He had a sudden image of her in bed with him, and he could feel his arms around her and his hands cupped over her breasts, feeling the smooth skin of her buttocks against his groin, as if she was really his and this trip down the highway was proof of that. He lifted up his left hand and put it on her waist just to touch her, and she pressed back up even closer against him. But then, just when he felt the magnetic pull of her body as if she were giving herself to him, the very suddenness of it made him see himself next to her, and see what Penny would see if she saw them!

He stepped back away from Anne Marie, and to cover his move, said, "Why don't we walk out of this business section for a few blocks, then stick our thumbs out? We'll have a better chance."

"All right," she said, but looked closely at him, as if she thought something was wrong.

After walking several blocks, then walking backwards for over an hour, he saw that they were still in town, near his old pension, in the crowded older section of town, and he really began to fear that Penny might see them together. Then, any chance he still had left of getting her to come back with him would be lost for sure.

He had to smile wryly at himself at the irony of his predicament. He had come all the way to town to find Penny, and now, at this moment, he didn't want to see her. It was all so neat! So fake! All of them in Las Palmas today just as Anne Marie had suggested the day before! And he wasn't writing! And here they were, he and Anne Marie, walking down the street like lovers! He was being handed a new girl to take the place of the old girl right away, before he could miss her too much. And everybody knew what was happening! Everybody knew it was a setup!

He began to walk faster down the street, trying to get out of the area as soon as he could, making Anne Marie hurry to keep up.

10

"What's the matter, Roger?" Anne Marie asked as they walked down the dusty street of the village after six long hours on the highway, getting only two rides and having to walk the last ten kilometers into town. "Do you miss Penny?"

She was exactly his height and looked right into his eyes. It was such an honest question, it shocked him, after what he'd been thinking about her.

"Yes," he answered.

"Are you sorry I'm with you?"

Another honest question and a clear brown eye which shamed him, and he said, "I do miss her. We've been together a year and a half. And I didn't want her to see us together. She's so jealous of you, I'd lose all chance of getting her back."

She looked down as if she had to make sure of her footing, then said, "You're sorry I'm with you then?"

"Oh, no!" he said, and she looked up, a hint of a smile on her lips. "I miss her and want to find her, but I like being with you and that's the truth."

"I understand," she said, and touched his hand as if she really understood.

A wave of tenderness for her swept over him. "Would you like to go to La Rubia's and have something to eat with me? Or are you going back to the cave with Robey?"

"I don't want to," she said, pressing up against him as they walked.

He felt an urge to grab her and kiss her, but the thought that she was being put up to it, that he was being manipulated again, whether for herself, the police or both, stopped him. But she was so lovely, walking so close to him, he shook his head at himself. If she were trying to manipulate him for herself, wasn't that normal? Wasn't he the one who wasn't normal? Then, trying to be considerate of her, too, he asked, "What will you do? Where will you stay if you don't go back to the cave?"

This time, she stared at him as if she questioned his motives, but then asked, "Are there any rooms at your pension? I could rent one," as if she knew that there were.

He had trapped himself again and knew it. But then, though he wanted to say, "You don't have to rent a room! Why not stay with me?", and knew that's what she expected, he kept himself from giving into his urge to take her and make her his, now that he was all alone, now that he was lonely, and answered, "There's one right across the hall."

A sense of fatalistic doom gripped him when they reached the street corner of the inn and turned down along the rocky shore. He knew that just by taking her to the pension to get her own room, he lost all chance of being reunited with Penny, and that no matter what he did, the secret police would end up having it their way.

"Those fucking pigs," he said to himself as they reached the row of cedar trees. He wanted to send her away, just to prove they couldn't do it, take one away and give him another one just as quick. He saw a police state as implacable and unrelenting and inescapable as the Fates of the Greeks or the Gods of Shakespeare in controlling his destiny, any man's destiny who dared to fight back.

He wanted to fight back and stubbornly didn't ask her to stay with him in his room. Yet, when he asked the landlord's tall son for a room for her, a deep sense of foreboding, of loss still saddened him. He knew he was losing Penny and felt panicky.

This was it! Even if Penny did come back, she'd leave if she found Anne Marie just across the hall. She'd think they were lovers! Yet, following Anne Marie up the stairs, seeing her shapely bottom swaying just so slightly above him, he shook his head at himself. They were taking one away from him and giving him another. And he liked her. He couldn't be cruel to her either, even if she was an agent for the police. He had to smile when the long-nosed young Arab pointed at Anne Marie's door and said, "*¡Ella aqui!*", and stepped across the hall and knocked on Roger's door and said, "*¡Y usted aqui!*"

The Arab then stood in the middle of the hallway and made an imaginary line down it with his shoe and, pointing to each side of the line, repeated, "*¡Ella aqui y usted aqui!*"

"I guess he doesn't want us to sleep together," Anne Marie said as they stepped down from the porch to the street and started walking down the row of cedar trees, around the cove to La Rubia's.

"Yeah, he was pretty persistent on that, wasn't he?" Roger said, but he hid his relief that, at last, a final breakup with Penny had been postponed. "I wonder if it was because of his morals, or his reputation in the town, a concern for his business being respectable, or because he just wanted to rent two rooms instead of one?"

"Probably not his morals," Anne Marie said, and they both smiled.

Yet, Roger couldn't shake a sense of entrapment, of being a pawn, of everything being counterfeit, including her love, including her willingness to sleep with him. He was sure she would. It was all so neat it depressed him, and he didn't speak anymore all the way to La Rubia's. He was full of his longing for Penny, somebody he could trust, an irony that hurt more when he thought of why she finally left him: "Because you don't trust me in the end, your words."

"You're worried about Penny, aren't you?" Anne Marie said as they sat down in the main dining room.

"Well, that, too, though it's a little bit more selfish than that," he said. "She's my best friend."

Anne Marie smiled and looked up at him from the menu as if she really liked that. The light from the windows across the room was soft on her cheek and cast the other side of her face into shadows with a straight line down her nose. Her eyes were large and magnetic, full of feeling for him, making him trust her.

"Would you like to see the letter she wrote?" he asked.

"Yes," she said, and took the letter with a stiff, uncertain reach. She stared at the page to avoid his eyes, as if sensitive to reading something so personal. She didn't look up once as she read and he studied her face, the incredible smoothness of her complexion. But glancing down to see where she might be in the letter, he suddenly realized that he was letting her read about his most secret relationship with Penny and about his thoughts on the secret police! A sense of entrapment touched him again, but she immediately made it vanish with her first words: "I never knew Penny was so deep. I thought she was a little timid, she's so quiet most of the time around you."

She folded the letter back into the same crease marks and pushed it across the table.

"She can write," he said, putting the letter in his jacket pocket. "You ought to see her poems! She writes good prose, too, though she doesn't quite have the stories to tell yet."

Anne Marie smiled at his enthusiasm, then said, "Take good care of her if she comes back, Roger."

"I will! I will!" he said, full of love for her at her goodness, then froze when he saw the front door push back and Penny step down onto the landing! She held the door back with her hand and stared at him, then glanced at Anne Marie and stepped swiftly back outside, pulling the door shut with a slam behind her.

"Penny!" he called, and jumped up, knocking the chair over backwards. He leaped up on the stone landing to the door, threw it open, saw her just reaching the top of the stairs, jumped up them three at a time and caught her arm only a few steps from them.

"What's the matter? Why are you running away again?"

Her face was white and her mouth quivering when she looked up at him. He was glad they were in the shadow of the building and no one could see them.

"So, she's your new girl already! That's what you wanted, isn't it? You didn't waste any time getting together with her, did you? So soon, Roger? So soon?"

"That's not true!" he said, grabbing both her arms. "I met her in Las Palmas today, where I went looking for you. I was just heading back and she went with me, that's all. She's not my girl!"

"She's moved in with you already! The landlord's son said you had a new girl!"

"What?" he said. "That dirty bastard! Now, I know how it all happened. I suspected this! I thought it was a plot all the time!"

He squeezed Penny's arms and leaned his face down close to hers.

"I'd given up hope. I thought there was no chance left of your wanting to be with me! I went to the post office to catch you this morning, but I was too late. Then I went to our old pension and when you weren't there, I thought you really didn't want to be with me. Then I went to the park and stayed there until I gave up, and then, only then, I saw Anne Marie and she hitchhiked back with me. I felt like I was being set up all the time, I swear it!"

She squinted at him for a moment, then asked, "Did you really go looking for me?"

"Yes! I spent the whole day looking for you!" he said. "I waited in the park because I thought I might see you there. As soon as I saw Anne Marie there in the park, I suspected her. By the time I got here, I wished I was with you, somebody I could really trust."

"Do you mean that?" she asked, and when he nodded his head, she said, "Do you want me? Do you really want me?"

"Yes, I want you," he said.

"Then, let's move out of there tonight! Right now!" she said.

When he nodded, she threw her arms around him.

Episode Six

INCOMMUNICADO

1

"*¿Nada?*" Roger asked, his teeth showing through his parted lips as if still shaping the word. He couldn't see the plump mail clerk's eyes through the brown-tinted glasses and felt as if the guy was hiding his eyes from him.

"*¡Nada!*" the clerk said, then shut his lips tight together.

"*Pero, varias personas me escriben,*" Roger said. "There's got to be some mail by now!"

But the clerk kept his mouth shut, shrugged his round shoulders and slouched away, his gray sweater wrapped around him like a cocoon.

"Come on, Roger," Penny said, putting the letter from her mother into her straw bag and pulling him away from the window.

"Goddamnit!" he said. "That's five fucking Mondays in a row that we've hitchhiked a hundred kilometers from the village into Las Palmas without a letter for me! And you've gotten a letter every time! Don't tell me that's some kind of coincidence! I didn't go for Ruth or Anne Marie so they try to get me this way, that's what!"

He let Penny pull him away, but he didn't stop talking.

"Either they're holding up my mail or all my mail's getting lost, which isn't very probable, or neither my agent nor my wife nor my father nor my son nor my editor is writing to me! That's one hell of a coincidence! Especially since it coincides so neatly with my writing this novel that pulls the covers off the CIA and their subversive, not to say, treasonous activities!"

"Keep moving," Penny said, pulling him through the swinging glass door of the Lista de Correos office and out onto the sidewalk of the narrow street that sloped steeply down toward the harbor a mile away.

The cars were parked bumper to bumper, facing him on both sides of the narrow, one-way, one-lane street. There were so many three- and four-story buildings with iron trellises and balconies and fire escapes sticking out of them, filling up the narrow sky, that he couldn't even see the harbor.

The strip of sky he could see was hazy with clouds. A cool breeze swept up through the canyon-like street, chilling him a little in the deep shade of the post office building. He saw a tall, young man with thinning red hair leaning against a car with a camera at his waist, facing him. He noticed how Nordic he looked with his milky skin, long nose and big-boned height. He wore a short-sleeved, flowery sports shirt open at the neck and khaki pants. He was almost unclassifiable and looked a little like Fuzz, too, except for the thinning hair, which made him see even more sinister and threatening. The guy looked down at the top of the camera, aimed it at Roger, quickly took his picture with a flick of his thumb, then turned away.

"Hey, y..." Roger started to say, but got jerked around by Penny.

"Come on. We've got enough problems," she said, holding his arm and pushing him downhill with her shoulder.

"Who do you want or need a letter from most?" she asked.

He watched her for a moment as he walked in step with her, letting her lean against him, glad he had her around to tell him what to do sometimes. And nobody, not anybody, was going to take her away from him again. But his face tightened behind the mask of his dark glasses when he said, "My agent, Rob Welscher. He's the one who's supposed to know everything. But my editor, too! He was supposed to tell me exactly when the book was going to get published. Maybe they're holding up publication because they know I'm writing this book about the cops and their dirty tricks."

Roger expected her to deny it, but her tiny mouth didn't speak. With her tiny chin and big eyes, she looked a little like a pixy.

"And what about my ex-wife Lenora? I wrote to her, to all of them, four months ago. I asked her to send me all that research material on revolution, copies of the *Gadfly* and those books by Marcuse and Paul Goodman. And my son! He's never answered me either! And my father! I wrote to them, too! I don't even know if my editor, Kurt Deaver, even got the edited manuscript of *Kilo*, because nobody's answered me!"

He held up his hands. "I'm afraid they're either not writ-ing to me or my mail's being held up because of the cops!"

She pulled his hands down. "Well, the only thing you can do then, is write again," she said. "You've got to write to each of them and ask them why they haven't answered."

"All at once?" he said, throwing his hands up. "What a fucking job!"

"Begin with your agent. Then take them in order of importance. Write one letter a week. Some might answer before you're through with the last one. You wouldn't have to do it all at once!" She pulled away from him when they reached the flat, busy street at the bottom of the block and faced him on the corner, just a foot away.

"But this week that means hitchhiking back to use my typewriter, then hiking back again tomorrow if I want to get a letter off quick, and not writing on my novel two days in a row!"

He held up two fingers, but she said, "You could mail it from the village and give our address there!"

He shook his head. "That change of address could cause more problems than it would solve. Everything could get lost in between."

He took her hand and stepped off the curb, leading her across the street towards the bus stop.

"No, you're right. Let's go back and I'll write the letter and we'll come back tomorrow, then come back once a week after that. If their intention was to stop the novel on a day-to-day level, they're making me lose one day a week for the next month or so, at least."

She squeezed his hand when they stepped up on the curb and smiled when he looked at her, making him smile, too.

He started walking faster down the street to hurry back to the village and write his letter. He had her and that was a lot! Half of it! Real love! The other half was his book. Without either one, life wasn't worth living.

She must have seen his feeling on his face because she asked, "Do you love me, Roger?" And when he nodded, she kissed him.

2

Roger sat down at his typewriter and began to type the letter to his agent with a pattering racket of the keys, quick and full of anger.

Dear Rob Welscher,

I received a letter dated October 11, 1968, from Susan Flanagan in which she stated you would be writing to me about magazine and book publication of *Kilo* by the end of the month. That was four months ago. Where's the letter? Where's the contract? I don't want to suffer over this lingering problem any more. The same thing occurred with *Every Mutha's Son*, and so thoroughly ruined the publication of the book for me that I've had a taste of ashes in my mouth ever since.

You've been a fairly good agent.

He stopped with his fingers on the keys. Rob Welscher, a guy he'd never seen, who had an ivy-league softness to his deep voice, the only human thing Roger could associate with him. It made him picture a tall man in his mid-thirties with a soft, pink face, thinning hair and glasses—rimless glasses— for some reason, a sign of his conservative lifestyle, like his soft, easy, educated voice. But Welscher hadn't written to him in months. Roger began to type again.

I think this is the first potentially best-selling material I've ever sent you, so I can't expect miracles. So, let's give it another go-around. Let's try to start from a new beginning, and I'll forget about the past if you will. I hope Forest Press does, too. But if I don't hear from you by the end of the month, I'll take action to get myself another agent. This silence is ridiculous. I hope you can see this from my point of view.

Yours, sincerely,
Roger Leon

3

Just as he pushed the side post office door open, Roger again saw the redheaded guy who looked like Fuzz press his thumb up and down on the button of his camera. Roger stopped, but remembering how Penny had pushed him away the last time, he stood watching the guy, camera dangling from his waist, push off the car he was leaning against and walk off up the sloping sidewalk toward the busy boulevard which ran in front of the post office.

To say something might lead to a fight. With the kif pollen on him, it could only lead to big trouble. He had mailed his letter to his agent and somebody in that office had to actually sign for it when it got back there. Proof that it had been received was supposed to come back to the Canary Islands. He'd settle for that. To hell with the guy and his camera.

"Feel better?" Penny asked when the guy reached the corner of the big marble building and walked around it, out of sight.

"I did until that guy took my picture," Roger said.

"He might not have," she said.

"Don't say that now or I'll get mad," he said. "Let's go have a beer or something. I need to have fun as a stopgap. But, really, everything depends upon my getting an answer to that letter. Then, I'll be able to tell you if I feel better. Only then, and I'm not going to write to anybody else until I see if I get an answer to this one first!"

4

"Nothing? Not even a letter with the name of this person? No letter with my name? They didn't even send back the card?" Roger asked, but the clerk just shook his head, shut his mouth and stared at Roger through his brown-tinted glasses.

Roger pushed through the door again and saw the redheaded guy standing just across the sidewalk from him with his camera dangling from his neck, as if he'd already taken his picture. Again Roger wanted to say something to him, but he had deep regrets about the tone of his letter to his agent, and, bothered by that, he started down the sloping sidewalk without saying anything to the guy. He was afraid he was too demanding of his agent, even if justified. He had probably turned Welscher off.

"Do you think I ought to write a more conciliatory letter to Kurt Deaver?" he asked.

"That might be a good idea," she said.

Roger walked without looking where he was going, wishing he'd met Deaver so he'd know how to approach him. He pictured him from his letters and from what he knew of the liberal house he worked for as another man in glasses who looked maybe like a party man, but smaller, neater, more efficient, with white shirt and tie, like some high-level civil servant, somewhat like a theoretician, well-ordered, somebody who did not like wild, passionate men.

By the time Roger got back to the village, he decided to write the letter right away and be as restrained and unemotional as possible. And, above all, not egotistical. He did so very much want to get along with everybody, particularly his editor. But he wouldn't mail the letter until the following Monday when he came back once more to see if he'd gotten a reply from his agent.

Dear Kurt,

I wrote to you about forty days ago asking you for your criticisms of *Kilo* so I could rush the corrections back to you. I also wrote about the possibility of my going to New York City for the publication of the book. I could pay my own way back and stay there and edit the gallies, help publicize the novel and learn a little about the literary life of New York, groove on the culture there, too, and meet, I hope, all the members of the Forest Press staff, get to know them and come to an understanding of them. I think it's about time I made the big splash for a little writer and went to the big city so I won't have problems of communication and can grow up a little bit. This pressing book business has brought me to this and no word from my family back home, either.

I'm afraid I put you on the spot with the last letter. I thought the book was going to come out in the spring. I guess it's not. Too bad. Please let me know when you expect it to come out though, and what happened to the proposed publication of the chapter in Forest Press Review. And how about the French contract again? Man, questions all over again. Maybe I can resolve them all in New York City. Please, answer this letter, Kurt.

Yours sincerely,
Roger Leon

5

Hands on the typewriter keys, Roger remembered Lenora when he had left her for good. Even with tears running out of her huge blue eyes, she was pretty, really pretty. His chest tightened as he pictured her back jerking with sobs, walking away without him. But he couldn't love her anymore. Her cooperation with the police had hardened her and made her cold to him. She hadn't kissed him in three and a half years. He remembered her last letter now and how she had told him she had a chance to marry Wes, her boss, the junior partner of the junk company.

Dear Lenora,

That was quite a mind-blower about you and Wes. I guess you've made it with him, though you don't say so. And Wes must love you, if he's willing to give up his family and that business. You've known Wes for ten solid years. It was his influence that took you away from me, that made you lose belief in me. You're close to him. You know him and he's good to you and always has been.

But that doesn't mean you have to marry him either. Who says you have to get married? Who says you have to either settle down with a man or be a bum? Personally, I don't think you need a husband. You're a modern woman. You can take care of yourself without any complications and do very well. Don't get married because other people want you to get married. Get married because you want to get married and for no other reason. You're very young. You will always be beautiful. You're probably the most beautiful woman I've ever known in my life. Only marry someone you want to give your life to. That's the meaning of marriage for a woman. If you don't want to give your life to some man, if your need isn't so great that you can't live without him, well, then, don't give your life to him.

I left you because you weren't willing to give your life
to me anymore. You had a life down at the office which was
more important than your life with me.

Go to college. Don't get married. Fuck it! You're young
and beautiful and intelligent and that's where you'll meet a
groovy guy with culture and education and enough money,
too.

Now, I've got to ask you some important questions all
over again, the same questions that I asked you in my
long-unanswered letter. Did you get the manuscript of
Brothers? I sent it last October.

Please find out how Daddy is. He wrote to me last
August and said he was going to the doctor twice a week for
checkups. That's a lot, but it could go on for twenty years or
more if he's not seriously ill. Please find out. I wrote to him
twice since I received his letter, once in California, once
here, but I have not had one reply yet. I've been suffering
much over him. I love him. I don't want him to die. I'll come
back if he's seriously ill. But find out for me about Daddy,
okay?

And I might go to New York for the publication of the
book anyway, whenever that is. I've only got two thousand
left of the advance on *Brothers*. I've got another book, a controversial one, going good but it won't be done until September at least. I never received that fifty dollars you said
you were going to send me for Xmas. As you can see, Spain
is no place to receive mail for a radical writer.

Man, it seems like things are breaking apart back
there for me. I'm glad Brad has got a girl who loves him.
But the lack of a father is sure showing now. There's no
symbol of authority for him to depend upon. And I told you
he'd need me sometime and I wouldn't be there, remember?
What's he doing? Tell him to answer my letter! By the way,
with his juvenile traffic arrest, he might be able to get out
of the service. Get a psychiatrist to testify that he isn't suited for regimentation because of his whole artistic upbring-
ing, the way he was taught to talk to snails and draw
pictures of their world.

Now, write to me and tell me when you have problems.
Remember that I love you, too, and would never have left
you, never, if you'd still believed in me and would have
been willing to follow me and live my somewhat poor life
style. But you didn't, and now my heart still aches for what
once was. But everything you do is important to me and I
don't want you making big plans that might ruin your life

without asking me my advice first. I can at least give you a different viewpoint on them. And that will help. So don't do anything drastic yet, and keep in touch. Answer this letter! With love, Roger

6

Roger turned away from the mail clerk without getting any mail. He remembered the redheaded guy, hoping he wouldn't see him. He had looked for him when he first walked up and he wasn't there. But when Roger looked out the glass doors for him now, the redhead was leaning against a parked car, his camera hanging in front of him, hands on it, waiting like Doom, like Big Brother, to take his picture.

Roger stepped to the door facing the guy, saw the guy lean his head down to look into the camera, and, at the last possible moment, Roger pushed Penny out first. He saw the thumb press down and up and the guy's head suddenly pop up and stare at them, surprised at the trick. He then turned, dropped the camera on its strap and walked away. Roger had beat him just this once, which gave him some satisfaction. But when Roger had walked only a few feet down the narrow sidewalk between the parked bumper-to-bumper cars and the high stone wall of the building, feeling that he'd, at least, finally outwitted the guy, he glanced back to see the guy standing in the middle of the sidewalk with the camera pointed at him and his thumb going up and down.

7

Dear Brad,

My son, I answered your letter over three months ago.

Roger stared at the page, but it blurred with memory and he saw Brad now at the side of the pool in Orinda, smoking hash out of a wooden pipe, his ruddy cheeks sucked in with the drag, beautiful brown eyes furrowed together over the high bridge of his nose. Muscular in his bathing suit, he looked good lying around in the sun. It seemed to Roger that was all he ever did since Roger had left three years before.

The idea of meditating in jail on weekends for your traffic ticket sentence is beautiful, man, because if you succeed in doing it you'll build some creative wellsprings that will last all your life. Although, it's too bad you've got to make that jail scene even if only for traffic tickets. It's nowhere. The best you can do is make something out of the evil you've experienced, but the evil itself is deep and lasting, even if you've finished your sentence. Those days you did in juvenile hall isolation under questioning over me when you were sixteen made you into a man, baby, and don't think not. But they'll always hurt.

Strangers always thought they were brothers, they looked so much alike, but Brad was finer-featured and prettier, with his mother's beauty.

So, why'd you drive with a suspended license and get into an accident? I don't want a defense again, but I'd like to know, if you can tell me. Your meditating ought to be able to take you deep enough into your own behavior so that you can come up with some answers, even though you might miss some other contributing factors, like the fact that you don't have a father symbol of authority in your life to even object to and rebel against now. And the only alternative is joining the army and getting an institutional father-figure, though God forbid you should be trained to kill.

In their last years living together as a family, Lenora had spoiled Brad, and Roger had to be the heavy to keep him from becoming spoiled rotten. Then, Brad didn't like him. He said he was glad when Roger left to live alone.

But remember a long time ago when I told you you'd need me sometime when I wasn't there? Well, believe it or not, I believe your driving fuckups are an attempt to bust loose because you don't have a father to even attack and are also attempting to emulate the reckless behavior of your father, me, who's a pretty fucked-up cat himself and will probably always act a little like a kid.

Though they had reached a state of mutual caring in the last two and a half years before Roger left for Europe, the closeness was gone. Roger ached with doubt that it would ever return. He pushed the thought out of his mind, and when the page came back into focus, he made himself type again.

I taught you to be brave and to risk yourself in a manly way by diving from the trees into my arms when you were four and zipping down hills from Sequoia Park on a flexi at 35 miles an hour when you were five, and I never hurt you, because, paradoxically, I was never reckless with your safety. I was sure of everything I did. I wanted you to become a man, not a punk. So, now, catch hold of yourself, and don't die because of some romantic image of yourself in some horrible accident, and don't drive without a license so the man can't fuck with you.

Okay, no more advice and questions. But answer me, man. Answer this letter!

With love,
your father and partner, Roger

8

Blind eyes through brown-tinted glasses, the slit mouth, the shake of the head, like some dream. The post office clerk doesn't like him, Roger can tell. He's tired of being the object of Roger's anger. He wraps his gray sweater around himself like a blanket, like layers of sleep Roger can't penetrate. It's like yelling in a nightmare and there's no sound.

Roger turns and walks out into the camera eye like a sleepwalker. He's tired. All the brave words in the letter to his son are now gone, on their way to America, he hopes, then realizes with a pang of despair that the letters might not even be leaving the post office. It's too much to fight week after week. He says nothing to the red-haired man. He doesn't even bother to stare at him. He can even see the camera still pointed at him after he turns down the sidewalk, but he doesn't care. He's too tired. It hurts too much.

He remembers long hours on the highway, under a hot sun, watching the occasional cars swish by. He remembers Penny reaching out for his hand and holding it as she sticks her other hand and thumb out. He thinks of himself as a poor father. Then he thinks of his own father. He thinks of his own father all the way home. His father's voice on the phone the night when he called him up and screamed at him: "I wish you were dead! I wish my mother was alive so she could see what you've done! Cooperating with the secret police against a son who's doing nothing more than living by the values you taught him! I wish you were dead!"

"What-what-what!" he heard, then nothing, nothing, nothing. But that hurt too much. He loved his father too much. He went to see him and kissed him on the cheek and hugged him and sniffed his round, bald head. The big man's beautiful smile suddenly came over his stiff face, then broke as he started sobbing. Roger just wants him to be alive now. He just wants him to live.

Dear Daddy,

I've been thinking about you a lot these days and I hope you're alive and well. I've suddenly become afraid that you're dead. You haven't answered my letters and I'm afraid that I'm writing this letter to a ghost and that you'll never read these words. Sorry. We're being treated cruelly in Spain these days. I get no mail at all, not even from my agent or my editor and I feel like committing suicide. Spain is a place of contradictions, like all places. But if you're a foreigner, or extranjero, you get the extremes of good and bad. I get to smoke here all I want, though the police know what's going on and merely tolerate it, since Africa's only 50 miles away and the influence of the hashish-smoking Moors is long and deep. So that's a very good thing and I wish America was like that. It will be someday when grass is legal. Some day.

Suddenly a strong feeling, like a wave of love, comes over him as he stands next to the window. He feels like he's talking to his father. He feels like he's reaching out to him, that he can almost touch him and lean in close and sniff him, smell the warm odor of him, a smell he'd associated with security since he was a little boy. He wishes his father were near, really, so he could touch him with his hands. He wants to rub his head and back and chest. The thought makes him feel strong.

I feel better writing to you. Boy, I hope you're well,
Daddy. The sun comes up in my window in the morning
with a great rosy glow and lights up the face of Hemingway
on the giant poster I have on my wall. It's 5:15 in the afternoon and a motor scooter just buzzed by, sending up clouds
of dust on the dirt road. I love you, Daddy. And I'm not crying anymore. Write to me, Daddy. Please answer this letter. Please. I love you. I want to hear from you. Please,
Papa, please answer.

Your son, Roger

9

The birds were singing in the cool air of mid-morning
when he got back on the highway, unable to wait until the
next week to mail the last letter. But without hope, he felt
worse than he had on all the mornings, but he just couldn't
wait. He had to do it now and find out if he had any mail, too.
And sure enough, the thin-lipped clerk turned away again,
without even looking at him, and again Roger walked out into
the iron eye of the camera. Somehow he'd hoped that the
break in routine, by doubling back the next day instead of the
next week, would throw them off. But though he saw the guy
above the blink of the lens, he didn't look at him, didn't care,
just turned and slouched down the street to hitch back to the
village again.
    Penny put her arm around him and walked in step with
him, not speaking either. He remembered a couple of rides
and the flat desert land sliding by, then walking into the room
and stalking back and forth in the darkness, without going
out to eat. Then Penny dozed off in her clothes on top the
blankets, so he didn't turn on the lights, just stood there and
stared out the line of windows at the full moon just over the
big eucalyptus trees of the hippy camp on the other side of the
bay, the shiver of stars all around it, his mouth dry with bitterness. Why couldn't he just be happy with her and not have
to suffer this shit? He'd been under the gun his whole life in a
country that kills its great liberal leaders. Nixon was now
president over the bodies of two Kennedys.
    Nixon? Suddenly he realized that tomorrow was January
20th, 1969, and Richard Nixon was going to be inaugurated.

The darkness hung over him like a premonition of his own death, of something very bad happening to him. They weren't going to stop, and he wasn't going to stop. The handwriting was on the wall. He was going to die one way or the other, through suicide or murder, without even leaving a will. He had to at least say something about it! Desperation had brought him to the edge of nothing again, to the thought of suicide. He must fight back, must write or die.

He turned away from the window and stepped to his little portable lamp on the barrel next to the typewriter, wishing he could muffle the keys to keep from waking Penny. But she had slept through many long night sessions of him clattering away on his typewriter. He slipped five pages and four carbons in and began to type. He must write or die.

LETTER TO MY AGENT, MY EDITOR, MY FAMILY, EX-WIFE, LOST SON, FORMER FATHER, AND FORGOTTEN FAMILY: LAST WILL AND TESTAMENT

Today, this very early morning, not long past midnight, is January 20, 1969, the day of infamy in which Richard Nixon finally gets to the White House over the dead bodies of two Kennedys. Today is the day in which the right wing of the military-industrial complex finally legitimatizes its coup d'etat in America. Today is the day when America loses its democracy. Today is the day I might die because I am writing a book about that tragedy of classic Greek proportions and refuse to stop. I will never stop! If I love my country and myself and my art, I will be true to what I believe.

I believe there is treason in the land. I believe it exists in the highest office. I believe my president was murdered by men who now take control of my government, the oldest living democracy in the world. That democracy is now gone. It dies today. Of course, it really died the day President Kennedy was shot. It was just a slow death and the coup de grace didn't come until the bullet to the brain of his brother Bobby before he could become president.

On this day it has been four months since I have heard from any of you, and I have plenty of reasons to believe it's no accident. I've been followed and harassed and had my picture taken and my European trip manipulated since I set foot on foreign soil, meaning England. I was followed on the plane. An agent rode with me. I have not been able to escape the presence of Nixon anywhere I've gone. His first official diplomatic act after he becomes president today will be to come to Spain where I am! I left the country to get away from this monster and all he represents, and I might as well have stayed home.

In addition to the long silence from all of you, especially you, Rob Welscher, which is incomprehensible to me, I have received no research material from my ex-wife in Berkeley, and no word from Kurt Deaver over the KILO manuscript I carefully edited and sent to him, and which he has never acknowledged receiving. It, my second novel, was supposed to be published in January, 1969, to take advantage of the topical interest in Haight-Ashbury. This is January and not one word about it has come from anybody. I have reached the end of the line.

If you, Rob Welscher, aren't interested in handling this book, notify me by telegram at this address and I'll get myself another agent. If I don't receive an answer from you by the end of the month, I'll take action to get myself another agent, if I'm still alive. You might think this action odd. I don't. You might think my inference of your silence unfair, I don't. After what's happened to me because of my radical activities and the subject matter and viewpoint of my writings, your silence is only too easy to interpret as just another facet of the total suppression I suffer. But I'll try to let you know just what I am, what kind of a person and writer and why I believe what I believe and why I must fight to the end for those beliefs.

I worked like a slave in the California presidential primary for McCarthy the whole month of May, 1968, trying to work within the political system for my own particular view of things, meaning to get a strong showing for McCarthy so the Democratic Convention would have to stress a strong peace plank in the platform. I lost all hope the night of the primary when Bobby Kennedy was killed and the following week I joined an illegal sit-in at the State College Administration Building. We held it for one week, right into finals, forcing the college president to grant all but one of our fifteen demands, failing only to get ROTC off campus—The Pentagon was too strong for that even then.

We won by extra-legal means after our legal attempts to change the forces of power were declared null and void by the crash of bullets into the brains of great men, liberal leaders of the people. But I fought so many agents in the sit-in alone I became convinced that our country's democracy was at stake, and I left the country rather than vote for either of the two puppets of the military-industrial complex, Humphrey or Nixon, and found myself unable to even think about writing about anything but the personally traumatic and nationally most tragic experience I/we had undergone the previous spring.

Unable to work within the system politically when the right wing nullified the democracy with the barrel of a gun, I now fight back. I fight back as a democrat, small "d", fight for my country, for everybody I love, for the world, for myself, for art, for freedom, for our freedom, with the written word, the most, eventually, powerful weapon of all. "In the beginning was the word!" No idle statement. Civilization was not built upon the wheel but upon the ability to communicate, which produced a society which then needed the wheel, especially since it was nomadic.

I see my function in the evolution of man as one of raising the level of awareness, of consciousness. Ho Chi Minh said there must be many cadres. I am a soldier of the word, with the weapon of language in the war for freedom against fascism of all kinds, of whatever color, whatever party, Southern Democrat, Republican or Stalinist. I believe in the worth and dignity of the little man, in local control of government within the framework of a social democracy, meaning the right to choose my own leader of whatever political persuasion, not have it chosen for me by the events of the last year in our country.

I write you this letter in the probably naive hope that you might understand me and not think me your enemy just because I fight against the present administration which has brought us to this ruin. I still believe in democracy and that's why I write my book and why I write to you. I will take the chance that this letter is misunderstood and that I'll suffer for it, in many ways. But I believe that only by writing this letter will I keep alive that belief and myself. I couldn't live much longer not believing in what two Kennedys and King died for. I would take my own way out, choosing death rather than a spiritual hell, with or without success or money. I lost my wife because of the corruption of my family by a police state which sought to stop me from practicing that very democracy our country was founded upon. I find it exceedingly difficult to trust anyone now, even the girl I love. But I must continue wanting to believe in people, or my soul will surely die and my writing will be without spirit, without hope, which I believe uplifts the bitterness of the novel I write now and those I've already written, and which all of you have liked.

I've been under the gun for many years. If I seem paranoid I must point out that paranoia is an illusion, the murder of two Kennedys a fact. On this day, I'll take this letter and hitchhike a hundred kilometers to Las Palmas to mail it, to all of you. But if I don't get an answer from you, in particular, Rob Welscher, by the end of the month, I'll take action to get myself another agent. I must if I want to live and keep writing. As for the rest of you, my family, I mean, I won't write to any of you again until I get answers from each of you.

A sense of death makes me an artist forever. Agnostic like my father, I can only have cultural immortality at the very best, so I give it my best and only shot. I write so I won't die.

With all my heart,
Roger Leon

10

Everything seems to buzz with sleep, like he's high, when he reaches down and shakes her shoulder under the blankets to wake her. There's a slight surreal sense of heightened reality to everything, as if the sleep he hasn't had hangs like a gray narcotic over his brain, a fine veil spiderwebbed over the gray matter, barely holding down the demons beneath.

His face is thin with hollows under his cheekbones and dark shadows under his eyes. He doesn't look at his eyes in the mirror when he shaves. He hasn't eaten since his wheat germ and *café con leche* breakfast the day before. He's not hungry. His belly's flat and hard and his hipbones stick out. He's tired, a weak fatigue inside his bones, yet he's full of energy when they walk out onto the small strip of highway and stick out their thumbs. She carries the letters in separate envelopes in her bag, smiles at him, then holds his hand and hitchhikes with the other. He's glad she's with him.

The smell of the sea is strong this morning. Birds chatter at a high pitch in the trees near them, all down the highway. The driver of the first car that stops for them lets them sit in the back, and Roger lets the cool air from the open window blow over his face, keep him awake, keep his mind from wandering. Penny leans her head on his shoulder and holds his hand. Their warm fingers intertwine. He can feel sweat on his palm. He swallows. His mouth is dry, and he hasn't even smoked any kif pollen yet. He will when they get out.

The scent of the smoke is sweet to his nostrils in Las Palmas. But he feels exactly the same after he smokes up. He walks to the post office with the same buzz of sleep in his brain, the same sense of heightened reality, as if he steps on a sidewalk far below him.

The slit-mouthed clerk doesn't even turn around to check for any mail for him, just takes all the letters, with the last will and testament in them, fills out the forms, takes his money and doesn't speak once. It's like some nightmare. Across the counter behind the iron-barred cage, the gray bug of the man in front of him performs mechanical rites without words. He's as far away and unreal as a figure up on a screen in a silent movie, yet close and sinister and too real.

Roger pays and steps out into the eye of the camera, huge in the tall man's hands. It reminds him of a gun. The same unreal quality, small and black and harmless-looking, yet deadly, with an unerring, killing aim. The thumb goes up and down, once, twice, three times. Yet he keeps looking at it until Penny pulls him away, without him once looking up at the tall, red-headed man, who vaguely resembles Fuzz. He seems unimportant now that Roger's mailed the letters with his last final try to reach them all.

He walks down the sloping street with Penny, sleep buzzing in his ear, his belly stretched taut and stringy as meat jerky. His legs move mechanically. Something is over. He has said something final. He needs to relax. He'll stay in town and walk around today.

But the sense of doom that prompted him to write the letters, that hung over every word, steals over him again with the first sight of the redhead in the park near the artist's booths taking his picture when he steps up on the curb from the street. The guy's followed him downtown! He tries not to look at the redhead, but can't help glancing at the stark white cheeks, their ghastly paleness, flesh white enough to be dead, yet with the strong jaw of Fuzz and Ted Kennedy. He looks quickly away, turns and hurries off down another path to avoid him.

Penny looks up at him, but doesn't speak, as if she understands. He takes her hand, aches to have her with him, but begins to feel as if he's wasted his time, that his long letter won't make any difference, and wishes he were back in Arguiniguin. Tonight, on this day, January 20, it'll be two full days since he's eaten a full meal, two long, unhappy days.

Yet, he's not hungry, but light and weightless with no need of food. The kif pollen has blended with the subconscious part of his brain and the turmoil of the dream images has been kindled by the strong weed. He winces when he walks out from the shrubbed and flowered path into the camera eye, pointed at him from a table under an awning. He sees the long pale fingers clutching it, the beveled mask of the pale face under the thinning red hair over it, and turns away down another path to escape.

Penny hurries after him, grabs his hand and squeezes it when he looks down at her. She clasps his arm with her other hand and presses herself close to him.

"Let's sit down," she says when they reach a round tile bench that circles a tree and some small shrubs like a large flowerpot in the middle of the park.

She keeps her arms around his waist and leans her head on his shoulder. He kisses her head, very conscious of how much she means to him.

Yet, it's hot, at least in the eighties, and he feels a little fatigued, too, though he can barely detect a sea breeze. A slight hum of chatter and auto traffic hangs in the air. He lets his head lean on Penny's and thinks of how brown and healthy she looks. He coasts a little, loses some of his fear, some of his anxiety. Yet, Nixon is probably now being inaugurated.

He lifts his head and looks in a vague, daydreaming way through his dark glasses across the gardens at the aisle of greenery on the edge of the park where the artists booths glimmer with color like some flower garden. Penny suddenly sits up next to him and says, "Roger! They just took our picture again!"

"What?" he says, still dreaming, and turns to look at her, then spots the wink of the shutter like an iron eyelid only a couple of feet from his face. His eyes blink with wide whites. He blinks again. He can't believe it! The green eyes of Fuzz, not the redhead, stare at him from above the camera! It's not the redhead this time, it's Fuzz. He's hunched over like he's aiming a gun at Roger! His mouth a thin line, almost a smirk!

Roger leaps to his feet, knowing that he's overreacting but too angry to care. "What're you taking my picture for, Fuzz?"

But Fuzz sits back down on the tile bench next to the redhead and starts talking in Spanish to him, as if he hasn't even heard Roger, as if he doesn't even know him, as if he's the guy with the thinning red hair! But he's not the guy with the red hair! He's talking to the guy with the red hair! They're trying to trick him!

"Give me that film, Fuzz!" he shouts.

But Fuzz leans back on the bench as if to get a better look at him, then speaks in Spanish with fluttering lips and bright green eyes as if he can't speak English, as if Roger's crazy, as if it's not Fuzz sitting right there in front of him. A pang of doubt shoots through him. Is he crazy? Has he gone crazy from no sleep and worry?

But the bright green glare of Fuzz's eyes saves him. Hard as marbles, they stare at him. No friend sits there, Fuzz or no Fuzz. No human being who cares for Roger. Roger knows that. He can see that, no matter who the guy is.

Suddenly everything pops. Sick of being turned away every week for four long months without mail, sick of being tailed down every street, into every room, by this bastard of the police state, sick of this pig pestering him, his hand streaks out and cracks across the cheek of the lying face. He sees an eye shut with the slapping sound and the face twist around with the force, then he sees Fuzz spring up and raise his fist.

Roger can see it coming, see the fist come down toward him, and, even though he's tired, has time to slip his body to the right and make it miss, he lets the guy hit him. The punch catches him right on the left eye. His dark glasses fly off with the smack. A patch of sky flashes in front of him and he lands flat on his butt on the white tile, Fuzz glaring down at him.

It's a fight now, and he leans his hands on the smooth tile and springs to his feet before Fuzz can step in, but feels the blood rush out of his head with a wave of dizziness and Fuzz shiver in front of him, blur like an image on a screen. Tight pain starts in his left eye, like it's puffing up.

He watches Fuzz punch again. Sees the fist fly toward him, big knuckles blurring, but still just stands there and catches it right between both eyes with a smack that knocks him flat on his butt on the tile once more, Fuzz standing above him.

Penny charges Fuzz, swinging her arms like a windmill, face red and puffed, mouth open, screaming, squinting, catching him with two or three closed-fist punches before the red head and another man who's been sitting on the bench, too, grab her and pull her off. But she keeps fighting, screaming and sobbing, struggling to get loose.

"Pennyyyyyyyyyyy! Get out of the wayyyyyyyyyyyyy!" Roger screams, mouth wide, face hot from the effort, with what feels like the last bit of his strength fading out with his voice in the clamoring roar of the crowd, the shouting men and Penny's high-pitched screams leaving him breathless and weak.

Penny suddenly stops struggling and screaming as if she's heard his hoarse cry, and lets the men pull her away. A wave of relief sweeps over Roger, and he leans over on the tile and starts to get back to his feet again, but slowly, trying to preserve what's left of his energy, knowing he's got to find some way to get back into the fight and that it's all uphill any way he goes about it.

He's not scared at all. He might have been hit good and dropped twice, but he hasn't been really hurt once. He might have felt the pain of the punches, but he's seen no stars nor felt the buzz of being stunned nor been made dizzy by the force of them. If he'd lost his senses, then he'd be worried, but he didn't and right now, he's not even in real trouble, just in a mean fight. He only lacks strength, and he can make up for that by making every punch count.

A mass of people surround him, a large blur of tourists and Spaniards in a big circle, when he finally stands up and faces Fuzz. It is Fuzz. Big, powerful Fuzz, looking like a halfback on a pro team in front of him, head down, brow wrinkled, brown hair waving back, charging at Roger again.

Though he's too weak to even lift his arms and put his guard up to protect himself, Roger steps to meet him and snaps out a jab from his waistline with all his weight in it that catches Fuzz right in the mouth, snaps his head back and stops his charge, makes him stare with wide, green, surprised eyes. Then, with his arms still down by his waist, Roger starts

circling Fuzz to get his back to the wide space in the center of
the *medina* where he can have room to move.

Fuzz charges him before he can finish the move and
Roger steps toward him and snaps out another solid jab from
below, catches Fuzz right in the mouth, knocks his head back
again with a spurt of blood, but Roger catches another right
hand punch over his jab this time, right on the bridge of his
nose that drops him back on his butt again. That big guy can
hit, Roger thinks, and sits there for a moment, taking a rest,
trying to preserve energy, expecting Fuzz to wait until he gets
up.

But Fuzz kicks at his face instead, and Roger falls back
out of the way and blocks his fall with his elbows. Fuzz starts
kicking his legs and Roger rolls over once to get away. Fuzz
keeps kicking at them, and Roger can't get enough room
between them to risk standing up and has to roll over again,
then scoot backwards on all fours, catching first one, then
another kick in the legs.

Roger wonders how he's going to get up, feeling so weak,
when Penny suddenly dashes out of the crowd behind the
Fuzz and screams, "You dirty bastard!" and kicks out with her
hiking boot, catching Fuzz between the legs from the back,
making him grimace and grab his balls and twist around with
a frown of pain on his big face.

Roger jumps to his feet just as the redhead and the other
man jump out of the crowd again and grab Penny's arms and
pull her, still struggling, away. When Fuzz turns back around,
Roger is standing with his guard up, the strength of both of
them equaled a little by her well-placed kick, even though the
redhead did help Fuzz again by pulling Penny off him.

Roger backs up, further into the wide open tiled space of
the plaza and leads the guy far out from the crowd where
there's plenty of room to move. Then he shuffles forward with
his head down and his hands up and snaps out three straight
cracking jabs to drive Fuzz back, stepping in with them, then
falls in close, crouched, arms up, guarding his face and body,
intending to left hook to the open body and right cross to the
face.

But big Fuzz suddenly drops down and cracks Roger on
the forehead with his forehead, knocking bone on bone, and
Roger sees stars for the first time, blocking any chance of getting in. Then Fuzz, seeing that Roger's been hurt and is a sta-

tionary target, jumps in again. Roger skips back out of range, but slips on the smooth tile with his worn boots. Fuzz jumps after him once more, trying to take advantage of the awkward slide and catch him off-balance, really showing the killer instinct in him. But Roger stops where he is to keep his balance, steps forward, and snaps out another jab. He connects with a spurt of blood from Fuzz's nose and knocks Fuzz back, stopping his charge, giving himself a chance to get set again.

Roger now sees a target. But it's a long way away and has to be reached from a distance, with only a long hook of some kind, maybe an overhand right, he thinks, and shuffles in toward the guy, with his puffed left eye sighted on Fuzz's chin. Suddenly he spins to his right and steps away as if he's going in another direction, then just as his right toe touches down, he spins back around on it with a twist of his whole body, and loops an overhand right through the air with a swish that just misses the chin but connects to the throat with a loud "splat!" and drops Fuzz with an open mouth and wide eyes flat on his stomach on the tile plaza.

Roger can kick him in the face now, play Fuzz's game and hurt him bad, as helpless as he is, but doesn't. He steps back instead and waits, lets Fuzz get to his hands and knees, then rise up on his feet, then finally straighten nearly all the way up, with his back hunched and his head down low between his arms now.

Roger steps in again. He can see the glazed look in Fuzz's green eyes, knows he can't see well and that his reflexes are slow, and he drops forward over his right hip so he can get under Fuzz's guard, and swings his right hand up between Fuzz's arms and right-hooks him under the chin from underneath, catches him flush on the point of the chin with a clack of the jaw, and drops him flat on his face again.

The crowd cries out in astonishment. Roger feels a sense of satisfaction. He's made another one count. He's now winning.

He waits again, hardly any strength left in his arms, his legs like water, while Fuzz gets up more slowly this time. When he's completely up, his green eyes watching Roger apparently unable to focus clearly, hunched over with his arms low now so his lowered head is exposed and in reach, Roger steps in again, more slowly this time, hands up high, ready to one-two with a left jab and a right cross and finish

the guy off while he still has the power left in his punches to
do it.

Roger faces him with a blue lump the size of an egg in the
middle of his forehead, a bluing eye puffed nearly shut, blood
trickling from his nose, and his hands down low near his
waist, not wasting any strength trying to hold his hands up.

He takes one final step in with his left foot and jabs at the
same time as his foot comes down on his toe so that all his
weight is in it and catches Fuzz right on the point of the chin
with a crack of bone on bone, knuckle to jaw. Fuzz's eyes shut
with the punch and he drops flat on his face with a splat, completely out cold this time, without Roger having to use the
right cross.

The crowd roars again and closes in around the fallen big
man lying on the shiny white tile with his eyes closed. Many
arms reach down and lift him to his feet, but his head hangs
and his eyes are still shut and his big, heavy body sags. They
hold him up for a few seconds, but since he can't stand, they
have to lay him back down again. Then legs and bodies close
around the tall figure sprawled on the tile flooring. Roger
can't see him anymore. He turns around and with his left eye
puffed and blue, and blood running out of his nose, his mussed
hair looking thin along the hairline, without any strength left
in his body, he pushes his way through the crowd and walks
back across the tile plaza to find Penny.

He's surprised at how far it is. It's been a long and
far-ranging fight. But he can't see her near the bench, and he
walks around it, scanning the people staring at him, then
spots the camera lying where Fuzz had been sitting, and
something in him snaps again. Enraged, he snatches it up and
tries to open it to get the film out, keeps fumbling with the
knobs and latches on it, but can't find the right one or press it
the right way, partly because he's so angry and partly because
he's never been interested in mechanics and knows hardly
anything about cameras.

Turning the camera over and over, he gets frustrated and
lifts the camera up and smashes it down on the tile to crack it
open, makes it bounce once, but only leaves a small dent in
one end of it.

He picks it up again, even more angry and cursing "God
damn you!" smashes it down again with what feels like his

last bit of energy. But it bounces once with another dent and stays closed.

He fumbles with it again and tries to pry it apart with his fingers, then on his knee with the heels of his hands, then with his thumbnails, still cursing "Goddamnyou! Goddamnyou! Goddamnyou!" but still can't pry it apart. He then lifts his hand high above his head and smashes it down with all his weight and strength, only to see it bounce once more and still remain closed—a small impenetrable metal box.

His strength all gone, he kicks at it with his boot toe, then turns and watches the men carry Fuzz away, head hanging back, blood running down his face, mouth gaping, eyes shut, through the flowery paths, past the artists' booths and off toward the green men's room on the southern edge of the park. The redhead is holding one of Fuzz's arms. Then, totally exhausted, drenched with sweat, his hands so slippery he has to wipe them on his thighs, wanting to just drop down on the red brick and seep like hot water into the porous surface, he finally sees Penny step out of the crowd near him.

She squints up at his puffy face, looking all freckles to him, then hides her face in her hands and begins to sob. He puts his arms around her and, hugging her to him, pats her back.

"Good boxer," a dark Spaniard says, showing perfect teeth with his smile, dimples in his brown cheeks, and reaches out to grab Roger's hand and squeeze it, making Roger wince.

He looks down at his hand and sees that it's swollen over the right index knuckle. But before he can even study it, a tall cop in a blue uniform and thin mustache steps up to him and says, "*¡Vamos para allá!*", and nods his head in the direction of the green men's room.

"He bothered my wife. *Molestó a mi mujer*," Roger says as they walk toward the building, knowing he has to have a good reason for what he's done or he's going to jail.

"Wait close by," he says to Penny when they reach the low green building, which reeks of piss.

"He took my wife's picture," he tells the cop when he steps inside. Several men stand in a circle around him while others wash Fuzz's face, who, seated on a bench, sags against the wall. The redhead stands to one side staring at Roger.

"He took a picture. He bothered my wife," Roger repeats, knowing he's on trial right there, that the cop's going to decide what to do with him right away, and that he must stress the bothering of his woman, which is a common social problem that all Spanish men will understand. But he's astounded when the cop stands still, doesn't speak and lets a short Spanish man about thirty-five or so with a thickening body question him. He saw the whole fight and had held Penny with the redhead and helped carry Fuzz into the men's room.

"Why did you punch him?" he asks.

"I slapped him, I didn't hit him," Roger says, holding out his open palm. Then he realizes he's speaking in English, and that's why the cop is probably letting the other man handle it.

"He bothered my wife," he says again. "He took photos without our permission. I didn't hit him until he hit me three times. He knocked me down three times before I even got a hit in!

All the men nod their heads as if they believe him, and the Spanish man looks at the cop then says, "Well, pay for the camera, and that's it!" Then staring at Fuzz, who is now standing next to the cop with his big head and green eyes, he adds, "*en precios canarios*," meaning pay for the camera at Canary Island prices, lower in a free port without customs duties.

"*Gracias*," Roger says, then adds, "but I want the film. *Quiero los fotos*."

The man nods his head, talks to Fuzz in Spanish, turns back to Roger and says, "Fifteen-hundred pesetas," and opens the camera, takes the film out, gives it to Roger, takes Roger's money and hands it to Fuzz.

"*Gracias*," Roger says, realizing that he's now free, that it's over, and he stuffs the roll of film into his pocket, glances at the redhead, steps to the trough-like washbasin and washes the blood off his face. He then tears some paper towels out of the towel box and starts blotting his swollen face with tender pats, when he feels someone grip his arm. He turns to see Fuzz staring at him with gritted teeth.

"Again?" Roger asks without even bothering to struggle, glad that the men and the cop can see who's the aggressor. They all grab Fuzz and pull him off into a corner by the toilet stalls and argue with him in Spanish as Roger walks out, past the redhead, who has still not said anything.

"You really ought to see a doctor, Roger," Penny says as soon as she sees him.

He looks at his puffed right hand with its index knuckle
swollen three times its normal size. It hurts bad, too, and he
can't begin to close it. His long fingers and their white moons
look stubby now, and he's afraid he's broken the knuckle. But
though his left eye's closed and blue as a ribbon, and he has a
lump as big as an egg on his forehead, he says, "No, let's go
home now. I've had enough for one day," and he walks off
toward the boulevard.

Episode Seven

THE OATH OF HYPOCRISY

The skeleton of his hand stood out against the black screen of the x-ray machine like an omen of his own death. The white bones were shaped so neatly, even the knuckle that was out of place and tipped just slightly out of line between the finger and the long bone at the back of his hand.

"Yes, it is a dislocated index knuckle, see?" the tall, handsome doctor said with a high-pitched ring of impatience and a furrow between his brows. His brown wavy hair was cut close to his scalp in a militaristic style common in Spain.

The treatment room with its machines, table, and medical supplies was as starkly bare as the waiting room of the storefront office, which only had hard wooden chairs for furniture. He was the only doctor between Arguiniguin and Las Palmas, and the village he worked in was not much more than a couple of blocks of low, pastel-colored houses on the lightly traveled highway near the sea.

When the doctor just stood there, pale-faced and thin-lipped, without speaking, Roger, trying to keep the impatience out of his own voice, asked, "Well? Should it be set?" He'd waited two hours with Penny after taking two hours to hitchhike the forty kilometers from Arguiniguin to the doctor's office. He didn't expect the doctor to smile at him, but he did want to be treated decently, at least.

"You can buy a ready-to-put-on bandage at the *farmacia*," the doctor said, nodding his head toward the street on the other side of the frosted glass window.

It was as good as a slap, as good as telling him to get out. He looked at Penny. Her tanned face looked gray in the frosted light, her lips looked white.

"Put it on myself?" Roger asked, holding up his swollen right hand between them, squinting up from under his swollen forehead with his puffed left eye, still blue-black.

"*Sí*," the doctor said. "Don't boxers know how to wrap their own hands?"

"What?" Roger said, glancing at Penny, knowing only the cops could have told the doctor he'd been a boxer. Penny tilted her head at him with a curious stare.

2

"Does it hurt really bad still? Can I help?" Penny asked, grabbing his wrist and trying to hold it steady while he tried to wrap the slippery bandages around his hand, but they wouldn't grip.

"No. I know how to do it better than you do. But it's too sticky and wet and I can't control it," Roger said, aware of the face of the silvery-haired pharmacist watching him through the drugstore window.

Roger couldn't make the bandage grip, and, cupping his fingers over the slimy wrappings to keep them from sliding off his hand, he said, "I don't have much chance by myself. Doctors don't send people down to buy their own bandages and set their own hands one-handed. And there's only one way he knew I boxed. There's nothing I can do."

"Let's go back and get him to do it," Penny said, and, putting her arm around his waist, started leading him back down the sidewalk, ignoring his comment on how the doctor knew he boxed.

Roger didn't want to go, but let her push him down the narrow sidewalk to the doctor's office. Just before he turned into the waiting room, where he could already see the doctor standing in the doorway to his office, as if waiting for him to return, a sputtering sound made him turn and see a motorcycle cop put-putting slowly by, staring at him through the dark glasses of his aviator's helmet.

It was the only time he'd ever seen a motorcycle cop in the Canary Islands. Then, as he held his swollen hand in front of the doctor's white smock, he remembered, too, a station wagon parked across the narrow, empty highway that morning when they first started hitchhiking. A fat Spanish cop with frizzy blond hair then got out and, before he walked away, sat a German Shepherd police dog in the back, facing them across the two-lane road. The dog watched them through the window the whole time they were there, and never once changed position or took its eyes off them.

Suddenly the news item he'd seen near the bottom of the front page of last week's *London Times*, which announced Nixon's inauguration and his projected European trip, beginning with Spain, flashed in his mind, and everything seemed connected:

> One hundred arrests in Madrid. There was uncertainty and puzzlement in the Spanish capital yesterday, the first day of a three-month State of Emergency decreed by General Franco. A number of arrests were reported in Madrid. Strong police forces guarded the deserted campus of Madrid University, which was closed on Friday, but life in the rest of the city went about normally. In Barcelona, police raided the house of Alfonso Carlos Comin, a progressive left-wing Catholic writer, and detained him and 21 other persons, including five Jesuit priests. Information Ministry officials were censoring in advance all Spanish newspaper and news agency reports. The reason for the shock decree worries the majority of the 33 million Spaniards. What is the international conspiracy Franco referred to? The Minister of Information, Senor Manuel Fraga Iribarne, has referred to Franco's old enemies, the Communists and the Anarchists, who were about to launch some sort of challenge to his power, aiming at disrupting Spain's internal security. It is believed that Franco's enemies have been plotting a revolt similar to the one that paralyzed Spain last spring.
>
> —Christopher Morris, Madrid

"I can't do it. I tried," Roger said.

But the doctor didn't speak. He didn't once look at Roger's hand or at Penny, who stood next to Roger with a frown on her face. All three of them stood around the lifted hand, a big puff where the index knuckle should have been. They didn't speak until the sputtering sound of a motorcycle driving past the frosted window—as if the cop had turned around to come back by for a second look at Roger—seemed to shatter the yellow light in the bare room and spark the doctor into action.

He reached out and took the swollen hand and began to unwrap the slimy bandages, hitting Roger's swollen index finger and making him wince each time he touched it.

3

A great roaring sound burst over Roger and woke him with a gasp, sat him up in bed, his face all mouth for a moment, left eye no longer puffed but still black, the lump on his forehead just a shadow under the skin.

He jumped out of bed and ran to the end window. He opened the shutters and stuck his head out, squinting his eyes in the morning sun. He ducked back in when a small fighter plane swept low over the village from the sea. It came from where an aircraft carrier sat on the edge of the horizon with warships flocked around it like decoy ducks. Roger ducked his head down, expecting bullets to hit around him from the strafing run. But none came, and he lifted his head up as another plane came diving down, swooping in from the sea over the rooftops, the gray underside of its metal wings and tucked-up wheels as clear to him as if he were standing right next to it.

He turned to call Penny, but she was already standing behind him, her face, with wide, wondering eyes, pink as her pajamas. Without a word to her, he grabbed his bathrobe and ran out the bedroom door, then out the front door where he could see lots of people from the village standing in clusters outside their doors, on the roofs of their houses, and in the streets watching the airplanes swoop in low over the village.

But Roger was still afraid and pressed himself up against the wall of the house with one arm around Penny. She had both her arms around his waist. The sun hurt his eyes though, and he let go of her and held his one good hand over his still bruised left eye and slightly swollen forehead. They both watched the planes dive down in formation over the village in what seemed to be an air show meant to demonstrate the invasion maneuvers of the Spanish armed forces. Roger wondered if the whole thing had something to do with his being in Spain and fighting Fuzz.

"Ooooh!" Penny moaned, and hid behind him when a plane seemed to drop out of the sky over them with a horrifying roar. It scared him so much that he doubled up in a ball and fell back against her, pressing her against the wall. When he straightened up again, he thought that it must cost a million dollars to stage the maneuvers. Thorn in the side of the police state that he might be, he was much too small to be worth that much. It couldn't be just for him.

"Roger, look!" Penny said, and he turned to follow her finger pointing at big-bellied cargo planes flying in very high from over the sea. He wondered if they were going to drop bombs, thankful they weren't right overhead.

"Oh!" Penny said again as bright puffs of silk began to pop up in the wake of the planes and drift down like wind-fluttered white flowers over the sea and white sands of Más Palomas, a tourist resort fifteen kilometers away.

It couldn't just be for him, Roger knew. Not this show. Not by any stretch of the imagination could he be that important yet. Maybe later if he ever achieved great fame like Sartre and produced many controversial books. But not now. No way.

Still, as he stood there watching, fascinated by the parachutes, wondering if any of them would land in the sea, ducking down instinctively every time a dive bomber came too close to them, he felt that his problems were tied to the show, that it was all related to the State of Emergency decreed by Franco and Nixon's inauguration and their just finished Chiefs of State meeting. Even if this was just a show of force by Spain, some kind of pattern of action was being formed and slowly defined. This was part of that pattern. He was sure of that. He knew as he squinted up at the planes that he had to find the wits to solve enough of the pattern to save himself.

4

The electric voice crackled through the dark air with the crisp accent of an English newscaster. It broke through the static of the van's radio with broad A's, as if stretching tongues of invisible current over Roger's head and out between the shadowy trunks of the big trees in the hippy camp.

He paused with the hash pipe halfway to Penny when it announced, "...the invasion of the Spanish Sahara by the

Spanish Army and Navy to protect the lives of Spanish citizens. The Spanish forces had been maneuvering in the Canary Islands and had seized control of all coast cities by nightfall. Spain gave up the Spanish Sahara in 1948 in order to gain admission to the United Nations..."

A flash of perception hit him. Now he knew why Nixon came to Spain right after becoming President, why there'd been a State of Emergency, and why they had tried to harass him out of the village and drive him from Spain! He, as a radical Berkeley writer, had become an unwitting eyewitness to an international conspiracy!

He shoved the pipe at Penny with an urge to tell her. But when she turned and stared at him as if she thought something was wrong, he caught himself and just handed her the pipe, as if that's all he wanted, unsure if he'd tell her at all, even in private. But she leaned so close, to look into his eyes, so sensitive to his feelings and changes of mood, that he said, "Listen! Listen, you guys! What you just heard is why Nixon came to Spain first thing on becoming President. He came over and gave Franco permission to retake the Spanish Sahara in violation of international law, in return for U.S. military bases in Spain. And that's why there's been a State of Emergency here, to lock up all the radicals and keep them from demonstrating over it, bringing it to the world's attention. That's why they tried to drive me out of the country, too! So I wouldn't pick up on it, since I was right in the village where they were going to practice doing it. So I wouldn't write about it! On top of that, I'm writing a novel about the murder conspiracy that pig Nixon is already mixed up in! Don't you guys see what I mean? Don't you see?"

Vague, blurred faces looked up at him now standing above them. But not one face spoke, not even Penny's. She took the smoldering pipe in her hands without moving, without taking a hit, as if what he'd said was too shocking and unbelievable to comment on.

5

He held up his hand, puffed as a snowball, in front of the doctor's face. For a brief moment, when the physician's stern straight features broke and contorted and his mouth dropped open with shock at the sight, Roger felt the doctor's humanity. But when the doctor stuttered, "I...uh... We can... I can send you to somebody, a specialist in Las Palmas, who will fix it for you. Do you want that?" a tremor of fear quivered in Roger's stomach. One contact with this guy had made his whole hand swollen, not just the knuckle to his index finger. He'd only come back to show it to him because Penny insisted.

"I don't know," he said. "What will he do?"

"He can reset it," the doctor said.

Before Roger could answer, Penny said, "Yes, Roger. Let's go see the specialist."

He could only nod, believing the doctor had misset his hand on purpose. He noticed that the doctor said, "I'll write you a letter of..." and sat down without finishing his sentence.

Roger studied his fine, handsome features as he wrote in a tiny script, and wondered how a young good-looking man, who was probably as young, or younger than himself, could be so cruel. Then the doctor took the page, folded it, sealed it in a small envelope, wrote the name of the other doctor with his address on it and handed it to him. Roger studied the small, cramped handwriting and wondered if the envelope was a ticket to another trap set for him.

"Thank you," he said, trying to be polite, but when they walked back out and crossed the highway to begin hitchhiking again, he stared at his puffed hand, then at the letter in his good hand, and felt the urge to tell Penny about his fears. But when Penny stuck out her thumb, then looked back at him trustingly, he was torn between not wanting to hurt her and his need to tell her his fears, and of his worst fear that she might be in on it.

But he couldn't keep his eyes off the letter in his hand even as the car of the young Spaniard who picked them up droned down the highway. Roger wanted to go someplace where he couldn't be seen and open the letter, find out what was hidden in it. But he was too afraid he might antagonize the doctor if he saw the letter had been opened. He might then make his hand even worse.

Roger kept the fear of a trap, the horror of his puffed hand and his urge to rip open the letter smoldering inside him until they reached Las Palmas and were walking up a tree-lined sidewalk on a hillside of the old section of town. When they were only a few doors from the address on the letter, he couldn't stand it anymore. He stopped and said, "Penny! I'm afraid to go see another doctor! I'm afraid he's going to hurt the hand even more! Maybe we better open the letter first. Not take any chances!"

She shook her head, saying, "No, no, Roger. You might offend the doctor if you open the letter, and no doctor would do that to you. They've all taken the Oath of Hippocrates, haven't they? And promised to be ethical?"

She took his good hand and pulled him along with her. "Come on. We're almost there. He can reset it for you right. There's still time. It's only been three weeks. Let's go in and see him."

She tugged at his hand and led him up the stairs of the building to the office on the second floor. Inside to the waiting room, a man in a pinstripe suit with short, stubbled side-burns, sat on the far end of a couch. He stood up when Roger stepped in, then walked through the opening in a white wood-en partition into the doctor's office. He looked like a plain-clothes cop to Roger. He could see his blurred figure and the doctor's hunched over a desk through the thick, marbled glass at one end of the partition. Roger's hands began to sweat, and he had to keep wiping them on his pants. The man stood up after only a minute or so, walked past the doctor and out through the opening in the partition, keeping his eyes from meeting Roger's as he walked past him in a stiff-backed mili-tary step.

The plump, olive-skinned doctor appeared at the entrance to the partition in short shirt sleeves and brown slacks. He stared at Roger for a moment through his rimless spectacles, motioned with his finger for Roger to follow him, then turned and walked back into his office. He was already sitting down when Roger and Penny walked in, too, and still without speaking, pointed at the chairs opposite him. His short, coarse black hair stuck straight up like brush bristles from his round, tanned face, and gave him a severe military look, which increased the sense of dread that Roger felt. There was absolutely no friendliness in the man.

Roger handed the doctor the letter and sat down to watch him read it without making any attempt to speak. He heard a sound from one of the other cubicles in the white-partitioned office, and he stared through the doorway of the office and listened. But he could neither hear nor see anything. He began to suspect that there might be a cop hiding in one of the other compartments to jump on him in case he tried anything violent.

Finally, the doctor lowered the page to the desk, stared at Roger, and still without even the slightest hint of a smile or any kind of warmth whatsoever in his voice, said, "We can reset your hand at the hospital."

He then stood up, slipped the letter in his pocket, and, without putting on a coat or sweater, wearing only his slacks and short-sleeved shirt, he led them out the door. He closed it behind him, didn't check to see if it was locked, and took them downstairs to the sidewalk, where his small car was parked along the curb. Still, he didn't talk, didn't utter one word to them while he drove the mile or so to the hospital.

The doctor turned Roger over to two other doctors, both in white smocks, one tall and blond and the other tall and dark. They led Roger into an operating room, but stopped Penny from entering. The blond doctor didn't speak. He just held up his hand like a traffic cop and shut the door in her face.

"Arriba!" he said, pointing to the operating table, and Roger got up on it and lay down with weak, trembling movements. He almost gasped when the blond doctor stuck a long needle into his arm, then felt panic sweep over him when they wheeled him under the big, monstrous eye of bright light on the ceiling. Roger knew it was too late, that he'd come too far already, that he should have read the letter, that he should not have even gone to see the plump doctor, that he shouldn't have ridden to the hospital with him in his car, that he shouldn't... A dizzy blackness swept over him, and he looked right up at the bright light above him and said, "¡Me voy!" and blacked out.

6

"¡Mucho dolor!" Roger said when he woke up on the operating table and felt the terrible pain in his hand. It looked strange in the cast. His index finger was bent down against the palm instead of sticking straight out as he'd expected. And all of his hand hurt, not just the knuckle as before, or even just the finger, but the base of his thumb, too.

A tremendous pain ached there, and he knew that he'd made a mistake, that he should have read the letter. Yet, he was too dizzy to reflect on that for more than a moment, as Penny helped him off the table and guided him over to the desk to pay the bill. Penny paid with his money. But he had to sign the receipt personally with his left hand in a wobbly scrawl. He fought the woozy feeling that distorted everything he looked at. He could see that the plump, round doctor wasn't there, and that he'd been treated by two complete strangers, neither of whom he'd probably ever see again. His hand ached as if it had been badly mangled.

He realized that it was dusk when they walked outside, and that for some reason they had no trouble catching a minibus back to the village. He appreciated this, though it surprised him. He'd never seen one before. He couldn't remember getting on, and he drifted in and out of consciousness on the ride, his head on Penny's shoulder, lights from passing cars flashing softly through his eyelids, while he suffered the burning, excruciating pain without a sound.

But he had to catch deep breaths to keep down the moans that kept coming up to the surface of his mouth, deep breaths that buckled in his belly like hiccups, but kept him from crying out, from moaning, from pleading for some relief from this terrible, terrible suffering, from the pain in his burning, broken hand. He woke once to find Penny staring at him in the darkness, and he realized that he was in his own bed, that he'd already come back to the village, then forgot it all like a bad dream as he slipped back into merciful blackness again. He awoke in the morning with a loud moan that rang in his ears. Penny was up on one elbow next to him, stroking his face.

"Come on. You've been moaning in your sleep all night, and it's getting worse. We better get dressed and go to the pharmacy and get you something for your pain," she said. She then kissed him and threw the covers back.

7

"*¡Mucho dolor!*" Roger said to the young pharmacist at the other end of the counter. He had turned away from a young couple and asked "What do you want?" in English.

Roger pointed at his hand cradled in the thin, white sling which hung from his shoulder, and said, "*Necesito medicina. What do you have?*"

"Aspirin? Codeine? Morphine?"

Out of the corner of his eye, Roger could see the young man and woman watching him when he said, "Aspirin isn't enough, and codeine dulls my brain so I can't write or read. I'll just lie around like a sick man with a fuzzy brain."

He turned to Penny, who was holding onto his arm, and shook his head. "I don't know if I want morphine. It's too dangerous. You can get hooked or even O.D. on it."

She nodded.

"Besides, I don't know how to inject it. Can you inject it?" he asked the pharmacist, meeting the handsome dark eyes of the man, so striking with his pale skin, white smock, and dark hair.

"No," the pharmacist said.

Roger guessed that the young man and woman peering over their shoulders at him were spying on him and wanted to see if he'd take morphine and stick it into his body, if he'd risk getting a habit just to relieve the pain in his hand. He might O.D. or commit suicide with it, too, something the Spanish police might want.

"Is there anybody in the village who can do it?" Roger asked, the dark circles under his eyes making the squint of pain on his face more pronounced.

"No," the pharmacist said.

"You won't do it?"

The pharmacist shook his head.

"Then, I don't want it," Roger said, turning to leave the small one-room building. He noticed the astonished faces of the young couple, still peering at him with a fearful squint to their eyes, as if afraid he might hurt them.

8

Roger stopped typing with his left hand and the one middle finger of his right, cast hand, with a flash of pain that made him grimace. He turned his head to look out the window. He didn't want Penny to see him suffer, to notice the small frown that seemed ingrained with the dark hollows under both eyes.

He sat down on a milk pail that he used as a stool and leaned his elbows on the big box they used as a table. But his hand kept throbbing, and he stared into the corner of the room where the high, iron bed sat flanked by a chair on either side. The pain still wouldn't go away, and he tried to concentrate on the sounds he heard to take his mind off it. He could hear some birds trilling in the branches of a tree near the *pensión*. He heard footsteps go down the hall, then come back up, then go back down, then come back up in an endless sound, as if the same person were stalking back and forth. His hand still ached.

Then a fat blue fly started buzzing around his head and landing on him, first on his ear, then on his left hand, and he couldn't slap at it because of the cast, so he tried to shake it loose. It flew right back down on him and he cursed "God damn you!" under his breath and jumped up and ran out into the hall and grabbed the fly spray kept by the front door and ran back in. Holding the can in his left hand and pushing clumsily on the pump handle with his cast hand, wincing with pain every time he shoved it in, he chased the fly around the room, past the closed door, and finally caught it in a corner of the window where he kept spraying and gradually brought it down, still buzzing, though much slower, to waist level. He lost sight of it when it got near the floor and had to look for it until he finally found it on a square of tile five feet from the window where it buzzed when he touched it with the spray, then turned over on its back and withered up.

"You didn't want him to live, did you?" Penny said when he straightened up.

"I guess not," he said. But his hand really throbbed with pain from using the fly-spray can. He tightened with expectation with every pulse beat. The pain seemed to fill his whole

body. He put the can down, stepped to the typewriter, put a
page in and started typing:

> Spain has its flies
> They snuggle into your hair
> speckle the light bulbs
> bead the silver toilet chain
> leave welts like mosquito bites
> and buzz around your head at night
> after the lights are out
> then wake you in the morning
> with their first sunlight attack
>
> They spread out on the bedspread
> which holds the warmth
> and cluster in angry clouds near toilets
> where
> if you look closely
> at the back edge of doors
> where they shut flat against the frame
> you'll see the flattened black husks
> and fishscaled wings
> of the slower ones
> who didn't buzz away
> in time

9

Roger stood in the room in front of the windows after dinner, staring out. The house was set on a hill just above the
pebble-beach cove, on the high side of the dirt road which
curved around the cove from the stucco buildings in the center
of the village. Just across the road from the Shantytown with
its plywood shacks, the house looked like a poor adobe hovel,
built like a box and brown as the earth around it.

From that road, the back of the house resembled a junk
yard, with packing crates and old rubber tires and sheets of
tin covering the holes in the chicken coop and goat pen. But
the front of the house was protected from the damp sea wind
which blew in from the cove behind it. It had a small, neat
garden of flowers and cactus, and next to it by the gravel path
that led to the front door, a thick wooden bench where you
could sit in the sun. Just inside the big, hand-carved doors

was a ten-foot wide hall with a beautiful tile floor and pale, rose-tinted stucco walls. It stretched the hundred-foot length of the house. Two wrought-iron chandeliers hung from the ceiling at each end of the hall. Beautiful rosewood doors opened to the hallway from each of the four rooms at either side of it. But Roger wasn't in any mood to contemplate the beauty of the house.

"Why are you frowning?"

"Am I frowning?"

"Yes," Penny said softly, looking sad in the soft light of dusk coming in from the unshuttered windows. She sat in front of the big box they used for a table, her now empty plate in front of her.

"I wasn't aware of it."

"Does your hand hurt?"

"Yes," he said.

"That's it then," she said. "Do you want to lie down? Maybe if you rested you'd feel better."

"Okay," he said, and they lay down in the fast-settling darkness at the back of the big room and stared out the windows at the stars just beginning to appear in the eastern sky. He closed his eyes for a moment and let the tears well up, then squinted until the wave of pain passed and opened them again.

"Are you crying?" she asked, and put her arm around him.

"Sort of," he said, his eyes shining with misty tears.

"It hurts that bad?"

"It's more than the pain," he said. "It's what they've done to me. The way they've punished me for trying to write about the evil in my country, the killing of my president, his brother, and Martin Luther King. I'm crying because I'm afraid the doctors have set my hand wrong again and maybe crippled me for good."

"Don't say that."

"Penny, I'm telling you that they might have done *just* that to me. Why else would it hurt so bad? It didn't hurt like that before they put it in this cast! And look at the way it's bent! Everything hurts, too. My thumb, my finger and the original displaced knuckle, which is the only thing that hurt at first and not very badly."

She was quiet for a while. He could just see the faint dark shimmer of her eyes.

"Maybe I'd better go see that pharmacist again and get something for your pain. That might make you feel better."

"It won't be worth it," he said. "It'll just dull my senses, and I'll waste the time because I won't be able to read or write. I'd rather take the pain. At least I can create on it."

"I don't mean that," she said. "I mean without the pain you might feel better and less pessimistic."

"Pessimistic! How could I feel anything else but pessimistic?" he said, and grabbing his cast with his left hand, he started pulling at it. "I feel like ripping it off to save myself. I feel like I'd better rip it off or I'm going to be sorry. By God, that's what I'm going to do! I'm going to take this sonofabitch off! I'm going to cut it off!"

He rolled over, dropped his legs off the bed, and pushed himself up with his left hand when she grabbed him and held onto him, crying, "No-no! Don't! Do what the doctor said, Roger! Please! It's only three weeks more. Wait! Roger, please!"

But when he pulled free of her hands, she started sobbing and cried, "I'm afraid you'll hurt yourself! I'm afraid!"

"Don't cry! I won't do it, if you feel that strongly about it," he said, and twisted back around, reaching out to stroke her hair. "But I've got to tell you that I'm afraid they've messed me up. It really hurts."

"I wish I could do something," she said, and pulled him down on the bed next to her, kissing him with an open mouth.

He hugged her to him, but lay awake cradling his aching hand against his chest for long hours. He was still awake at midnight when the voice from the tiny radio cried "¡Viva Franco! ¡Arriba España!" and he remembered how he'd mocked that cry only a couple of days before and made Penny laugh.

He still didn't fall asleep for a good hour after that, and he woke up several times during the night, too, to the throbbing in his hand. But no matter where he put it, near his chest or down along his leg or hanging over the bed, it ached. Finally, he cradled it against his chest and drifted off to sleep.

10

"*¡Viva Franco!*" Roger heard, jerked his head up from the book and stared out the front window. He could see the deep blue of the eastern sky above the tips of the eucalyptus trees on the horizon and long shadows on the ground, but not who had cried out.

"*¡Viva Franco!*" he heard again and saw a man's arm stick up at the foot of the hill near the house, then saw that the stump of the man's other arm was pinned to his side through the folded sleeve of his suit coat.

"*¡Viva Franco!*" the man yelled again, and jammed his hand into the air again, then squinted at Roger and focused the two little black dots between his slitted eyelids on him, sending a spurt of fear through him. Roger had mocked those very words a week ago.

The guy looked like some kind of an apparition, some kind of bad omen in his old, ragged clothes, rumpled hat, and a shoe sole that flapped when he took a step closer. His thick upper lip curled back in a crease, showing pink, gummy gaps between his teeth as he shouted "*¡Viva Franco!*" again and began to sing some garbled song in an off-key mumble. He tapped his foot to the beat, shoe sole clapping every time his foot came down, and Roger felt the hair on his arms rise.

Suddenly the man stopped singing and frowned, took off his hat and stuck it under his stump, held it there, then stared at the ground and rubbed his thick dirty fingers over his lined face and head, exposing patches of white in the short, brown stubble of his hair.

Roger couldn't guess his age. He looked both young and old. He could be either thirty or fifty.

Finally, the man lifted his head up again and again rubbed his hand down his face, harder this time, pulling the wrinkling skin tight over the hollows of his eyes and cheeks. Then he shouted, "*¡Me voy a trabajar!*", meaning "I am going to work!", and a loud burst of laughter came from the front of the house, too far down for Roger to see.

Roger stood up and moved further down the row of windows until he could see down the gravel walk in front of the house in the other direction. When he pressed his face against a pane, he could make out about ten tanned Spanish children in short pants and dresses and three Spanish peasant women with sallow skin, in black kerchiefs and long black dresses.

"*¡Me voy al trabajo!*" the madman said again, and all the children laughed and jeered and pointed at him, and the unpainted faces of the women wrinkled with laughter, too.

The madman frowned again, looked down and again rubbed his hand over his face, stared at the ground, then suddenly snatched his wrinkled hat out from under the stump of his arm and slapped it on his head. He pulled it down tight over his forehead, then looked up at Roger again, jammed his good arm in the air and shouted, "*¡Viva Franco! ¡Viva Franco! ¡Viva Franco!*"

Roger's right hand jerked in its sling with an urge to mock the cry, too, but nobody jeered this time, and he was glad his arm was in a cast. The whole thing smacked of a trap.

The man was silent for a moment, then stared at the children, the women and Roger, and said, "*¡Me voy al trabajo!*", and all the children burst out laughing again.

He squinted up at them above him on the hillock, curled his upper lip back, showing his gums, doubled his fist and, shaking it in the air and shouting "*¡Golpe! ¡Golpe!*" meaning "Hit! Hit!", started running clumsily up the hill at them, shoe sole slapping.

Some children screamed and ran past Roger's windows, but some bigger boys bent down and picked up pieces of gravel and pelted the madman, stopping him halfway up the tiny hill as he slapped awkwardly at the pebbles with his good hand like some clumsy bear pawing at bees. When the pelting stopped, he shouted, "*¡Golpe! ¡Golpe!*", and started charging up the hill again. But a hail of tiny pebbles peppered his face, stopped him again, forced him to cover his face with his arm, turn his back on them and stumble back down the hillock again.

He looked at the children and looked at Roger for a moment again, as if trying to figure out who he was. Then he jammed his hand in the air again and shouted, "*¡Viva Franco! ¡Viva Franco!*", and hurried at a stumbling trot, dust slapping up with his shoe sole, down around the hillock and behind the house.

11

The sallow-faced women in black stepped back into their houses. Two boys in short pants, thin brown legs bare to their shoes, glanced at Roger as they walked by his windows. Roger stayed by the window, watching some of the children linger for a moment in front of his house. But there was no laughter or chatter, and he felt goose bumps creep over his arms again.

The monster was for him! He had just escaped some dangerous trap. He saw a web of intrigue behind the scare. It was surreal. He was living a nightmare. It was like being in Hell, having to always look out for what might happen to him next, for some new surprise from the secret police.

He heard Penny come in and turned to face her.

"Some nut was just standing out there in front shouting, '¡Viva Franco!' like I did last week," he said.

"What?" Penny said, putting her bag down in the middle of the big square box—their table.

"Some tramp with one arm was here, trying to get me to shout '*Viva Franco*' publicly. Did you come in the back way?"

She nodded and asked, "You mean that man with one arm?"

"Yeah," Roger said. "The room's bugged for sure. They must've heard me mocking Franco and came to try to get me to do it in public, then they'd have a reason to jail me and deport me, maybe give me some time. It's scary."

"Oh?" she said, and took some oranges out of the bag and put them on the table, leaving the open bag standing there, too. Then she turned away, sat on the bed and started folding the laundry. Taking a pair of pajamas from the pile of wrinkled clothing, she folded the top neatly, put it down on the other side of her, then picked up the bottom and folded it, too. She never once looked at him nor showed any interest in what he'd said.

He could see her little double chin in profile, the way her nose tilted up, and the wide sweep of her nearly closed lashes, but she wasn't cute to him. He turned and stared out the window at the darkening sky and wondered if she was in on it, if she'd egged him on to do the mocking in the first place, or if she was just tired of all the misery and didn't even want to talk about it.

Maybe being tired was the real reason or the biggest one. But he was trapped either way. At any moment of the day, of any day, of every day, he had to be prepared to fight for his life. He felt as if a wave of darkness was slowly seeping over him, smothering him. He wanted to scream with anger. But he suddenly turned and grabbed a sheet of typing paper, turned the portable lamp on over the typewriter on the bottom of the oil barrel he used for a desk and began to type, to write out his feelings. He pounded hurriedly for several minutes, all concentration, eyes narrowed, then snatched the page out and turned to Penny to read it to her. But she kept folding her laundry and didn't look up at him.

12

"We came to visit the patient," Anne Marie said, smiling, all golden and tanned, bringing some sunshine into the sad room.

Roger smiled back, the deep shadow under his left eye vanishing into the creases of his lid, taking the darkness out of his face.

"We thought we'd cheer you up some," Robey said, showing his crooked front teeth. He walked up and hugged Roger with his skinny arms.

"Glad to see yuh," Craig said, setting his big brown bag down on the big turned-over box. Ruth, stepping in behind him, smiled and popped the top of a beer can, then kissed Roger on the lips, held the can to his lips and began to pour.

Roger tipped his head up and opened his mouth, letting the cold liquid fill it. He gulped, pulled away, and lowered his head to cut the flow, swallowing the last of it. It left a cold trail clear to his stomach. He reached up with his left hand and took the can from her, smiled and kissed her, then tilted the can up and gulped some more. He lowered the can with a grin just as Fuzz stepped in.

Roger squeezed the cold can and stared at the big man standing there in front of him with a bag of beer in his hand, too. Trap! Roger thought, but Fuzz smiled and said, "Cheers!" and Roger saw that his teeth were wired! That he had a broken jaw!

"I'm suffering, too, Roger," he said, slurring his words, and Roger stared up at him. His green eyes weren't hard. There was no hate in them, like in the park. No glare. But not softness either. Caution, but not fear in them. Roger had to smile at him. They both had fought and lost. He couldn't refuse him. "Cheers, Fuzz!" he said, not hating him anymore.

"I've got some more beer in my van," Fuzz said, "and it's cold. So drink up. It'll only take a minute to get it."

"I feel like having some fun. I'm glad you came," Roger said, and took another deep swallow, then another, then tilted the can up and drank it down until his throat burned with cold and he finished the can. "Awwwwww," he said. "I'll take another one."

"Roger!" Penny said, but he snapped the top off as he turned to face her. "Don't forget you've been sick and taking those pills for declotting today."

"That shouldn't hurt the booze," he said.

"Maybe it might cause some changes in your blood chemistry," she said. "Maybe they won't mix with alcohol."

"The pharmacist would have said something about it," Craig said.

"You can't depend upon them. You can even buy morphine without a prescription," she said.

"Just this one," Roger said. "I feel like having some fun for a change. I want to get high! I'm tired of being down all the time."

When she frowned and shook her head as if she still didn't like it, he said, "I'm tired of feeling sorry for myself." And when she turned away, he said, "Say! I wrote a poem about this, but Penny didn't want to hear it. Do you guys?"

When nobody answered, he repeated, "Huh?"

"Sure," Robey said. Roger put the full can down on the box table and picked up the poem from the typewriter stand. He stood with his back to the door, said, "I dedicate this poem to Fuzz," and smiled at him. Then he began to read in a soft voice, speaking slowly so that the emotion he felt writing the poem would come through.

BE MY VALENTINE

A strange thing
an image of myself

keeps coming back to me
a self-pitying one
bringing with it a flush of tears
seeing myself
as some persecuted
trapped creature
in some room
with the walls listening in

Picture of secret police
with their heads bent
to my baby talk with my chick
and my sobs when I cried
maybe hurting them too
anonymous frowns on their faces
white shirts and ties
tracking my lifeline across the globe
spiking it dry

There's a danger there for me
Mist over my eyeballs for myself
could drain me for good
have no spine left
to stand up with
and shout
Fuck
you!

He looked up and saw Fuzz look down to keep from meeting his eyes, a frown on his face as if the words hurt him. A
spark of warmth leaped up in Roger, a sense of victory that he
had pricked Fuzz and drawn blood. Yet, there was warmth for
Fuzz, too, for being human, like the first roadside doctor had
been when he was shocked by Roger's puffed hand.

"Ballsy!" Robey said, and Anne Marie smiled at Roger,
but Craig just said, "Hmmmm," and Ruth kept her head
down. Penny frowned.

"Don't you like it, Penny?" Roger asked.

"I...I...I don't know," Penny said, and looked down at
her hands in her lap.

"I don't care. I feel like having some fun. I feel like enjoying myself," Roger said. He picked up the can and took another swallow, then danced back, shuffling his feet, sanding the
soles of his shoes on the tile. Then he shook his shoulders and
finished off with a stomp.

"Come on, drink up! Let's get out of here. Let's go have some fun!"

But Penny shook her head and said, "I don't want to, Roger."

Her mouth was puckered with determination.

"You don't have to," he said. "But I'm going to get stoned out of my skull."

He tilted the can all the way up and, gulping without stopping, kept it there.

13

Roger's breath whistled as he toked in on the big briar pipe at the table in Fuzz's van on the edge of the cliff. The fuzzy white sun in the center of the Coleman lantern seemed to hiss with his breath, sizzle on his cheeks. The dark waves far below shimmered with moonlight.

"I can handle this stuff," Roger said, his left eye dark as a ghoul's in the fluorescent glow.

The others all drooped around the table with heavy eyelids and dreamy stares. Roger handed the pipe to Ann Marie, who sat with her back to the open door of the van and took the pipe with a smile and a heavy-lidded look of her dark eyes. She pursed her lips and sucked in the smoke as if she were slurping soup, like he'd taught her. Then slowly, she closed her eyes.

Dark hollows appeared on her cheeks, making a sculpted mask out of her face, beautiful with the soft light and sharp shadows on it. But she pressed her hand to her chest and fluttered her eyelids as if she were having trouble keeping the smoke down. She quickly handed the pipe to Robey, whose blond natural flickered in the sputtering lamplight as if it were on fire.

But Robey, too, seemed to be having trouble, and he pinched his pointed nose to keep the smoke down in him, his pale eyes watering. After only one hit of the deep-bowled pipe, he passed it to Craig. The smoke hurt Craig so bad he glanced at Roger, then clamped his fingers over his nostrils. His eyes bulged out and his cheeks puffed up, as if he were going to burst. But he swallowed slowly as if he were drinking hot coffee and kept the smoke in, then burst out coughing and spewed spit across the table. He wiped the water from his eyes and handed the pipe to Ruth.

Ruth put the pipe in her mouth and, smiling so that the dimples in her cheeks showed, sucked in smoke through tight lips. The sweet smell of the burning ember spiraled out of the pipe with curling smoke. She drew slowly as the others sunk down around her, and seemed to have held the smoke in until she handed the pipe to Fuzz and burst out coughing.

Roger watched closely as Fuzz sucked in one light toke through his wired teeth, took a breath, then another toke, then a breath, then another toke, then a breath, his short goatee flickering like a bird's tail. But he kept the smoke down and was the only one besides Roger who downed the smoke without suffering, though he took it in short hits.

Roger had never smoked it in the huge briar pipe before, only in a thimble set inside the pipe bowl. But he was sure he could handle it and took another deep toke, drew in deep, deep, deep until his lungs ached. He wanted to rise above all his heavy troubles. He was tired of never leaving the hole of his room, of days and nights of great pain, great sadness, and great unhappiness. He wanted to thrust his brain into a beautiful dreamland. But when he pulled the pipe out and handed it to Ann Marie, his head suddenly dropped down below him and smashed against the table with a starry flash in his brain, just like he'd been punched in the chin. His body tingled all over with a numb feeling, and his stomach buckled with nausea. It took a few moments for him to realize that he couldn't lift his head off the table, and he suddenly remembered picking his way stilt-legged out of the door in the hut in Formentera the first time he'd smoked kif pollen, how the panic had gripped him when he felt his mind lose control of his body.

He lay with his face down on the table, unable to focus his eyes, dimly aware of the floating sun sputtering with fuzzy edges in the Coleman lantern and of the lamp bending out of shape along the tabletop, which itself was a wavering horizontal line next to his face. He closed his eyes to stop the bitterness and the nausea that buckled in his stomach. But his stomach buckled again as if he were going to vomit, and he forced his head around on the table so he could see the door.

Every person swerved out of shape, though he could tell that everyone of them was slumped down, too. Ann Marie sat next to him with her head hanging forward and her eyes closed, as if she were asleep on the little portable chair. Fearing he'd throw up on her, he slurred "I've got to get out of here," through his closed teeth, his jaws shut by the weight of his head, then lurched out of his seat and fell over Anne Marie's lap, mumbling, "Sorry."

He scrambled on all fours, hit the dirt and crawled a few more feet to spill his mess away from the van, dimly aware that everyone was knocked out by the dope and that he had to keep away from the edge of the cliff.

He felt a retching wave buckle up in his stomach and rise to his throat. He opened his mouth to vomit with a hoarse retching sound, but his body bent and straightened, bent and straightened, with muscular contractions ripping his stomach, yet no vomit came out. It stopped for a moment, then started again—a racking cramp in his stomach and a gagging feeling at the back of his throat, a retching sound from his open mouth—but still no vomit. Then it happened again and again with ripping, tearing pains in his gut.

Finally the wave passed. He could see the vague shifting light from the van and the cliff that towered over the highway behind the van and the fuzzing of stars in the clear sky above the cliff. He could make out some of the others sprawled out on the shoulder of the cliff, like they had passed out, not making a sound.

His stomach started buckling with horrible cramps again and his body jackknifed with the unbearable pain. A ball of vomit gagged him, and retching cries and groans spewed out his mouth again and again and again, until his body was a tight band of unbreakable pain. He was sure he was going to die when the cramps suddenly stopped and he fell flat on his face on the dusty shoulder.

He lay with his mouth open, tasting dirt, trying to keep the wave of nausea from sweeping over him again. But it came back again and again and again with shorter and shorter moments of relief between the jackknifing convulsions, until, finally, seizing on a moment of rest between the racking seizures, he called out, "Help me, you guys! I'm dying! Help me! Help me!"

He jackknifed into another convulsion as the dark figures struggled to their feet and made a circle around him. The wave finally passed and, when he was lying with his cheek down in the dust once more, Anne Marie bent down near him, stroked his hair and asked, "What can we do, Roger?"

He was grateful to her for stroking his hair in front of Robey, but he was also ashamed of the way he looked: so ugly, with his mouth open like a gaping fish. Then he went into another convulsion, which went on and on, finally leaving him exhausted, face down in the dirt again. Finally, he managed to say, "I'm dying like the villain of my first novel, from strychnine poisoning. I'm dying! Help me, please! Please! Please!"

Then another wave of convulsions, body-racking, jackknifing, stomach-aching dry heaves, hit him, and he writhed in the dust on the edge of the cliff, under the star-filled sky, the bright moon shining down upon the waves. When the convulsions finally stopped, he felt himself being picked up by his arms and legs and carried into the van, where Anne Marie squatted down on her knees next to him and stroked his head. Fuzz kicked the motor over and started driving the van down the winding cliff-edge road the five or six kilometers to the village and the *pensión*.

Roger could feel the drone of the motor in him even when he went into convulsions two or three more times before he finally felt the van bump onto a dirt road, go a short way and then stop. When they picked him up by his arms and legs, stepped down out of the van with him and carried him to the *pensión* door, he went into convulsions again, and they almost dropped him on the gravel walk.

Anne Marie squatted down and stroked his hair again when he stopped. Then more people came out of the house and stood around him in the dark. Anne Marie suddenly stopped and stood up. He wondered what was wrong when Penny knelt down next to him and asked, "What's wrong, Roger? What happened? What can I do?" Then she started stroking his hair just like Ann Marie had done, and he was aware, even down on the gravel, gasping through his mouth like a landed fish, that he was somehow fortunate to be liked by the two women.

"I love you, Roger," Penny said, and kept stroking his hair until he went into convulsions again and her hand slipped off.

"I'll leave, Fuzz! I'll leave! I surrender! I'll go! I'll get out
of Spain!" Roger cried, suddenly aware of what was wanted of
him now. He was sure that his novel on the assassinations,
the mail that never came, Nixon's visit, the State of Emergency, the dive bombers and the invasion of the Spanish
Sahara, the pictures and the redheaded man, Fuzz and the
fight, the broken hand still aching so badly, the morphine he
wouldn't take, the dark ring under his eye, the alcohol and the
fly spray, the pharmacist's pills and the convulsions were all
connected.

"Help me, Penny! Help me!" he cried when Fuzz didn't
speak, and he jackknifed into the gasping, hoarse-voiced,
stomach-buckling dry heaves again.

"Help me help him, you guys," Penny cried, and Roger
saw her lift her face and look up at the circle of young people
around her.

"We've got to get him to vomit," Robey said. "Get whatever poisoned him out of his stomach."

"Raw egg whites and warm milk," Anne Marie said. "Tell
the landlady to mix some up. That might do it."

Then Robey said, *"Claras de huevo y leche, Señora."*

A few minutes later, during one of the pauses between
convulsions, Penny bent down and lifted his head up. She
poured warm milk and eggs down his mouth, and he went into
convulsions immediately. But this time warm vomit spilled
out his mouth, easing the ball of pain in his belly, and kept
spilling out until he was finally dry.

14

The thin rosewood shutters glowed with sad light when
Roger woke in the morning. The grain of the wood was a red
network of veins and cast a sickly glow over everything, colored everything a pale, pink color, giving a faint anemic aura
to every object, the walls, the iron foot-railing of the bed, the
clock on the bed stand.

His hand still ached where it rested against his chest, and
a frown tightened his sleepy face. He had beaten his cast
against the gravel walk and promised to leave Spain last
night, in front of Fuzz, to Fuzz. He hugged the cast to his

chest and slid out of bed, frowning, not sure what to do, but sure he'd been poisoned. Drugged by the doctors or the pharmacist, made allergic to alcohol, which with fly spray and strong kif pollen sent him into convulsions, like the villain of his first novel! And they'd broken his thumb, like Jonas in his early poem, *The Prophecy of Jonas*! "Quarter him from his right hand to his toe! Crack his thumb!" Fear shot through him. They were following the script!

He wondered what he looked like, picked up the little round shaving mirror, scanned his face, but tried not to look into his eyes. Yet, he still saw the dark circle under his left eye. It'd been over a month already and it was still black. Maybe the little dark pills he was swallowing to take away the blackness actually kept it black. Maybe they were giving him some drug that kept the dead blood from dissolving into the blood stream. Maybe the pills were poisoning him like he'd been poisoned last night.

He made himself look away from the mirror and saw the cast below him. He hugged his aching hand to his chest, walked across the cold tile to the shutters, opened one of them, and stared out through the glass at the small bay between Shantytown and the gravel dock a mile away, the eucalyptus trees of the hippy camp sticking up halfway around it. He hunched his shoulders with a chill and hugged his aching hand to his chest, glanced at the cast and stared with sad, sloping eyes out over the silvery blue water and the morning sun sizzling on the sea like a fish scale. He wondered what was going to happen to him next. Then, suddenly, he winced with pain, held his cast to his chest, but couldn't stop the throbbing, and was barely able to keep himself from crying.

He hugged his cast to his chest to help him endure the pain, then, through the window, near the corner of the house, noticed a pigeon pecking his way around the yard with the chickens, dangerously close to the sharp hooves of a goat with full udders and long teats. The pigeon had a deformed wing that looked like a dislocated shoulder, pure gray and smooth as a molded fender on a hot-rod car. But it stuck up at an odd angle and kept the pigeon down on the ground, where he had to take his chances with the roosters and goats.

"What the hell am I looking at this for?" Roger asked himself, then realized that the wounded pigeon had touched him by its courage. The pigeon was braver than he was. He looked down at his cast, the misshapen lump of it, the plaster gray and fraying at the edges. "I'm going to take this fucking cast off right now. It's not going to hurt me anymore!" he said out loud.

Penny sat up in bed, startling him.

"No, Roger! You've only got a few more days and the doctor can take it off!" she said, jumping out of bed in her pajamas.

"What's a few days then? You're not stopping me anymore," Roger said, and grabbed a razor blade out of his shaving kit on the bed stand.

"Roger, please!" Penny cried, stepping in front of him when he walked toward the box table. But he stepped around her and said, "I'm going to take it off. I'm going to find out right now what they've done to my hand! Why it hurts so badly! Right now! Right now! And I mean now!"

He started scratching a straight groove down the back of his thumb with the blade, digging deeper and deeper, blowing the plaster dust out of the hole, pushing harder and harder until Penny cried, "Be careful! You'll cut yourself!"

She had such an anguished expression on her face, he stopped. He then took out his boy scout knife, and using its screwdriver, started prying the cast apart, not caring if he hurt himself. When he finally had cut all the way through, he stopped and put the knife down, pried the cast all the way off with his fingers and pulled his hand free.

"Oh, no!" Penny cried when he held it up.

His thumb was puffed up like a cue ball at its base, as if the joint had been broken and permanently healed that way, and his forefinger dangled as limp and swollen and curled as a fat worm from his imbedded index knuckle. There was a bloody ulcerated sore on its middle knuckle where it had been bent down by the cast.

A puffed pink sausage, that's what his index finger looked like. With a bloody hole in the middle knuckle from rubbing against the cast. Trust of the doctors had crippled his hand. He had a cue ball for a thumb, the bone hanging off the edge of the wrist. They'd crushed his hand, broken the bones for daring to fight back. He tried to move the finger, but the pain was too sharp and the finger too weak, too unattached to its knuckle, which was imbedded in the puffed flesh. He couldn't move it.

"I can't even move that finger. It's hanging there as if it doesn't even belong to me," he said.

"Oh, Roger, I'm sorry, I'm sorry," Penny cried, then covered her face with her hands and started sobbing.

15

"This is very unusual," the plump, olive-skinned doctor said, but made no attempt to touch or examine the claw-like lump Roger held out in front of him.

"I can't even move the forefinger. It hangs like a bloody sausage. When I move my thumb, the cord snaps back and forth over that lump of bone at the back. See?" Roger snapped his thumb back and forth to show what he meant.

"The whole hand hurts too, now," he said, squinting at the plump man in front of him. His voice was calm because he knew that he couldn't blast the guy with his good fist and hurt him good because the two men in dress suits in the waiting room would come in and shoot him. He knew that even if he just hurt the doctor a little bit, they'd toss him in a Spanish jail, maybe for a long time, and that there'd be no hope at all of saving his hand. It would wither in its claw shape and cripple him for life. He wanted his hand more than he wanted revenge. Revenge could wait, his hand couldn't. When he had a hand, he'd leave Spain.

"If I just touch the finger against anything, it stings like I've been shocked. Can I still save my hand? Can it still be saved?"

The small eyes stared through the rimless glasses at Roger without a blink. His cheeks were smooth and round and polished as fruit. The tiny mouth was thin and tight. "There is a physical therapy clinic in town where you might exercise it. You must exercise it, if you want to save it."

The doctor glanced at Penny now for the first time since she'd come into the softly lit office with Roger. Still staring at Roger, he reached down and opened the desk drawer below him, stuck his puffy hand in and lifted up a pistol which he pointed at Roger's face. He aimed right between Roger's eyes.

Roger could see the round iron eye of the barrel right between the glassed eyes of the doctor.

"Like this," he said, and pulled the trigger three times with three distinct clicks.

16

Lit by the rosy morning glow, the spider was a tiny spark against the backdrop of the pink wall. It was so tiny it looked like a minute speck of lint. Roger hesitated to press the alarm button before the alarm clock went off. He didn't want to wake Penny and he didn't want to break the web and bother the spider either. It had spun one strand from his alarm clock to his black portable lamp. But when he saw that the spider was dangling by a separate single strand from the little plastic lamp that was not connected to the clock, he reached around it and pressed the button down on the clock without touching the strand.

The spider's life was so fragile, so totally dependent upon Roger's whim, it depressed him. He stared at his right hand lying limply on the bed next to him. It was very ugly. His forefinger looked as pink and soft as a shelled prawn, with a deep hole with a scab in the middle of its curled back where it had bent against the cast. Big Brother was going to kill him, bit by twisting bit, one long, slow, crippling death. There was no way out.

He stared at the rosewood shutters, but the rosy glow that illuminated them didn't lift him now like it sometimes did. He was too tired and hadn't slept more than three or four hours at best. He'd sat in the darkness all night, tossing and turning in the bed for a good hour or so before falling asleep. His stomach felt hollow, too. He hadn't eaten since the wheat germ and *café con leche* the morning before. Penny had fallen asleep with her clothes on again when they came home from Las Palmas. He'd thrown a blanket over her and didn't put his own pajamas on till four in the morning. He was thirsty, with a strong urge for orange juice. He must have become dehydrated during the night.

Roger slid out of bed, slowly, so as not to ruffle the blankets and disturb her, trying to keep a little of the bliss left from when she came back to him from Las Palmas. He was convinced he loved her, but all the suffering of the last two months had almost wiped it out. He stood next to the bed in his nylon pajamas and looked down at her cute doll's face, round cheeks and long, upswept lashes. He was touched by the childlike look of her, small-boned and petite. How sad that their lives should be so sad together when they cared for each other so much. Monumental problems, full of politics and the police.

His lips moved with a soft whisper: "Those fucking pigs want to keep me from writing my book even if they have to kill me. They're going to shut me up one way or the other. That's why no letters nor a second book published."

He heard his own voice and pressed his finger to his lips, shut himself up and watched Penny's face for the least movement, but couldn't stop his mind from churning, seething like a can of maggots in his brain. His crippled hand! The eye of the gun barrel! He'd never be free! He couldn't even run.

He picked up his towel, razor and comb, opened the hand-carved door quietly and walked down the hall. He never had problems getting the bathroom first in the morning, because he was the first one up. The other hippy tenants all got up between ten and twelve and had to wait their turn.

His face was hollow-eyed and sunken-cheeked in the mirror. He didn't particularly like his face anyway, and when he was down, he disliked it. He looked ugly. His eyes were too far apart, and he could see tiny wrinkles near the corners. His upper lip looked puffed and sullen. It was too big. His face was lopsided, too, because he used to crack his left jaw hinge when he was nervous, and he'd created a hard, muscular lump there. His wavy hair looked awfully thin on top, too. He usually combed it so the thinning hairline didn't show too much.

The sad fact of his own mortality showed too much now. He was getting old, even if he did look ten years younger than his age: thirty-eight. A good part of his youth was gone, and there weren't too many years of it left, even if he was in good shape at a hundred and twenty-four pounds or so, probably less after not eating yesterday. There was no hope. He knew now why his brother killed himself nineteen long years before.

His eyes shut at the memory of finding him dead in his blanket, lips cracked and closed, eyes a deep, deep blue, in the back room of the pharmacy. Roger had to take a deep breath

to keep a sob down. How bad he must have felt to kill himself!
He chose rest. How sweet and appealing that choice seemed
now.

When Roger sprinkled water from the little hose attached
to the faucet over him in a cold, miniature shower, and saw
goose pimples spread over his legs, he gagged at the futility of
washing his slowly dying body every day. His stomach buckled
and a wave of dizziness swept over him. He had enough of it.
He'd go join his brother.

Shakily, legs wobbling, weak from lack of food, he stood
up and washed himself, got every part of his body with quick,
practiced motions, without thought, just moving to keep the
sadness away.

After toweling off, he slipped back into his pajamas and
shaved with his good left hand, succeeded in never looking
himself in the eye by keeping his sight focused on all the little
motions of skin-spreading and blade-lifting. He quickly finished by running his comb through his hair without the usual
artful moves that covered the thin parts of his hairline.

He stepped into the hall, but stopped and stared back at
the waste basket for a moment, then at his crippled right
hand. He stepped back into the tile bathroom and picked the
razor blade out of the waste basket, held it carefully in his left
hand, then stepped out the door again. Instead of going down
the hall to the kitchen and asking the *señora* for a small bowl
of *café con leche*, he turned toward the front end of the hall
and his room.

He stayed on his toes when he stepped into the room and
changed from his pajamas to his Levis and green-striped
T-shirt. He kept watching the huddle of Penny's sleeping body
as he dressed, ready to stop all motion at the slightest movement from the sleeping figure, like a low hill on the bed. When
he was dressed, he didn't open the end shutter of the window
over his typewriter, which was propped on a small box on top
the small barrel, as usual, to get the light he needed for writing. He picked up the razor blade and slid it into a small
matchbox with a colored picture of a toy clown with a tragi-
comic face on it, slipped his green cardigan writing sweater
on, and very carefully stepped out the door, closed it softly,
then stepped to the big front door.

He opened one side of it, but when he stepped out into the
morning sun and saw the lovely view—the ocean glittering sil-

very-blue out past the tip of the headland of the shore—he let the door slip out of his hands and bang shut behind him.

He caught his breath, stared at the door for a few seconds, hoping he hadn't awakened Penny, then swallowed and realized how dry his mouth was. Should he go back in and brush his teeth? Just another futile act, he thought, and turned toward the dry, bare hills. He saw a cop just outside the bakery in the long, low brown-tile building a dirt lot away from him.

The black, patent leather, three-cornered hat gleamed in the morning sun. He'd never seen a Guardia Civil cop in the village before. And so early in the morning? Then he saw the glint of the long black camera as the cop lifted it to his face and aimed it at him.

"Fuck you!" Roger said in a low voice, braced himself, squared his shoulders, stuck out his chest, and kept walking straight at the cop, without flinching, giving him every possible shot at him. He even straightened up so that the cop could get a full picture of him and stifled the urge to punch him.

"Stick it in your file, you pig! And see what good it'll do you where I'm going!"

When Roger got within fifteen feet of the cop, threatening him, too, by walking straight at him, the cop lowered his camera and stepped in through the big door of the windowless bakery, closing it behind him.

"Back away, you chickenshit bastard," Roger said, and managed to hold a forced smile for a few more feet. He kept moving down the dirt road to the empty highway a block away, crossed it and began to walk up a path that went near the top of the long, sloping hill in front of him. As he climbed, he had to stoop more and more, and as he stooped, his spirit sank. He felt all thick upper lip by the time he stopped near the top of the hill and turned to look back at the village below him.

The rooftops and the rocky cove seemed swept over by a veil of damp sea air, a soft, just discernible mist, that gave it an ethereal look. He stood staring at it for a long time, trying to take in everything he could with this one last view. He would rather live, but he wasn't going to live in terror, without spirit. If he wasn't going to be free, he didn't want to live. They'd never stop torturing him. The cop with the camera was all the proof he needed of that. Well, they wouldn't torture him anymore. He'd choose his own fate and set Penny free. Penny! Sweet Penny. Penny! His heart jumped at the sight of a small figure coming over the rise of the hill below him. Penny, with her long hair swept back from her turtleneck shirt, hands on her thighs as if using them to push herself up the hill with every step, lifting her head with every step to squint up at him.

His first impulse was to start running and ditch her, which he could do once he got over the top of the hill, about a block above him. He could run so much faster and farther than she could. But he didn't want to run. It seemed preposterous to run away from his girl into the hills so he could kill himself. It didn't fit together. His intention was not to run away. But he wanted to kill himself in private, without an audience. And he didn't want to be rushed, either. Everything was too precious these last few moments.

He sat down on a small stone fence and watched her work her way up to him. When she got close and he saw her squinting to see him better, he couldn't meet her gaze.

"Whatta you doing, Roger?" she asked, and sat down next to him, panting.

The collar of her turtleneck shirt was folded under on one side as if she'd dressed hurriedly. Then he remembered she'd fallen asleep with her clothes on, and that he'd let the front door bang when he stepped out. That's what probably woke her up. Her eyes were bright and green, and there was a perfect sensual shape to her lips that was strikingly beautiful to him. It was as if he could see all her beauty now that he wasn't going to see it ever again. He saw her eyes switch to the matchbox in his left hand and her lips move before he heard her words: "What's that?"

He hesitated but it seemed ridiculous to lie. "A razor blade," he said.

"Whatta you going to do with it?" she asked, her face pale, lips tight.

"My whole life's controlled by the secret police, Penny," he said without looking at her. He turned and looked back up the small, bare hill above him, trying to choose which direction to go.

"They'll never let my book be published. They'll starve me on *Kilo* to keep me from writing this one. That's why my agent hasn't written to me. That's why there's no word from my editor. There's no hope for me. They've got too much power over me. They make my life miserable. They break my bones. They point guns at me. It's not worth it," he said, and threw his legs over the small stone fence and started climbing the hill again, taking long steps to get away from her.

"Roger!" she called, and climbed over the fence, bell-bottomed dungarees flapping, and ran up the hill after him, catching his hand with the matchbox in it.

"Roger, stop! You can't do this!" she cried, and her face seemed all freckles and mouth, her long, reddish brown hair blowing back from her shoulders, green eyes shot through with red veins.

Roger jerked his hand free and started leaping up the hill, taking still longer steps, making her run at full stride to keep up with him. His stomach was a tight knot, as if it had shriveled up into a ball from no food and was now contracting with the suffering he felt. He hurt. He ached, but he didn't feel like crying. He felt like... killing himself!

He reached a giant outcropping of rock and had to climb straight up or go a long way on one side to get around it. Penny grabbed his pant leg from below and pulled on it, wouldn't let him climb up. He jerked free, but she grabbed his foot with both hands and held on. Her eyes were red, but she wasn't sobbing. Her face was tight instead, white.

"You can't do this!" she said, hugging his foot to her body, as if she knew once he climbed over the rock, he'd get away from her.

"Let go!" he said. "I've got to have some control over my life, even if it means ending it, goddamnit! They're not going to kill me bit by bit, torturing me every second of the day! They're not going to rule me! Nobody's going to rule me! I'm a free man, goddamnit! a free man!"

He pulled the razor blade out of the matchbox, dropped the box and tried to jerk his foot loose. But she held onto it, squinting her eyes, and yelled, "Don't, Roger!"

Suddenly she looked ugly and repulsive to him, and he shouted, "Remember your part in this! Remember how you got me to fight that guy and kept telling me to trust the doctors! Remember what you did to me, too! Remember how you helped kill me!"

He stood poised above her with the razor held up, staring at her. He jerked his foot back again to get loose, and when she held on, he suddenly kicked out at her, caught her in the chest, saw the shocked circles of her mouth and her eyes when she fell backwards and her legs flew up, then the shut-eyed grimace on her face and heard the coughing sound of her breath when she hit the ground on her back.

He became aware then of the whole hillside below her and the sloping bare fields and tomato patches and the village in the cove between the headlands of the cliffs, the sun glittering on the sea, and Penny on the hillside below him, knocked down by him, hurt by him, suffering over him. Roger flicked the razor blade away and jumped down the hill to her, bent down and put his arms around her.

"I'm sorry, Penny. I'm really sorry," he said, and pressed his face against hers, stroked her hair, and rocked her in his arms. "I didn't mean to do it. I didn't mean to."

He could feel her chest throb against his and the wet tears that ran down her cheek. He could smell the sweetness of her hair. His eyes misted with the pain he'd caused her.

"Please believe me, Penny. I'm really sorry. I was too hung up on myself and didn't think of you. Please believe me."

Her sobs softened. She leaned back away from him so she could see his face, and said, "Why don't we hitchhike to Las Palmas today?" She hiccuped with a little suppressed sob. "We could go see the physical therapist. We can still save your hand, Roger. There's still a chance." She wiped her pale face under her eyes with her hand. And we'll go tell the U.S. Consul all about it. You don't have to die! You don't have to kill yourself, Roger!"

Her rising voice broke with a sob at the end. He pulled her to him and stroked her hair, saying, "Yes! That's what we'll do! And I'll keep writing the book, too! I won't let them stop me! I'll keep writing! I'll keep writing!"

17

Roger leaned against the counter, looked into the consul's pink-rimmed eyes, and, noticing the big red nose and the webbed cheeks, thought: lush! alcoholic!

"My name's Roger Leon. I'm an American novelist."

He hesitated. He really wanted to trust the guy but couldn't make himself do it. There was a red ring around the guy's bloated neck, just above the rim of his stiff collar, and his belly ballooned out, stretching the buttons of his white dress shirt and pressing against the counter. He looked sweaty and uncomfortable in the hot weather, and not about to help him.

"Yes?" the guy said in a husky whiskey-rasp.

"I'd like to talk to the consul. Are you the consul?"

"Yes," the guy said, then turned to Penny. "Who's she?"

"Penelope Lawson."

"She should register then," the guy said.

"What do you mean, register?" Roger asked.

It was as if the alcohol was poisoning the guy, seeping into the outer layers of his pink skin, splaying the skin with red veins, and turning his blond hair gray around his red ears.

"She's under age. All underage minors should register with the U.S. Consulate. It's the law. It's our way of checking on runaways."

"I'm not a runaway and I'm over eighteen," Penny said, raising her voice, her eyes sharp-green. "And we didn't come to see you for that."

"What did you come to see me for?" the consul asked.

"Uh..." Roger stopped. He could see a Spanish man in a pinstriped suit sitting in a chair behind the consul, listening.

"Can we talk in private?"

"About what?"

"I...uh..." Roger said, then just lifted his hand up above the counter to show him instead.

But the consul just glanced at Roger's hand, opened a counter drawer, plucked two tufts of cotton from a box, turned his head to one side, stuffed a cotton in an ear, turned his head the other way, did it again, then looked across the counter at Roger and said, "Yes?"

18

Ringing the doorbell sent a shock like electricity through his hand and curled his sausage-shaped finger up against the black button. But he gritted his teeth and squinted his eyes at the pain and kept his finger on it, kept pressing with his weak, trembling hand, as the shock burnt through his pulpy finger, making his knees bend, his legs quiver and his body twist sidewards with his silent scream.

Finally, he let go, crouched over, and cradled his burning hand in his left hand, wanting to fall flat against the wall for support. The pain ebbed away and he could straighten up, but he was so weak he could barely stand. When he looked at the wall-long row of physical therapy contraptions—doorbells, latches, doorknobs, window hooks, miniature finger stairs and light switches—then at the room-long parallel bars, waist-high, he had to walk with his hands, at the fifteen-foot rope hanging from the ceiling in the other room, which he was going to climb without the use of his legs, and then at the long row of weights and pulleys, wheels and dumbbells, he cringed at the pain he was going to suffer.

He looked down at his crippled hand. It was still a malformed lump. And his tendons were beginning to ache above the elbow, a sure sign, the physical therapy doctor said, that they were shortening permanently, and if they did, he'd never be able to straighten his hand out again. He had to save his hand no matter how much it hurt, without any thought of self-pity.

"Without any thought of self-pity," he said to himself, then arched his back and squared his shoulders so that the muscles on his wiry body showed through the black nylon T-shirt. He pointed his finger at the next button, then pressed down and gritted his teeth with the first shock.

19

Roger stopped typing, using only three fingers of his right hand, when he saw the workman still watching him from the empty shell of a second floor room in the small hotel going up across the street. He was a working man with a paunch in powdery gray work clothes and gray hat, more gray still from the fine white plaster dust that floated around the concrete rooms. The building had no inner walls yet, so Roger could see past the man into the shadowy hulls of the rooms behind him, where plaster-spattered wheelbarrows and other workmen stood.

Roger stood by the window, with his typewriter on a clothes bureau, where the sun streamed in and warmed him as he typed and stared at the dark eyes of the man. He concentrated all his energy into staring past the horn-rimmed frame of his glasses to let the man know that he was tired of this ten-hour-a-day surveillance. It had been going on for a week already. The workmen traded off in shifts so that at all times of the workday, even when Roger got up in the morning, there was a man standing not more than fifty feet away on the second floor of the building, watching, trying to see everything he and Penny did in the privacy of their own room. The man kept staring though, leaning against an unplastered wall with one hand, the other hand on his hip.

Roger took off his glasses and stepped to the window. He stood with both hands on his hips and stared at the man, threatening him with all his silent force, with all his will, meeting dark eyes with dark eyes until the man finally blanched, then colored and turned his head away. Roger kept staring until the workman turned his whole plump body around and faced the downtown Las Palmas street, pretty and sunlit in the late morning, with the crowds of tourists already starting to fill the sidewalks and cafes. Roger then stepped back to his typewriter, feeling strong and satisfied.

20

Still sticky with sweat from his pushups, Roger stepped into the shower and turned on the hot water handle, but nothing came out.

"Goddamnit!" he said. "This morning there wasn't any cold water and yesterday no water at all. Tomorrow we'll probably have steam only. I didn't get to take a shower until I was up two hours yesterday. Nobody else seems to have this problem in this hotel. I asked a couple of people about it."

"I'll go down and check on it," Penny called back from the room. He waited in the shower until he started to shiver before she came back.

"He says it will be a while, Roger," she said, standing in the bathroom doorway.

"What did he say, *momentito?*" he said, his lips parted with sarcasm, then caught his breath and turned the cold water on.

"Something like that," she said as he turned his body around under the cold spray. Then, still shivering, he turned the water off and stepped out to towel himself dry. The funeral organ music started up in the suite above him again. "There it goes again, Penny," he said. "I still think they're doing it on purpose."

"Not on purpose, Roger."

"Well, didn't you ask them to stop yesterday?"

"Yes, but he said he works in a band. The whole band lives up there. All four of them."

"Well, how come the others don't practice, too, then?"

"I don't know," she said. "Maybe too much noise?"

As the organ music rolled in slow, mournful waves through the big front room, he put on his black T-shirt, summer Levis, and hiking boots, then swiftly combed his hair, trying to avoid looking at the black ring under his eye to keep from getting even more depressed. Finished, he turned and walked slowly back through the room toward the tall, floor-length windows overlooking the busy street, then realized that he was walking in step to the sound of the funeral march. He stepped next to the window, hoping to see some sight that would blot out the music and make him forget the constant pressure on him, the unrelenting, never-ending pressure from every person he made contact with at every turn. But he caught his breath at the sight below him of an old man in a white T-shirt that showed all his fat belly, picking his way slowly down the sidewalk with a cane. He looked just like his father! When the old, bald-headed man looked up at him standing in the window, he had his father's same deep brown eyes and arched gray eyebrows and hooked tip to his nose. He stared up at Roger with burning eyes, as if pleading with him, while the funeral music rose to a rolling crescendo.

Roger couldn't breathe. It could have been his father tapping his way along the sidewalk below him, staring up at him.

"God! Penny!" he cried out, and touched his heart with his crippled hand.

"What, Roger? What?" Penny asked, sitting up on the edge of the bed, where she'd been reading.

"I'm having trouble staying alive, Penny," he said. "Just staying alive."

21

He'd just put his hands back on the typewriter keys, it seemed, holding up his right index finger and thumb, when he heard the door jerk and the knob rattle. He turned to see Penny come rushing into the room, out of breath, her face all white.

"What's wrong?" he asked, stepping toward her, fluttering waves of anxiety in him.

"Leave me alone! Leave me alone!" she said, breathing heavily through her mouth, her bottom teeth showing through her pale lips.

He stopped and forced himself to keep his hands down at his sides, but kept watching her, head bent, peering up past the upper frame of his horn-rimmed glasses as she walked past him, sat down on the edge of the bed, and stared out the window.

"Penny?" he asked with a hesitant tremor in his voice, stepping toward her.

"I told you to leave me alone, you bastard! Goddamnit! Leave me alone!"

"But what's the matter?" he asked.

"Shut up! Shut up!" she screamed, and jumped to her feet. Then, with her eyes squinted nearly closed, her mouth a round ugly circle of hate, she screamed, "I hate you! I hate all men! You bastard! You sonofabitch!"

"But tell me what's wrong, Penny!" he said.

"Leave me alonnnnnne!" she screamed, and charged him, started striking him on the chest with both fists. The first punch knocked the breath out of him, made him hunch over in pain, his whole breastbone aching. He expected her to stop when she saw that he was hurt, but she kept pounding, and he had to grab her wrists, hoping that the man across the street couldn't see them.

Then she started screaming as if he were hitting her, a
chilling, high-pitched wail that rang in his ears. Then she
started kicking him as she screamed, and he had to jump back
to escape her kicks. He lost his grip on her wrists, and she hit
him in the cheek with a solid blow that hurt him so bad he
reached out with his left hand and yanked her by the hair,
jerked her to the floor with a snapping motion and cut off her
cry with her mouth still open. He then threw himself down on
her and grabbed her wrists, and, holding her pinned down
under him, tears in his eyes, asked, "Penny, please, Penny,
tell me what's wrong!"

"No! No!" she yelled, her eyes ugly white circles.

"But don't you see?" he said, his voice breaking with a sob.
"How they've turned us against each other? Don't you see
that? What the Spanish cops have done? By tempting me by
myself and in front of you with girls and by pestering you
when you're alone? Don't you see?"

She closed her mouth, though she kept staring at him
with bright green eyes, then suddenly twisted her head to one
side and sobbed, "Today...today, twice...twice guys came up
to me on the street. One, a pretty boy, kept getting in my way
and wouldn't let me by. Every time I tried to step around him,
he stepped in my way. I kept saying, '¡Dispénseme! ¡Dispénseme!', but he wouldn't stop, and finally I hit him in the
face like you showed me, and he grabbed his jaw. Then he hit
me on the head with his open hand and let me go by."

She paused for breath, and Roger wanted to smile, but
didn't for fear she'd think he was mocking her. He didn't let go
of her either, but sat on her, holding her wrists down, and
asked, "What else?"

"On my way back from the post office, where there wasn't
any mail again, a guy followed me down the street, trying to
get me to talk to him, and when I wouldn't answer, he slapped
my ass, then grabbed ·my tit. I hit him right in the jaw and
knocked him into a store window and started screaming,
'¡Policía! ¡Policía!' He called me some names in Spanish and
hurried off down the street." She looked at Roger and pursed
her lips with satisfaction.

"Good! That'll show the sonofabitch!" he said, and loos-
ened his grip on her wrists.

"But when I came home to tell you what happened and I
was still mad, too, those dirty bastards across the street, the

young one who always pushes the wheelbarrow around on the bottom floor, he called me *puta* and poked his finger through his thumb and forefinger of his other hand, as if he were screwing, and he got me so mad. He got... He got..." She broke off sobbing, squinting her eyes closed and turning her head so as not to look at him.

Roger let go of her wrists and lay down next to her on the tile floor, putting one arm around her, pressing her close to him, patting her shoulder and rocking her back and forth to console her. "I ought to go break the dude's ass right now," he said.

"No! Don't! They'll just put you in jail, and I'll be more alone than ever! Don't! Don't do it!" she said, and leaned back to look at him, her eyes red and watery. "Don't do it."

He stared at her for a moment, then said, "Then we better get out of here! We better leave Spain! Otherwise I'm going to hurt one of them, or all of them, badly, the way I feel now, and then I'll really be in trouble. And you will be alone."

He showed her his right hand. It still looked lumpy and crooked, but not soft and pale anymore.

"I've got a lot of grip in it now. If I keep exercising it with that handspring I bought, I can keep improving it. We better go, now!"

Episode Eight

MORROCAN SHADOWS

1

Roger heard the screech of the loudspeaker echo in the big Las Palmas air terminal building just as he saw the red neck-scarf. It was early morning, and he'd barely slept all night. Sight and sound occurred simultaneously in a surreal sensation. The man's pale throat under the scarf seemed to scream with hoarse static. Roger twisted his head around to see better, senses prickling as if his subconscious were simmering close to the skin, warning: Cop! Cop! He could sense cop! He was clean, but he still got scared. He stared at the guy. A thin, obviously artistic man stood at the airline counter. His wild blond hair stuck out around his head in long curls and he was dressed in the fashionable, hip, arty style of the Spanish Gold Coast, with his striped polo shirt, bell-bottomed trousers, and red scarf. He turned to meet Roger's eye. His long, slender hands had skin as pale and transparent as porcelain. Roger saw the skeleton beneath the flesh, as if white rubber gloves had been pulled over the bones, and felt a crippling sense of weakness. They'd put a grotesque artistic freak on him. He was living a nightmare. He turned to Penny with bloodshot eyes and started to reach out with his crooked, still-crippled hand, but she was holding a bag in each of her hands. With only a glance at the pain on his face, she turned away with a frown.

2

"We should catch this cab together. It's the only one, and it's fifteen kilometers into Agadir," the blond man with the red scarf said as soon as Roger and Penny stepped out of the airport customs room into the warm Moroccan countryside. Wide green fields stretched out around them. "We'd each have to pay twice as much if we went separate. We should share the cost."

Roger could tell he was a Spaniard even before he heard the slightly stiff formal Spanish manner in the blond man's speech. Even through Roger's dark glasses, the blond man's hands were pale, and he couldn't stop glancing at the skeletal bones that gripped the brown, tin suitcase. Fine as an artist's hands, but knobby and grotesque as a skeleton's. The hands gave him a bad feeling. Cop! Cop! he thought, and took so long to answer, the cabbie took Penny's backpack from her and put it in the trunk of the cab, then reached for her straw bag and briefcase and put them in, too. Roger let the cabbie take his typewriter and briefcase without objecting, but felt as if he were falling into a trap. He got into the front seat with Penny, leaving the blond man to sit in the back seat alone.

"My name is Tony, Antonio," the blond man said, and reached over into the front seat, poking his hand between Roger and Penny to shake Roger's hand.

His touch was so cool and bony that Roger pulled his hand free right away, even though it no longer hurt. "Roger. *Mucho gusto.* This is Penny," he answered.

Tony smiled, then, still staring at Roger, spread his bony legs and showed the bulge in the crotch of his tight-fitting, low-waisted duck pants, then asked, "Is there a chance that all of us could get a suite of rooms together?"

Roger turned back around in his seat as if he'd been slapped, angry heat in his cheeks, and stared out the front window of the cab, sure the guy was a cop-plant now. He remembered he'd seen a big customs guard in a gray uniform holding hands with a little Moor in white robes the first thing on landing. The Moors were bisexual, like a lot of Moslems.

He wasn't going to take it though, and when the cabbie cleared the airport gates and picked up speed through the flat, crepe-green fields, he slipped his arm around Penny so he could turn around and look at Tony in the back seat. His face masked by his dark glasses, he said in a hard voice, "Franco uses the communists as an excuse to suppress political opposition in Spain, and to drive the rebels out."

Tony blushed a bright pink and slapped his legs together.

3

Tony's bony hand reached out like a grappling hook for Roger. Standing on the cobblestoned street in Essouerra, still damp from the night's misty rain, he smiled good morning above it. Roger stared at the outstretched hand, hesitating, not wanting to touch it. That hand was the last thing he'd seen of Tony when he thought he'd ditched him in front of the Agadir bus station the day before by saying they were heading north to cooler weather. He felt his right hand lift from his side now like a mechanical claw, then stop, then lift again and reach all the way out and shake the cool flesh. But as he touched the bones through the rubbery cover, he asked, "What are you doing here?"

"It was too hot in Agadir, so I came up by bus yesterday," Tony said.

"So did we," Penny said, squinting at him. "We didn't see you."

"Going to have breakfast?" Tony asked as if he hadn't heard her, still smiling, still holding on tightly to Roger's hand.

"Yes," Roger almost whispered with just enough wind to be heard, pulled his hand free, reached for Penny, and started moving down the curving cobblestone street.

The street wasn't more than ten feet wide between the three-story high stone wall of the city with its gun turrets and the three-story high plaster walls of the houses, all jammed together in an unbroken line, with blue-painted window shutters and doors.

He didn't invite Tony to join them, but could hear him behind them. He saw the pained frown on Penny's face, a tiny squint to her green eyes, almost gray in the dull light, which seemed to indicate that she was suffering, too.

It was the same look she had when she woke up with him on the bumpy bed under the high ceilings of a once luxurious hotel. The skylight in the hall was splintered and the furniture on the balcony above the lobby was worn, threaded and broken-legged. But it was the toilet bowl that didn't flush and that was full of shit piled on shit that bothered him the most, that almost made him vomit. He hurried back to his room, where he quickly sponge-bathed all over with the pail of

water. Then he saw the self-conscious pained look on Penny's
face when she came back into the room after going out to the
toilet, and saw how carefully she scrubbed her body down, too,
before putting on her jeans and turtleneck sweater.

He felt sorry for her. But when they reached the main
street and a horse-drawn black carriage with the top down
came creaking and rocking behind the clopping hooves of a
black horse with two veiled women in it, he squeezed her hand
at the exotic sight. He continued to hold her hand tightly as
they turned down the wide thoroughfare, followed closely by
Tony, through a marketplace teeming with brown men in
robes, many of them with little skull caps on their shaven
heads, and women in long white robes and black veils. The
women stared out with dark, sexy eyes at them as they
walked past brightly painted goods, chickens, fruits, vegeta-
bles, all manner of rugs, flowing robes, and multicolored
drums.

He held onto her hand until the street narrowed just past
the marketplace, where it was lined by little shops with
awnings and blue doors. They found a French cafe with tables
out in the open, some of them in the spotted sunlight that was
beginning to break through the gray blanket of clouds. They
sat down, only to be joined by Tony, who acted as if he were
invited.

A thin, dark waiter with a narrow face and white jacket
took orders for coffee all around, and stepped quickly away.
Roger sat opposite Tony, who lay his pale, blue-veined hands
on the white tablecloth. They could have been a dead man's
hands for the dead whiteness of the skin. A shaft of sunlight
fluttered over the table and highlighted them, made the
prominent bones shine for a second. Roger had to turn his
eyes away.

4

"How do you do? My name is Omar Khayam and I'm one
of the official guides for our sssity. Do you mind if I sssit with
you?" asked a slender young man as he stepped up to their
table. He wore European clothes: orange shirt; blue, narrow-

kneed, shapeless, very cheap dress slacks; and black wing-tipped shoes.

Roger was more taken by the young man's voice than he was by his name or even his features. It hissed like a snake and put him on guard right away. Omar looked more Portuguese than Moroccan with his olive skin, black curly hair and European dress. "Are you greeting us officially?" Roger asked.

"I would like to be of ssserviccccce to you," the man said.

"Sit down then and have some coffee. We need a place to stay, an apartment, at least a room as soon as possible. We don't want to spend another night in that messy hotel we're in now," Roger said, willing to take a chance in spite of his suspicions

"We can ssstart assssssoonassss you're ready," Omar said.

"Let's go now," Roger said, pushing his chair back and standing up to get rid of Tony.

But Tony stood up quickly, too, scraping his chair and said, "Do you mind if I go with you? I'd like a guided tour around town, if that's possible."

"I...uh... Well, all right," Roger said, but felt a quickening inside him, as if he were making a serious mistake and should just break it off.

5

"Could I talk to you, Omar?" Roger asked from the front room of the two-room apartment, with its bed, rattan couch and easy chair, where Tony stood, still looking the place over.

"Sssssertainly. What do you want?" Omar asked.

"Well..." Roger said, seeing Tony looking at him, then stepped past him into the kitchen and outside into the stairwell.

"Yessss," Omar asked, his eyes bright and cold as ball-bearings under his bushy black brows.

Roger felt another quiver of fear, although he knew most Moroccan men smoked weed, as he asked in a low voice, "Could you get a kilo of kif for me?"

"Sssure," Omar hissed.

"How much?"

"Ten dollarssss," Omar said. "Or fifty durham."

"I'll take it," Roger said, just as Tony stepped out of the kitchen, staring at him.

6

"Is *everybody* here?" Roger asked, looking up from the package wrapped in newspaper cupped in Omar's arm. Over Omar's shoulder Roger saw a well-dressed young Moroccan in a blue suit and brown overcoat step into the room, followed by Tony's wild blond hair. Two witnesses to his buy! To the package in Omar's hand! And, hypocrisy of hypocrisies, kif was against the law in Morroco!

"He works in the post office," Omar said, and stepped aside so Roger could see the neat black mustache of the young man, his plump brown cheeks, his well-groomed hair combed back in shining black waves. He looked like a Mexican-American with a lot of Indian in him. But he could be a cop no matter what he looked like.

"I was coming to see you and ran into Omar in front," Tony said, sat down on the rattan couch and immediately spread his legs.

Roger just looked away, but they had him, and he said, "Let's have it, Omar!" and reached out for the package. He put it down on the coffee table, snapped the string and started unwrapping the newspapers, folding each page back until he saw a thick sheaf of plant stalks about two feet long, cut just like they stood in the field with one swipe of the scythe. Nothing like the pressed bricks and pound bags of loose commercial dope in America. Before he touched it, he asked, "Why'd you bring this guy over, Omar?"

"He works in the possstofficcce and can mail some hasssshissssh back to America for you, guaranteed to get through," Omar said without looking away.

A quick, queasy feeling of discomfort hit Roger, a shaky lightness to his body, and he picked up a stalk to stall them, stripped some green buds off and packed them into his briar pipe, then lit a match, touched it to the pot, took a hit and asked, "How?"

"He'll put it in the bottom of a leather bag so that nobody will be able to find it," Omar said, and Roger glanced at Penny, who frowned and shook her head.

"I don't think so," Roger said, handing Omar the pipe and blowing out a cloud of smoke.

"Yeah, don't!" Penny said.

Omar took a hit, passed the pipe to Tony, and said, "He's got to get back to work," then led the Morrocan right out. It was so quick, Roger wondered if the guy really was a narc, just a fink, or maybe even a legitimate post office worker trying to make some extra money. A slow buzz settled in Roger's brain, and he didn't speak, not even after he took a toke a second and a third time or when it went out. He just smoked and passed the pipe to Tony, and, as the grass took hold, ignored Tony, more convinced than ever that the whole sale was staged in front of a witness who just happened to come in when the kilo was being delivered. It was a crime to smoke dope in Morroco! He could go to jail.

He saw Tony glance at the typewriter, then get up and step over to it. Roger stood up quickly and stepped in front of the typewriter.

Still, Tony stared over Roger's shoulder at the page in the typewriter, a description of an undercover cop at the student strike. Roger pushed him back with his shoulder and kept turning until he blocked the whole typewriter with his body, then stared right into his pale blue eyes until Tony finally turned and, without saying goodbye, walked through the doorway into the kitchen, where Roger heard him cross it then close the door behind him.

7

"Let's go to Marrakesh," Tony said, holding tightly to Roger's crooked hand, showing all the teeth in his skeletal face.

Roger just shook his head in disbelief, but couldn't help smiling. He'd come back so quickly, only two weeks after he'd walked out, knowing Roger didn't trust him. Agents were nothing if not brazen. But when Penny said, "How?" he knew she wanted to go.

She had let Tony in, but now talked from the kitchen doorway, her green eyes dark in the shadow of the room.

"By car. I rented a car from an American hippy," Tony said. "So I can go to the Atlas Mountains. Would you like to go there, too?"

Roger started to shake his head again when Penny asked, "How long will it take?"

"A few days, maybe a week...or two!" Tony said, complexion pale in the overcast light. "It'll be warm!"

"That's too long for Roger to stop writing. Could we get back by ourselves if we only went to Marakesh with you?" Penny asked.

"By bus," Tony said. "It's only nine now. You could spend the day and come back. It would only take one or two hours."

"Can we go, Roger?" she asked, speaking past Tony to Roger by his typewriter. When she asked like that he wanted to say yes, but fear of another trap filled him.

"You really want to go, huh?"

"Yes," she said, and smiled. "I could use something to do besides walk around this little walled city every day. We covered the whole town in two days!"

He turned to look at Tony, who looked right at him as if he meant it. "You really want to, huh?"

She nodded, without smiling this time, and he suddenly realized how much she wanted to go, specially when she knew how he felt about Tony. He felt sorry for her.

"All right," he said, and when she grinned and reached for her green cloak, he added, "But we'll come back today!"

Tony nodded and smiled, showing those teeth again, and Roger hoped he wouldn't regret it.

8

Roger kept hearing a rattling sound from under the old Chevrolet as they drove inland, away from the fog-bound coast and into the dry, hot land of the interior. Green fields looked like crepe bouquets, and endless rows of orange trees stretched out on all sides around the two-lane highway. Tony and Roger smoked kif and ate hash candy mixed with nuts that was soft as taffy. Roger was enjoying himself, but couldn't shake the feeling that he was caught in a trap, that he was being led to the slaughter.

Penny, squeezed in between Roger and Victor, looked so happy at finally getting to go somewhere like a tourist that Roger didn't want to say anything about his fears or the constant knocking and rattling from under the car. Finally, the pounding got so irritating that he asked, "What's making that noise?"

"The muffler," Tony said, leaning around Penny and smiling. "It's loose and makes a lot of noise."

He waited until he caught Roger's eye, then leaned back and kept his eyes on the two-lane road, and Roger caught an implied hint to keep his mouth shut about what happened to him in Spain. It was subtle, even gentle, but it was there.

Penny smiled at him and touched his hand with her fingers. He smiled back, trying to keep from frowning. Then he wondered if he was too high and making too much of everything, but when he looked down at her fingers on his crooked hand, he couldn't help lifting his hand up for a better look. There was a lump for a back joint of his thumb. It had been shoved so far back by the cast that the base joint was nearly out of its socket. The tip of his index finger was still bent like a bird's claw, too, and though the sore had healed in the center of his middle knuckle, which had been bent against the cast, the knuckle was still twice as thick as a normal joint, and the finger looked as fat and knobby as a Coke bottle. The hand didn't hurt anymore. Still, the fist knuckle was so imbedded that when he tried to close his fist, the index finger stuck out in front of the other fingers, which meant that it would probably break or at least sprain if he got into a fight and had to punch with it.

When Tony asked, "What happened to your hand, Roger?" he suddenly realized that the Spanish doctors had set it wrong not just to punish him, but to keep him from punching on anybody, especially a Spaniard. "I'll tell you what happened to my hand!" he shouted. "It was broken by Spanish doctors! Spanish doctors took this hand and broke it because I dared to fight against pigs like Franco! That's what happened to my hand!"

"Roger!" Penny said, and covered his hand with hers.

"And what happened to me happened to my president and Bobby Kennedy and Martin Luther King and Malcolm X and to everybody in this world who dared to fight that pig Nixon and all his crowd. He just came over to see Franco! That's what happened to me!"

He sat up and leaned against the dashboard so he could see Tony, daring him to challenge him, ready to burst out and accuse him of being in on it, of being sent to tail him across Africa, of being a flunky for the fascist pigs.

"You're making friends with me because you want to either make me forget what happened to me in Spain and/or put me in jail, if I don't."

Tony didn't speak. There was only the drone of the motor and the knocking and rattling of the muffler underneath, the sight of the green fields moving by, and ahead, the vast, unbroken blue sky and the snow-peaks of the Atlas Mountains in the distance, with Marrakesh at their feet, the last barrier between them and the Sahara Desert.

Penny patted his hand and he lowered it, then turned back around on the seat, and said, "Still, I can't live in isolation, can I? I've got to live in some kind of society because I'm a social being, a social animal like all men. We socialize for survival, and we can't survive without socializing."

She leaned her head on his shoulder, and he reached up and touched her cheek with his bad hand, patted it and said, "I find myself in a position where I can't refuse your offer of friendship without being unfair to Penny, who deserves some joy in her life with me, or ungrateful to you for trying to be friends! I've got to go with you, if I love Penny and want to keep love alive in me. I've got no choice. The only other choice is to be consumed by bitterness and hate!"

She gripped his fingers, cupped them in both her hands, still leaning her head on his shoulder, as if still trying to console him.

"I've got to return good for good, even if I still have my doubts, don't I?"

He turned his head to look at Tony, forcing Penny to lift her head so he could see him. Tony kept driving, eyes on the road, keeping his profile to Roger. Penny put her head back on his shoulder and patted his hand again, then pressed it gently and cupped it in both her hands, cradling it as the car rattled and droned over the highway.

9

Really high off the hash candy, Roger turned in a circle in the Medina looking for Tony, but couldn't see anything but a blur of bright silken stands and multicolored flags. An old-fashioned marketplace, the Medina lay just between the newly paved streets and fancy sprawling homes of the French Quarter and the gates of the old walled city—a rusty-colored, stone-walled fortress with gun turrets. The old city's narrow cobblestoned streets curled like snakes in some labyrinthine puzzle away from the gates toward the icy Atlas Mountains which towered above the city like some great giant wall to keep out the Sahara Desert. "Can you see him?" Roger asked.

Penny turned in a slow circle, too, and said, "Not anywhere."

"I shouldn't have flipped out at him," Roger said, his eyes glazed from the belladonna in the candy. "He probably went straight to the mountains because I bumkicked him shouting about my hand. I'm sorry I yelled at him. I'd like to get along with some people sometime."

Penny stepped right in front of him.

"You might have chased him away. He should have been here by now. He said he was just going to park the car." She gripped both his arms. "But don't worry about him; have fun instead."

"All right, to hell with him then. I'm going to eat that other piece of hash candy he gave me, too, so I won't have to worry about carrying it."

She dropped her hands. "Maybe you better not, Roger."

"I'm really tripping, it's true," he said with a tremor of fear that Tony might have poisoned him like they did in Arguiniguin. "But I want to enjoy myself like you said. I feel like it now. For a change. Let the worries stir in their own juices."

He pulled a cake of brittle, glass-like green candy out of his pocket and bit into it. He smacked his lips at the slightly bitter taste, like biting into an orange peel, then stuffed the rest in his mouth, crushed it with his teeth, and swallowed it quickly. Then he wandered off with Penny into the tent city of the Medina. As they walked through the narrow, curving, crowded, carnival-tented streets of the marketplace, he was dimly aware that they had to catch a late afternoon bus back to Essaouerra, but was too entranced by the exotic place to care.

He stopped to buy some snails boiled in their shells, and used a safety pin the man gave him to pluck the gooey body out of each shell and pop it into his mouth. The man, in robes and baggy pants, a turban wrapped around his head, smiled and said, "Hubba-hubba," then offered one to Penny. When she turned her face away with a scowl, he grinned again and said, "Fucky-fucky."

Roger stared at him, wondering what he should do about it, but the guy kept grinning at him and offered him another snail, so Roger turned away when Penny said, "Forget it, Roger. Come on."

He caught up with her. The colors of the stands and the silken finery and the multicolored handmade goods entranced him. He stepped with Penny along a sunny street where bright forty-yard strings of yarn were dipped in boiling black story-deep vats of different colored dyes—bright red and green and yellow and purple and blue—then hung on ropes ten feet high to dry. Their shadows created a soft, picket-fence effect on the hard earth below them.

Roger stared as if he were high on acid, as if his whole body were a live receptor, as if he were taking everything in through all his senses at once. It was as if he could see the dazzling luminous glow that emanated from the bright silken colors of the stalls under the deep blue of the sky and feel its heat like an electrical field that touched him with its invisible force when he walked by, raising the hair on his arms.

He seemed to float through a section of small food stands, the fish scents touching his nostrils and filling the membranes of his nose with their tasty smells, making him stop by a smoking charcoal brazier of shish kabob with its simmering squares of beef impaled on sharp-pointed iron rods. He bought one each for him and Penny. She licked her lips in ecstasy as she ate.

Then they saw some young boys carving furniture with their hands and bare feet, one guiding a chisel with his toes while another hand-turned a lathe set on the floor. The pungent smell and dust of the wood shavings floated into the air. Roger stopped and watched them for a while with a pang of regret thinking of the cramped toes the children had to endure. He then moved on and stopped in a circle of people around a flute player in a long robe. His turbaned head swayed in graceful synchrony to the mournful reed call and the swaying necks of hooded cobras. Roger became so entranced that he didn't realize he was swaying back and forth with the man and the cobras, too, until Penny said, "Roger!" and pulled him away from the circle of Moroccans staring at him.

Penny stared, too, when he stopped near a long line of blind men in burlap robes holding tin cups out in front of them, raising their blind eyes to the sky and chanting in a chorus for the mercy of the passerby and the glory of "Allah! Allah! Allah!"

He put a coin in the cup of each of the ten men in the line to thank them for the beautiful spectacle that they themselves couldn't see. And though he floated in circles in the bazaar for what hours, sometimes finding himself at the same place more than twice, he kept coming back time after time to the blind men, as if they had some magnetic pull on him. He was conscious of it in the upper realms of his dream world, where the sights and sounds that bombarded his senses and exploded inside him had symbolic shape and form. He saw the myth of it, the archetypal blind man of all time standing like a reflection of himself in a line with his cup out, in Morocco, in the Middle Ages, with time spanned for once, right there in front of him, in melodic chanting sound and burning, living color. It was living Art, with a capital A. Roger was *living* art. If there had to be a heaven, it would surely be like this, pure sensation rippling out into infinity.

He heard a loud rumble of drums and looked for the source of the sound through his dark glasses. Reminded of old Hollywood movies of the thirties, he expected to see a scene from out of darkest Africa suddenly materialize around him. A large circle of people out on the wide asphalt field between the Medina and the gates of the Old City caught his eye. He could hear the clash of tambourines and the jingle of bells. Excited by the carnival atmosphere, he grabbed Penny's hand and hurried over to the crowd.

He edged through the circle of people, sliding far enough into the crowd to see black tribal dancers in feathers and bells dancing in front of a row of black drummers and tambourine players. Just the glimpse of the high-stepping, black tribes-

men slapping their bare feet against the pavement, bowing
their backs in synchronized rhythm, baring their shaved
skulls and black turbans to the bright sun, made his heart
beat faster.

He felt a dizzying rush of blood to his head when he edged
into the inner side of the circle and saw the bells on the
dancers bare black toes and ankles, all over their black fingers
and wrists, and strung across their bare black shoulders so
that they jingled with every step, every jerk of shoulder and
sway of hip, every quiver of hand. Standing behind them were
a half dozen drummers and tambourine players and one white
hippy in a white turban, who held a tambourine next to his
ear and thumped it with the fingers of one hand.

A great buoyancy filled him, seemed to lift him up on his
toes with a tingling feeling that crept over his scalp and every
pore on his body, and he began to dance, too. He did a little
foot shuffle while standing in one place along the inner edge of
the crowd, then moved more and more until he was dancing
almost frantically with every part of his body, keeping time
with his shaking shoulders, his snapping hips, and his stomp-
ing feet. He was waving his hands in the air as a blurred
vision of black natives danced to the drum beat with much
slapping of feet, ringing of bells, glittering of teeth, popping of
tambourines, swaying of black robes, spinning of shaved
skulls, and shining of black skin filled every part of his being.
It went on and on and on until he could barely hear Penny's
cry, like some far-off call: "Roger! Roger! It's getting late! It's
time to go! Time to catch the last bus!"

10

He could see her eyes as they walked across the asphalt
field toward the gates of the old city, trusting her to lead him
to the bus, but for some reason, he couldn't seem to see beyond
her. Everything around them seemed far off and somehow
blurred. He couldn't focus on anything. He couldn't even look
into her eyes. He tried, but they were blue-green and cold,
without any depth to them, as if the sky were clouded over.
The day now looked gray to him. Everything had a shadowy
haze to it. He was sure the sky was gray. But he couldn't

make himself look up at it. He couldn't make himself look at the sky. It seemed to press down on everything like a wet gray tent, but somehow, it didn't wet him.

He was worried, though. He seemed to have no control over himself. He didn't know what to do about it and he was afraid he wouldn't be able to get off the edge of the Medina. If he missed his bus, he'd be stuck in Marrakesh. It seemed that if he didn't catch the bus right away, get on it, get seated safely and on his way back to Essaouerra and the cold little apartment above the Jewish family, he might die.

He stopped before he reached the gate with all the buses lined up against the wall to its left. He could see the cobblestoned streets beyond it, curling out into narrow earthen paths only a few feet wide a short walk away, between one-, two- and three-story buildings. Throngs of people in robes, veils and western dress moved, intertwining like ants between each other as if deep in some underground tunnel.

"Come on, Roger," Penny said, stopping a step beyond him.

"I don't want to go in there," he said, pointing at the gate.

"We don't have to go in there. The ticket counter is to the left of the path, in the wall. See?"

He nodded, but while Penny went up to the window, he stayed where he was, along the edge of the asphalt field of the Medina, right next to the wide cobblestoned circle in front of the gate. Steady streams of people poured in and out of the gate simultaneously, and the roar of buses and the stench of their exhausts hung like pale clouds in the air. Bus drivers and men in turbans and short white bloomers with skinny black legs stood around and carried peoples' baggage for them.

Penny came back within what seemed like a minute with two tickets in her hand and said, "Number fourteen."

Just at that moment, he heard a bus motor start with a roar. He spun around, saw a cloud of exhaust, and afraid that they were going to miss their bus, he started running to catch it, hearing Penny call out behind him, "That's the wrong one, Roger!"

But he kept running, trotting through the stinking exhaust cloud and up along the bus to its still-open front door. He started to jump up, but when he saw a sign above the door with the number 10 on it, he stopped.

Something was wrong. He could see a few men with beard-stubbled faces in turbans and bloomers standing bare-legged and dirty near a row of buses watching him with heavy-browed eyes. He wondered how he looked to them. He was afraid of them. He needed to get away from them.

Roger saw another bus about a hundred feet away, closing its doors and gunning its motor to drive off, and before Penny could get to him, although she was running, too, he burst into a dash. He ran with all his strength, scared that the bus would leave, knowing that his life depended on it, shouting "Wait! Wait! Wait!" and waving his arm as he ran.

But the bus pulled off in a big cloud of stinking exhaust, and he slowed to a trot and stopped, panting on the edge of the Medina.

"Please don't worry, Roger," Penny said in an irritated tone when she reached him, panting, too, and took his bare arm. "I think the ticket man said over there where that line of people's waiting. Please stay with me. Don't run off."

She pointed about a block down the Medina, where he could see a group of Moroccans sitting and standing at the side of the road. They seemed to be in shadow. Their figures were flat and dark as shadows, as if the grayness of the day and the distance from him made them blur and loose dimension. He knew he should walk over there and get in the group, but he was afraid he would still be dizzy and disoriented when he got there. He was afraid that he wouldn't find any warm place there for him to stand, that the figures he could see at this distance wouldn't exude any warmth toward him and he'd be a helpless stranger among them. He was afraid of them.

"Come on," Penny said, and pulled on his arm. And though he felt hesitant and kept wanting to pull free, he let himself be led along by her. He noticed that she had on her green cape, that she was warmly dressed, and that he was only wearing a mock turtle-neck T-shirt just barely covering his torso. He felt bare, almost as if he was naked, and this somehow exposed him to the gray weather. But he followed her. He let her lead him into the crowd of Moroccans. He grabbed her arm in fear when the bus pulled up and he saw how crowded it was. He was afraid they wouldn't be able to get on.

But the crowd kept packing on, moving in more and more until he and Penny were finally able to squeeze up onto the steps, even edge their way far enough into the bus to find an empty bench behind the driver. Yet still more Moroccans pushed up onto the steps of the doorway, so that there was not one foot of clear floor space left in the entire bus when the driver closed the doors with a big sigh of air. He gunned the motor and began to drive away from the gate of the old city and the Medina toward the wide boulevard and lawns and palms of the French Quarter. Roger finally let himself sink down on his hard seat with a big, relaxed sigh of his own.

11

Men in turbans and hooded robes and women in veils surrounded Roger and Penny. They rattled in Arabic and shaped all words with slender brown hand gestures, puckered lips, squints, frowns and wiggles of their eyebrows. The chickens tied to the roof squawked and fluttered their feathers, flapping their wings above the drone of the bus engine.

It was like going to a fair in the Middle Ages. He felt like he was in a movie; rather, that he was watching a movie from inside a movie. There was a light projector in the back of his own brain that shined out through his eyes and illuminated the scene. His senses were being bombarded and his mind was racing.

He kept looking from person to person, place to place, but it was only when the sunlight touched his hazel eyes through the dark glasses and the yellow flecks glittered against the green and gave his eyes a sputtering, almost delirious excitement, that he showed any of the effects of intoxication.

He was squeezed between Penny on his left next to the window and a woman in a silken tan robe and transparent tan veil across her chin and mouth. She had a small boy on her lap and was pressed so close to Roger on the crowded bench that he couldn't move his arm or leg without touching her. Seated behind the broad back of the bus driver in his gray European uniform and the wide bus window, he had a panoramic view of the countryside, with fields and trees on all sides and the highway dead ahead. He could see every car that came down the road toward them. When the bus driver made a good move to avoid a near collision with a truck on a curve, Roger said, "Wow! Far out! Man, that was close! Where'd you learn to drive, man?" The bus driver glanced back at him with a dark look, then muttered something to himself, and Penny nudged Roger to keep still.

The beautiful young woman sitting next to him looked into his eyes with hers and smiled just ever so slightly, just the tiniest spread of her perfect lips beneath the thin veil, and he fought the urge to lean over and kiss her lightly. He knew she'd let him. Yet, he was afraid of getting Penny mad at him. The men on the bus, too, might take offense and get him in trouble. But she kept looking at him and smiling, and her mouth was gorgeous, so small and full, with a heart-shaped crease down the middle of her lips. Her nose was very thin, with a fine point to it, and her complexion was so golden it glowed even under the veil. He couldn't take the temptation anymore and turned toward Penny to avoid it when the driver suddenly pulled up, stopped, and idled the motor. He seemed to be waiting for some Moroccans to come out of a small mud shack that might have been a little store next to the road. Roger felt the need to take a piss.

"Excuse me," he said to the beautiful lady in the transparent veil. He walked stiffly and a little unsteadily toward the door, pushing his way through the crowd. He stepped out and down, but seemed to fall through space with his last step off the bus. He hit the ground with a jolt that shook his head. His teeth clacked together making him grab for the door and hold onto the edge to keep himself from falling.

He didn't want to take a piss in front of everybody or do it behind the shack for fear of offending the owner. He started, instead, walking back down the highway to get behind the bus, only to find the little man who picked up the bags and put them on the roof staring down at him. He decided to walk to some trees a block back by the side of the road, but he'd only walked a few steps when he heard Penny call, "Roger! Come back! Come back!"

He turned and could see her by the bus door yelling and waving to him. She seemed unreal to him. Yet, he began walking back toward her, but couldn't seem to get any closer no matter how many steps he took. He began to worry that his steps wouldn't stretch far enough to get him back to the bus door in time. It was like walking on a treadmill. Time was flowing by as he paced in one place. Penny ran to get him and grabbed his hand and pulled him back to the front door of the bus and up the stairs to his seat. The bus driver muttered something and started off, throwing him against the lady with the baby.

"Oh! I'm sorry! I'm sorry!" Roger said. "Excuse me, please!"

As the woman smiled softly at him, he sat down and saw the wrinkled face of an old man not more than a foot from him, in the row behind him. He was leaning in close to Roger as if trying to hear every word Roger said. An alarm bell rang inside Roger. He quickly took in the old man's face, the very narrow nose and narrow cheeks with wrinkled brown skin sagging in the hollows, and the dark-brown, deeply set eyes, which looked off to avoid his gaze. He probably had a badge in his robe folds and was on the bus to watch him. Turning around, Roger noticed a man in a checkered sportscoat and slacks. He was beefy and heavy like a cop. The only thing missing was a Dick Tracy short-brimmed hat. He was the only Moroccan besides the bus driver wearing western clothes. Roger watched him move step by step up the stairs with each of the many stops the bus made to let passengers off or take some on. The man in the checkered coat finally found a seat right up against the front window, right next to the door, squeezed in above the stairs. Roger's gaze kept going back to him time after time, his thoughts racing along, wanting to say something to the man, imagining the actual words in his head, like "How are you? Who are you? What are you looking at? Do you know me?" Roger wasn't sure if he had actually spoken the words or even if the man was looking back at him.

Roger's bladder felt so full it ached, and the next time the driver stopped the bus, he jumped up and said, "I've got to go!" He hurried out the door, made sure he didn't fall on the last step and headed out into the green field to look for some place to piss in privacy. But there were no trees and only open fields and grass that reached as high as his thighs. No matter how far he walked, he couldn't see any place to hide. Yet, he kept on walking, feeling the wide green space around him, feeling immersed in tall grass, held up as if floating in salt water, as if he were just treading water. He heard the bus horn honk and he turned to see all the faces of all the people in the windows staring at him.

"Roger! Come back! Come back!" Penny jumped out of the bus and came running through the field toward him, seeming to bounce high in the air as she ran, bounding toward him with the long, graceful, slow motion leaps of a deer. She finally reached him, grabbed his arm and led him back toward the bus, which seemed to hover over the ground like a spacecraft with blue space and cloud shadow beneath it.

The bus driver muttered something again and gave Roger a hard stare when he stepped back on, but the pretty woman in tan smiled at him again. Penny held tightly to his hand every time the bus stopped and shook her head every time he tried to rise, and he stayed seated, feeling as if his bladder were about to burst. Then, finally, when the sun started to go down in a deep red horizon, the bus stopped at a bus station that had a cafe and little men out in front selling shish kabob from portable charcoal fires. All the men got off to bow down and praise Allah, and Penny let Roger go to the men's room.

Roger went out a door of the cafe into a courtyard behind the adobe building. He took a piss in a smelly place and then went back out the door, but froze with fear when he saw six doorways before him: dark, rectangular shadows that hid a safe passage to the bus from him. He was scared the bus would leave without him. He couldn't see well in the dusk. He could barely walk, but he went through one door and found that it just led back into the kitchen. So he went back out into the courtyard and tried another door, but found that this was just a single room without any other exit to the building. He was afraid to move. He was afraid he'd get lost. His heart sank when he heard the roar of the bus motor and the honk of its horn. He wanted to fall into a pile on the hard-packed dirt of the courtyard and cry, he felt so helpless. Then Penny suddenly appeared in a doorway and said, "Roger! Where have you been? The bus driver is mad and ready to go! Come on!" And his heart leaped in his chest with love for her.

12

Faint streaks of light stretched away into the blackness from an occasional street globe here and there on a curve or corner of the winding streets of the little walled city of

Essaouerra when Roger got off the bus with Penny. He pulled her along with him, still happy about her saving him. He walked with a bouncing step away from the city gate, down a twisting cobblestone thoroughfare to the narrow alleyway of their house. Some little children were playing on the narrow little street. They looked so fragile and innocent, fluttering like moths in and out of the light, they touched him. He hurried across the cobblestones to a little shop where he bought a large plastic bag of taffy candy and then hurried back across the street to the little dirt alley to give it to the little children.

The little children shouted with joy when he gave them the gummy balls rolled in little scraps of wax paper. Within a few seconds, he was surrounded by other children who came running out of the darkness of the street. About ten or fifteen little boys in short-sleeved shirts and knickers, and little girls in short dresses pushed and shouted. They grabbed at his hand and drove him back down the alley. He was reaching out and down to the smaller children when he saw a wave of big boys, some taller than him, sweep up and push their way through the smaller children.

They surged up against him and forced him back against a wall, reaching into the bag themselves, grabbing handfuls of candy. He couldn't keep their hands out, so he spun sideways and tucked the bag under his left arm, fending them off with his right arm. But one big boy got next to Roger and pretended to hold the others off, then reached back under Roger's arm and pinched a hole in the bottom of the bag making the candy fall onto the ground. Roger grabbed for him but missed. The boy started to run, and Roger, still cradling the bag in his arm, chased him down the alleyway through the crowd of children and caught him. The boy cowered down, but instead of hitting him, Roger only laughed and gave him some candy, then turned around and gave some of the other big boys some candy, too. He then took the bag and shook it in a circle so that the remaining taffy candy fell in a wide arch across the dark alleyway, giving all the children a chance to get some. He burst out laughing when they scurried to pick it up.

Still chuckling, with Penny standing by him, he shook hands with a little boy who showed him a handful of candy he had picked up and then with another. He was quickly surrounded by laughing and chattering children who wanted to shake hands with him. He laughed and shook hands with each and every one of them.

Then a little girl in a gauze-like dress and earrings reached out to shake, but grabbed his glove instead and slid it off his outstretched hand. She then started running away with it. Roger leaped after her and caught her in one stride, making her scream and drop the glove. He let her go, picked up his glove and turned down the dirty alleyway, followed by all the kids and their shouts of "'ip-pee! 'ip-pee!" all the way to his door. He could hear the kids still calling out in the street as he walked up the interior stairs to his apartment, feeling exhausted and a little bothered by the way the kids had tried to rip him off.

13

He could definitely see a cat, huddled up, its four feet tucked under it, lying squarely down in the middle of one of the brown checkerboard tiles near the bed. The tile was a little too small for it, and parts of its tail and shoulders stuck out onto the adjacent tiles. He looked away, his mind still churning over the way he was mobbed by the children. He assumed he had been thinking about a cat and therefore saw it in his mind's eye. But when he looked again, the cat was still there. He stared at it, waiting for it to move, noticing that it was mostly dove-gray, except for one white ear, half of its face, which was also white, and a white spot on its back. But it didn't move. It could have been asleep, it was so motionless, although both its eyes, gray like its body, were open.

He lay there and waited. Everything looked normal. The surreal bombardment of his senses had stopped. He was obviously sane again. At least, everything *looked* simple and normal to him. But so did the cat, which still sat on the tile floor without moving.

"Penny!" Roger called.

"Yes?"

"Is there a cat in this room?"

"No," she said, and was silent again. He guessed she was sitting at the kitchen table writing to somebody and didn't want to be bothered. He didn't blame her after taking care of him like some looney nut, but he could still see the cat.

"Are you sure?" he called out again.

"Yes!"

Perplexed by her answer, he looked around the room—the white stucco walls and the high white ceiling, the deep shelf of the window, nearly two feet thick, the wooden shutters that closed it, the long rattan couch and chair, the yellow and green porcelain Moroccan drum next to it, and an old coffee table with some books of poetry on it. His gaze swept back to the tile floor and the one brown tile where the cat still sat, motionless.

"Well, you may not believe it, but there's one sitting in here," he said, and waited. When she didn't answer, he asked, "Want to see it?"

He heard her chair scrape, then saw her head pop in the doorway and stare at him.

"Look!" he said, and pointed at the cat.

She stepped into the room in her green turtleneck shirt and blue bell-bottomed trousers, and, her face perfectly calm and expressionless, asked, "Where?"

"Right there on that brown tile," he said, poking a finger toward the cat.

"I don't see a thing," she said, her voice rising with impatience.

"Not right there on that brown tile?"

"Not there or anywhere else, Roger," she said, and looking him straight in the eyes, shook her head as if he were an imbecile then stepped back into the kitchen.

He closed his eyes and let his mind drift, not wanting to argue about it, but wondered if the hash candy had messed up his mind. Then he looked back down at the floor and saw only the flat brown tile.

"Hey, Penny!" he said. "That cat's..."

He stopped. He could see it now sitting on one of the cupboard shelves right next to the entrance. He could just make out the front of its body, the head, forepaws and shoulders. He blinked and looked again, but it was still there.

"What?" she asked, her voice sharp and short.

"I can see it on one of the cupboard shelves now," he said.

"See what?" she asked, her voice rising with irritation.

"That same cat. It's sitting on the shelf now, the second shelf from the bottom, where there's nothing else."

"Oh, Roger," she said, her voice dropping wearily.

"I swear it. It's gray. It has a white ear and half of its face is white," he said. "Do you want to see it?"

"No," she said.

"It's really there," he said, trying to get her to get up and look. But the doorbell rang and he saw her walk out the outside kitchen door. He stared at the cat until she came up a minute later and said, "There's a Moroccan woman down there with that little girl who grabbed your glove, and her face is all covered with iodine as if she's been hurt. The woman says you hurt the little girl and wants some money."

"What? Iodine on her face? I didn't touch that little girl. I only grabbed her arm."

"I know," Penny said, "but she's down there wanting money. What should I do?"

"Don't give her a damn thing. Tell her to split!"

She went back out the kitchen door. He heard the front door close a few moments later and then saw her walk back in the kitchen again.

"What did she do?" he asked.

"She complained and kept saying something that sounded like *gendarme*, but I closed the door on her and she went away."

"Good," he said, but smacked his dry lips at the bitterness he felt. Now, he was being harassed by the Moroccans, too. The whole thing brought him down; he didn't feel high anymore. Then he noticed that the cat wasn't on the shelf. He sat up, and still staring at the shelf, got off the bed and went over to look at it. He put his hand where the cat had been and ran his hand over the whole shelf. It was cold. Then he looked under the bed. There wasn't a trace of a cat in the room. He was cold sober.

14

"Did I hear you right?" Roger asked, head down, hands stretched out on his thighs. His voice was tight and high-pitched, his feet flat on the floor, his whole body tensed, ready to jump up and start fighting. The mournful wail of a man's voice floated up from a roof somewhere near the window. It was a plaintive, melancholy cry, with the ups and downs of a flute, which seemed to match perfectly his own sober view of a frightening reality.

"So I won't have to leave it in the hotel room where a maid might find it," Tony said in his perfect English, watching Roger with narrowed blue eyes from his seat at the end of the couch near the kitchen doorway.

They were trying to set him up now, the next act in a coldblooded attempt to break him with any kind of pressure, even to driving him nuts, anything to shut him up about what happened in Spain, not just to stop his book about what happened in America. Tony was the one who gave him the hashish candy that made him crazy.

"What?" Roger said.

Penny stepped into the doorway from the kitchen with her head lifted and her eyebrows up, as if alarmed by his voice. She'd hardly talked to Roger since they'd come back from Marrakesh and got irritated at every little thing he did. She seemed to want to fight over everything.

"You want me to hold your dope for you?" Roger asked, head still down, chin almost touching his chest, long fingers digging into his thighs.

Tony lowered his head so that long strands of his curly blond hair snaked wildly over his thin face. They concealed most of it, casting his whole face in shadow with just a few patches of pasty white skin showing, his deep-socketed blue eyes barely visible. He didn't speak.

Roger's voice had struck a high note of tension that seemed to freeze him motionless.

"Answer me, man! Did I hear you ask me to hide *your* kilo of dope for you in *my* apartment?" Roger asked, his voice ringing out.

But Tony sat without speaking, his silence convicting him in Roger's mind.

"You got me crazy on hash candy and then split on me when I accused you of working against me. Now you want to set me up! Give it one last try while you've still got a chance, huh?"

Roger kept his hands on his thighs, ready to leap up at Tony. Tony stood up quickly, and soft as a shadow, not saying

a single word, stepped past Penny and disappeared from
Roger's sight. Only the opening and closing of the kitchen door
told Roger he was gone. He didn't make any sound on the
stone steps that spiraled down to the front door.

Suddenly, Roger heard the mournful wail of the man on
the roof somewhere near them again. It was a high, rolling,
mournful cry, with the low tones of a deep flute. It seemed to
express all the pain and anxiety that he still felt about Spain.
He hadn't gotten away at all, but he'd get away from here.
He'd at least get away from this town and Tony. He'd try that.

Episode Nine

THE MARRAKESH EXPRESS

1

Water tapping lightly on the bedspread woke Roger. He could see a big damp spot up on the high ceiling of the room in the Hotel De France in the old city of Marrakesh. It dripped down onto him, tapping lightly on the blanket that covered his legs. He wondered if this was another trick, and it took him a moment to move. Then, finally, he said, "Penny! Let's get out of here," and he slid out of the bed without moving the blankets.

Penny opened her eyes and stared at him, then looked up at the ceiling where he was pointing. Her eyes widened when she saw the dripping rainwater, and she, too, scooted out of bed without moving the blankets.

"I'll go get the maid," he said, slipping into his robe. He opened the door, ran around the roofless balcony in a steady rain and into the building and down the stairs, where he spotted the big black woman who was wide as a tent in her gray jellaba. Beckoning to her, he ran back up to the second floor and out onto the rainy balcony and around it to his room. He ran inside and, when the woman ran in a moment later, he pointed at the water dripping onto the bed.

She looked at the ceiling, then down onto the bed, then smiled, showing all of her gold teeth. She beckoned to him to follow her and led him and Penny back around the balcony in the rain to the room at the opposite end, where the carpenters were working late the day before. On opening the door, she pointed to the ceiling, then to the floor, showing them how dry it was. With a wide grin of her gold teeth and a sweeping gesture of her orange palm, she offered it to them.

"*Merci!*" Roger said. He turned to Penny and said, "I'll give her a tip as soon as we move in, Penny. Come on!" He led her running back around the balcony in the rain, into their room, where they dressed, packed their backpacks, and hurried back in the rain to their new room.

"We're lucky the carpenters finished working on this room yesterday! Aren't we?" he said, and smiled at Penny, who was unpacking her backpack. But when she nodded without smiling back at him, he turned away.

She hadn't smiled at him since he went nuts on hash candy. He caught her blue-green eyes glancing at him quite a few times in the week they'd been here in Marrakesh, as if she kept expecting him to act crazy again and feared it.

Roger felt a cold draft and looked around for an open window. He couldn't see any, but the room was cold, and after he set up his typewriter and novel and hung up his coat and pajamas, he sneezed. Then Penny coughed and they both sniffled and looked at each other.

"I hope that rain didn't get us sick," he said. "We're both such sissies." When she squinted as if she didn't understand, he said, "We've both had respiratory diseases as kids. You with pneumonia and me with whooping cough."

She nodded but kept unpacking without saying anything. He remembered how much she disliked her dad showing pictures of her as a skinny, sickly, freckle-faced kid, so he didn't push it. He picked up the pages of the novel that he'd written the day before to edit them before they went out for their coffee. But as soon as he sat on the bed, his ears got cold and he could definitely feel a draft across his head.

He stood up and looked at the twin French windows, searching for cracks in the frame. Sure enough, the window frame had newly shaved edges which left half-inch gaps on all sides of it. He then turned and examined the floor-length windows on the other side of the bed, overlooking the patio. They had been shaved on all sides, too, creating a cross draft over the bed. He could feel his heart pounding hard in his chest as he checked the door, too, and saw the fresh, pink wood of an inch-wide gap under it and half-inch gaps running around its three other sides. He then turned and looked at the French window on the other side of the narrow room, by the table where he'd put his typewriter, opposite the door, and it had just been shaved to make gaps, too. It was hard to believe, but there was a constant draft in all parts of the room at all times.

He looked quickly around to see if the carpenters had done other work, but found nothing. Not anything else in the room looked new or worked upon or even reconstructed in any way. They'd only widened the gaps around the windows and the doors, as if they knew he'd be moving into this room when it rained. They'd done nothing else. Nothing else.

He turned around in a slow circle, and gritted his teeth to keep from screaming.

2

Roger stood in the new, drafty room above the narrow dirt road that wound through the old mud buildings, built flush up against each other, a quarter of a mile from the Medina.

The day before, Penny had asked him the time. After he answered, "Three o'clock," she asked him again only a few minutes later. His watch had said five o'clock. A full two hours had passed according to his watch, and he got so confused he didn't answer her. He was sure she was trying to see if he was crazy, and he was afraid that if two hours had slipped by without him noticing it, then the hash candy was still affecting his mind, he'd lost his sense of reality and he *was* crazy.

So, he went to the Medina and stopped at the bus-ticket window in the wall outside the gate to the old city and glanced inside, holding his breath. He let it out in a sigh of relief when he saw it was only three-thirty, only thirty minutes since he'd given her the time. He wasn't crazy. Yet, his watch still showed five-fifteen!

Something was wrong. Penny hadn't touched him in an affectionate way since they had left Essaouerra three weeks earlier. She could be working with them or...she could just be tired of him. But why was his watch off? Maybe when he had taken off his watch at night, she had turned it ahead? Or, maybe they had some kind of magnetic box that threw his watch off in the hotel? His mind was spinning. That was the possible explanation and it seemed to border on madness. They were driving him into madness. He didn't want to go back to see her. He was afraid she might pull something else. But there was nowhere for him to go. He wandered around the Medina until night, feeling as if doom were stalking him.

3

Roger turned away from the typewriter, which he'd put on a box on the table so he could stand and type. He looked out the window onto the black asphalt roof of the Turkish bath just across the narrow street from the hotel. A chimney sweep as black as the soot that covered the roof, with a skull cap on his stubbled head, ran a long, blackened bamboo pole down a chimney to keep it clear. The top stories of buildings stretched out beyond the Turkish bath in yellow and gold and rust brick to a tall, golden mosque tower, poking up out of a grove of trees about a mile away.

When he'd finally come back the night before and gotten into bed next to Penny in the darkness, she'd told him how she'd dressed up in her mother's dress and high heels as a little girl to tempt a Japanese gardener who looked just like him, Roger. It horrified him as much as the request for the time. It was a sexual story designed to convince him he was a sexual psychopath. It reminded him of the tricks they'd pulled on him in the nuthouse, where he'd been committed for smoking pot back in the early sixties. He lay in bed next to her for two or three hours in silence before he fell asleep, still brooding over it, not touching her.

He'd spent a lot of time in his room, working six to eight hours day on his novel, then staying in at night after dinner. He'd become a recluse again and let no one get near him for fear of them trying to bust him or drive him crazy and stop his novel. He suspected everybody and wanted nothing to do with anybody. He'd withdrawn into his book, and he and Penny rarely talked. He was suspicious of her, and she seemed tired of him.

He moved away from the window, still unable to make himself type, and stepped to the door of his room, opened it and looked out over the roofless patio. He then turned and stepped back into his room and up to his typewriter. But he couldn't make himself type. He felt surrounded by an unseen enemy who was trying to drive him crazy, break him so completely that nobody would believe a word of what he said. It was all so surreal, so horrifying: his watch and Penny's comments, the hash candy, Tony's hands. He wondered if he *was* going crazy.

He stopped trying to type at all now, put his pages away, and covered his typewriter. He then lit a pipe of kif and listened to the Moroccan prayer music curling up in the air like the smoke from the marbled end of his pipe, while the last rays of the setting sun streamed through the iron bars of the window. The song of prayer floated up from all the mosques and through the air in melodic ripples as deep and throaty as the blood-red horizon and as purple and soft and sad and lilting as the shadows that were creeping over the roofs from the eastern sky with the coming of nightfall.

He paused in his smoking, stopped and listened, in a state of pure melancholy, and thought he could hear a prayer wail from his own roof. But there was only the sputtering of a motor scooter, the ring of a bicycle bell and the hum of wheels on dirt from the narrow street below. He felt a sense of foreboding, as if something really bad was going to happen. He had only momentarily escaped the Spaniards when he left Spain after all. *They* had not stopped stalking. The Brigada de Investigación Social, Franco's secret police, was probably working with Interpol right here in Morroco.

4

A great shush of steam shot up out of the narrow pipe on the Turkish bath roof like an atomic mushroom cloud and caught Roger's eye through the barred window.

He stopped typing and watched it rise up and fade away into the blue air. He started to turn back to his typewriter when he spotted a soot-covered, yellow-striped cat suddenly snap to its feet on the brick ledge of the roof. It stood stiff and still for sixty seconds or so with its fangs bared, its back humped and its tail standing straight up as a flag. Then he saw a black cat at the other end of the ledge, looking as if it had just stepped onto it from an adjoining roof, standing stiff and watchful, too, but without a humped back or bared fangs, only his tail twitching.

Roger watched them, knowing there was going to be a fight. He could hear the slap of children's feet running on the narrow dirt street below and the sputter of the motor scooter as the skinny, raggedy cat began to stalk the black cat one slow paw print at a time, with a low, small, rumbling, warning snarl.

He thought of himself. He was being stalked like that, except he couldn't see his enemy. He did not have *an* enemy. Everyone was his enemy, even those he couldn't see, and even Penny. He was getting tired of being stalked. It wasn't a fair hunt. He couldn't fight a draft along his feet and one at his head. If he told anyone, they'd think he was crazy. Penny would never admit they'd shaved the windows and doors to make him sick, since they knew how strongly he reacted to drafts.

He sniffled. He did have a lingering, small cold. She'd tell him he was crazy. Maybe he was. He couldn't trust his own senses anymore, his own logic. He longed for peace. Even death looked good again. He was in a terribly weak position. He wished he were as able to fight back when his space and privacy were invaded as the yellow-striped cat.

Head bowed, eyes wild, fangs long and sharp, bent on defending its own territory, the striped cat got closer and closer to striking distance. It stopped, let out a deep and throaty warning growl, then leaned back and got set to leap.

Roger pressed his head against the bars to watch, then caught his breath when the yellow cat leaped with a screech, fast as an eye blink, hit the black cat, and tumbled him over once in a complete circle, still screeching, so that they both came upright again. Frozen for one split second with their fangs and claws in each other, but still fighting, still screeching, it looked like a stand-off, when the black cat suddenly broke free and streaked across the roof in a black blur, the yellow tiger right on its heels. The black cat flew over the side and out of sight as the yellow tiger skidded to a stop on the edge of the ledge, where it stood, snarling, its tail twitching, twitching.

Roger rocked his head slowly in admiration, then when the cat lay down on the ledge right where the black cat had dashed over the side, curled up and began to lick its wounds, he raised his lumpy fist and shook it in tribute to the cat, wishing he could score such a decisive victory when somebody invaded his space.

"Who're you fighting now, Roger?" Penny asked.

"Why shouldn't I fight?" he snapped, spinning around to face her.

"What're you shouting for?" she asked.

"Because I'm sick of you being against me all the time!"

"What do you mean by that?" she asked from the bed where she had been reading. She lifted her face, but her slanting eyes nearly closed as if she were already blinking against his next attack.

"I'll tell you what I mean!" he said, head down, taking a step toward her.

"What?" she said, and sat up.

"I'll tell you what! Your asking me what time it was and my watch being two hours ahead day before yesterday."

She blinked again.

"Do you think that's a new thing to me? They asked me the date in the nuthouse! To test my sense of reality under their stress! They wanted to see at what point I might break! They wanted to see if I had broken! Shit!"

He turned away from her and stared out the window at the cat still lying on the ledge, licking its dirty fur. "Right now the pigs have got me under stress over Tony and this drafty room, and they want to see if I've reached the breaking point. They want to see if that hash candy still has me off my rocker! That's what!"

"And what's that got to do with me?" she asked, but her voice was weak, as if she were afraid of his answer.

"You're doing the dirty work for them! You're the agent! You're the one who asked me the time the day before yesterday and told me how you tried to tempt a Japanese gardener who looked like me! They did that to me in the nuthouse, too! Why don't you admit you were trying to see if I was crazy when you asked me the time?

"I did wonder," she said. Then, with a hurt quiver to her lips, she asked, "Don't you trust me at all?"

He wouldn't let himself look at her mouth. "They try to get you where you're weak, through your love! They get you by the balls and twist your dick out of shape! They take away all human love from you. They don't let you love at all! They take all the joy out of life and then dole you out little fillips of love, little kisses, if you're a good boy and are willing to take any kind of love, just to have some love."

He stopped and studied her face. Her lip was tight now, as if she were keeping herself from crying. He ached inside with the urge to rush to her and kiss her, but he kept it down.

"That's what I'm talking about. You, the person I'm supposed to love and trust, asking me about things that fit right into a pattern of manipulation and deception."

When her mouth quivered again as if she couldn't stop herself and one single tear ran down her cheek, he spoke again, but softly this time, more in despair than anger. "How can I trust you, Penny? You got me to fight Fuzz in the park. You got me to trust the Spanish doctors, even after one of them mis-set my hand. You got me to go to Marrakesh that day I went crazy on the hash candy. You asked me the time."

He turned away from her and stared out at the cat, still on the ledge where it had chased away the black cat, and tried to explain himself, to keep her from hurting too much either. "I'm under great pressure, Penny. I'm sniffling now because of this strange repair job on the windows and door that the carpenters did. The Spanish Brigada Social still tails me. Kids steal from me and beggars harass me because I give to the blind men all the time."

"What beggars?" she asked.

"I mean that old beggar at the Cafe Sportif this morning, that supposedly blind, toothless old man with the slobbery mouth who was all dressed up in clean, white burlap rags. He aimed right for me at the table, and when I ducked out of the way, he leaned down and bumped into me anyway!"

"Well, just that, Roger! That could have been a slip!"

"Whatta ya' mean 'a slip?' He had to bend over from the hip to fall on me on his way by! He practically poked me in the eye with his turban! But I'm talking about more than that! I'm talking about everything! The total scene! The same kind of pressure that killed Hemingway!"

"Hemingway?" she said, and he glanced over at her, still on the bed, looking up at him.

"They drove him to suicide. The FBI! They were after him like he claimed. He was a left-winger since the Spanish Civil War. He fought for the Republican cause. He defended Communist party participation in it. And he lived in Cuba when it was in a state of undeclared war with the United States! He got his picture taken with Castro. If you were the FBI, wouldn't you follow him and tap his phone and try to find out if he was an agent for Castro? They don't believe in morality. They believe in money and power! They drove him to it. And the psychiatrists helped. They convinced him he was crazy for believing the FBI was after him and gave him twenty-nine shock treatments to cure his delusions."

Roger clasped his arms and looked out the window for the cat. It was still there, lying in the sun on the roof ledge, still licking its wounds.

"He must have really suffered. His insides were still all bruised up from his last plane crash. The booze had finally gotten to him. He had lost his fantastic body. He would probably never get well again. He doubted his own sanity."

"He quit," she said.

He spun around to face her. "He didn't quit in the sense of not being brave! He took the best way out under the circumstances, with a double-barreled shotgun blast. That wasn't a cop out, at all!"

"He killed himself, didn't he?" she said. "He didn't want to go on anymore. What do you call that?"

"It was his attitude. That's the difference!" Roger shouted. "He was a man of the jungle, an eye-for-an-eye, tooth-for-a-tooth kind of guy who knew that the weak got weaker and were finally destroyed by the world. So he did the killing himself. He didn't wait around for the world to do it. He offed himself when he gave up hope of it ever getting better. He pulled the trigger! If they had him trapped, he died strong even in the trap! That's what I'm talking about!"

She shook her head. "I don't think he died strong. He was a tired, old man," she said, then added, "though, it's true, he made the final decision."

"That's all a man has on earth, his free will! His right to do with his life what he wants to do with it! Everything else is bullshit! Suicide can be the only weapon left against a totalitarian state when there's no avenue left for hope, when there's only endless suffering ahead, when a man can't be honest anymore."

"Don't talk like that, Roger," she said, and stood up. Then she stepped toward him, put her arms out and hugged him to her, saying, "I don't want you to die, Roger." But he turned his head so she couldn't kiss him. He ached with love for her, but felt his tenderness would weaken him, make him forget why he started shouting in the first place.

"Don't you want to kiss me?" she asked.

"I want a love I can depend upon and trust when I'm in need," he said.

"But I do love you. Don't you believe that?"

"Not lately," he said. "You don't seem to even like me since I went goofy on hash candy that day."

"Do you want me to go?" she asked.

"I don't know," he said. "We're not happy."

"I can't stay with you if you don't want me, if you don't trust me," she said. "Oh, if you only trusted me! If you only trusted me!"

"I can't help it, Penny. Everything fits in."

"I'll have to leave you then," she said with quiet finality, as if there were no longer any question of it. She lowered her face, looked out the window to the horizon for a moment, then spoke with a heavy sadness: "I'll go to Paris. Maybe I can find something for me there, some place with somebody where there won't be all this suffering."

"Like mine?" he said, his mouth twisting with bitterness.

"No, mine," she said. "I'm burned out with all the suffering, all the time, never letting up...never."

He turned and pressed her tight against him, hugged her as hard as he could, trying to press the ache out of him and her. And though he said, "I'm sorry, Penny. I'm really sorry," he couldn't kiss her. He couldn't make himself kiss her.

5

Smiling and blond in the glow of the lights at the gate to the old city, Tony said, "It's a nice Italian restaurant in the French Quarter with checkered tablecloths and candles and ivy growing along the walls." His blue eyes were bright as if nothing at all had happened between them, as if Roger hadn't threatened him the last time he saw him in Essaouerra, as if they were old friends. "Why don't you? It would be a nice dinner for all of us."

Roger turned to Penny, who said, "Let's have some fun..." then dropped her voice and, her pink mouth puffed with sadness, added, "before I go," as if she didn't want Tony to hear her.

Roger felt the threat, too. He faced Tony and saw it under the veneer of friendship on Tony's ivory face, his pale, so pale complexion, the cutting edge in his white teeth, so bared and smiling, much too pleasant for all that had happened. Yet, he turned and asked, "You do want to go, Penny?"

There was a plea in her eyes when she answered, "We've never eaten in the French Quarter. We've never gone farther from the old city than the Medina. There's so little time. Let's have some fun!"

He smiled at Tony and nodded.

Tony pointed behind him and said, "Let's take that cab!"

Before Roger could even say yes, Tony had stepped past him, opened the back door and said, "Get in!", making Roger feel like he'd had it waiting for them the whole time.

Roger got in after Penny, stepped past her and sat on the far side of the back seat, leaving her in the middle with room for Tony. Tony had just barely closed the door behind him and the cabby had just started to drive off when Tony leaned out past Penny and said, "Did you know that I was in the hospital here?"

"No," Roger said, feeling a sense of fear. Penny sat stiffly between them, looking straight ahead as if she didn't want to hear it.

"Yes. The hospitals are really bad around here." He kept Roger's eye in full contact with his. "My temperature was higher than my head. I was sleeping on blood-crusted sheets in a ward with cigarette butts all over the dirty floors. The place stunk like rotting flesh. Like dirty, moldy feet!"

He kept leaning over to look at Roger as he spoke the most horrible words in the most matter-of-fact voice.

Roger couldn't answer at first, then, finally, trying to fill the gap of silence, said, "That doesn't sound too good."

"Yes, that's right," Tony said. His faced glowed stark white when they passed under a street light, and he added, "It could happen to anybody."

6

Sitting on the other side of the red and white checkered tablecloth from Roger, Tony picked up his goblet of burgundy wine and took a sip, stared at Roger over the glass rim, then lowered the goblet and with a stiff mouth asked, "Roger, what

did you do in fighting Franco that made the Spanish doctors
break your hand? It must have been very violent."

Penny glanced sidewards at Roger from her seat next to
the window, just in front of the open door to the wide sidewalk
in the French Quarter, then looked back at Tony.

Light chatter came from the people sitting at the candlelit
tables near them and waiters moved in white jackets around
them. Plants sat on the window ledges and pleasant, spicy
smells floated about. But two men in business suits sat at the
next table, not speaking to each other, as if they were listening, and Roger could feel the pressure on him as surely as the
humid, heavy night air. Sweat bubbled up on his hairline. He
felt helpless and hopeless and couldn't answer.

Penny kept her profile to him so she wouldn't have to look
at him. He couldn't see her eyes, only the high bridge of her
nose. She didn't surprise him by trying to stay out of it. She
wasn't his woman anymore, so why should she suffer? He
didn't even blame her. He'd worn her out. She would soon be
in Paris. She'd already left him in spirit, if not in fact.

There was silence at the table for a few seconds and a
clatter of dishes from the kitchen, small talk from the other
tables, and the studied indifference of the two dark men in
business suits at the next table. Roger studied the gaunt face
across the checkered tablecloth from him. Perfectly matched
eyes stared so directly at him he could detect the pale blue
around the black pupil even by the soft light of the candle in
the center of the table. But Tony was no nice guy, and in spite
of the two men at the next table, Roger finally said, "The
Spanish doctors broke my hand because I broke the jaw of an
agent provocateur in Las Palmas.

"Oh, no wonder they broke it," Tony said. "Now, I understand. You know, it's a common law all over the world that
violent people are dangerous and should be locked up."

Roger felt as if he were undergoing a slow, live quartering
of himself, but finally asked, "Just what do you mean?" His
voice had risen with the undercurrent of his anger and he was
close to losing his temper.

Tony looked at the goblet of wine in his hand, then put it
down on the table and spun it in slow, quarter circles with his
thumb and forefinger, his chin down so that his rangy shoulders stuck out, his silence now as much a taunt as his words.
Penny picked up her goblet and put it to her lips, without

looking at Roger either. He picked up his glass of Heineken beer and took a deep drink, struggling to keep himself from going for the bait and exploding, but felt the beer run down a throat so tight with anxiety that he couldn't enjoy the taste.

The long-nosed waiter appeared, handed Penny her raviolis first, then Tony his spaghetti, then set Roger's pizza down on the table in front of him and quickly turned away.

Roger's nose told him what was wrong before his eyes did. The pizza was burnt so bad it stunk and the big black bubbles all over the jelled sauce were as ugly as sores. He felt as if all the pores of his skin had opened up and even the light from the candle and the heat from the food had penetrated him, as if his sense of smell were so acute that the burnt smell stung the inner membranes of his nose and made his eyes water, as if his tongue had already tasted the charcoal edge of the burnt pizza, as if the blood that pounded in his head with the quick tripping of his heart would explode in rage. It was an old nuthouse trip they had played on him to see if he was crazy, since schizophrenic persons were supposed to smell burnt toast and even like their food burnt. His stomach tightened with anger. He wanted to scream and smash the pizza in Tony's face.

"That's a common law all over the world," Tony said, "that violent people should be locked up."

Roger stared down at the burnt pizza, the burnt smell rankling in his nostrils, fighting the urge to smash Tony, knowing that Tony wanted him to try. He guessed that the two big, dark men who sat at the next table were watching him and that they were probably cops ready to jump him and beat him up so badly that he'd end up in the hospital with blood-crusted sheets if he jumped Tony.

Roger couldn't stand it anymore. He jumped up with a sharp scraping sound of his chair, his face twisting into a grimace, staring down at Tony, who sat gripping the edge of the table, body tensed, head down and eyes narrowed. But when Roger glanced at Penny next to him, her mouth open in shock, as if afraid of him, too, he turned and ran out the open door and started running down the wide sidewalk of the darkened, palm-lined boulevard.

He ran past the lighted windows of the business section as fast he could so that Penny couldn't possibly catch him or even see where he went. When he turned on the corner and ran out of sight down a wide, darkened, curving street of the residential section with its sprawling Moorish-style homes, he started sobbing, knowing that no one would hear him or see him on the deserted street, and that his tears were falling for himself, alone on the face of the earth as long as he lived.

He cried without shame, allowing himself that weakness since he hadn't smashed Tony or fought the two men at the next table. But he knew that the tears really weren't a weakness, only release, and that he'd continue to fight fascism as long as he lived, that he'd never quit, that he'd kill himself like Hemingway before he quit writing what he believed was important.

He knew he was totally and hopelessly alone, like Hemingway, and that there was no escape anywhere, that the persecution would go on. It if weren't the Americans or the Spaniards, it would be the Moroccans or Englishmen, depending only upon where he was, which nation had sovereignty. He would not stop writing about the police as long as they persecuted him, and they wouldn't stop persecuting him as long as he wrote about them.

And running, running for block after block on the curving streets, sweating and sobbing, he became more determined than ever to risk fever and the blood-crusted sheets and jail, yes, jail, too, for what he believed, for his freedom to write what he wanted.

Chest heaving, he saw a wide boulevard ahead of him. He was surprised that there was another boulevard like the one he'd left in the French Quarter of town, but realized when he reached it that he'd circled back again to the main drag, hitting it maybe a mile from the restaurant.

There were so many people and cars on it, he stopped running and, still sniffling every few steps, he walked back towards the old city. He hadn't walked more than a block down the street when a cab pulled up next to the curb of the wide sidewalk, the rear door swung open, and Penny called out, "Roger! Get in!"

He stopped and leaned down so he could see into the cab. No one was inside but the driver and Penny. He walked over to the open door, got into the back seat and closed the door.

Penny looked at him as the cab drove off, her eyes large and moist. She touched the lids of his eyes with her fingers and wiped the tears from them, then said, "Do you know what

Tony said after you left? He asked me if you'd do anything violent! He makes me sick!"

When Roger just stared at her, she said, "The driver helped me look for you. I was so worried about you, I was crying and could hardly speak my French to him. I left Tony at the restaurant with money for our food. He acted as if he lived around there somewhere."

When he still didn't speak, she said, "Oh, Roger, you need me! You really do need me!" She threw her arms around him, pulled him to her and kissed him on the lips.

Roger slipped his arm around her, and kissed her back hard, feeling like her lover again. She was saving him from despair with her love. And Tony hadn't broken him. He had not smashed Tony nor surrendered. The secret police hadn't been able to put him in jail, nor the hospital for assault and battery. Their game had backfired and had brought Penny closer to him. He squeezed her tightly as they kissed. She kept him from going under.

Then, just at that second, the thought that to have him trust her now would be the best move the cops could make to catch him flickered in his mind. She pulled back away and squinted at him as if she'd read his thought.

Ashamed, he leaned down and kissed her again.

7

"Roger!" someone called as Roger and Penny, circling back around the Medina, reached the big intersection in front of the old city gate, where the only French style cafe in the Medina, the Cafe de France, was. The highway through town passed by at the broad intersection between the gate and the Medina, where nearly all people coming or going to the Medina would come by at some time of the day. Craig moved away from the cafe, through the streaming crowd toward them, glasses shimmering, smiling. Ruth's face showed behind the shoulder of a turbaned man, blue eyes bright and beautiful with her black hair and dark tan. Penny's mouth sagged and the smile lines around her eyes vanished. Roger squeezed her hand and smiled to let her know she didn't have to worry about Ruth. Penny squeezed back and even smiled when Craig and Ruth reached them. They all hugged each other as if there'd never been any trouble between them. Roger was surprised at how pleased he felt.

"What're you doing here?"

"We came over on a ferry from the Canaries. We never dreamed we'd see you," Craig said.

His soft words out of his soft face rang so false that Roger turned away, thinking that he had just escaped from one trap with Tony and he might be stepping into another one.

"Small world," Ruth said, showing all her teeth.

"Sure is," Penny said in an ironic tone, and there was a sudden moment of uncomfortable silence.

"Say! We're going to Paris in a van we bought!" Craig said. "Want to come with us?"

"In a van?" Roger asked.

"When?" Penny asked.

"Any time. That was our main intention, to have fun in Morocco, and score a little dope to help pay our way. Which we did. Wanna go?"

"You didn't know we were here?" Roger asked, his right eyebrow rising above the frame of his glasses.

"Well...uh...yes...no..." Craig glanced at Ruth, then said, "We heard you left Las Palmas for Morocco, but we didn't see you in Essaouerra, so we suspected you might be here, that's all!"

He glanced at Ruth again, who said, "We hoped we might see you over here."

Roger nodded. It made sense, but when he looked at her, he suspected a plot.

"I'd like to go, Roger," Penny said, sliding her arm through his. "I wanted to go anyway. It could be fun."

Though nearly his size, she looked so petite and cute next to him, he felt her need for some pleasure again, for companionship, for relief from the constant suspense. He glanced up at Craig and Ruth, who were both smiling, and knew he liked them in spite of everything that had happened, *because* of everything that had happened, which they'd experienced together and which made them close to him. And there was nothing else to do.

"When do you want to go?" he asked, still not decided.

"Any time, like I said. We've done our business," Craig said.

"I'd like to leave tomorrow!" Penny said.

"Done!" Craig said, and reached out to shake Roger's hand.

Roger shook it and hard, but felt a nagging sense of fear in him.

8

The white walls of Essaouerra above the palm trees and the strip of beach to his left were overcast with fog when they reached the ocean from the inland highway and pulled into the gas station.

Roger leaned forward to tell Ruth not to light her kif pipe in public. But just as a cop came out of the gas station with a clipboard in his hand, she handed Roger the pipe and blew her smoke out the window. Roger found himself sitting in the back seat of the van with a smoking bowl of kif in his hand as the cop walked right toward him. He just barely managed to get it under the edge of his seat cushion before the cop reached the door.

The cop sniffed outside the window with just a small twitch of his nostrils and his thin black mustache. Then his dark eyes slanted nearly closed under his stiff black cap brim. Roger quivered inside remembering that Craig had said that he had stashed seven kilos of high-grade kif pollen in the walls of the van.

"Car license!" the cop said in English, but looked in the back seat where the smoke came from. He smiled at Roger and said, "Kif?"

Roger just stared at the cop, couldn't move as the cop looked down at the stem sticking out from under his seat cushion and smiled. Roger smiled, too, then, trying to make the best of it, lifted up the pipe and offered it to the cop, saying, "Want some?"

But the cop shook his head and spun his forefinger at his temple and pointed at the pipe, then reached across Ruth for Craig's papers. He jotted down the name and car license number on his clipboard, then handed Craig his papers and stepped back as Craig paid the gas station attendant. The cop stared at the van as Craig started it up and drove onto the coastal road, heading for the white walls of the coastal city.

"Don't ever do that again!" Roger said when he couldn't see the cop anymore. "You might have got all of us busted, Ruth. We still might get busted. He might turn our license number into customs and they might shake us down when we cross into Spain."

"She didn't mean anything, Roger," Craig said, glancing at him in the rearview mirror.

"I don't care what she meant," Roger said. "I care about what she might have done to us."

Craig didn't answer, but Roger watched a slow smile come over Ruth's lips.

9

The black hulks of the ships and ferries in the black water off the waterfront road in Tangier and the dark windows of the little shops, bars and cafes on the other, city side of the road at four in the morning depressed Roger. They'd driven straight through from Fez in one long fourteen-hour trip, and he was really tired and sleepy as Craig drove the van through the strange port city, looking for a vacancy sign on a hotel.

"Hey! There's the ferry we'll be taking!" Ruth said, then dug into her backpack and held two, olive-green hash cookies out in front of Roger in the dark van. But when she added, a smirk coming over her lips, "I'm taking these over with me," Roger suddenly woke up again.

"Hey, Ruth!" he said, sitting up, not forgetting that she'd endangered him with dope already and could have had him locked up.

Ruth pursed her lips, like a kid about to get a lecture.

"You brought the heat down on us in Essaouerra! And you know we've got a lot of dope in this van! You and Craig have dealing weed stashed in here! And you know that I've got about a pound of dope, too."

Ruth turned her face away and looked out the window at the dark city.

"Listen!" Roger said.

When she turned her face back around, Roger tried to think of a way to say it without calling her a snitch and that it was all a plan to bust him. "I don't want you talking on that boat, got me?" he finally said. "You take your risks for yourself. Don't put them on me, on us!" He pointed at Penny. "When we get on that ship, you don't know us and we don't know you, got it?"

She smacked her lips and turned away again, but Roger said, "We'll talk again in Spain at that cafe on the pier in Algeciras, like we planned. Until then, you don't know us. Don't forget that!"

There was only the drone of the van for a few seconds and the faint glow of the dash lights to see by when Craig, his cheeks full and round, said, "You don't have to talk so hard to her, Roger."

Craig put the van into second gear to climb the winding hill up from the waterfront. A neon sign reading HOTEL was visible up ahead like a blue flame on top of the woody hillside.

"Look, Craig," Roger said, "I'm not going to jail for any so-called mistakes of this...this." He jabbed his thumb at Ruth's back. "She's acting like a kid, and I don't like it. I could've...we all could've gotten busted in Essouerra, and I'm not going to do six years in a Spanish jail for smuggling dope. I'd rather talk hard to her now than get busted on that boat!"

Craig didn't answer. Ruth kept the back of her head to Roger. Penny reached over and squeezed his hand, then yawned as Craig pulled up in front of the hotel. For just a moment, Roger considered telling them to go in separately just to play it safe. But it was too late in the night and everyone was tired.

10

Ruth stood with her nude back to him in the far corner of the sunny room, slipping a blouse on over her slightly plump, very brown body. Craig had gone to fill the van with gas and oil, and Penny stood between their cots, slipping a belt through her jeans when Roger said, "Penny, they might be watching us, or me at least, now."

"What do you mean?" she asked, without looking up.

"That cop in Essaouerra. I made a bad mistake offering him that kif pipe. There's a good chance they've got the license number of the van and might be waiting for it and watching me!"

"But lots of tourists smoke without smuggling it out," she said, buckling her belt.

"I know. But we're going into Spain with lots of dope. They've got seven kilos stashed in the van, and I'm going to be carrying a pound of kif across myself. I mean, the cops might try to bust me just on suspicion, shake me down hard."

She looked up right away, still holding the belt with both hands. "You mean, we?..."

"Not necessarily. You might not have anything to worry about, just me! For being stupid, simple," he said, seeing Ruth turn slightly to hear better. He could see the heavy sag of Ruth's breast, with a strip of white like a mask over it, the nipple for an eye, the only pale part on her brown torso. He briefly imagined the white strip around her loins, then thought, "She wanted that. She turned for that. She's trying to con me with sex." He kept his eyes focused on Penny's face to keep from staring at Ruth's breast.

"It's got me scared. I'd hate to have to do several years over that. Know what I mean?"

He looked at Ruth again. She still hadn't buttoned her blouse. "Maybe...I could carry it across for you? They're not after me," Penny said.

He shook his head.

"I didn't mean that! I meant I just didn't know what to do about it, and it's got me worried. I wouldn't want you to take that chance!"

"I'm not afraid, Roger. Ruth and Craig are carrying stuff in," she said. "They're after you, you say. I can do it some way. It's not very much, if you bunch it up."

"Why don't you wear one of my dresses, Penny?" Ruth said, and faced them, finally buttoning the bottom button of her blouse, but giving him a glimpse of both breasts. "They're too big for you anyway, and you could pad one out by spreading the pound around your body."

"A dressy dress?" Penny asked.

"Yes."

"I could do that," Penny said, "and wear high heels, too, if you have some."

"I've got heels and a long coat, too," Ruth said.

"I could put most of it in my panties, spread it out flat in a plastic bag and stuff a lid apiece into the toes of the heels, too. Yes! Let's do it!" she said, and turned toward Roger again, smiling.

Ruth smiled at Roger, too, all blue eyes and bright teeth, acting like a friend and an adult again, trying to make up to him, making him trust her. Yet he shook his head.

"I've never risked my woman over pot in my life. I've carried it on me and run across a field when I knew the cops were waiting for me in the Oakland hills, before I'd let my wife carry it on her, even though she wanted to. I wouldn't let her risk herself."

"Oh, Roger, that's beautiful," Penny said, and reached over her bed to touch his cheek. She held her hand there a moment, looking into his eyes, then said, "And that's why I want to do it. If she would, I will. And I'm not afraid. Nobody's after me. And, maybe, nobody's after you, either. You've never carried it across before. There's no reason to think you would now. I want to do it for you."

He grabbed her hand, kissed it, said, "I really appreciate it." He suddenly wondered if it was all a plot to make him trust her. Then, ashamed of himself, he asked, "Do you really want to? I don't want to push you into this! Tony..." Ruth was watching him, but he said it anyway. "Tony knew we bought a kilo, remember?"

He kept himself from looking at Ruth. "And you know what happened with him!"

"I know," she said, "but I want to do it for you. Ruth's not afraid, why should I be?"

He stared into the soft green of her eyes, the little indented puff at the top of her pouting lips like the cleft in a valentine, and said, "Okay. I'll put the weed into plastic bags, and you get dressed. Fix yourself up so you look really straight."

She smiled and reached down next to the bed for her backpack.

11

Penny walked up the gangway several feet ahead of Roger, with her hair piled high on her head, a small overnight bag in one hand and Ruth's coat over the other. She looked so strange and old. Roger carried only his backpack. His novel, typewriter and briefcase were in Craig's van.

At the poop deck, Penny smiled at him as he slipped off his backpack. He began to feel better right away. But when he sat down next to her, he saw that his backpack blocked the narrow passageway between the stairs from the main deck and the stairs to the top deck, and that all the rest of the room on the poop deck near them was taken up by empty chairs.

"Wait a minute," he said, and hooked his pack up with one arm and carried it back down the iron steps to the main deck. He stuffed it under a bench so he could almost see it from his chair next to Penny, then went back up the iron steps and sat down. He didn't think anybody would steal it, and there was no dope in it, so he wasn't worried.

In a few minutes, Craig appeared from the main deck and joined them right at the rounded bend of the deck rail, from which they could see in all directions on board the ferry. No one spoke. Roger still hadn't seen Ruth and kept glancing around for her as the North African shoreline gradually flattened out and finally disappeared on the dark gray horizon. Penny put Ruth's coat on, but though a threat of rain hung in the leaden clouds, there was hardly any wind and the dark sea was calm.

A tall, bald man in a black raincoat came down from the top deck that served as a partial porch roof over the poop deck and sat down just on the other side of Craig. Roger wondered why he sat so close when there were other seats further along the rail where he could have some privacy. He was a pink-skinned man with a long nose and a long jaw, very nordic looking. The man sat facing their little circle as if he were on the outer edge of their group, as if trying to listen, without looking directly at any of them. He was pure cop to Roger, the first sign he'd seen of them on board. But since they weren't discussing anything and sat in silence, he didn't sweat the man. And the guy sat there so long, Roger finally lost his suspicion of him. He began to think that he was too paranoid. Then another man came up the stairs from the main deck in a black raincoat and walked around the group and sat down next to Roger. Roger studied the man, guessed he was Spanish right away with his deeply tanned complexion, but paid more attention to the deep wrinkled eye socket where the man's left eye should have been. He sat parallel to Roger with only his blind eye and his graying sideburns to him. He had short hair, too. Now there were two men in black coats next to Roger's group.

Ruth finally came up out of the staircase from the main deck. His breath quickened, but he kept a stony, shut-mouthed look on his face to discourage any sign of greeting from her. He didn't want her approaching when there might be cops around. He'd snub her if she dared speak to him. No one else made a sign of recognition either, and she stepped past them and turned into the cafe under the top deck. Roger could see that her face was tight, no smile on her lips. Her cheeks looked pale, as if he might have scared her with his warning. Roger wondered where she'd been for so long, and for the first time he could see the effect of his hard talk. He was thankful for it, with the two men in black raincoats around.

The sudden movement of people standing up and moving away made Roger turn around and see that the ferry had entered the harbor of Algeciras. He saw Ruth move away from the table by the window and then appear again in the crowd of people going up to the top deck, heading for the van. Craig stood up, too, and, without saying goodbye, suddenly disappeared down the staircase to the main deck, heading straight down to the hold and their van, leaving Roger and Penny alone with the two men. They stood up, too, but didn't move away. Instead they stepped in front of Roger and blocked his view. Then, suddenly, he realized that there were three more men in black raincoats standing in front of him, trapping him against the rail!

"Ruth!" he thought, seeing the wall of black in front of him, knowing he'd been abandoned by Craig. He wasn't really clean! If they grabbed him and searched him, they'd find loose bits of kif in his jacket pockets and in the lining, too. And he could, maybe, be arrested just for having stone hash pipes in his backpack.

Penny squinted at him as if she could see the fear on his face, the sallow color under his dark tan, the frosty sheen to his dry lips. Only his dark glasses protected his eyes from exposure. He realized then that he was endangering her by staying near her. He pushed himself up out of his deck chair, his legs like water, his mouth dry, expecting to be grabbed and arrested.

But no one reached for him as he pushed through the two men directly in front of him. His mind was churning, his stomach fluttering, his legs shaking. He stepped over the deck to the iron stairs and grabbed the railing to keep his wobbly balance. He kept moving because there was nothing else he could do. When he reached the main deck, he glanced up once to see if any of the cops were following him, and was surprised they weren't yet. He dug into the outer pocket of his backpack, grabbed the stone pipes and dropped them into the rain gutter under the backpack. He glanced back again to see if anyone had seen him. But when he stooped down to slide into the arm straps of his backpack, he saw the stone pipe heads in the gutter at his feet.

"Goddamnit!" he said, then bent down with a grunt, sweat breaking out on his forehead, picked them up and, from where he was, threw them over the railing and into the water. He then turned, hands still shaking, face still white, to see the one-eyed man starting down the iron stairs toward him.

Roger walked quickly down to the opposite end of the main deck to where the passengers were backed up in line to get off. He moved past the end of the line and kept moving until he was at the midway point. He kept himself from turning around even once as the line moved slowly off the ship and into the custom's shed. When he finally reached the gangplank, he dared to look back only to find the man standing right behind him, staring at him with the one brown eye and the sunken eye socket, the pink of the inner lid showing.

12

Humped over from his backpack, walking fast, Roger guessed that the men in the black raincoats were still watching him. He looked for Craig's white van in the bumper-to-bumper cars which were moving down the ramp from the ferry. There was no sign of Penny in the thin line of people walking down the pier. No sunken-eyed man in a raincoat, either, thank God! He scanned the tables of the cafe across the street from the pier where they planned to meet, but still couldn't see any of them.

As soon as he started across the street, he saw Ruth sitting next to a big man, either Canadian or American, he guessed by the red plaid shirt stretched across his broad shoulders. But he couldn't see Penny, and his stomach fluttered!

"Penny! Penny! Don't get busted!" he said in a whisper, scanning all the tables, then recognized Craig sitting at the same table as Ruth.

"Where's Penny?" he asked as soon as he reached the table, ignoring the stranger.

"She's in the bathroom," Ruth said.

Roger sighed and slid his backpack off next to a wrought-iron chair with fancy patterns. He sat down and looked at the stranger. "Who's he?"

"George from New York!" the big guy said, held out his hand, squeezed Roger's crippled hand hard, and asked, "You're Roger?"

"Who brought you around?" Roger asked, without answering or smiling, sure the guy was a cop.

"I met Ruth on board," George said, and flicked his thumb at Ruth.

"George wants to ride up to Barcelona with us," Craig said, trying to smile.

"We told him we have room," Ruth said, without trying to sway him with a smile for once.

"No! There's not enough room. There's not enough privacy now!" Roger said. His words were sharp with a ring of finality.

Ruth made a sour pucker of her lips, but didn't argue. Roger, jaw set and eyes masked by his dark glasses, looked back out at the sunlighted pier.

13

Roger bristled in silence as Craig drove the van down the Mediterranean shoreline road. A golden beach lay on one side and a dry, desert landscape with scrub trees and rolling hills on the other. Everyone was down to their light T-shirts and summer blouses. He could barely keep himself from blowing up at Craig and Ruth for what had happened to him on the ferry, for what had happened since he'd joined them. He was sure that George was some kind of an agent, Interpol or CIA, and that Craig and Ruth were part of the plan to get him busted and stop his book. He was still fuming over it when Craig rounded a curve in the highway that cut through a low, bare hill. A small service station and a general store stood there.

"Anybody want anything? I'm getting a Coke!" Craig said.

Roger shook his head, still unwilling to talk to any of them. He didn't say anything when Penny got out the side door, closed it behind her and walked across the clearing behind Craig. He watched Craig's back, wondering what he was going to do.

Penny, who looked like his old lady again in her short-sleeved blouse and cut-off blue jeans, could have done everything for the right reasons, and yet, he found himself wondering about her, too. He was the only person who didn't carry dope across the border and the only one who got messed with.

Smelling smoke, he turned to see Ruth lighting a pipe of kif pollen, taking a deep drag, then two, then three, holding them down with pursed lips. Finally, she blew the smoke out in Roger's face and said, "Here! I want something to drink!"

Roger shook his head and held up his hand, refusing not just the pipe but any talk with her. She put the smoldering pipe down on the seat and jumped out of the van, leaving the sliding side door open. Roger reached out and closed it to keep anyone in the store from seeing the pipe. But Ruth had hardly gone into the store when the sputter of a motorcycle made Roger turn to see a cop come around the curve, look at the van, pull off the highway in a cloud of dust and sputter up to the driver's window. He stared through the goggles of his leather cap at Roger.

Grabbing the pipe, Roger slid towards the driver's window and leaned forward across the seat to block the cop's view with his body.

"¿*Qué?*" he asked, with a feeling of *déjà vu*.

"*Mueve el coche. Es muy peligroso aquí*," the cop said, pointing at how close the van was to the two-lane highway. When Roger lifted up his palms to show that he couldn't move the van, the cop kicked his bike stand down, and cutting off his motor, stepped up to the window and said, "*Sus papeles.*"

"*¡Un momentito! ¡Yo no estoy manejando!*" Roger said, frustrated by his clumsy Spanish. He pointed to the store. "*El chofer está en la tienda.*" Roger started to scoot across the seat to go call Craig, then remembered he couldn't move with the still smoldering kif pipe on the seat. He cupped his hands and shouted, "Craig! Craig!" then honked the horn, afraid he was acting too nervous.

Roger stayed tense even when Craig came running out of the store followed by Penny and Ruth. After listening to the cop, they got quickly into the van and Craig pulled back onto the highway.

When the van had only moved a half a block away from the cop, Roger said, "If you risk my life again, Ruth, I'm going to slap you! I don't care if you are a girl. You're playing too heavy. I won't let anybody put me in jail! I'll get them if they do. That goes for you, too!"

Ruth's lips looked puffy and sullen, but she didn't say anything.

"How did she risk your life?" Craig asked.

"By lighting that pipeload of kif and leaving it still burning with me just as the cop came up to the van, that's how!"

"You don't have to talk so mean, Roger," Ruth said.

"Whatta ya mean, mean?" Roger screamed. "You just risked my life! And you wanted that George, or whatever the fuck his name was, to ride with us, too! You act as if you don't even have any dope in this van and don't have a thing to worry about!"

"We could have given the guy a ride," Craig said without taking his eyes off the highway.

"And what about the dope in the van? What about the cop coming up right now? What if he got suspicious and took us in? You don't know that George! He could have been an undercover cop! I almost got busted on that boat! Don't you understand?"

Roger could see Craig's gray, colorless eyes in the rearview mirror, but Craig kept staring at the highway and wouldn't meet Roger's eyes or glance back at him.

"Did any of you get any rumbles when we came through?" Roger shouted.

Ruth turned to look back at him, her eyes very large and dark in the shadow, with the bright backdrop of the wide windshield behind her.

"Did you have any problems, Penny?"

"No," she said.

"Did you, Ruth?"

"No."

"And you had two hash cookies, right? What about them?"

"The guard just glanced in our van and waved us through," she said.

"That's what I thought! Everybody here brought dope into this country and not one of you even got a rumble."

Roger waited for that fact to sink in, then said, "Yet, I'm the only one who didn't bring any in, and I'm the only one who got the shit scared out of him."

"What do you mean?" Ruth asked, but looked out the windshield when he looked at her.

"I mean that as soon as you guys left, I was surrounded by five men in black raincoats, and that little one-eyed man who sat next to me on the poop deck followed me down into the line and even cut into line behind me when I tried to get away from him."

"That doesn't mean they were cops," Craig said in his low, common-sense voice, as if he were talking to an irrational child.

"It means something to me," Roger said. "And right now that big guy would be listening to every word we said about how much dope we carried in, and you two guys have seven kilos of high-grade kif pollen stashed in this van!"

No one answered for a few moments. The motor droned. The landscape passed, and Craig finally peered past the plastic temple of his glasses at the rearview mirror and said, "But Ruth still didn't mean anything by it, Roger."

"Goddamn! I've told you before! I don't give a fuck what she means! I care about what she does! I care about what she does to me! To meeee!" Roger screamed. "I don't want to go to jail for smoking a lousy little bit of pot!"

Nobody answered. There was only the drone of the motor. Roger felt as if he was the guilty one again, making everybody suffer, when all he wanted to do was survive to love and write.

"Goddamnit!" he finally shouted. "Let me out of here! Get me to a fucking airport and I'll fly to Paris! You can keep that fucking pound of mine! I'll buy me some new dope in Paris. Get me to an airport. I want out of here!"

Penny slipped her arm around him and said, "Let's stick it out to Barcelona, Roger. It's only a couple of days, and we can catch a train from there. You don't have to cross any more borders with them."

Roger let himself sink back down onto the seat, then said, "Okay. Two more days. Then Barcelona. I don't want to pass one more cop with Ruth. She's acting like a kid again. I'm afraid I'll slap her right in front of the cops if she gets me busted. I'm not jiving. Just Barcelona, that's all, if I can survive that long."

Episode Ten

A HARD ROAD

1

Bent over from his heavy backpack, briefcase and typewriter, the thump of Roger's hiking boots on the wooden steps of the Hotel Du Paris kept time like a slow drumbeat to the rhythm of his stride. The sweat on his face ran into the droplets of mist that spotted it, and he had to squint to keep the water out of his eyes when he looked up at the third-floor railing and saw how far he had to go. He kept telling himself that he was in Paris, in the Latin Quarter, the magic land of the great writers of the Lost Generation and of all the great painters of the nineteenth century; the original Bohemians. He should be happy, not on guard. Craig said Hemingway had lived here!

He looked down at Penny trudging past the shower and toilet doors on the landing below him. She had wanted to catch a cab instead of the subway. But he was really afraid they'd have cabbies waiting for them, and would know where they were going that way. So he and Penny had walked as long a distance from the subway to the hotel as they had from the train to the subway. Though he realized, even as they walked, that the cops would know where he was anyway, since Ruth and Craig had been the ones who had given them the address of the hotel. The plump, pretty, olive-skinned concierge was probably also notified. Yet, when he turned down the hall on the third floor, he didn't regret the walk even after a mile in the drizzle. It kept him on the edge of privation and hardship, kept him tough and sure of himself, confident he could take care of himself in Paris.

Still, he didn't know whether to be joyful or careful when he pushed open the door of the room with his briefcase and crossed the slightly sloping floor of the long room to the bed.

Penny put her bags on the wooden table between the door and bed, locked the door, jerked off her seaman's cap. She then turned to him and, smiling, said, "Aren't you glad we're in Paris together?"

Roger felt her joy. He wanted to agree with her, but he was afraid they were just waiting for him in Paris. And he couldn't forget that smirk on Ruth's face the whole trip from Marrakesh, not even when Penny walked over and sat down next to him, put her arm around his waist and said, "I'm glad we're here together. I'm glad I didn't come alone. Now, we get to have another chance at making it."

He nodded, but still didn't answer. Then he sniffled.

"You ought to dry your face off. And your hair, too, so you don't catch cold. You're sniffling," she said.

When he didn't move, she ran her fingers through his damp hair and said, "You have pretty ringlets. If you were a girl, you'd be lucky."

She made him smile. "I'd have it made, huh?" he said, stood up and jerked his towel out of his backpack, wiped his face, walked over to the sink by the window and hung it on a towel rack. Then he glanced out the window, which overlooked a small park. He gazed at the gray, damp sky over the rooftops of the stone buildings of the Sorbonne on the other side of the park and the gray apartment buildings just across the street which reminded him of Zola's novel *Gervaise*. Not a single person walked in the park, and only a few cars moved down the wide street between the park and the Sorbonne. He noticed, then, a storefront window on the street level of the building across the street with big red pictures of Mao and Che Guevara in it and suddenly realized that he was in a bourgeois democracy again. A rush of warm feeling filled him. He had escaped from the fascist state of Spain for the second time, and he was...almost...free.

He turned to see Penny standing near him, her arms out to him. He hugged her, aching with the thought that she loved him and that he had almost lost her. And now she was standing in a room in the Latin Quarter of Paris with him.

"Aren't you glad we're here in Paris together?" she said again, then pulled back to look at him, still smiling. When he smiled back, she began to kiss him around one ear, down around his neck, and up to his other ear, making his flesh tingle and pop up with goose pimples.

"I love you," she said, kissing him from his ear to his mouth, keeping her body pressed tight to his. Then she pulled him over to the bed, staring into his eyes all the time, her own face pink with anticipation. She pushed him down on mattress, fell on it next to him, and began to caress his body, while still kissing him.

When she pulled up his turtleneck shirt and kissed his right nipple, he cringed with the tickling thrill and felt his dick harden instantly. She then unbuckled his belt and the iron buttons of his Levis, reached down and grabbed his dick with her whole hand, then pulled it out of his pants so that it stuck straight up and began to pump her hand up and down on it.

His body twisted around with the thrill, until he couldn't stand it anymore and he slid his hand down into her pants and cupped her box in his hand, then stuck his finger into the moist, tight warmth and began to pump it back and forth inside her. Then she turned over on him, still holding his dick, his finger still in her, and kissed him with an open mouth, giving him her full tongue.

2

There was a sense of spirituality, almost like cellophane crackling around him when he awoke in the morning. The sun shone through the wall-high windows of the breakfast nook that overlooked the Sorbonne. He got out of bed and walked to the window. High on the third floor, he looked over the rooftops of the great university. It was like a new day for him.

He turned when Penny came up behind him, her face a pink smile.

"Let's go out and look for the French edition of your book," she said.

"What makes you think it's published here? My agent never answered my letter about it," he said.

"That doesn't mean it's not published," she said. "You don't know, Roger. We can look for it while we walk around. I want to walk around anyway. Come on, let's look. We might find it."

She pulled off her pajamas and started sponge bathing herself between the sink and the bidet, moving around nude like some wraith of the past, a ghost of all the nudes that

Rodin sculpted. She was so vivacious, he said, "All right. Why not? They said it would be published in France. Let's go!"

He rushed to use the toilet on the landing and pay seventy-five *centimes* for the shower, then back up to the room where Penny had already made his breakfast of honey, tea and wheat germ.

Paris. He was in Paris. And Penny was gorgeous. Her eyes softened with sexual allure in the shadow of her long, thick lashes when she looked at him. It seemed that he knew her by her sex, by the moistness of her box and the swell of her pale breasts, the way she pumped against him and wrapped her legs around his for leverage for her thrusts. Yesterday, they had made long, slow love in the gray light of the rainy day and had heard the soft patter of the rain when they slept. They had awakened only to eat sardines and crackers from her pack, then fell back in bed to sleep.

He saw only her love when she looked at him and reached out and grabbed his hand. "Let's go walk around the Sorbonne and see if we can find it there so we can have some fun, Roger!" she said, and smiled when he nodded his head. Then wearing his brown corduroy jacket, turtleneck shirt and sweater, hiking boots and Levis, and Penny her turtleneck, jeans and cape, they walked out and he locked the door behind them.

The wide wooden stairs that led down in long flights seemed to echo with Roger's sense of time and history. It spoke of the long-dead, great writers who had walked down them. Roger didn't really know the names of any of them except for Hemingway, but Craig had told him that other Lost Generation writers had lived in the Hotel Du Paris.

Outside, the street was still damp but sun-washed like a watercolor, clean and sparkling and cool. The gray-brown buildings of the Sorbonne were only a short block away, but Roger had to stop and stare into the big store windows of the Young Communist League at the blood-red background of the Che Guevara poster. Just the fact that it was displayed gave him a thrill after what he had suffered at the hands of the Spanish fascists and the despots of Morocco.

Che looked like Jesus taken down from the cross when he died: his beautiful gaunt face, the long dark beard, the large, soft eyes, eyes of a saint, eyes of a martyr. Mao, on the other side, looked like a fat general who thrived too well on the good life of success.

Che had gotten fat in Cuba, too, and didn't look like Jesus there, but here, now, in this classic photo, lying spread out on the table where he'd been shot, he looked like a beautiful apparition, his eyes slightly parted and dreamy, distant but beautiful. Roger turned to Penny, who met his gaze, but pulled him away. Though he went along with her, he couldn't forget the sadness he'd felt when Che died.

At the very next corner, when they turned to walk onto the Sorbonne, he saw a big khaki-colored bus parked just across the street. The smoked-glass windows kept him from seeing inside until they got up near the open door. Four cops in riot gear were playing cards next to a row of automatic rifles behind the driver's seat. Across the street was another bus with a couple of cops standing outside the open doors, sunning themselves and chatting with each other. A chill tingled over him. The political cops were here, too, like a crack in the beautiful, quaint veneer of the Latin Quarter.

When he looked further down the street, he saw a bus at every other corner, at every other intersection, with cops outside some of them. It looked like the whole campus was ringed by cops and had been since the student revolt the year before. The battle he had left in America to stop the war in Vietnam still went on here, and he had to remember to stay on guard and protect himself.

When he and Penny started down one of the streets onto the campus, a loud roar made him turn to see two more buses driven by cops. He wasn't the only one who'd been fighting, he could see. At least, he didn't fight alone.

"Don't let the soldiers bother you, Roger," Penny said. "It's not like Spain."

He nodded and turned onto the campus, trying to do what she said as they walked deeper onto it looking for a bookstore. He did enjoy walking in the sun, squandering the time. They walked for an hour, looking at the big buildings, mostly nineteenth-century construction, without seeing anything even resembling a bookstore. Finally, deep within the Sorbonne, they found themselves in the middle of a modern complex of buildings four stories high. They were pale-blue and white with hundreds of windows. Paper banners with political slogans hung across them. Roger hoped they might find a store

and his book, too. It was possible. It could have been published without anybody telling him about it.

Roger was surprised to see students milling around tables
set up outside and inside the foyer of a cafeteria, looking at
pamphlets, politicking and engaging in spontaneous debate. It
was the first evidence of large-scale student political activists
he'd seen, and he wondered where the cops might be sta-
tioned, since he couldn't see any around. On their wandering,
rambling walk, he and Penny must have passed ten or twelve
buses full of cops parked at different places in the Sorbonne.
But he was pleased to see that there were still signs of political freedom here in spite of all the cops.

Roger and Penny stopped in front of the glass wall of the
foyer and stared up at the large posters of Mao, Castro, Che
and Marx. He began to hope that he could really be free in
Paris, here on the campus of a great university. He then
looked inside the box-like passage toward the main room of
the cafeteria, trying to spot a bookstore, and noticed a tall student with horn-rimmed glasses watching him from behind a
table. Their eyes met and the student smiled, so Roger nodded
his head in greeting and watched the student step around the
table and walk out to him.

"You're an American, aren't you?" he asked in perfect
English. "Don't you live by the Hotel Du Paris?"

Roger hesitated before answering, on guard again, then
answered, "Yes, I'm an American, and yes, I live at the Hotel
Du Paris. How did you know?"

"I saw you looking in our office window—The Young Communists—across the street from the hotel, about an hour ago.
I thought you were an American then. What do you do? I
mean, you seemed to be interested in our...place!"

Again Roger didn't answer right away, suddenly wary of
being suckered. He glanced at Penny, but she was reading a
poster. The student's explanation sounded reasonable, so
Roger said, "I'm just glad to see a society free enough to allow
dissent! I've been in Spain and Morocco, where everybody
keeps their mouths shut. Though it still looks like a war zone
here with buses and buses of cops everywhere."

"The Sorbonne has been occupied since the student revolt
last year," the student said.

Roger waited a moment, then said, "At least it's in the
open though. In Spain it was undercover. There's no tolerance

of dissent. It makes me realize what I'm fighting for and against. It's really a war! But it's fought more fairly here. This is a Paris in the turmoil of revolt. Yet they give you the liberty to have a chance. I'm back in a bourgeois democracy, even if it's a democracy at war with itself. You make me feel that I'm not alone. You give me hope!"

"I seeee," the student said slowly. "I like your ideas, but what do you do? Why is this so important? Most Americans, tourists, have little interest. Why are you different?"

"I'm a novelist. I write books about outlaws in America. I'm writing a book now about a radical writer who fights all sides in a campus riot. You make me realize once again that the whole society's at war, in turmoil, not just me. When I see you students aroused, battling, I get hope once again. It's invigorating to be here in Paris. I read all about your revolt soon after our student revolt in the U.S. It's all very exciting. It's the authorities against the students who want to make them cut up the pie more fairly. It's all about money in the end, though I see it in a spiritual way, like you do, except I express it, or try to, through my art."

"Oh, very interesting," the student said, smiling again. "Are any of your books published in French? I'd like to read them."

Roger shook his head, regretting the letter to his agent over that question, a question never answered. "Not that I know of," he replied. "But that's what I'm trying to find out right now. Whether or not my first book's been published over here."

"Why don't you come back and talk to my comrades and see if they might know about it. But you won't find it on campus if it is. You'll have to look in the Latin Quarter," the student said, and gestured with his hand for Roger and Penny to enter before him.

Roger stalled, wondering if he was falling into another trap, if the encounter was as spontaneous as it seemed, but then walked in.

"I am Anton and this..." Anton said, stepping past Roger and Penny to a table where a pretty, slender girl with long blonde hair sat, "is Nicole."

"Hello," she said. "American students?"

"Novelist and radical," Anton said, his brown eyes very large behind the big horn-rimmed frames of his glasses. "He writes about outlaws and is writing about a student riot in America. He wants to see if his book's been published in France."

"About outlaws or radicals?" she asked with a shrill tone to her voice that was a sharp as her features.

"A radical in the United States is an outlaw," Roger said. "Right now I'm writing about some student revolutionaries." He stopped and looked from the girl to the guy and switched the subject off himself. "I really would like to know what happened during your *real* revolt last year."

When neither of them spoke, he said, "I fought the police by myself, an undercover war, in which they held all the cards. You guys had the whole university and labor unions with you. You did the real thing. Tell me what it was like. I want to know from a personal view, not the so-called objective generalizations of the press."

Anton's soft brown eyes seemed to fill his horn-rimmed frames as if he really understood, then he said, "I reacted to the sensations. When I was up on the barricades and could see the tear gas welling toward me and smell the sting in the air before it even reached me, hear the yells of my comrades around me, it seemed as if I was experiencing life at its greatest. That was my reaction."

"No fear?" Roger asked, squinting through his dark glasses, remembering how scared he'd been when the riot troops charged down on them at State College.

"No," Anton said, shaking his head. "I was much too excited to feel fear."

"And what did you do when you weren't actually fighting? Here at the Sorbonne, I mean."

Anton nodded as if he liked the question and said, "I see you really are writing about a student revolt."

"We set up revolutionary classes in everything that was pertinent to our revolutionary society," Nicole said. "We had classes on the intellectual and society, on labor unions and classes on woman's role in a revolutionary society and on how to administer a revolutionary university." She sat back in her chair, cold blue eyes on him.

"We made a university that was relevant to our society, not one dedicated to only classics and scholarship, an ivory-tower syndrome."

"Ah, that sounds good," Roger said, liking her now in spite of the shrill tone of her voice, the surface coldness of her features. But still mistrustful, he asked, "Where are all the police now? Why can't I see them here? They're everyplace else!"

"They are with their buses on the closest street corner," she said, and smiled at him. Her blue eyes and blonde hair and tall, slender figure were almost beautiful. But her eyes were too cold for him and her facial features too narrow and sharp to be really pretty. She lacked Latin femininity. Still, she was attractive and committed, and he enjoyed being around her and hoped Penny didn't get offended. But Penny, too, listened to Nicole, apparently just as interested as he was.

"Well, the CIA must be around here undercover then," he said, still mistrustful, and saw Nicole's eyes blink as if he had either frightened her or exposed her. He felt sure then that he'd touched something hidden in her which kept him wary of the whole scene. He spun around when a shaggy-haired student with a long, dark, hawklike face, wearing a black coat with sharp lapels and tails that could fit in a movie set of a Dickens' novel, stopped at the table and said, "What will the workers think about this waste of their money?" He swept his arm around at the idling students and the banners up on the walls of the building complex.

"What's the big deal about the workers?" Roger asked, thinking party man, dogmatist. "In America, the workers are the enemy at this point in history. When we see the hard hats coming, we run."

"Without the workers there will be no revolution," Anton said.

"I can grant that," Roger said. "But you needn't be sentimental. If the workers get enough money here as the skilled craftsmen do in America, there won't be any revolution here either. They vote their pocketbook, and morals always runs a poor second. You need leisure to be moral. And don't forget, cops are working men. Don't sentimentalize an abstraction. The unions sold you out in the revolt last year, according to the newspapers."

"True. True," Anton said.

"How do the intellectuals fare over there?" Nicole asked.

"Right now they fare badly. The pressure's been on since Johnson took over. But now it's worse, with Nixon as president, according to what I've read in *Newsweek* and *Time* magazines. The students who demonstrated during the Johnson years are now being run off the campuses, and the only revolutionary proletarian group, the Black Panthers, are being shot down all over the country."

"Who are you?" the thin dark student asked.

"A somewhat radical American novelist," Roger answered, and had to smile at Penny.

"Did they run you off?" the student asked.

"You might say that. I've been arrested about ten times in my life, though I've never been in prison and the busts weren't for politics on the surface, though they were certainly for rebellion. And, besides, if you're a famous radical you can get hired at other universities if you get fired, but if you're an unknown, like me, then you starve when you lose your job."

"What's your name?" the student asked.

"Roger Leon."

"Roger Leon, hmmmmm. I've seen the name somewhere."

Roger tensed himself, alert for a trap again, but asked, "It wasn't in French, was it?"

"Yesss, I believe I saw a book by an American advertised in some publisher's list. I don't remember the publisher, but... That's it! I remember! Did you write a book about a street fighter?"

"Why, yes!" Roger said, his pulse quickening, beginning to hope it was true and not a trap.

"Then I saw it advertised only last week as an explosive novel by a young American. *Les Enfants de Bon Dieu*. I did see it. It was the only novel by an American. That's why I read the blurb."

The thin student was so excited that Roger wanted to believe him and discount his suspicions that this was a little skit all prepared for him, so he asked, "What does the title mean?"

"The Children of God," Anton said.

"That doesn't sound like my book," Roger said, disappointed. "My book was called *Every Mutha's Son.*

Anton thought for a moment, his eyes up in the corners of his thick frames, then said, "But 'Les Enfants de Bon Dieu' means 'Every Mother's Son.'"

"Is that true?" Roger asked, and looked at Penny, who smiled, giving him hope again.

"That's correct," the dark student said. "That's what it means. Why don't you give a copy to our group? We would like that."

"Are you with this group?" Roger asked. "You seemed to be critical of this activity."

"I was merely playing the devil's advocate," the student said, and smiled.

"Why don't I get a copy for myself then?" Roger said, but still suspicious, asked, "Are you sure it said Roger Leon?"

"If I'm right, will you give us one?"

"Sure. But first I've got to get me one. If there is one."

All three of them smiled, and Nicole winked at him and asked, "Will you autograph it for us?"

3

A thin veneer of clouds covered the sun and the air was cool, so Roger kept his corduroy coat zipped and his gloves on to keep himself warm. As they walked along the Seine, he looked for his book in each of the bookstalls along the concrete railing of the Seine River. He longed for it to be true, that he was published in one of the greatest cities in the world—where he might even be able to meet the great Jean Genet, one of his outlaw heroes. He had visions of finally finding a home for himself here, where he'd be accepted, respected, and loved, where the writers would save him from the secret police, the same way they had joined Sartre to save Genet from a life sentence as an habitual criminal.

But Roger quickly tired of skimming blurred titles in a foreign language and of asking tight-lipped bookstand clerks if they'd heard of *Les Enfants de Bon Dieu*. With Penny following in her green cape, he pushed his way through the pedestrians browsing over the flat book counters and onto a bridge for a better view of the Seine, where he noticed the big, white-stone police station, a block long and several stories high, across the river from them. They'd passed it earlier and he had asked an American about it. He'd told them it was the jail. Now Roger thought of the bars inside, the jingling of the guards' keys, the hollow echoes of voices down the long corridors of cells, and felt fear quiver in his chest.

Then he turned and looked at Notre Dame cathedral. It was a block away, on the same side of the river as the jail, but upstream, next to a bend of the river. He could make out the row of bishops' heads high above the tall doors of the great cathedral. Stepping down off the bridge, he noticed a sign, *The Bookshop*, across the river from the cathedral, just on the other side of a little park, and he felt a pulse of hope rise in him again that he might find his book in there.

"That's the first bookstore we've seen, even if it is English. Come on," he said, pointing at it. They skirted through the tiny park and walked right into the small store.

The large window with its small Tudor-style squares flooded the inside with light as he walked down the aisle, skimming the books, hoping he might see his book in French, but saw only English titles and English and American imprints.

"Can I help you?" a middle-aged man with a white goatee and black beret asked.

"Looking for the French edition of a Forest Press book," Roger said.

"I have no books in French. All American and English. Which book?"

"*Every Mutha's Son*. I mean *Les Enfants de Bon Dieu*," Roger said, and sighed, shaking his head, beginning to doubt that it was even published in French.

"Don't have it," the man said, shaking his head, too. "Can I show you some other books?"

"I really wanted that book. I mean, I wanted to see if you had the French edition."

"You don't want to buy it?" the man said, and smiled, his goatee flicking like a bird's tail.

Roger had to smile, too, and glanced at Penny, who said, "He wrote it!"

"You're Roger Leon then?" the man said in a high-pitched voice, his white eyebrows peaking, nearly touching on his forehead with the question. "Read about your book in *Time* magazine," the man said, then stuck out his hand and took Roger's. "Pleased to meet you. My name is Guy Whiteman. I bought it as soon as it came out in French last week. It's a classic, the best book about a juvenile delinquent ever."

Pink with the flush of pleasure, Roger said, "Thanks! Can I see it! Do you have it with you? Here?"

Guy stood tall in front of him, very thin, in a vest and a heavy brown cardigan sweater and a white shirt open at the neck with a wrinkled but once fine ascot around his throat. He was lined, but in a pleasing way, and his pale, very pale, blue eyes were clear and almost transparent as water within their rims of wrinkles.

"Sure, why don't you come into my office and look at it?" he said, and looked around the store, glancing at a couple of customers browsing through the books. He then turned and led Roger and Penny back through the shelves to a small, closet-sized room. He reached on a shelf up above his desk and pulled down a shiny pink quality paperback book and handed it to Roger.

It shocked like electricity when he touched the shiny pink book. It was like the first time he had touched the first American edition. He had sent it to his son, who quickly lost it. Now, he held the rose-colored book in his hand, looked at his name on the thick, paperback cover, then the title, *Les Enfants de Bon Dieu*. It was a marvelous sight. Suddenly, Paris looked as rose-colored as the cover. James Jones lived here. He might even get to meet him. He glanced at Penny, her eyes wrinkled at the corners with smile lines.

Roger then turned the book over, but there was no picture on the back, and he glanced at the three paragraphs of script-like French, which he didn't try to decipher. He opened the pages and looked at the print, stared at the first paragraph and deciphered the French translation of the first few words. He tingled inside. He'd made it to Paris, and if they treated him fairly, he'd never go back to America. He noticed Penny looking over his shoulder at the book now, and he turned and handed it to her.

She skimmed both covers, then flipped open the first page and said, "Here's the publisher, Products Incorporated, Roger! Is it around here, Guy?"

She looked up at Guy, who nodded and said, "Not more than half a dozen blocks or so. You should be able to get a copy from them. Just go down the river to the next bridge after this, San Michele Boulevard, two blocks more on the other side of it, then up a block or two and you'll have it."

Guy smiled and Roger could see he had false teeth.

"I really appreciate it," Roger said, taking the book from Penny, then, handing it to Guy. "Thanks, Guy. Let's go, Penny!"

They started to turn around when Guy said, "Wait a moment!"

Roger faced him again in the tiny room, afraid of a trick.

"Would you like to read here? I have a reading about once a month. They're usually well-attended."

"Sure," Roger said. "When?"

"How about July first? In the evening at eight?"

Roger turned to Penny, who smiled.

"It sounds good to me," he said. "You know, this is my first day out in Paris, and I've seen all the students fighting for democracy. Quite a sight after being in Spain, where they imprison them for it. Then I heard from them about the publication of my book! Then I find it and you invite me to read! That's a lot of goodies for one day! All I've got to do is go find the publishing house now and it'll be a perfect day. I want you to know I appreciate it." Roger smiled and held out his hand and shook with Guy.

"Pleased to have you," Guy said.

"Say, how long have you been in Paris?" Roger asked, wanting to show some interest in him now and not just rush off.

"Twenty-four years. Since the end of World War II."

"My brother was here then!" Roger said. "He was a cultural attache to the U.S. Embassy here. He was a budding writer, too! I don't know where he lived, but it could have been around here! You didn't know him, did you? John Leon?" Roger smiled, anticipating another pleasing response when Guy's long, narrow face seemed to slide down to his goatee and his pale eyes hooded over. It was all so quick, but so convincing, Roger guessed he knew John was a homosexual and didn't want to be thought one himself. This meant he already knew about Roger and his brother and that's why he had the book! Which meant the cops had told him! They could guess he'd eventually end up in the only English bookstore in the Latin Quarter, just across the street from the landmark cathedral, Notre Dame. And if that was the case, then his book and the reading and the good luck, maybe the students, too, were all just another trap.

They all stood in a circle for a silent, stiff moment, then Roger said, "We better go see if we can find that publisher. Can we copy the address, Guy?"

Guy nodded and flipped the cover back to the title page.

4

When Roger saw the number 8 on the door of the red-brick building, one of the tiny shops pressed up against each other on the curving, narrow street, he wondered if it was a bad sign, that once he stepped inside, he'd be behind the eight ball. Guy's long face and hooded eyes when Roger asked about his brother John were still looming in his mind. Roger checked behind him for someone watching him, waiting for the person to appear, but saw no one, and he did feel some sense of satisfaction in finally finding the publisher of his book.

A beautiful blonde woman with short, straight hair stood behind a counter. Shorter than Roger in high heels, her blue eyes looked up at him as he stepped to the counter. She tilted her head and watched him approach, as if wondering what a hippy would want in a respectable place of business like hers, and asked, "Yesss?"

"Do you publish the novel, *Les Enfants de Bon Dieu*, by Roger Leon?" he asked.

"Yesss," she replied, tilting her head even more, sizing him up with one eye.

Still bothered by Guy's hooded eyes, he was of two minds: one engaged in action; the other watching, on guard, trying to analyze the emotions on her mannequin-smooth face for any kind of ulterior purpose. "I'd like to know if I could have a few copies at a reduced, uh, author's rate," Roger said before she could shake her head.

She blinked, then before she could speak, he said, "I wrote the book in English. I'm Roger Leon."

Her head straightened up and she said, "One moment, pleassse," and stepped around the counter and hurried up some carpeted stairs.

Penny nudged Roger with her elbow and both of them grinned, then squeezed hands when she came quickly down the stairs and said, "Would you come upstairs, pleasssse."

She led them up the soft, thickly padded stairs to a carpeted floor of offices where a nice-looking man in his forties, tall and well-dressed, stepped toward Roger, holding out his hand and smiling.

"Pierre De Puy," he said, taking Roger's hand. A long, thin nose was the most prominent feature on his soft, round face.

"Roger Leon," Roger said, taking his hand, then gesturing with the other, said, "Penny Lawson."

"Hello," Pierre said to Penny, then pointed to an inner office. "Would you like to come in and sit down?"

He followed them in, opened a filing cabinet, pulled out a manila folder and sat down behind the desk. He flipped the folder open, spun it around so Roger could read it, and said, "As you can see, you've been published with some good names: D.H. Lawrence, Henry Miller and Nabokov, which certainly won't embarrass the high quality of your work."

Roger looked into his eyes, which were soft and brown, to see if he were trying to flatter him, but Pierre looked right back at him and added, "Unfortunately, though, there haven't been any reviews so far."

"Well, if it means I have to help publicize the book, I'm ready and willing."

"And I'm sure you'll do well," Pierre said.

Roger stood up to leave, wanting to get away, feeling like he'd just been kicked. "I think I'd better go."

"No, I don't think so," Pierre said. "Why don't you wait just a minute? I would like you to meet the translator of your novel. She also did the translation of James Jones' *From Here To Eternity*, and we have a nice gentleman agent in the offices who'd like to meet you, too. Wait here a minute, won't you? And I'll go get the two of them."

Roger sat back down, blushing with pleasure. Pierre returned with a very large man with a big, blond, walrus mustache and a tall, attractive, young blonde woman. "Hans Mahler and Beverly Mohr, meet Roger Leon and Penny Lawson," Pierre said in an economic manner that pleased Roger and made him relax a little. He wondered if they had been waiting for him though, since they were already in the office. It was all so neat.

"I suggest we all go out for a drink. But, first of all, I must say that Hans is a literary agent, and Beverly is a well-known translator with several great books to her credit already, including yours."

Pierre's brown eyes seemed as earnest as his voice, and Roger reached out and shook Hans' large hand with a tight grip. There were slight blue bags under his eyes as if he drank too much. He must have been about forty.

"I really enjoyed translating your book," Beverly said. "It was quite an experience for a woman. A genuine work that compares favorably with Jones' *From Here To Eternity*."

"Thank *you*, very much!" Roger answered, and, as everyone laughed, he guessed that she was only in her twenties. Her hair was almost as long as Penny's, but she wore high heels and conventional clothing.

"Say, should we go now and have that drink?" Pierre asked as he gave Roger a slip of paper. "By the way, here is James Jones' phone number. You call him."

Pierre led them down the stairs and out onto the winding street a couple of doors to a cafe. They all walked through to a back room with big, black, soft-leather booths and walls lined with mirrors. Roger, in spite of the pleasure of having James Jones' phone number in his pocket, felt instantaneously uncomfortable. There was almost no place he could look without seeing himself. He noticed, though, that Hans and Beverly both looked full at themselves, then at him before and after they sat down, and a horrible feeling came over him. Everywhere he looked he saw himself reflected in mirrors. He had to stare straight at a person to keep from looking into his own face. He felt as if he were in the nuthouse and everyone was looking at him, watching him, trying to see how he'd react.

"I just broke a contract for a writer on his second novel. He didn't like the contract, so I broke it for him and got him another publisher," Hans said, looking at Roger with pale-green, almost yellow eyes.

Roger couldn't think of anything to answer, and there was an embarrassing lull of silence. He felt it was an almost direct reference to his own situation with his agent and publisher, which meant that Hans, again, knew the predicament that he was in. He was being manipulated again in Paris. He flicked his broken thumb back and forth with a nervous motion, snapping the tendon over the lump at the base. Pierre glanced down at it with a severe look, and Hans switched his eyes away and looked at himself in the mirror again. But the waiter appeared, took their order and returned almost immediately with glasses of wine on a tray.

"On me, please," Roger said, and Pierre suddenly laughed and said, "A traveling writer who insists on paying the bill. He should be successful. And do you know that there is going to be a book fair in Marseille in a...two weeks?"

"That sounds nice," Roger said, finally beginning to feel welcome. "I'd like to go. It might be a good place to start advertising my book."

"Oh, yes," Pierre said. "We could start here first. We could put you on TV and get a nice review for you in *Le Penseur*."

"Is that an underground newspaper?" Roger asked, nervously snapping his thumb.

"There are no underground newspapers in France," Pierre said. "Everything is above ground here," he added, and laughed.

"Well, I'd like that," Roger said.

"Oh, I think you'd do well on TV. Articulate. You won't have any problems at all. All we have to do is set it up. Don't forget Jones' phone number. Why don't you call him tonight?"

Pierre pressed Roger's hand as if to impress the point on him, then his eyebrows went up like antennae in the middle of his forehead and he said, "You know Carson McCullers was one of our writers!"

"Beautiful," Roger said, thinking he still might make it in Paris.

"She enjoyed herself very much here in France. Maybe she drank a little too much. She was afraid of getting old, you know," Pierre said, and lifted his eyebrows again and stared at Roger's high hairline as if hinting that Roger better get with it while he was still young.

Roger snapped his crippled thumb back and forth again, feeling self-conscious again, and Penny nudged him with her knee to make him stop. Roger felt as if he wanted to scream when Hans suddenly looked away from the mirror and asked, "What are you working on now?"

Roger stopped snapping his thumb and sat up. "I'm writing about the underground war going on in America between the students and the secret police. It's all about the seizing of a college in San Francisco, where the secret police infiltrate and corrupt the movement and cheat and turn everybody against each other so much they cause a riot. I'm down close to the last couple of episodes. I've been working on it since I left San Francisco last September."

He couldn't help but smile, expecting them to smile and ask him questions about it, but Hans frowned, the thick folds of his cheeks sagging. Beverly's face was sharp and pointed, and Pierre avoided looking at him. Finally, Hans said, "What do you think of Malraux?"

All three of them seemed to lean in over the table and wait for his answer, making him feel as if everything, his whole future in Paris, depended upon his answer. Yet, he answered truthfully: "I love *Man's Fate*, but what's with Malraux? I thought he was a revolutionary. Has he forgotten his youth? The wars he fought for the people of China and Spain? He's become part of a semi-dictatorship by going along with De Gaulle's censoring of Olympia Press and Sartre's magazine."

Pierre's face suddenly lost its soft look. He pursed his mouth and took a deep breath, and his eyes looked hard and brittle as if covered by thick lenses. Both Hans and Beverly looked away, although neither of them looked in the mirrors.

"Evidently," Roger said. "it's uncool to criticize the Minister of Culture of my host nation or to refer to De Gaulle's government as a semi-dictatorship, even if the Latin Quarter is an occupied city."

His words seemed to send them into silent paroxysm of dislike. They all frowned and none of them spoke. They didn't like what he was writing about, and they didn't like what he said. He was right back where he started from. Trying to change the subject, he said, "I'm supposed to read at The Bookshop next week. Are you interested?"

"Of course," Pierre said. But he didn't smile, and then he added, "I really must be getting back to the office now." He stood up to leave.

5

"Hello?" Roger asked over the phone. "Is James Jones there?"

He had dialed James Jones' number as soon as he got back to his hotel room, but hadn't turned the lights on and stood in shadowy darkness of dusk. He would try to make up for scaring Pierre, try to prove that he could be a responsible writer who was willing to cooperate and work hard. He was in a shaky position, trying to survive under their pressure and yet be honest.

"Yes, but Jimmy's sleeping," a woman's voice answered, and Roger remembered the picture of the blonde beauty queen he'd seen in Time magazine when James Jones married her.

"Could you tell him when he wakes up that Roger Leon, who used to work with Lowny Handy, like he did, called. Pierre De Puy gave me his number and told me to call him."

"Oh? Is that so? Why don't you call him back? He should be up in about an hour."

Roger waited, feeling as if he was being tested, as if she was seeing how enthusiastic he was, if he was willing to pay homage to the "Great Man," in quotes, which meant a willingness to kiss ass, the first step in conforming to the powers that be that ruled the literary establishment. Man could be bought as well as broken. Then he answered, "I have to go out for dinner, but there's no reason why I can't call. But if I miss him, could he call me? Just in case?"

The line hummed with silence, and Roger said, "I'll call…"

"Give me the number," she said.

"Thank you, 84 32 22," Roger said, reading the number off the phone base. Then he heard the line click without a good-bye and he hung up with a weak feeling in his legs that he'd blown it. He was afraid he'd never know Jones, the wide-jawed guy with the broken nose and thinning hair who shot to fame with his World War Two novel, *From Here To Eternity*.

"Maybe we should eat here, Penny," he said. "Just in case he calls back, so I can be here. I said I'd call back in an hour, if he didn't call, but I don't want to take any chances."

"I'll go get something if you like, but it will take longer to eat," she said, looking up at him from the bed where she lay in dark shadow.

"Thanks, Penny. I'd rather do that," he said.

He watched the little traveling clock hands for the next hour. Penny had come back within a half-hour and prepared the ground steak, which took five minutes. She then fixed a salad, which was ready to eat ten minutes later, leaving fifteen minutes to go.

"I don't want to eat until I talk to him, Penny. The steak won't be ready for a while, anyway," he said. He paced back and forth in the slowly darkening room, watching the hands of his wrist watch until an hour was up. He was vaguely aware that *they* had him on his toes, that *they* were running his life.

Roger dialed the number again and waited. The phone rang, a low buzz on the line. Then it rang again and again and again and again and again and again and again. When it rang fifteen times, he hung up and bitterness welled up in him. He was being punished for his political views and his non-cooperation. He was being taught his place. Penny turned on the portable lamp on the table for dinner.

"Turn it off, will you?" he asked, and sat down to eat his salad in the fading daylight, in total silence, catching sad glances from Penny every once in a while. He finished his ground steak in darkness. Soon, only the street lights gave light to see by in the room, and Penny laid down on the bed and appeared to fall asleep.

Roger walked around the dark room as she slept, seeing her face down on the mattress, feeling the slow suffocation of their love. It was like a slow constriction of his breathing, heavy in his left side, his belly muscles bunched up so tight it felt as if a fist was doubled up down there. Waiting, waiting, and hoping, really hoping that the phone might ring, that it would ring. On principle, he could not call back again himself. They would not make him play that game. He suffered over his cross, but he was determined to carry it all the way.

6

"Sign that," Michelle, the blonde publicity girl, said, and pointed at the sheet in front of her. When he looked up and laid the pen down, she stared in his eyes and said, "You are not to give these copies to any person but those who can help you publicize the book!"

She lifted six pink copies of the book, tied with string, onto the counter. Her stare was as hard as the tone of her voice, as shocking, though she hadn't done more than glance at him one time since he'd entered the office in his best black

polyester T-shirt, clean summer Levis, and lightweight sandals.

As cold and pretty as a mannequin with her pointed nose
and pale skin and blonde hair, she twisted her red lips in a
snarl as she said, "Mr. De Puy will not be able to attend your
reading at The Bookshop, and, furthermore, you will not be
able to attend the book fair in southern France. There is no
room for you."

He stepped back with his books. He was hurt, like taking
a hard shot from a big guy, glad his dark glasses covered his
eyes. He saw her look down at his bare toes then scan his body
upwards to his face, her lips still twisted.

"All right," he said, taking another step back without
turning around, as if he couldn't break away from her gaze, as
if hypnotized for a few scathing seconds.

7

"Guy," he said, "I'm not giving that reading. I'm getting
out..." He stopped, seeing the wounded twist of the older
man's mouth, and he was sorry. But he wasn't going for any
dangling carrot at the end of the line anymore. He wasn't
going to start catering to politicians now, especially literary
ones, and that included James Jones. Not when he'd been
fighting so long at such cost, with a broken hand and a black
eye.

"I'm sorry, Guy, but I've got personal reasons," he said,
and turned around to walk out.

8

He saw the publicity girl, Michelle, coming out of the
Young Communist offices across the street on high heels as he
typed standing up. His typewriter was just at chest level, and
he had to bend his neck to see the page well. In a close-fitting
short tan coat, short blonde hair exposing her pale neck, she
stood on the corner for about five minutes without once glancing up at his window.

He watched her all the time, mind teeming with the urge to open the window and call out to her, then run down the stairs and out onto the sidewalk and across the street to her to ask about his book.

But he knew they brought her around to tempt him because he hadn't ever called James Jones back or returned to the publisher's office. Because he'd cancelled his reading! Because he wouldn't stop writing on his novel! Because he was getting close to the end! To finishing it!

Though he could taste bitterness like blood in his mouth, he wouldn't call out, even when a cab pulled up and she stepped into the back seat with shapely legs. He'd broken forever with his publisher. There was no chance to make it in Paris as a writer now. But he'd finish his book! He'd finish his book!

9

Penny's mouth pursed just after they left the hotel for the American Express office, when Roger saw a girl who looked like Anne Marie and couldn't help staring at her. She was the same small size, with blonde hair combed straight down like Anne Marie. Then when she turned and looked right into his eyes, her eyes were the same pale-brown color, and she even had the same slight bump in her nose and the cleft in her chin.

He grabbed Penny's hand right away and kept right on walking down the street, without looking back, to prove himself to Penny. He didn't trust girls when they flirted with him anyway, especially now, when it took dark glasses to cover the dark line still under his left eye, and when his nose was still a little thick between the eyes from the punches he caught. He was sure the girls had been put up to it, that they didn't really like him. Instead of making him feel loved or wanted, they made him feel like an unattractive fool.

He stared down at his crippled hand, holding Penny's hand. It looked unsightly up close. The thick lump on the middle knuckle of the index finger was still there, with a pink scar in the middle of it from the ulcerated sore that had developed in the cast. And the very tip of the finger was bent and he couldn't straighten it without using his left hand. The lump at the back of the thumb, which he could see well even down below him now, gave his whole hand a lopsided look and made him want to cover it with his black glove or stick it in his pocket when someone glanced at it. Though not always. Sometimes, he didn't care. He did now.

He didn't feel attractive to women, and when he and Penny got on the subway and a slender blonde girl pushed into him as she got off, he looked down into another version of Anne Marie's face, the same pale-brown eyes and bump in the nose. He wanted to hide his face so she wouldn't see how ugly he looked. When he turned to stare back at her, she turned on the platform to look back at him, too, and his heart sped up with longing for her as the train pulled away.

"She's gone now, you know. We might as well sit down; you can't see her anymore," Penny said. He spun around to face her, feeling that he'd played the fool again.

He stayed on guard on the subway ride through the smooth, soundless purr of the Paris metro. He was afraid that he might see another girl who looked like Anne Marie and might stare again, fall for the ruse and get Penny really mad at him this time. He was caught in the web again. They wanted him to lose Penny and find himself alone in Paris.

She glanced up at him from her seat next to him, as if wondering what he was feeling for her. He made up his mind right then not to look at the next girl who looked like Anne Marie to prove his love for Penny. But as soon as they walked up onto the low-ceilinged mezzanine floor of the American Express office, a small blonde girl in dark glasses and a long tan coat walked toward him, stuffing some letters in her purse, as if aiming for the stairway behind him after getting her mail. She snapped her purse shut, looked up and stared straight at him through her large dark glasses. He could almost swear it was Anne Marie and wondered if he should say hello. Her sunglasses were so large and dark, he couldn't see the eyes behind them without staring at her. He turned quickly away to follow Penny to the Poste Restante window without looking back.

"That was Anne Marie in those dressy clothes, wasn't it?" she said as they got in line. She pulled her letter to her mother and father out of her purse.

"I thought so," he said. "I thought she was going to talk to me. So it must have been her."

She put her face right in front of his. "If you had talked to her, I would have left you right then," she said.

"That's not fair," he said. "Why can't I be expected to say hello to her? I know her. The only reason I didn't was I wasn't sure it was her."

"I don't care. I would have left you," Penny said in a dry tone.

10

Her face was soft and sensuous in the faint light that came through the curtained windows from the street lamps below them. He could hear the nighttime traffic picking up again with the mild night. People were going out to the cafes, but he still hurt from the whole day. The carrot had now become a club that hit him when he tried to take a bite. And Penny wouldn't talk to him. She didn't speak throughout dinner, and they both went to bed in the darkness when they finished. He wanted to talk to her about Anne Marie, but he didn't want to talk about anything important when he felt so negative. He was afraid the room was bugged, sure of it.

"Let's go for a walk," he said.

"I don't want to," she said from the other side of the bed.

"I'm too down in here. I want to get out." He wouldn't say *talk* to her in the room.

"Go on and go then. Maybe you'll see Anne Marie, and you can talk to her when I'm not around, since you seem to want to."

She stared at him from her pillow for a long time. He wasn't sure if she was really looking right at him or in his direction, for her eyes were in the shadows and he couldn't see where they were focused. He ached inside. He wanted her to know how sorry he was for hurting her feelings, and that she should go out with him and let him tell her what he really felt about Anne Marie and all of those look-alike blondes. Then she could tell him what she thought. But he held it in, because of the suspected bug in the room and because he didn't want to fight with her.

Finally, she said, "You'd know if it was Anne Marie because she's so pretty."

"I'll stay with you," he said, touched by her honesty, and reached out and put his hand on her waist.

She pressed his hand with her fingers for a moment, then let go and said, "No, I want you to go out. I don't want you to stay in. And if you see her, talk to her. Get it out of your system, at least. Find out who you really love: her or me."

"I know who I really love," he said. "But I do want to go out. I feel depressed in here."

"Go out and have some fun then," she said. "I'd rather be alone."

"Do you really mean that?" he asked.

"Yes, I do. I mean it. Go on out. You don't have to stay in here. I want to rest. I'm tired."

"From all the walking today?"

"From everything," she said, and closed her eyes.

11

He stood on the corner near The Bookshop and the bridge in the little park, watching the people crowd the cafes and the wide sidewalks, wondering what was going to happen to him, afraid of the unknown, yet wanting to have some fun, maybe even see Anne Marie. The pattern of seeing her that day made him guess he'd see her tonight, or somebody who looked like her, especially if the room was bugged. Yet, he would enjoy seeing her, and he found himself in a funny position: courting danger just because he wanted to be happy and have fun like any normal person, any tourist in Paris.

He had kept himself from going back into The Bookshop, although there was nothing else to do. He hardly drank when he was writing a book, and he busied himself now watching the crowds, listening to a long sax solo float out of a jazz club across the brightly lit street. A small blonde girl with long hair came out of a cafe on a corner a couple of darkened doors from The Bookshop, flipped a cigarette into the gutter and stepped off the curb. He watched her cross the street, torn between calling out "Anne Marie!" and keeping silent. He was sure it was her this time. But he mistrusted Penny's words now, too. Was she pushing him onto Anne Marie so she could break up with him?

Was Penny collaborating with the police against him? He thought of Che Guevara and Tanya, who was supposed to be spying on the Cuban revolutionary for the Russian KGB, even though she died with him.

He watched the girl, determined not to call out, determined to let her walk away. But the girl stopped at the little cafe across the street and sat down at a sidewalk table. Her long hair hung down over her face so he couldn't see it well, and he began to doubt it was Anne Marie. Still he got so curious that he started across the street to find out. As he stepped up onto the sidewalk, he saw her staring down at her cup and recognized the smooth sheen of Anne Marie's face. He caught his breath and held it until he stopped next to the table. "Anne Marie?" he asked.

His heart beat hard when she looked up and said, "Roger! It's so good to see you!"

Her heavy lids gave a sexy slant to her soft eyes, and the counterplay of lights from the street and the cafe highlighted her high cheekbones and the cupped shadows in the hollows under them.

"Sit down," she said as she reached up, grabbed his hand and pulled him down onto the chair next to her. He found himself wanting to press his mouth down on her pink lips.

"How are you?" she asked, but before he could answer, she stared down at the crippled hand she was holding and held onto it even when he pulled on it. "How does it feel? Does it still hurt?"

Moved by her words, he let her hold it, saying, "No. It doesn't ache anymore, only if I hit it against something or pick some heavy thing up in the wrong way. It works all right, too. It's just a crooked lump yet, that's all. Just like this dark ring still hasn't gone away yet, either. See?"

He pointed to the shadow under his eye with his left hand.

She squinted at it, then pressed his cupped hand in hers and said, "They really hurt you, didn't they?"

He swallowed, unable to answer at first. He was moved by her sympathy, the first time anybody besides Penny had even hinted that he'd been wronged. It was as if she'd plucked a heart string. He reached out and covered her other hand with his. Brimming with feeling, he said, "Yes! Yes! They really did! Do you know that the doctor pointed a gun right between my eyes and pulled the trigger three times?"

She shook her head as if it were unbelievable and gripped both of his hands.

"And when I left Spain, they even followed me to Morocco!"

"The Spaniards?" Anne Marie asked in a slightly doubtful tone.

"Yes!" Roger said in a loud voice, trying to convince her. "And you know something? You're the first person I've told this! See that big white marble building across the river? That's the Paris police station, and yet here I am able to tell you this!"

Anne Marie glanced down the river where the very top of the white building showed, then looked at him again, her face alive with the counterplay of lights, her slanting eyes glittering as if she were intensely interested. There was a constant buzz of voices from the other tables on the wide sidewalk, which was crowded all the way to the corner with people. Only a couple of cars were moving down the street.

"If I talked to you like this in Spain, if I dared, the cops would show up and stop me. They would. The cops would show up. That's not so crazy. You know how they are in Spain. Everybody's quiet. *¡Tranquilo! ¡Tranquilo!*' they always say, and pucker up their lips and press their fingers against them to shush you. They'd put me in jail for talking like this in Spain! They'd be around so fast, your head would spin!"

"Maybe you shouldn't talk so loud, Roger," Anne Marie said, and squeezed his hand again.

He stopped and stared at her, and she smiled, showing her slightly crooked front teeth, and he felt love for her fill him. Only Penny would warn him like that. He felt the urge to kiss her again and stared at her mouth for a while, then looked up at her eyes, so soft and heavy-lidded and sensual that he sat there without speaking for a long time while she held his hand.

Finally, the screeching, "Hiiii-loooooo, hiiiiii-looooooo, hiiii-ii-looooo," of a police siren made him turn and see a Black Maria rolling over the bridge from the police station toward him. He watched and waited for it to pass, but it pulled right up next to the curb, parallel to his table, with its lights blinking and its siren still whining. A cop in a blue uniform jumped out each side of the wagon, then they stood next to each other in the street, staring at him, trying to scare him into silence. Threatening him! They were threatening him so he'd shut up! He couldn't believe it! They had to be bugging the table or she was wired! Then he realized that Anne Marie was staring at *him*, not at the cops, as if to see if he were frightened! The cops stared at him for one long minute then got back in their Black Maria and drove away. Roger pulled his hand free, stood up, waved once at her and walked off.

12

Anne Marie was out on the sidewalk in front of his hotel as soon as he stepped out the next afternoon. He was sure she was waiting for him, that she was bait for him. Yet, when she waved at him and caught his attention with her heavy-lidded eyes, with her straight blonde hair glistening in the sunlight, and her perfectly shaped, tanned thighs, she looked so exquisitely pretty in her brown miniskirt, his heart started beating fast. And when he walked up to her, he found himself speaking nicely, even apologetically to her: "I didn't want to stay around last night. That police wagon...I..."

"I understand. It's all right," she said, making him like her instantly. "Why don't you walk with me?"

"Uh... Where you going?" he asked.

"Home," she said, smiling at him, arousing him with the slanting sexiness of her large brown eyes. She then turned and stepped away, forcing him to fall in step with her.

They're starting all over again, he told himself. But he kept walking down the broad sidewalk with her anyway, across the street from the little triangular park, toward busy St. Michelle Boulevard and the moss-green ruins of the Bastille.

"Where do you live?" he found himself asking, expecting a lie from the evasive way she turned and stared at the busy traffic of the big intersection ahead.

"I keep house for a bachelor," she finally said.

Roger felt a little sag of disappointment, yet wondered why he cared, if he thought she was bait. Still, he asked, "Do you make love to him, too?"

She blinked but kept staring straight ahead without answering him. He walked silently along next to her toward the intersection, busy with afternoon traffic and crowds of people. Then, telling himself that he had no right to care, that she wasn't his, he smiled to hide his feelings and make her feel better. She smiled back as if they shared some intimate secret, then, with one quick motion of her hand, she grabbed the elastic band of her panties through her skirt and pulled it up and snapped it against her flesh so that he could hear it pop as well as see the motion. He was suddenly alert again, remembering what it was all about.

"Well, I guess I'll see you around sometime," he said, and stopped at the corner.

She turned big hurt eyes on him. Then the heavy lids quickly covered them again, and though a slight frown that barely creased her smooth complexion tightened her eyebrows, she waved slightly with a single flick of her hand.

He watched her walk away, taking his regrets with her, wishing he could let himself love her. But he whispered to himself, "It was just a game, pure sex without love, without a feeling of real love."

Still, he felt the ache in his chest.

13

Anne Marie was standing on the corner right across the street from Roger's hotel room with Robey, staring up at his window where he was typing standing up, his typewriter propped on the table drawer. Robey stood a little sideways. He looked like a suspended question mark above the sidewalk, his lanky body had such a pronounced slouch to it with his sunken chest and hunched shoulders. Roger wanted to push the curtain aside and wave to them, but there was no way they could have known his address or exactly where he lived but through the police. And there was no way *they* wouldn't know that he knew it. They were being open about it. She wasn't pretending the way she did yesterday. *They* were giving him a signal through the invisible wall they had wrapped around him: If you don't take her, Robey will. But he couldn't risk it, and he leaned back from the window, away from his typewriter so they couldn't see him through the gauze curtain. Anne Marie frowned as if she were straining to see him. Then she turned and looked at Robey, lifted one arm and wrapped it around Robey's neck. She kissed him on the mouth and put her arm around his waist. Robey put his arm around her and they walked up the street toward the Sorbonne, turned on the boulevard and went around the corner out of sight.

Roger ached a little. He wanted love. He wanted somebody who loved him so much they wouldn't cooperate with the police against him in whatever benign manner. It was benign on the surface only. Underneath it was slavery and dictatorship. He wanted loyalty. He wanted somebody who was willing to die for him as he was willing to die for her. He couldn't trust anybody, really. He couldn't even trust Penny.

He turned away from the window and smashed his crippled fist in his palm, winced with pain, then did it again.

14

The two-inch hole of the little alcohol burner flickered with flame. It shrank down to a low, steady transparent blue glow as Penny reached across the table and closed the small air holes. Roger tried to fill the silence in the room. He tried to reach out to Penny, to tell her how he felt, but he only asked, "You going to cook now? So late? It's after eight."

"Would it make any difference?" she asked.

"What do you mean?" he said.

"Whether I had tea with or without you!"

"What're you talking about?"

"You've got Anne Marie around now, don't you?" she said with a slight, wry twist of her mouth.

"What're you talking about?" he said, wishing he'd gone with Anne Marie now, but knowing Penny knew some way, either by being told or guessing from seeing her at the American Express, that the cops had brought Anne Marie around.

She turned away to the darkened window behind her, making him turn to look at her, ready to accuse her of being in on it, of putting him up to it, of knowing he'd seen Anne Marie and of using it as an excuse to break up with him. But he suddenly felt sorry for her, seeing her there in semi-profile looking so sadly out the window, her eyes burning with reflections of the blue flame. Finally he said, "I saw Anne Marie last night, and you know it."

She twitched her mouth, a little twist of hurt sarcasm, but didn't deny it.

"I left her when a police wagon pulled up with siren wailing right next to our table at a sidewalk cafe!"

She faced him. He could see the blue glow of a flame flickering in her eyes.

"And she appeared again today, just very neatly when I went out for a walk this afternoon."

Her eyes widened and her lips parted.

"But I didn't go with her then, either! I walked away, and an hour later she appeared with Robey on the sidewalk across the street! Then, when I stepped back away from the window, she kissed him and put her arm around him, and they walked around the corner and out of my life, I hope!"

Her long lashes swept over her eyes and she looked down at the table, then up at him again. The blue glow in them was soft and low.

"Why don't we go out for a walk? It's too depressing in here," he said.

She looked up and asked in a soft, conciliatory tone, "How about my tea?"

"Just turn it off. We'll stop and get something to drink in a cafe."

She stepped to the table and turned the burner off, then closed the lid to keep the alcohol from evaporating. She turned back to him and, smiling, said, "Let's go!"

15

When he opened the door and Ruth stood smiling at him with crinkled blue eyes, he saw in his head both Anne Marie and Michelle down on the sidewalk. Trap, he thought, and

didn't invite her in, knowing she'd only appeared because he
didn't go for them, because he'd kept writing, because he was
writing right now, because he and Penny were reconciled last
night. And she wasn't going to stop him. He hadn't forgotten
the trouble she'd caused him.

"Aren't you going to let me in?" she said, and pushed a
brown bag with a rubber band around it at him. He recognized
his pound of kif.

When he reached for the bag, she let him grab it, but used
it to push him back. She then kissed him on the lips and
didn't let go until she had stepped past him. She stepped over
to the table by the window where he was writing, glanced at
the typewriter then down at the page, and leaned over to read
it as he asked, "Where's Craig?"

She straightened up and turned around, and he couldn't
keep himself from staring at her nipples, which stippled the
transparent black skin of her leotard like blossoms at the tips
of her big breasts.

"Craig and I broke up," she said, smiling.

"Where is he?" Roger asked, too suspicious to believe anything she said, but sure that showing her body to him and
bringing him his kif had something to do with it. He was
determined not to get sucked in.

"I... I... I..." she stuttered, then stopped and said, "Here
in Paris."

"How long since you've seen him?" Roger asked, still not
smiling.

She stared at him with a drooping mouth, obviously unhappy with his questions, then answered, "Yesterday."

"You just broke up yesterday?" he asked, his voice rising
with his mistrust.

"Yes," she said, and squirmed uncomfortably. She then
spun around to face the window next to his desk and said,
"Oh, what a nice view of the park here! You've got a good
room."

He knew she was changing the subject, and without com-
menting on her compliment asked, "Where are you staying?"

"Right here in the hotel. Up on the top floor, four-twelve,"
she said, showing all her front teeth in a smile.

He wanted to say something sarcastic, but they'd told him
about the hotel in Morocco and that they'd meet him here with
his kif, even though he said they could have it. She had every

right to stay here, too, no matter what he thought of her. He
relented a little and said, "Thanks for the kif," keeping himself
from asking about their dope-selling trip to Ibiza.

"Oh, that's all right. It was yours. Where's Penny?"

"Out shopping, I guess. She goes out in the afternoon
when I write."

Ruth stared over her shoulder at him and her breasts
stuck out in profile. The black leotard was almost off her
shoulder, her waist curved down to her Levis.

"When do you expect her back?"

"A couple hours more, at least. She stays out till dinner
time, so I can be alone and she can be alone," Roger said, then
stared at her breasts when she turned to face him again.

They were a little too full and sagged somewhat, though
she'd never had any children. He knew she was trying to get
him to look at them, to stop his writing, one way or the other.
Yet when she swayed near him and leaned her body ever so
slightly against him, he put his arm around her waist and felt
the soft flesh of her stomach and it turned him on. But when
she pressed against him, he caught himself and pulled away
from her.

"Let's smoke some of that kif," he said.

When he slipped the rubber band off, opened the brown
bag and the heavy hay smell hit him, all the memories of his
suffering in Spain and Morocco came crowding into his mind.
He remembered how scared he was when they had surrounded him on the ferry, just because Craig and Ruth didn't offer
to put his small bag of dope with their seven kilos in the van.
Now, they'd brought it to him after selling their own dope in
Ibiza.

He rolled a big joint without talking to her, even when
she sat down next to him and put her arm around his shoulders.

They passed the joint back and forth in silence. He could
hear the soft hum of the traffic and street noises from outside
as the strong smell of kif filled the room around them. Ruth
kept staring at him with her deep, blue eyes, tempting him,
trying to draw him to her, to make him turn and kiss her and
stop his writing.

The sunlight came through the gauze curtains, but over
the gabled roofs of the Sorbonne a block away, he could see
what looked like rain clouds forming on the horizon, and his

bitter determination to keep writing kept his desire down. He'd just shaken off the temptation of Anne Marie and convinced Penny of it, so he wasn't going for Ruth.

"I better get back to my writing," he said when they finished the joint and he flipped the last shred of cigarette paper in the bidet and flushed it down.

Ruth, who hadn't spoken once either, stood up, and slouching her body, propped one hand on her outflung hip, looked full in his eyes, puffed her mouth in a pout, and said "I'm constipated," and walked over to the door.

16

He watched the windows streak with rain as Penny took the ground steak out of its wrapper, made two thick patties and put them in her mess kit pan, then poured some alcohol in the little burner and lit it. She then blew out the match, quickly adjusted the flame on the burner, put his mess kit frying pan on top of her own frying pan to keep the heat in, and started taking lettuce and carrots and tomatoes out of her grocery bag to wash for a salad.

All through dinner, he didn't mention that Ruth had been there and only spoke when they had finished their yogurt and honey.

"Ruth was here today."

"What?" She put her spoon down in her tin cup. "Why didn't you tell me? How did she get here? When?"

"A couple of hours ago. She moved in yesterday. She said she broke up with Craig." He saw her eyes narrow at him as if she didn't believe it and suspected it had something to do with Ruth and him. "Don't forget they've stayed here before. They gave us the address," he said.

"I wonder what she's up to?" Penny said, still eying Roger. He blushed when there was a knock on the door and she said, "That's probably your girlfriend now."

"Whatta ya mean, 'my girlfriend,'" he said, his face hot, thinking of how he kept Ruth off, wishing for a moment he'd screwed Ruth. "You get it then."

Penny got up and went to the door, but wouldn't look at him nor answer him.

"Hello, Penny," Ruth said when Penny opened the door. She hugged her and said, "Why don't we smoke some Red Lebanese hash I've got and go for a walk? The rain's stopped, and it would be fun."

Penny frowned, but Roger was still annoyed at her for accusing him of something he'd tried to avoid. Though he suspected Ruth of being up to something, as usual, he said, "I haven't been out all day, and I've got a lot of writing done. I could use some good hash. I'm game for both."

He smiled at Ruth and pretended not to see Penny's sullen mouth.

17

Two large men in trench coats, a half block behind on the narrow, wet street next to the Sorbonne, had been following them for two blocks already. Roger was high on the hash and understood with lucid clarity that Ruth had brought him outside so they could follow him and maybe start some trouble. The point was to expose him in whatever way, maybe jump him. He purposely led Penny and Ruth around the next corner and down a broad boulevard on the other side of the Sorbonne with lots of street lights and cars swishing by so he could have people and lights around to protect him. He hoped they weren't fascist Spaniards, or it could be real trouble.

They had barely gotten a quarter of a block down the boulevard before the men came around the corner, walking fast, saw him looking back at them, and slowed down in midstride. He stopped under a street light and watched them approach with slow, casual steps across the long, wet expanse of sidewalk. When they stepped toward him through a big, shining puddle, shimmering like a small sea in the pale moonlight of a street lamp, it suddenly struck him: They were like Roman soldiers chasing Christ! Walking on water after him! He suddenly saw them with spears pointed at him. The perception glowed like some inner light that flared through his limbs, and he knew he had to capture the sight on paper somehow. He reached around behind him and pulled a small notepad and ballpoint pen out of his back pocket, looked around for something to lay the pad on, and saw the flat roof of a car parked next to the curb. He stepped over to the small car, leaned over on its wet top, and began to write.

The emotion burst out of him: Ruth and cops and dope and dark streets and dying Christs and Roman soldiers marching toward him. It was all controlled by the super-fine mentality the hash gave him, the perfect harmony between his conscious and subconscious minds. Yet he could barely keep up with the thoughts ripping through his brain with machine-gun rapidity. He withdrew from everything around him, even the two men drifting slowly as boats across the wet sidewalk toward him.

"DOWN WET PARIS STREETS. I'm with you, baby! Yeah, Eldridge, you and me and Leroy and every other crazy motherfucker! Kiss my ass! Those fucking bulls tail me in trench coats down wet Paris streets!

Shiver! and write these words down on a damp car top
Raindrops on my palm
follow this heat in my hand till I get this down
and leave some blood on their hands
All these paddy poets
And I mean Ginsberg too
Cop-outs all of them..."

"Roger! What're you writing?" Ruth asked. Her voice broke into his thought, shocked him out of the purified state of mind he'd fallen into. He stared at a blank line. The words vanished from his brain. He looked up at her, confused, then realized that she'd stopped the flow, that his mind was now a blank, that she'd stopped him from writing about the two cops following him. He saw her stepping toward him to see what he was writing, and hate blazed in him.

"Get awayyyyyy!" he screamed, and kicked out at her to keep her away, almost getting her breast, but stopped his foot just short of it.

He looked quickly back down at his tablet again, tried to pick up where he'd been, re-read his words, whispered them out loud to himself, but he was so filled with anger at her that he couldn't concentrate. He had lost the illuminating tie between his vision of Roman soldiers walking on water and the sinister men still approaching him like spectres of doom. He re-read the lines, trying to pick it up again. But the feeling

of frustration that had spurted up in him kept him from
thinking, and he lifted his head, put the pen and the notepad
back in his rear pocket and stepped over to Ruth.

He noticed that the two men had stopped only a dozen or
so feet away and were staring at him, as if they'd seen him
kick out at her and were now going to protect her if he dared
touch her.

"You didn't fool me, Ruth," he said in a low voice. "I know
what you were doing. I know you tried to stop my writing
about those thugs there." He pointed at the men. "Remember
that."

She stepped back from him, as if afraid he'd kick at her
again, then, without answering, turned and started walking
away. As he watched her move off, a great sadness filled him
that they were enemies, not friends when they had shared so
much together.

18

There was something familiar about the silhouette in the
bright daylight of the open hotel doorway. Some woman in a
man's checkered cap swayed into the hotel at the bottom of
the wide flight of stairs below Roger. She had the cap pulled
down so low on one side of her head that it almost covered her
right eye. Her face was in shadows, her hair tucked up under
her cap, and her body covered by a big, man's blue workshirt.

Then, as Roger stepped down, he saw Craig step in
behind her and realized it was Ruth. She stopped when she
saw him and waited for him in full view of the concierge.

"Hello, Roger," she said, when he reached the bottom of
the stairs, in a low, throaty, conspiratorial voice, so different
from her normal, high-pitched tone.

When he saw the concierge frown, he felt like kicking out
at Ruth again to keep her away and protect himself. Yet, the
frown on the concierge's dark face made him think of the need
to be civil, and he stepped to meet them and reached out to
shake hands with Craig. He seemed even more hunched over,
even more round-shouldered and subdued.

"Can we talk, Roger?" Ruth asked in the same, low, conspiratorial tone.

Roger noticed the small green box in Craig's hand and guessed it might be dope so they could smoke the peace pipe together and Ruth could make up for distracting him the other night. It was all the more reason not to talk in front of the concierge. He said, "Come on. I've been writing all morning and was just taking a break, going out for a little walk."

He started to step around them, but Ruth didn't move. "Can we talk in your room?" she asked, and glanced back at the concierge again.

Annoyed, Roger spun around and started back up the stairs to get away from the concierge. He then ran up them two at a time so Ruth couldn't speak to him until they got inside his room. He made them run to follow him. They both had red faces and were breathing hard when they finally reached the third floor. He liked seeing the discomfort on their faces for making the concierge suspicious. He knew Ruth was in some way trying to cause trouble for him with her, but he couldn't quite figure out what. When he closed the door behind them, he just waited for them to turn and for Ruth to tell a lie about why she spoke to him when he was writing that night.

But Ruth said, "Craig got this box of shaving gear from his mother. He doesn't need it. Could you buy it? It'd cost about ten or twelve dollars here in Paris."

"What?" It took him a moment to understand, the subject was so out of line. "Buy them from you?" He frowned. "Don't you have any money? I thought you made money dumping that dope in Ibiza?"

Craig just shrugged his shoulders.

"It must have cost more to mail them here than to buy them back in the States," Roger said.

"You know how mothers are!" Ruth said, showing all her teeth, as if he hadn't kicked out at her just the other night.

Roger looked down at the box of cologne, aftershave lotion, shaving cream, and talcum powder in fancy green bottles. He was sure he was being used in some way, forced to buy something he didn't need. Yet, he felt guilty over her amiability when he felt such intense anger. He smacked his lips, took a deep breath, then blew it out and said in a near whisper, "How much do you want for them?"

"Five dollars would be nice," Ruth said, slanting her eyes again, as if there was something mysterious to it all.

Roger hesitated, regretted asking. But when Craig said, "I could use the money," he asked again, "Didn't you just deal some kilos in Ibiza?"

"We owed a debt," Ruth said, and Craig nodded.

Still, Roger asked, "Are you so bad off, you have to penny-ante hustle?"

"I don't need the shaving stuff," Craig said, still pressing.

Roger pulled a twenty franc note out of his pocket, but Ruth snatched it out of his hand before he could hand it to Craig and stepped past Roger to the door. Craig gave him a weak wave as he closed the door behind him. Roger felt sure that they'd taken him and only then remembered that Ruth had said she'd broken up with Craig.

19

"Look what Ruth and Craig just sold me," Roger said when Penny stepped into the room and pointed down at the open green box on the table. Sunlight made the fancy green bottles glow like cut gems.

Penny walked over to where he was typing near the window, glanced down at them, said, "Hmmmmm." Then she looked up and said, "So she's with Craig again, huh? As soon as you don't go for her, she goes back and gets him again."

"I don't care about that," he said, shaking his head. "What bothers me is I'm afraid they stole them and they're trying to involve me in a crime. It's a felony to receive stolen goods and only a misdemeanor to steal something as cheap as these."

"Steal?" she asked, showing her front teeth. "Why would they do that?"

He shrugged his shoulders.

"To stop my writing like she tried to do the other night, like they tried to get me busted for dope in Algeciras, remember? If you hadn't carried it in, I would've gone to prison. Remember? And they wanted to bring that agent along in the van with us, too. If they got me arrested, it would stop my writing or at least break the momentum I've got going on my book, maybe even discourage me so much I wouldn't ever finish it. In France, you have to stay in jail until the case's settled."

"That's pretty far-fetched," she said.

"She's acting far-fetched! Remember how she acted in Morroco? You should see the way she's dressed! She doesn't even look like Ruth. She looks like a gun moll! She even made the concierge suspicious."

When Penny didn't speak, he said, "It's got to be a trap! I had something like this happen to me once before in Bolinas! I took the furniture the girl gave me back to her to keep from getting sucked in."

"They could put you in jail for buying that junk?"

"Yes," he said.

"Then take them back and get your money from them," she said.

"Go with me to keep it calm and be a witness," he said, and finally stepped away from his typewriter, put the cover on the green box, and walked out the door and up the stairs to the fourth floor with her. He felt the tension building with each step to Ruth's room, and when he finally reached her door, he was ready to explode with each knock of his knuckles on the old wood.

Craig opened the door. Ruth was preparing some kind of fruit salad on the table. She smiled at Roger when he stepped in, but he gave her no chance to charm him.

"Here's your stolen junk! You can keep the money! But if you ever mess with me again, Ruth, involve me in some crime again, and try to stop my writing, I'll bust you in your mouth, woman or no woman!"

She froze with her smile still on her mouth, a half-cut apple in one hand, a small paring knife in the other.

20

A strange moaning sound midway between ecstasy and pain, like a woman either coming or in misery, floated down from the floor above them, raising goose pimples all over Roger's arms.

"What's that?" Roger said. "What's she doing now?"

"Sounds like she's crying," Penny said, then cocked her head and said, "or is putting it on."

"We heard her do that before when Craig hit her in San Francisco, remember?"

"Too well," Penny said. "And the big fuck scene afterwards, too, with creaking bedsprings and all."

Roger smiled and said, "Well, *I* didn't hit her, and no matter what she does, I'm still going to keep my book going."

The moaning kept up for about five minutes, then finally stopped. Roger began reading and Penny finished fixing their salad. She had just put their tin plates on the table when there were heavy footsteps in the hallway, then the squeak and rattle of the doorknob as someone shook it, trying to get into the room, then started pounding on the door.

Roger jumped off the bed, sure it had something to do with Ruth, and asked, "Yes?"

"*Ouvrez! Ouvrez!*" a feminine voice called out, then in English with a French accent said, "Open door!"

Roger recognized the concierge's voice, and, afraid she'd brought the police, opened the door on her plump brown body balanced solidly on her high heels. When he saw she was alone, he asked again, "Yes?"

She pushed past him and stomped toward Penny, large breasts bobbing obscenely through her transparent silk blouse, wide hips jerking, lips puckered, shouting at Penny in French.

Roger hesitated, unsure about whether or not he should close the door. Penny stood with her back to the window, her lips pressed tightly together. He wanted to give the concierge the benefit of the doubt and try to keep from doing something he'd regret later. But her face puffed with dark blood and she kept screaming in a scornful, insulting tone, reaching a coarse, guttural screech.

"Hey! Stop!" he shouted, stepping toward her.

She caught her breath, then looked at him with scared, white lips.

"What's she saying, Penny?" he asked, keeping his eye on the concierge.

"I don't understand all of it, but she says that I was moaning and crying just now and bothering the other tenants."

"Tell her it wasn't you! Tell her it was...uh, someone on the floor above us," Roger said, not wanting to tell on Ruth.

Penny spoke in a soft voice to the concierge, leaning over a little from the waist, spacing her words: "*Il n'y pas moi, madame. C'est outre femme a là...* upstairs!" She pointed at the ceiling. *"N'est pas moi!"*

But before she could finish, the concierge stepped toward her, shouting again and shaking her fist at her.

"Hey, stop it!" Roger shouted again, and stepped between her and Penny.

The concierge's eyes were smooth-lidded, large and dark, like his father's, and gentle with fright for just a moment. But before Roger could speak, she said, "You move tomorrow, she not quiet."

"What? Move out? You're threatening us with moving out?"

She puckered her mouth with a scornful expression as if to speak, but something about him seemed to stop her, and she squinted her eyes at him instead.

He turned his ass to her and slapped it with a cracking sound, once, twice, three times and said, "Take your fucking room and shove it up your ass!" Then he turned around and laughed.

Her mouth quivered and she stepped back toward the doorway with fright, where Roger saw a slender, young Chinese man in a white dress shirt and cheap dress slacks, staring at him.

"Crazy," Roger said, and twirled his finger at his temple, then pointed at the woman and smiled at the man, embarrassed at being seen shouting at a woman.

But the Chinese man didn't smile back. Roger took in his lean face and his small-boned body, which he guessed was hard under the loose shirt, and then saw in a flash that the guy had been outside all the time to protect the woman. If that was so, then he probably knew judo or some other form of martial art, and if that was the case, then either she was getting out or Roger was closing that door. He stepped toward the concierge and, pointing at the doorway, said, "Get out! We'll move tomorrow! Now leave!"

But she didn't move, as if she'd seen him hesitate in front of the Chinese man, who continued to stare at him with a lock of long black hair hanging over one eye.

"Move!" Roger said, and bobbed his body in a feint at her, making her step back with a gasp and clasp her arms over her breasts. She was so funny in her fear that he couldn't help smiling. When she saw his grin, she let out a long string of curses in French which he couldn't understand. Then she caught her breath, turned her back, and stomped heavily out the door. He closed it behind her and caught a glimpse of the Chinese man still standing in the hall, watching him.

21

Penny tugged his hand and said, "Look, Roger!" just as they reached a gap in the line of thin-trunked trees, bushy and green with spring leaves. She pointed past him at the big truck parked parallel to the curb with its side panels down and a big movie camera trained on him. It turned as he turned to stare at it for a couple of seconds or so. He could hear its whir even after he walked past it and behind the trunks of the trees again—a low hum that rose above the noises of the street, the cars and voices, the low clamor of the big city, and felt a weakening sense of despair in him.

22

A young man, who looked like a Spaniard, with curly dark hair, dark eyes and a narrow, pale face, was outside the American Express office when Roger and Penny walked out. There wasn't a single letter for Roger from any of the people he'd written to in Spain, though he had left a forwarding address for Paris in Morocco.

Roger saw the Spaniard again when they stepped onto the subway. He saw him again near the Eiffel Tower. He tried to forget him when they walked along the neat gardens next to the Seine. Then, when they reached the bridge near the Arc D'Triomphe, he saw the Spaniard standing right at the railing with his camera aimed at him. His thumb went down and up, then he turned and looked over the railing as if he hadn't taken the picture. Roger kept walking, trying to ignore the guy. But when he was in the middle of the bridge, right over the Seine, he turned and saw the guy following him, hiding behind an old French couple, both so fat he could barely be seen.

"Keep walking straight ahead, Penny," Roger said, suddenly hot with anger. Then he stepped into the middle of a large family moving in the opposite direction, toward the guy, and managed to pass by the Spaniard without being seen. Once past the guy, he stepped away from the family group and started walking up behind him, measuring the man as he stood on his tiptoes and twisted his head around, apparently looking for Roger. The guy was only about five-eight or nine and couldn't weigh more than a hundred and fifty pounds. The urge to throw him over the railing gripped Roger. It would be easy. One arm between his legs and over he'd go. He could throw him, he knew that. He'd thrown lots of big men in fights, sometimes through the air.

Roger tensed himself. This was Paris, not Spain, and he didn't have to take any shit. The guy wasn't going to bother him anymore. Just as Roger stepped up behind him and started to crouch down to grab the guy, the guy turned around, saw him and jumped back against the railing with a gasp, one hand out in front of him to hold Roger off, his mouth open, scared.

It was the twisted fear in the guy's pale face that stopped Roger. He'd already won. There was no need. He watched the guy turn and run past Penny and over the bridge, then out of sight in the crowd on the other side.

"What were you going to do to him?" Penny asked.

Roger turned to face her.

"Were you going to throw him over the rail?"

"I was until he turned around," Roger said.

"What if he drowned?"

"He wouldn't have."

"How do you know?" she said, hands on her hips.

"I don't *know*," he said, "but I scared him so much, I'll bet he doesn't mess with me again."

"That's dangerous, Roger," she said. "You might hurt somebody sometime."

"They're hurting me, bad!" he said, and looked back around at where the Spaniard had disappeared into the crowd on shore. Roger then turned back to her again and said, "Let's not fight each other. I want to have some fun! Let's walk down the Seine to that cafe by Notre Dame and get something to eat. Let's not fight each other."

She shut her mouth, but it was still tight. Then she smiled and said, "Okay."

23

With the moaning sound of a jazz sax curling out the open door of the nightclub in a lonesome solo, and with people moving forward into the club in a slow-moving line just fifty feet or so away on the broad sidewalk in the glow of a street light, Roger sat with Penny at the very same table, in the very same cafe he'd sat with Anne Marie. But this time he noticed a hollow-faced, dark-skinned man staring at him from another table. Then he saw that all of the men at the next table were staring at him. Five of them. And they all looked like Spaniards with short hair and epaulets and military styles to their dress coats.

He looked them over quickly, then looked away. They kept staring at him with hard eyes and tight mouths, and he glanced around him and saw that, with his back to the street and the Seine, he had room to maneuver and even run if it came to that. He then noticed that a tall, rangy, wide-shouldered man coming around the dark corner near the Seine was staring at him, too. As he drew near, Roger could see the thickened bridge of his nose and his scarred eyebrows. He was slim and hard, in shape, trimmed down to bare muscle, like a professional fighter. Roger noticed, too, how close the guy was coming, walking as if he didn't intend to stop. When he stepped past Roger, he let his knuckles just graze Roger's shoulder.

Roger jerked around to face him with the touch, expecting anything, but the guy kept walking up to the counter where he ordered a drink. He then turned and stared at Roger again, his black, wavy hair combed down flat on his narrow head.

"What's he want?" Penny asked.

"A fight, I think," Roger answered.

"It looks like it, but what for?" She kept watching the man as she spoke. "You don't even know him."

"He knows me though," he said. "Take a look at the table behind you."

She looked back, then faced him again and said, "They do look menacing. Maybe we'd better go."

"Yeah," Roger said, and stood up, "maybe we'd better."

He put his hand in his pocket for some money for the check, keeping an eye on the men at the table, meeting their stares briefly, calculating that he might be able to get one or two or even three of them, but down he certainly would go against the six good men he'd have to fight. Besides, the heavyweight might be able to take him by himself.

All their faces turned with him as he walked by. Roger didn't speak as he and Penny moved past them and the nightclub where the combo was rippling with some slow, subdued beat, the crowd of people still at the door.

"Why do we always have to live in fear?" Penny asked. "Something always happens just when you and I feel good together."

Roger grabbed her arm and said, "I'll tell you why! They're after me for threatening that Spaniard with the camera on the bridge! And not going for Anne Marie's bait!"

"Oh!" she said, and stopped. He glanced back to see if the Spaniards were following them, then said, "If I'd gone for the bait, they wouldn't be threatening me because of the Spaniard! You know how the Spanish, meaning Tony, followed me to Morocco and harassed me near to death there?"

"Yes, I know," she said. Just three little but oh so important words of agreement, and he bent to kiss her lips, but she murmured, "But it makes me so sad."

He looked into her eyes, his face so close to hers. He could feel her breath on his cheek.

"If you're with me, I can take it," he said.

Her mouth spread in a surprised smile, and not caring at that moment what the cops did, he bent his head and touched her lips with his.

24

It was the same Chinese man from the hotel: a wiry, small man with a bony face and dark shadows under his eyes. He stood next to Roger in the subway car and didn't take his eyes off him for over five minutes. Roger was surprised to see him so close now and he tingled with fear. He wished he had his dark glasses on because of the dark ring still under his left eye, but he left them home because it was an overcast day.

Roger had seen him following them from the Hotel Du Paris to their new room, a clean little place with red velvet drapes and rose-colored wallpaper that overlooked the tree-lined St. Michelle Boulevard, on the very edge of the Latin Quarter. There was a Red Chinese bookstore run by a blue-eyed blond man across the street. Roger saw the Chinese man again when they got on the subway to go to the American Express. Now, as the subway hummed along the tracks, he got annoyed at the man constantly staring at him. He lifted his crippled hand and held it in front of him so the man couldn't miss it nor his intentions.

The man stared at the hand as Roger first held it flat and spread-fingered in front of him. Then he glanced at Roger's face when he closed the hand slowly, squeezed it into a tight fist, and kept it squeezed for a long time. The big lump on the base joint of his thumb popped up like a ping-pong ball. His index finger was still so puffed at the middle knuckle that it looked like a cigar. The fist index knuckle was so imbedded it barely showed.

He opened and then slowly closed the fist again, kept it squeezed for a long time again, really tight so the broken knuckles turned white, to let the man know it was a warning. Finally, the man looked away and Roger let his hand relax with a surge of satisfaction.

When the car stopped at the station before his own, a blonde woman stepping toward the open doors suddenly stopped and held her head out in front of her. Roger wanted to shout at her to get out of the way and push her through the opening. But he was afraid he'd hurt her and could only clap his hand over his mouth when the closing doors slammed together on both sides of her head with a thump. Before he could shout, the doors bounced open again automatically. She staggered out onto the platform and turned around and looked right at Roger with glazed eyes as the doors closed once more and the car pulled away with a loud hum.

"Did you see that?" Roger said, and Penny nodded with a tight mouth and looked over at the Chinese man, who was staring at Roger again.

Roger and Penny got off at the next stop, and Roger, with sweating hands and anxiety fluttering inside him, looked back to see if the guy was following him as they walked upstairs to the street. He wanted to tell Penny about it, but he could see by her sullen face that the accumulation of misfortunes was having an unhappy effect on her. He was sure she blamed him for the concierge shouting at her and kicking them out.

He didn't say anything to her when they came out of the subway and he saw an ambulance parked along the curb before them. The driver and his assistant both stared at him from the front seat. He was sure he was being threatened again. He kept his mouth shut about it even when they stood in the American Express line and a strange little man with wire-rimmed glasses that had one shattered lens and his hair cut in clumps so that his scalp showed, came over and stood behind him for a while. The man then pushed next to him and started mumbling, "CIA! CIA! KILL! KILL! CIA!"

Roger spun around to face him, fists hanging at his sides, ready to punch, sure this was it! He knew he could drop him with a left hook to the chin from underneath. But when the guy just kept mumbling and staring at him with pale eyes and didn't push into him with his shoulder again, didn't try to hurt him, Roger stepped back. Still watching the guy, Roger walked over to the wall, a good twenty feet away, to keep from having trouble. The guy might be crazy or just pretending to be crazy, or both. But, in any case, it only meant trouble. Roger waited until Penny posted her letter, then led her quickly out and down the stairs before the guy could move away from the Poste Restante window after her.

Roger walked quickly back to the subway with Penny, keeping his eye out for the guy and for the Chinese man, sure all this was happening because he threatened Ruth. Though he couldn't tell Penny and risk an argument over it. But when they got back on the subway and had only gone a couple of stops, he suddenly realized that he was surrounded by about ten men in business suits, all with small briefcases in their hands, all staring at him, and he said, "Penny, I think I might get jumped."

She cocked her head and looked into his eyes. He switched his eyes from side to side to signal without moving his head. She turned her head and slowly looked around her, then answered, "I don't think so."

Anger boiled up in him at her blindness *or* her lying, but he couldn't argue as the men edged closer, so close that he saw he was going to have trouble even raising his arms, that he wasn't even going to be able to fight back. They were going to pin his arms so he couldn't punch any of them.

"Do what I do if they jump us," he said, making sure he'd caught her eyes. Then he suddenly dropped down to his knees on the floor and doubled up like a ball, covered his head with his arms and hands, tucking his elbows into his sides like he'd learned in the Civil Rights marches, protecting the inner side of his body so that he could only be kicked or clubbed on his arms and legs or on the back of the head and body.

He waited for the kicks. Nothing happened and he quickly stood up again and looked around at all the men. They all stared at him with expressionless faces, not a smile or a frown or a sign of astonishment at the bizarre act he had just committed. That only convinced Roger that they were indeed cops, and he pushed through them and moved down into another car where there were lots of empty seats.

"Now, don't tell me you didn't see that?" he said when they walked out of the subway and down the Boulevard St. Michelle, next to the fenced-in, blackened, moss-covered ruins of the Bastille.

"See what?" she said as if he hadn't just run a gauntlet of bizarre threats, including the gang of men with briefcases. Anger leaped in him again, and he started to say something sharp to her when he felt someone pressing against him. He saw a dark-complexioned man built like Atlas in a tight sweater walking in step with him. He tried to step aside but was bumped by another husky man on the other side of him who was wearing casual clothes, too. Fair-skinned and blond, he was just as muscular as the other man.

Roger then realized that another husky man was right in front of him, and when he stopped to drop back and get away, another man with a big chest bumped into him from behind and made him keep walking. He was penned in! He twisted his head to look for Penny, saw her several feet back, walking down the street as if nothing was happening! When he had just spoken to her! As if she didn't even know that he wasn't walking next to her or that he was surrounded by four men who were going to jump him!

Heart pounding and his face white, lips dry and chalky, barely able to breathe, Roger shoved between two of them on his left and jumped up against the wrought-iron fence of the Bastille. He pulled out his boy scout knife, and, hands trembling, jerked the blade open and held it in his shaking hand, stuttering, "Try-try-try and get near me and-and-and I'll kill you! I'll kill whoever gets near me!"

All four men glared at him with angry frowns, the closest, a thick, dark, Arabic-looking man, showing his teeth in an angry scowl. But they kept walking and disappeared into the crowd on the wide sidewalk. Roger stayed up against the fence with the knife still open in his hand. When Penny stopped and stared at him, he said, "You keep your fucking friends off me! I'm warning you! I'll get whoever gets near me!"

25

"Like to talk to you," Fuzz said in a deep voice, without smiling. His green eyes drilled right into Roger. His blue and white checkered wool shirt blocked the doorway. Red threads ran through it. A streak of fear shot through Roger. Was he going to have to fight Fuzz again! Fuzz had shaved his sideburns and cut his dark hair short. It took a moment to recognize him. The *knife*, Roger thought. He's mad about the knife I pulled an hour ago. But Roger wasn't even surprised at seeing Fuzz at his door in Paris. Nothing surprised him. They followed him everywhere. The room was bugged. They knew everything.

"Sure," Roger said, and stepped back on his right foot to let Fuzz in, his weight balanced in case he had to move, thinking he'd better bring up his favorite sneak punch—a left hook from inside—if Fuzz turned on him. When Fuzz stepped in with his back to him, Roger stepped past and led him over to the breakfast nook.

Fuzz looked more like a rough Canadian or a football player out for a fight than a traveling American student. There might not have ever been a hippy movement to look at him. No more disguise. Everything was in the open now, evidently. They had fought fist to fist and knew each other well.

"What's on your mind?" Roger asked, and realized that there was no space in the room to dance around in if Fuzz charged him. Fuzz could use his big body to smother him. Fall in close, Roger thought. Punch from inside his arms and loop hooks around them to get him on the jaw.

But the big man stepped across the thick, burgundy rug without making a sound, pulled a chair out, and sat down at the table in the three-sided window nook. Roger didn't sit down, just kept his eyes on him, watching.

"What's this you're reading?" Fuzz asked, and picked up the book on the table, glanced at the cover, "*Tradition or Treason? A Look at The New Left Radical Personality In America.*" He scanned the open page, a deep wrinkle creasing his forehead. Yet, he put the book down on the open page and only said, "Not writing, huh?"

But Roger asked, "How's your jaw, Fuzz?"

The big brow smoothed out as Fuzz leaned back in his chair, threw one arm over it and said, "It was wired for six weeks. I couldn't eat solid food the whole time and lost eighteen pounds."

"I'm sorry," Roger said.

Fuzz kept his eyes on him without speaking.

"I mean that," Roger said in a tight voice, and Fuzz nodded, then said, "I'm sorry I pushed you so hard, but you weren't getting the message. You're still not getting the message."

Roger took off his reading glasses, put them upside down, templates spread, on the table, then looked at Fuzz, his hazel eyes flickering in the window light, and answered *his* question: "Yes, I'm writing. I'm nearly finished with the second draft of my novel."

"The one about the FBI infiltrating the student movement?"

"That's right."

"Think you'll make any money on it?" Fuzz asked.

A wave of fear splashed over Roger. Was Fuzz giving a warning?

"Not if the sales of my first novel and the way my second novel has been postponed is any indication," he said. "It was supposed to have been published last January."

"Why don't your books sell?" Fuzz asked.

"Because I don't play the game."

"Meaning what?"

"Meaning I've been cut out so long from the real world by Big Brother controlling me, keeping me down, that I don't even know how to operate in the commercial world."

"Are you sure that's the real reason?" Fuzz said. "Or is it that you just won't compromise and want everything on your own terms?"

Roger had to nod, then said, "There's truth in that. I want people to do the right things for the right reasons. I want to be published because I write the truth well, not because I play social games that end up being money games."

Fuzz snorted. "What do you mean, truth?"

"I mean..." Roger paused, hearing a sharp edge of irritation in his voice, then went on in a softer tone. "I mean that instead of just giving society what it's used to, I try to give it something that, though hopefully entertaining, makes society face its problems and, by facing them, then take steps to improve that society. The whole point of a serious novel is to teach people how to live better. It's a spiritual experience like Greek tragedy. It's a moral view of life in the form of entertainment. It's not just entertainment, but like going to church. It is a spiritual experience. I try to speak out for the downtrodden in order to make their lives better, and by making their lives better, make society better."

"What do you mean 'Make society better?'" Fuzz said, touching his jaw with the tip of his finger.

Roger kept an impulse of anger down and said, "You might call it teaching. Does that sound better? In my first novel, a small boy goes to a reform school for a street fight and ends up a multiple murderer in a couple of months. My point is that the reform school deformed him, and, therefore, something is wrong with juvenile justice in America. So, people read it and then, maybe, hopefully, might feel more compassion for juvenile delinquents and change the society so something like this doesn't happen anymore."

Fuzz shook his big head. "Pretty ambitious and pretty optimistic, too. That could take years and years. You could be dead by then. You could die any time."

The fear of the four men on the street gripped Roger again. He *was* being warned! But he met Fuzz's stare and said, "You mean beaten to death in the street? I'm not afraid to die!"

Fuzz kept his eyes on Roger. His mouth was tight. "Fighting with fists is one thing and fighting with a knife is another."

Roger felt that pulse of anger again. "I've got a right to protect myself," he said.

"You don't have a right to threaten to throw people over a bridge who take your picture, and you don't have a right to pull a knife."

"You don't have a right to harass me, manipulate me, and totally ruin my life," Roger said. He stood facing Fuzz, tense, still standing with his left foot forward, barely conscious of the traffic streaming past the tree outside the window. They were enemies, but Roger didn't hate the guy—he had gotten even with Fuzz for taking the pictures. He didn't want to have to go through it all over again though. There was no sound in the room, and just the motion of the slight fluttering of the leaves outside the window gave Roger the sense of sound. It was as if he were in a vacuum, a sealed room with no exit, a microcosm of his whole life, his imprisoned state.

Fuzz pointed a big finger at him. "Roger, if you hurt somebody again, you're going to really be sorry. That broken hand and that circle under your eye could just be starters. You understand?"

"Isn't that what you've been threatening to do to me all along? One threat after another? Aren't you trying to get me to fight back and do me in?"

Roger's full upper lip was tight now, too. He held his finger up.

"You can do anything you want, but I can't fight back, huh? Just like in the States. You club us in our peace demonstrations and then charge us with assault. Is that it?"

Fuzz blinked, then looked quickly down at the burgundy carpet as if he couldn't answer that, sat with his legs spread and his fists curled on his thighs as if trying to keep his temper. He was a very big man, had gained back his weight again and must have weighed over two-hundred pounds, at least. Roger tensed, in case Fuzz jumped him, wondered how he'd been able to beat him, and hoped he wouldn't have to fight him again.

"Do you really expect to ever get that book published?" Fuzz finally said.

"Listen, man. Melville wrote about the authoritarian state in BILLY BUDD, a state, like ours now, that destroys its good, natural men for the military security of the state. That book wasn't published for eighty years after it was written. I've got to write the book I'm working on, which is about the same subject, or die. I'll worry about getting it published later."

Fuzz sat with his big square chin up, still staring at Roger, but not speaking. But when Roger said, "Dissent is the essence of democracy," Fuzz spread out his big hands and answered, "Do you really think you can sell a book like that in America? Even here? There's no more Olympia Press in France, and there's no press that would touch it in America. You ought to write something that can sell, that can help make people feel better, not worse. A book like that doesn't deserve to be published."

Roger blinked, but didn't answer.

"You're going to throw your life away then, huh?" Fuzz said.

"You'll do anything to stop me from publishing that book, won't you?" Roger answered.

Fuzz looked away.

"You're trying to do me in just like you did Hemingway," Roger said.

"What's Hemingway got to do with this?" Fuzz said.

"Hemingway was, and still is, a hero in Cuba, and he was hounded to death by the FBI for his sympathies when he came back to the U.S. The FBI did follow him and did tap his phone and harass him when he came back from Cuba because we were in a state of undeclared war. And they had doctors convince him that he was imagining it and give him twenty-nine shock treatments, which didn't make the so-called delusions go away, and he killed himself. He was hounded to death by the secret police in America, one of our greatest writers."

Fuzz slid his chair back against the side window, spread his legs, and put his hands on his thighs as if he were going to stand up. Roger watched and waited, tingling inside.

Finally, Fuzz lifted his head and, his brow furrowed with a deep crease, said, "You won't compromise in your books then. You'll use them to preach violence. 'He who lives by the sword, dies by the sword.' Remember that!" When Roger didn't answer, he shook his head and said, "You've chosen a hard road, Roger," and stood up.

Roger stared at the burgundy carpet until he heard the door into the hall click closed and Fuzz's heavy tread on the stairs. A mood of sadness gripped him. The dark-grained wood trim and the chandelier, the window nook, with the green-starred leaves of the tree outside the window, talked of years and lives past, of people dead and forgotten, like he'd soon be. He felt like he was standing on the rim of the world with a vast emptiness facing him.

26

Roger stayed in the room a half-hour after Fuzz left, waiting for Penny to show up—he'd left her standing by the fence with the ruins of the Bastille in the background. He didn't see her and, even though he was scared, he went out looking for her. He checked both ways when he came out of the apartment building, seeing if he could spot Fuzz or any of those muscular goons. When he didn't, he looked for any other suspicious men or cars and, seeing no one on the street, he started walking down St. Michelle toward the Bastille. He kept looking around for her, but stayed on the lookout for any kind of a trap at all. When he saw a car with men in it parked along the curb, he moved to the other side of the broad sidewalk and looked carefully into the car when he passed it. Two Frenchmen sitting inside looked at him, but not with any particular hardness. He glanced back at them though, several times, until he was far down the sidewalk from them. When he got to the moss-covered blackened stone ruins of the Bastille and she was nowhere around, he decided to head back to the room in case he'd missed her. He crossed the wide street first to check on that side on the way back. He kept looking for cops, too, though, and had to fight the despair that swept over him. As he was passing the golden-barred gate of the Luxembourg Gardens, he had a hunch she might have gone into the park to think things over, and he turned in to look for her and to escape from anyone who might be following him. He could easily see them coming at him in the open spaces inside the park.

As he moved down a flowered path, he thought of how much he loved the garden. It was beautiful, even if it was too neat. And they wouldn't let you walk on the lawns either, as they did in the United States. Still, they surrounded their lawns with the busts of their poets on the tops of tall columns. Without even thinking about it, he went to a small circular lawn and sat down on a bench where he could look up at Verlaine, a fool and a damned soul, who'd sell a tinkling minuet of a poem for a glass of absinthe in his old age.

He got some small consolation from the lawn, but he was still scared he might get jumped and kept glancing around him. He still seethed inside at Penny for forsaking him, too, for letting the men surround him, for not even fighting for him like she had in Las Palmas when she kicked Fuzz in the nuts and gave him a chance to get up and drop Fuzz with the next punch. There was no way she couldn't have seen what happened. He hated her. She was a fake! She was cooperating with them to get him. Still, he loved her and she was all he had, the only person in the world he had a close relationship with and he wanted to find her. He wanted to be with her. And he'd be with her right now, if it weren't for the harassment.

Yet, they didn't jump him. This was perplexing. Why not?

He looked up and saw the Uzi machine gun a guard was carrying around the Chamber of Deputies. Lots of cops in Paris. Then he saw a busload of cops drive past the front of the Chamber, turn left on the corner of St. Michelle toward the Seine, and, probably, he guessed, to the police station.

Then he saw another bus right behind it, then another and another and another. He sat up, then stood up and watched eight buses of cops come past the Chamber, then turn left on St. Michelle. He noticed, too, that many of the cops had different colored caps on, as if they came from different police forces. Some wore multicolored caps with stiff brims and others plain caps, while others had on riot gear, with bubble helmets to protect them from blows to the head.

He stood up! Something was going on!

Then he remembered. This was election day! And Pompidou was ahead and predicted to win! The right-wing forces were going to have a celebration, he bet, and they expected trouble from the students, who were expected to demonstrate and riot.

Fascism all around him. No wonder the French police tailed him everywhere, trying to provoke him. He remembered what the police had done to him in Spain. Still, they hadn't jumped him in Paris, only threatened him. Why not?

He frowned and sat down, even though he saw more buses coming down the boulevard and more coming down St. Michelle, too.

Why not? Why hadn't they jumped him and, maybe, beat him to death?

Then he saw another string of buses roar through the intersection at St. Michelle Boulevard and realized that they didn't kill the students either, like they would in the United States. Why not?

Because it was still a democracy and the secret police had to be secret?

Not very secret, he thought, then suddenly remembered some words he'd read, in some article on the authoritarian state, that somehow seemed to fit, if he could only remember them. He thought of the cops all around him in the subway and the words popped into his head: Hostile surveillance! "Hostile surveillance is a technique used by police to pressure a suspect by letting him know he is being watched."

Hostile surveillance of radical outsiders, writers like him who were conspicuously followed in France. Conspicuous on purpose to scare him and get him to quit fighting them, quit fighting for freedom to report on what he'd experienced.

Hostile surveillance!

So this is what tortured him! It all became clear! He was under hostile surveillance in Spain, Morocco and now France! Here, the right-wing government was fighting a war against a popular revolt. They considered him a threat to the status quo, but because it still was a democracy, they threatened him to warn him not to use violence or they'd provoke him into it when they could handle it, when he'd lose, when they could beat him up and arrest him. He now realized that he must not give them a cause to use violence against him! He could not let them provoke him! He had to keep from getting hurt like they had hurt him in Spain!

His lips spread in a tight smile. His smile vanished. He still suffered! And the suffering was very great! The psychic turmoil they caused him was nearly as bad as being hurt physically, and it made him want to strike out. But if he fought back, they'd hurt him like they had in Spain, where the hostile surveillance had pushed him over the line.

His mind churned with that thought when he saw another line of buses go by and knew now they expected trouble. Then he leaned forward and reached back into his pocket, pulled out his note pad and pen, rested the pad on his knee and began to write as full of fire as he had been on the wet streets with Ruth, who had stopped it, but there was nobody here to stop this, yet.

He recalled the words of the letter he'd gotten from Amnesty International and heard the roar of buses as he started writing

> THE POLITICS OF POETRY
> Dedicated to James Jones
>
> After a while
> they disconnected the wire from my finger
> and connected it to my ear.
> They immediately gave a high dose of electricity
> My whole body shook in a terrible way
> My front teeth started breaking
> At the same time
> my torturers would hold a mirror to my face
> and say:
> 'Look what is happening to your lovely green eyes
> Soon
> you will not be able to see at all
> You will lose your mind
> You see
> you have already started bleeding in your mouth
>
> Torture tactics in Turkey
> an urgent appeal
> on behalf of hundreds of thousands of innocent victims
> now suffering the tortures of the damned
> Amnesty International
> USA

He gripped the ballpoint pen hard and wrote faster than ever with his crooked hand, aware that there seemed to be an unbroken line of buses groaning by, but was too engrossed, writing too quickly to even glance up.

But there is more to torture than the cell
There is a different kind of Hell

Secret hush of the police sighing
over the snail trails of bookworms
sticking
to the leaves of the library
Those fakes in pipe and tweeds
just as hard as the street dudes
only wearing a sheepskin over the weeds

He thought of Ruth for a moment, and Craig, both acting like close friends, lots of teeth.

or the lines of your smiling face
the sense of the lie
behind your grinning teeth

Take them out and dip them in a glass
swimming with solvent
murky clouds of lime
that will dissolve them in time
Dark sores on the calcium
Can't you see it?

He remembered Ruth's hurt look when he told her he had to write, then she'd said she was constipated and walked out!

Think
of never being able to say a word
for fear it will be heard
and transmuted and computed
and filed in the appropriate place
deep underground
with leaden walls to shrink your balls
catch even your cocktail chatter
or the privacy of your bedroom
where you grimace at the mirror
and cry in your secret heart

He remembered how he had sobbed over his broken hand in Spain, when the ache was so bad he couldn't stop the tears from streaking out of his eyes, then the way he had feared everybody who walked into the room.

Caught in the web
gossamer traces of it brush your face
when you enter a doorway
whispers
that still hang in the air
faint fluttering of skirts
and hum of static
the pretty girls with robes on
beckoning
beckoning

Anne Marie's beautiful sculptured face flashed in his mind, the offering of sex she gave him, and the heat he felt when he got near her.

You
like the animal come home from the hunt in a heat
the battle fought
needing love
and the musky smell of sex
carrying your offering
wrapped in puffs of cotton
with a red silk ribbon and a bow
the selfish beast
caged down inside
and the angel
let loose with beating wings so hard
it makes you thirst.

He could see her in his arms, the lovely body she'd shown in her bikini at Pata La Vaca beach, and the desire he felt. He breathed deeply now, feeling himself kiss her.

Cushion the force of my lust with your lips
the surge up the middle
the love like bone
holding my head up
and my dick

He gripped the pen, feeling the tense pressure in his groin. He could still hear the traffic and more buses coming by and he glanced up at a long line of them on the other side of the Chamber of Deputies, then leaned down and wrote.

But she doesn't love you
Secret Agent of the Police State
set out to warm your heart

He felt the desire slacken in his groin, then the bitterness
grip him again.

Listen
There is more to torture than the coffin of the cell
of that Hell
There is more to torture than the blow
the kick in the nuts
the knee in the groin
the smash in the face
the broken nose
the blood in the pee
the stiff bones and the puffing muscles
the cattle prod and the bottle up the snatch

Dear Reader
how would you like to wake up in your own
        windowless room
with your heart's blood wetting the bed around you?
the mattress seeping through to the springs
with your guts?
blank wall above you?
stone brick around you?
sunk in a concrete hole to keep the worms out?
with only the dampness to decompose you?
skin a dull yellow in the cold air?

His pen flew across the page, a ragged scrawl that he
could barely decipher, though he could have quoted the words
from memory already.

Waxy odor
The Ghoul has a painted face
With powder and rouge like an actor
he lays in the bed without flowers
without sniffling mothers
and suffering fathers with hands on their hearts

He glanced up at the wide face of Verlaine looking down
on him and thought that that man, however unhappy, had
had a better life than his own.

Without family the poet lies
The Holy Days click by
Soon his time will be up
Fold him into a drawer
some marks of his name and number
the day he died
just his scratch on the wall
and the unread poem under the bed

The bitterness of his unpublished novel, the suffering he was going through to write this one filled him and he wrote:

There is more to torture than a cell
There is a worse kind of Hell

Then the sadness of his own life hurt too much to bear to write it any longer and he looked up, saw Verlaine still looking down on him with that impish grin on his wide face and thought: What a happy guy! He lived out his life in the run-down mud hovels of the poor because he had left a rich wife to run off and write poetry with Rimbaud, only to have Rimbaud leave him. He did eighteen months in a Belgium prison for shooting Rimbaud in the wrist over it, and yet could still publish Rimbaud's poetry out of love for him and even reach out to the society that spat on him. The man's spirit was overwhelming.

Roger bent down to his notepad again, forced himself to reach into himself for some joy, some reason to keep on writing and fighting with love like Verlaine. He had to find something worthwhile to live for or he might as well kill himself. Find it! Find it! he told himself, then suddenly remembered a horse he'd seen outside Santa Cruz, California, in the foothills only a mile or two from the ocean, and how glossy its hide had shimmered in the sun and how good that had made him feel, then began to write again.

Still
a brown horse shivers his glossy sides!
twitches his mane!
swishes his tail!

Look!
I can see my shadow!

It gathers at my feet!
moves when I do!
jumps! steps! stops!
trots a little!
turns with me!
as if my toe were the axis of the sun!
and all things good!
and all things fun!
turned with it!

He looked up at Verlaine and smiled back at the man, the poet who created beauty even in his degradation, then sat up and closed his notepad. He pressed the button on the back of the pen so the ballpoint vanished in the narrow plastic cylinder, then stood up to go home and show his poem to Penny, whom he still loved, no matter what he thought she did. He hoped she *was* home.

27

She was just putting her rolled-up towel in the backpack on top the big four-poster bed when he stepped in and asked, "What're you doing?"

"I'm going home, Roger!" she said. Her green eyes were striking, highlighted by her pale-green turtleneck, but the beauty of them only made him ache when he saw the look on her face.

"The streets are filled with cops!" he said, trying to divert her, trying to keep feeling good. "I saw where they parked their buses! They've blocked off some small streets. They take up a whole public square by the Seine, two full blocks. The cops are all over the streets, not just the corners! Like an occupying army! It looks like they're expecting trouble!"

"I don't care," she said. "I'm going home."

The leaves of the big tree in front of the window screened the view of the street and the passing cars, and the sunlight glowed in broken shafts of light through the tree branches, giving him a feeling of seclusion. He could see why she hadn't seen the buses and wasn't excited.

"But, don't you hear what I'm saying? The streets are full of cops! Like an army!"

"I don't care! I just want out," she said, staring at him.

He could hear the traffic from the door where he was standing and he was conscious of the movement of cars by the glimpses of them passing through the bare branches between the leaves. He didn't see any buses.

"You mean you didn't know what you were getting into, don't you?" he finally said, and let himself face it.

She lifted her head. The glow from the windows from behind her bathed her face and made it seem very young, fresh and virginal, even childlike.

"What do you really mean?" he asked.

The green of her eyes was still sharp, but her face tightened as if she were trying to smile and soften the impact of her words. Yet she couldn't get the mournful expression off it when she said, "I went with you when I was really young and didn't know what I was doing."

She tried to smile again. "I was only eighteen and a virgin."

"Come to the point," he said. "Tell me if it's about what just happened on the street. Don't bullshit around."

He couldn't make himself tell her that he knew what was up, that it was hostile surveillance and that he'd never pull a knife again. Instead he said, "If you don't think I was justified in pulling that knife, you've got some soul-searching to do."

"But what about what you said to *me*!" she said, and jabbed her finger at her chest between her breasts.

"By the Bastille?"

"Yes! 'Tell your friends,' you said." She frowned as if she might cry.

"I'm still capable of saying that when I'm in danger," he said, all the joy he'd felt when he finished the poem and hurried home to read it to her gone now. "I've got to walk out on the street again. I'm justified in what I did! I have a right to survive!" He couldn't make himself tell her about hostile surveillance and the poem.

She looked down at her pack in front of her and shook her head. When she looked up again, her eyes glistened with tears. "Yes! Yes! But you don't trust me!" She cried and put her hands over her face and spoke through her fingers. "You treat me like an enemy!"

He walked around the foot of the bed and up to her, where she stood right next to the window nook, and reached out and touched her head, felt the fine, silky strands, then cupped his hand over it, pressed it and stroked it twice, lightly.

"Penny, I..."

He looked out the window upon a street he had no ties to, in a city where he knew no one, in a land where he, as usual, was the enemy, though it looked like he had a lot of company by the number of cops around. Then he looked down at her head again and stroked her hair and said, "In order to survive, Penny, I can't trust anyone. I have to assume that everyone is working against me or I'll be destroyed, killed or co-opted, stopped from writing, from doing the only thing I want to do, from trying to write meaningful stories and somehow, through that, make a better world. I can't take the chance on anybody, even you, stopping me."

She lifted her head and slid her hands off her face. Her fingers clung to her long neck and covered the collar of the turtleneck shirt. "But you really should get someone new then. Somebody more like you. Now that you're here. I should go home and go back to school in the fall. So I can develop myself more. So I can be my own kind of person. I don't really experience things except through you. I should go and live my own life."

His right brow arched up as he stared into her eyes. "Do you really mean that? Do you really believe that I dominate you so much you don't have your own life? That you only experience things vicariously? Or is it that you suffer so much with me you can't stand it anymore?"

She looked down at the thick rug between them, and he saw the rough lump of her thumb nail, which she kept in that permanent condition by sucking her thumb in secret.

"You said you wanted to leave me in Marrakesh because I suspected you of working with the police. Is that the main reason now?"

"We're not one! You don't trust me! It's everything!" she said.

"Do you love me?" he asked, and when she hesitated and her eyes glistened, he winced inwardly, afraid of her answer.

When she said, "Yes," he reached out and cupped her face in both his hands and said, "Don't you see what *they've* done?"

"What?" she asked, a tear spilling over her lid and down her cheek.

"They've beat us by suffering, by making both of us suffer. Me getting so much pressure I can't trust anybody, and you getting it from both ends, from concierges who jump on you to drive you away, and from me, who blames you sometimes for what happens to me, when they couldn't beat us by trying to seduce me."

"I don't understand," she said.

"I mean that they tried to get me through sex, by getting Anne Marie then Ruth to hit on me here when you weren't around and even when you were, trying to get me to choose one of them and drive you away. Then when I wouldn't go for either of them, they put me under big pressure, threatened me on the streets and made both of us so unhappy that they succeeded in breaking us up!"

She turned away and looked out the breakfast nook, surrounded on three sides by windows. He saw how her lashes seemed to sweep beyond the strong bridge of her nose in profile.

"I don't know..." she said.

"Unless you really are in on it," he said, drawing back from her, brows wrinkled together in accusation.

"No-no, don't say that!" she said, and cupped her hands over her face and began to cry again.

He caught himself, hesitated for a moment, then said, "But don't you see I'm losing you because I wouldn't go for the bait? That they punished me for not going for it and tried to get rid of you that way then? Through punishment and threats and trying to provoke me into attacking them? It's called hostile surveillance. I remembered it in the Luxembourg Gardens, trying to figure out why they didn't attack me. But it's all because I wouldn't stop writing my book, and now they don't want me to tell what happened to me in Spain either! I solved it all and came home to tell you what they were trying to do."

She looked through her tears at him and asked, "You didn't do anything with either of them? Ruth or Anne Marie?"

"No! And that's a fact! And that's why I caught so much hell after I put both of them down."

"A lot of things did happen all together," she said, facing him again.

"Penny!" he said, and put both his hands on her shoulders. "I figured it all out in the park! And I wrote this poem! Do you want to hear it?"

Her eyes were murky now, the whites streaked with red. "Yes," she said, so softly he barely heard it. But he let go of her and reached into his back pocket and pulled the note pad out. He looked up at her once, then began to read from the small pad on which he'd filled pages with the familiar scribble, written as fast as he could get it down.

He glanced up at her eyes with the harsh words, "Look what is happening to your lovely green eyes," and saw just the slightest, quickest blink, but kept reading, his voice rising and falling and softening and coming near a shout at times. He glanced up at her face after each stanza, and again, too, when he read "the sense of the lie/ behind your grinning teeth."

But she didn't blink; her gaze was steady, her attention complete. He went on and on, feeling the hypnotic sound of his own voice, and saw that she never at any time looked away. And his voice full of power, he saw her eyes narrow as if she loved it when he said, "...and the angel/ let loose with beating wings so hard/ it makes you thirst!" They widened when he said, "But she doesn't love you/ secret agent of the Police State/ set out to warm your heart."

He gave it all then, full of warmth for her warmth and, just when his voice dropped into a drone with "Without family the poet lies," he felt her sympathy, and he finished off the last two stanzas of hope with a rousing tone. He then lowered the page and looked up at her, smiling.

She had tears in her eyes, but she was smiling, too.

"It's beautiful, Roger!" she said. "You're beautiful!"

"Don't go home, Penny," he said in a soft voice, and made no attempt to touch her. "My chest aches with my love for you. I'm almost through with my novel anyway, but it's not worth it without you."

She swallowed and asked, "Do you really love me that much?"

"Yes, I do," he answered. "That much."

She wiped her eyes with the back of her hand and said, "Then, I'll try this one last time, Roger. I'll try just one more final time. But just one more time! That's all!"

He nodded and took a deep breath to keep the tears down.

28

There had to be ten-thousand uniformed men with different uniforms for different police corps thronging the main center of the Latin Quarter where the Boulevard St. Michelle crossed over the Seine. The cops with the plastic bubbles over their heads were the scariest. In their hands, they held long rubber clubs that curved like sabers at the ends.

Other cops wore small caps like Foreign Legionnaires and also carried long, rubber truncheons. There were cops in pale-blue helmets and uniforms who looked like American cops and carried wooden clubs at least four feet long. There were variations of these uniforms, some cops wearing differently colored caps and carrying different kinds of clubs. But they all lined the boulevard and gathered in groups at corners, and their buses filled the two small blocks of the square.

"Fascisti! Fascisti!" the Devil's Advocate yelled, beckoning to Roger to join him as soon as Roger and Penny reached the open-air cafe on the corner across the street from the bridge over the Seine. Roger hadn't seen him since that day at the Sorbonne when he'd told him his book was published in French. His narrow face was dark and as sharp and pointed as his nose as he raised his fist now at the people in the blue, open convertible which was leading the Pompidou victory parade at night. It had pictures of Pompidou on its doors and its horn honking. All the cars behind it were honking, too, far up brightly lighted St. Michelle Boulevard.

Nicole, the blonde with the cold face, and Anton, the soft-eyed kid in the horn-rimmed glasses, shouted, too, then looked at Roger and jerked their fists to encourage him to shout, too. Several other young students who seemed to be members of their Young Communist League stepped out of the crowd around Roger and Penny.

But Roger kept his arms down and his mouth shut. The Devil's Advocate was Lucifer himself, tempting him to explode against the fascist state that was destroying him. But he and Penny barely clung to each other in sadness and pain. And she was trying to brave it out one last try. He did not want to fight if he could help it. The handwriting was on the wall. He could lose her. Besides, he'd never seen so many cops in one place in his life. They formed an unbroken mass of men that filled the whole square in front of the Seine so that there was hardly any room for the civilians, who had to stand against the walls and sit in the cafes to find room for themselves.

"Fascisti! Fascisti!" the Devil's Advocate yelled at an open car, then ran out into the street, a fast, wiry figure, the full sleeves of his white shirt billowing with the movement.

Roger watched him turn to his right with the parade, run parallel to the convertible for a second, just in the very middle of the big intersection, then hop up on the back bumper.

"Fascisti! Fascisti!" he shouted, jerked on the tricolor pole, struggled with a young man in a suit and tie in the back seat, hit the young man in the face, ripped the flag off the pole, leaped off the bumper as the car reached the bridge, then ran back across the wide intersection and up to Roger, where, panting, he asked, "A match!"

"What?" Roger asked.

"A match! Do you have a match!" the Devil's Advocate said, still breathing hard.

"A match? A match won't burn that flag," Roger said, thinking of how slowly rag burned.

But the blonde, Nicole, reached into her purse, pulled out a cigarette lighter, held it under one end of the flag and snapped it on. She kept it under the tip for a few moments as Roger watched, expecting nothing. He was even disappointed that they blocked his view of the parade and was even trying to see past them when he suddenly smelled cloth burning and looked down to see smoke rising from the flag.

Astounded, he stepped back in shock when it burst into flames. A sudden crowd movement around it made him look up to see a wall of people falling on him, driven back by a force of bubble-helmeted cops with raised truncheons charging down upon the circle of students around the flag.

Roger grabbed Penny's hand but only took a step back, feeling guiltless, trying only to keep from being trampled by the crowd, when the cops suddenly burst through the outer circle of people, knocking down everyone in front of them, and one cop in a bubble helmet dashed at him, too. He turned and jerked Penny into a run across the wide, one-way street next to the darkened Seine, into the lanes of slow-moving cars bunched up at the boulevard, trying to get on the other side of the cars and out of danger, hearing the thump of clubs and the cries of the people behind him, seeing one guy go down just to the side of him, as he and Penny zigzagged from lane to lane, between the slow-moving cars, the glare of the headlights bright in his eyes, pulling Penny with him, not letting go even when, to keep from getting hit, he had to leap over the front fender of a car that screeched to a stop, but finally making it past the cars to the curb on the other side, where he jumped up onto the wide sidewalk next to the concrete railing above the Seine, dropped Penny's hand and finally slowed down. But hearing the sound of running feet, he turned around to see the same cop in the bubble helmet he'd been running from dash around a car right behind them and jump on the sidewalk, club raised to hit him, with other cops behind him, all running right at them.

"Run, Penny!" Roger shouted, and took off without trying to grab her hand this time, hearing the swish of the rubber club cut the air behind him and feeling it just touch the back of his coat with a downward slash.

"Run!" he screamed, knowing he had no time to help her and save himself, too. "Those are real cops with real clubs!"

He ran, expecting the club to hit him at any moment, sure he was finally going to get it now, as he had in San Francisco when he was clubbed and busted, wishing he didn't have on his heavy coat and boots which weighed him down, seeing all the young people next to him running, too, hearing the thump of clubs and cries behind him, lungs bursting with pain and legs aching, aching, so weak he was sure they'd collapse under him, yet finding the strength to shout, "Keep running, Penny! Keep running!"

Although hearing the pounding steps of the monster man in the space helmet right behind him, Roger looked behind him to see if Penny was safe. The face of the Devil's Advocate seemed to float along in the darkness next to him, stared at him as he shouted and suddenly jabbed out with the heel of his hand in a straight-arm that caught him on the shoulder and knocked him sidewards. Roger's legs crossed and his heart sank. He'd been set up after all. He should have listened to Fuzz's warning and stayed home and off the streets! He was going to lose Penny!

Roger staggered sidewards off the sidewalk into the glare of the blinding headlights, knees buckling, expecting the crack of the rubber club on his head, no hope of getting away. Sad, sad he'd been sold out, but fighting it out to the last step, bent

legs or not, he lurched like a drunken man further out into the
street, into the oncoming cars, bent over sidewards but still
running, body weak with fatigue, trying to make it into the
next lane where there was a gap in the cars before he fell, so
he wouldn't be killed.

Hearing the screech of the car tires in front of him, but
too much in danger to even scream, he managed to get his feet
under him and keep up, keep running until he could straight-
en up again, lungs bursting, chest burning, legs tired and
aching, but still running down the now deserted street. When
he realized he couldn't hear the thumping sound of the cop's
shoes behind him and that no one was even running next to
him, that he'd out-distanced everyone, he dared to look back.

He saw that he was a good fifty feet ahead of everybody
still running almost a block from St. Michelle, and that Penny
in her cape and sandals was still running down the wide sidewalk, too. There were no cops behind her and he couldn't even
see the cop who'd been chasing him. He was safe, safe, safe!

Roger slowed down, but kept trotting to get some distance
between him and the cops until he reached the cross street
and bridge by The Bookshop and Notre Dame. Only then did
he slow to a complete stop and lean his hands against the concrete river railing and duck his head down between his arms
and gasp for breath, trying, trying to fill the aching hole in his
lungs while still standing so he could still run if he had to.

Penny ran up to him and leaned against the railing, too,
and gasped for breath. Her face was so twisted with agony
that he didn't even try to talk to her until they had both finally caught their breaths. Then completely exhausted, legs
trembling with weakness, he said, "That was a setup if I ever
saw one. If I ever saw one, that was a set-up."

She nodded, eyes glimmering with reflections of the
streetlight on the bridge, but was still unable to talk, still trying to catch her breath.

"I couldn't help you anymore. You know that, don't you?"
he asked, reached out, and touched her hand with the tips of
his fingers. She nodded again, then put her hand to her chest
and tried to suck more air down into her lungs. She managed
just the slightest glance at him to let him know she'd heard
him. Then, after she took a few more deep breaths, she looked
up at him and gasped out: "I'm...going...home...Roger, and I
mean...all...the way...to...America."

29

The door opened and shut, and Roger knew that Penny had come back from the toilet and was about to fix her breakfast. He kept typing at the end of the table in the window nook with his back to a side window so he could get the full light of the nook on the page. He planned to stay in and write all day, afraid to leave the hotel until he finished his novel. He was sure they were watching for him and would try to get him if he stepped out as they almost had the night before. They might even try some trick to get him in the room as they had with Ruth and the Chinese guy at the last place.

"I am going home, Roger," he heard Penny say.

With his hands still on the keys, he looked over at her. She had her hands on her hips, her legs spread like a sailor, bell-bottomed jeans flaring out above the thick toes of her hiking boots, her small mouth pinched. He knew it was the last inevitable step of the trick they'd pulled last night.

"Why? I thought you'd agreed to stay and try?" he asked in a quiet voice, a sinking feeling in his chest.

"Because of last night! I told you last night. We almost got clubbed and arrested. I almost got clubbed and arrested by myself! You ran off and left me behind!"

He dropped his hands from the typewriter. "I did as much as I could, Penny. If I had held onto you after we got across the street, we would have both been caught, instead of both of us getting away. We couldn't have made it if we kept holding hands. We couldn't have run fast enough."

She shook her head, the motion rippling her reddish-brown hair. "I don't mean that you did anything cowardly. You didn't. You did the best thing under the circumstances. But still, I almost got clubbed, and I almost got caught, and I almost got put in jail, just because I was with you! Because I was following you! If I'm going to get hurt and maybe killed, it's going to be for something I believe in, not for what you believe in or say you do—though you did run off from me at the moment of truth."

He blushed and turned away from his typewriter to face her for the first time. "You have to take some risks to be free," he said, trying to keep her from leaving. Although her accusation hurt, he didn't really believe she believed it herself.

"That wasn't freedom last night. That was theatrics! Those students weren't about to challenge that huge army! I...we, you, too, almost got clubbed and arrested just so they could pretend make-believe revolution! They were playing, and you were serious. The only thing they seemed to be serious about was getting you hurt and arrested."

"You've never agreed with me so openly before. Say more!" he said.

"You said yourself it was a set-up! You always say I never believe you when things like that happen. Well, I believe you this time! I saw that guy who asked you for a match to burn the flag push you when you were running and almost knock you down in front of that car!"

She pointed her finger at him. "I thought you were going to die!"

She put her hand back on her hip. "You're just a poor sucker! You go around getting yourself beat up and bothered and persecuted and unpublished for things that nobody else even cares for! They all play the game but you! They all try and get ahead but you! You beat your head against the wall! You don't even come out comic like Don Quixote! I don't want to end up like you! I don't want to be thirty-eight years old and sad like you. Even if I looked younger like you."

She took her hands off her hips and kept talking in a softer tone.

"I'm afraid, Roger. I have a feeling that something really bad will happen to me if I stay with you. I had nightmares last night: cops with clubs chasing me. I've always been worried that something would happen to you. But last night made me see that it could happen to me, too. I don't want to throw away my life, Roger. You're on a collision course, and you're going to lose. You're going to die for nothing, Roger, and I don't want to die with you."

The plea in her voice touched him, eased the bitterness that bunched like a fist in his chest. He took off his reading glasses and rubbed his nose where the frame rested on his bridge, unable to think of anything to say.

"Look at the way they've treated you with your book! They don't want any idealists! They want people who go along and play the game! They're never going to let you be anybody until you decide that you want fame more than truth! Then they'll let you get a bestseller and glory and all those things.

Don't you see that? They treat you like dirt everywhere you go because you act as a reminder of what they're lying about! The publishers in New York and here! You've got a reputation as an *enfant terrible* that hops from city to city even without the cops! And I do believe there's cops around, maybe following us, you, I mean! The way those students set you up last night! I admire what you do, but I don't want the same fate. Can you blame me?"

"No," he said in a barely audible voice. "No, I don't blame you for that. I really don't. I can understand that. What I don't really understand is why you didn't say all this at the beginning instead of pretending that you couldn't live through me, that I was dominating you so much you couldn't live for yourself. Then, you seemed to be satisfied with our arrangement until the publishers messed me up and those cops chased us."

She blinked, then stared at him with wide eyes.

"Why didn't you say it sooner? Maybe then I could have gone and screwed the publicity girl and had it made. I wouldn't have minded screwing her and I could have gotten some new clothes and made the scene! Instead you covered up the real reasons and now I'm screwed worse than I would have been."

She pointed her finger at him again. "Don't blame me for that! You wouldn't have screwed her because you wouldn't sell yourself! You didn't want to kiss James Jones's ass either, and they didn't like your radical politics, besides. So don't blame me for that. And it's no fun going with your lover and having him see his would-be sweetheart everywhere."

"You mean Anne Marie?"

"Yes."

"Why did you say the night I met Anne Marie at the cafe that I'd recognize her anywhere, because she was so pretty then?"

"I saw you looking at those girls who looked like her. I thought they might have sent her around to take you away from me. I made the complimentary remarks about her to test you, because you hurt my feelings, because you were hot for someone else."

"Is that the real reason you're going home now?" he said, and stepped away from his typewriter.

Her mouth trembled. "It's all of them, Roger! Don't you see? They're tied together. Politics, this quest of yours, has destroyed your personal life. They'll always bring girls around you because they know you go for it. So you don't trust them or me. You don't trust anybody! You said that yourself. You idealize politics like you idealize girls, but you don't like the real thing. You want the one you don't have and mistrust the one you do have. Don't you see that?" She tilted her head with the question.

"Oh, don't you see that you're never going to find that ideal girl and that ideal land? Don't you see that?"

When he didn't answer, she dropped her hands off her hips and straightened up. "I want to learn how to live and survive in the real world. That's why I'm going."

He turned away from her and looked out the window at the tree-lined street. The maple tree in front of his window made him feel as if he were in a garden most of the time, but now he only stared blankly at it. He heard her come up behind him, but he didn't turn around.

"Yet, maybe I have a spirit like yours. I don't want to lead the dead life of my parents, either. I want to be a writer, too. I want to try and produce great art, like you try to."

He turned around now, saw her staring at him with a soft, tender expression in her eyes, as if she really did love him. She reached up and touched his cheek, stroked it softly with her fingers and said, "Beautiful, Roger." Then she suddenly dropped her hand and said, "I still want to go home, Roger. I can't let you lull me into staying here any longer. I've got to think about the future. I'm still afraid. I am really going home. I'm going to write home for money this morning."

The hard determination of her tone was too much for him to fight, and he said, "They couldn't get to me with sex and they couldn't get me with the carrot of success, but they got to you by suffering."

"Don't you see how close you came to dying last night?" she said, and reached out and touched him again with just the tips of her fingers, as if to keep him off. "I don't want you to die," she added in a low voice. "You told me Fuzz warned you yesterday about dying by the sword, and that cop almost killed you with that rubber truncheon. You almost got it then and when you nearly fell in front of the cars. About three of them almost hit you!"

She raised her voice. "Don't you see, Roger? You're risking your life!"

When he kept his lips squeezed tight to keep a sob from breaking out of him and didn't answer, she said, "I'm sorry, Roger, but I don't want to die with you. I want to live."

He swallowed, then said in a tight voice, "Everything you said might be true, yet, I love you."

Her pretty mouth seemed to open and blossom with feeling then, making him want to crush her against him.

30

"Kurt Deaver, please," Roger said in a quavering voice, trying to hold the phone close to his mouth without shaking too much, hands sweating. Fuzz and Penny had forced him to take stock, to count, to find that he had only fifteen-hundred dollars left from his advance on his second novel, a car he could sell in America, and a father who might help him, if his father was still alive. Penny was still packing in the room.

Roger was up against the wall, literally as well as figuratively, he thought, leaning against the wall by the door and staring at the life-size paper roses on the wallpaper. He was even more afraid to go out now, after he almost got clubbed and Fuzz's threat. And he was forced, if he wanted to be read, to finally kiss ass and try to communicate again, by phone, if they wouldn't write to him. They'd won in their way. Both Fuzz and Penny had made him see that. He would finish his book, but he wanted to be read. He didn't want to get hurt either. He couldn't forget that last threat about dying by the sword, then almost getting killed that very night.

"May I say who's calling?"

"Roger Leon, long distance from Paris."

"One moment, please."

He heard the line go blank, then caught his breath with a click on the line as if the phone had been picked up on an extension.

"Hello? Is this Kurt Deaver?"

"Yes," a voice said in a flat, non-committal tone.

"This is Roger Leon."

"Yes," the voice said in the same flat, unenthusiastic tone, and Roger guessed where he now stood.

"I'm almost out of money and I wondered if my book, *Kilo*, was going to be published soon so I could get the last half of my advance."

"Not that I know of."

Roger stared at the wallpaper and tried to think. He wanted to ask about the Paris publication, then. Wasn't he due an advance on that? And he wanted to know if they'd like to see his new political novel, too. But the guy was so unenthusiastic that Roger stuck to the point about the book they'd already given him money on.

"Wasn't it supposed to be published last January, according to your letters? And serialized or at least previewed in *Forest Review?*"

"I don't remember," the voice said.

Roger pictured a bespectacled intellectual speaking over the phone. He'd never met Kurt Deaver, as he'd never met his agent, and he could only fantasize how they might look. But he was hurting too much to worry about that. Fuzz was right. So was Penny.

"Then you have no plans to publish it? No specific date?"

"No," the voice said.

Roger ran the crooked tip of his swollen finger around the lined mouth of the rose, around and around, trying to keep his temper, trying to be sensible and stick to business.

"What do I have to do to get a date set for it?" he asked.

"You'd have to talk to the editorial staff, probably."

"You mean in person?"

"That's the best way."

"You mean come to New York City?"

"That's where we are," the voice said with a sarcastic ring.

Roger backed his crooked finger out of the rose, twirled it around and around the petaled lips in a widening circle, then stopped.

"Can I talk to the publicity manager now?" he asked, picturing the tall, bald, pleasant man he'd met twice in San Francisco.

"He's out to lunch."

"How about the sales manager?" Roger asked, thinking of the short, husky, very young man who was dynamic but very egotistical, and who wouldn't say hello unless Roger spoke first.

"He's out to lunch, too," the voice said.

Roger poked his finger into the very center of the rose's mouth, pressed down with it, bent the crooked tip of his finger back, then let up and said in a trembling voice: "I...I...guess everybody's out to lunch. All right, thanks for the information. I...I'll be contacting you, probably soon."

"All right," the voice said.

"Thanks, then," Roger said.

"All right," the voice said.

Roger hung up and squeezed the phone until his fingers turned white around it to keep from screaming. Then he smashed his crippled fist against the rose and, keeping himself from crying out, said, "I swear I'll finish this book, even if it never gets published. Nothing's going to stop me. I don't care if they kill me! I don't care if they beat me to death!"

31

A soft rose tone permeated the room from the burgundy rug to the rose-patterned wallpaper to the window nook with its soft velvet drapes and gave off a sweet melancholy when Roger stepped back in. He didn't feel like fighting with Penny; he just wanted to go with her. But when he said, "What if I finished my book and went back with you?" her mouth shut in a tight line.

"I want to make a clean break, Roger," she said, turning away. "If you go back with me, it'll just drag out and I'll still be involved. I want to go back and live my own life."

"He followed her around the foot of the bed, past the dark, lustrous wood posts shaped like big tulips to the window nook.

"When do you want to leave?" he asked.

"Soon as possible. I can't wait until you finish your book! Besides, with my student-body card from State, I can get a charter flight at a cheap rate." She put some alcohol in the burner, lit it, filled a small stainless-steel mess-kit pan with water and put it on the range, then adjusted the flame with the movable grill.

"When does that leave?"

"July third. I've already checked."

"Look, you just convinced me that I better get out, too," he said, not saying anything about her keeping her decision secret from him. "What should I do? Just catch a separate plane?"

When she looked back at him, he said, "I can finish the book by then. I'm almost done now. As a student, you can get a reduced fare for me, too, on that charter plane you're taking. It'll cost me twice as much to go alone on a commercial flight. I've got to go to New York now in order to get my second novel published anyway. Kurt Deaver just let me know that in simple words. I'll try to see if I can get the book I'm working on published, too. There's no way I can get it published here in Paris now."

He stepped toward her. "I don't want to stay here without you. I'll finish the book and go with you."

She shook her head, and, without taking her eyes off him, said, "I want a clean break, Roger."

His mouth drooped. She couldn't have hit him harder with a punch. "I promise I'll let you go in New York. But you convinced me. I've got to go back anyway, if I want any chance of getting any book published at all! Fuzz gave me the word and Kurt Deaver confirmed it."

"But what if you don't finish your book? Then I'll be stuck here." she said, tilting her head, then quickly straightening up. "No! You're not going to tell me when I can leave. I'm leaving July third and that's it! I'm not going to be dependent on you finishing or not finishing your book!"

"You've got a right to leave when you want to. I'm not disagreeing with that. But I know I can finish my book by then!" he said. When she started to shake her head, he added, "What if I promise to buy the tickets now!"

She stopped with her head turned and looked out of the corners of her eyes at him, then asked, "Today!"

"Yes," he said, and added, "That's how sure I am. I can be done in a week if I work eight hours a day! And I can do that! I don't want to go out anyway. The next time, they might make sure they club me!"

She nodded her head very slowly, then said, "That might be true! You almost got it, all right. And you really did get a lot of threats before that. I saw that myself."

Roger glanced at the water in the mess kit. It was just beginning to stir. "I have to go home, Penny. You've convinced me there's nothing else to do. They might even kill me when you're gone, even by accident, just like you said. One of those cars could have got me last night! I still might not even make it to a plane!"

She looked up at him. "Okay, I'll let you go back with me, if you let me go buy the tickets today while you stay in and write... so I can depend on going whether you finish your book or not, and you can't back out."

He grinned and breathed again, but tensed when she said, "But when we get to New York City, I'm catching a plane for home. I'm not staying there with you."

He swallowed, but nodded, his mouth tight, then saw that she felt sorry for him when she said, "You'll be better off without me there. Then you can screw the secretaries without feeling guilty and have yourself some fun, and maybe they'll publish your book without persecuting you so much."

He felt his mouth tighten and he swallowed again, then heard the bubbling water in the pan. Penny turned the little wheel so the flame puffed out, then put her finger to her lips, tipped her head toward the hall, walked around the bed, opened the door and stepped out onto the carpet. He followed her out and she closed the door behind him.

"What are you going to do with your dope?" she whispered.

"I don't know. My big worry's my novel, not the dope. If they've gone to so much trouble to harass me over the book, I don't want to let it out of my sight. I'll carry it all the way to New York on my body."

"How?" she asked.

"I'll stick it down the back of my shirt. I'm afraid to even leave it in my briefcase where they can touch it and get to it. I can't carry it in my hands or they'll see it and want to look at it for sure."

"What about the dope?" she asked again, still whispering.

"I've got a good half-pound left of cleaned stuff. It's too big to carry. And they'll be watching me. I could maybe trade for some hash with that Dutch dealer I've met. That would only be a tenth the size, which would help."

"They'll send you to prison if they catch you, you know."

"I know, but I do use it to write, and there's a good amount there, which would mean I wouldn't have to try and score in New York, where I don't know anybody and could get myself in big trouble. I could start working on another draft right away, without having to worry about it."

He turned toward the door, saying, "I better get working on my book now, so it's done in time. I'll worry about the dope later. I've got time." He put his hand on the knob. "You take some of those travelers' checks I've got and go buy our tickets. Since you're letting me go with you, I'll pay your way. You don't have to ask your parents for anything."

"Oh, Roger," she said, and stepped next to him, leaned her body against his and put her hands on his shoulders. "You're so good to me. I'll try to be as good to you. I'll carry it in for you. They're not after me, and I've done it before."

"You're not afraid?" he asked.

"A little bit."

"Don't do it then," he said. "I'll carry both my book and the pot in. That's better than exposing myself to the drug scene in New York, where they'll be watching me and can easily set me up. It's supposed to be real hot there. I'd hate to get busted!"

Her eyes looked a clear green in the hall light when she said, "I'll carry it in for you. I'll do that last thing for you. I really wish you luck."

"I'm going to need it, huh?" he said, and smiled.

She nodded but didn't smile, then took his crippled hand away from the doorknob and squeezed it.

"I wish I felt as strongly as you do, about everything. I wish I was as sure I was justified as you are, I mean the writing and the pot, then I'd go along with you. I'd even risk my life for you."

He took her face in his hands and lifted it so he could see it in all its rosy pinkness, then kissed her lightly and said, "I wish you did. I really wish you did, too."

Episode Eleven

SHOWDOWN

The door opened just a crack and the tall blond dealer looked down on Roger for a moment with slightly hooded, pale-brown eyes and a beak-nosed, expressionless face. Roger looked him over, too. With a good half pound of kif tucked into his armpit under his brown coat, Roger had as much to worry about as this tall Dutchman that he'd met at the sidewalk cafe by The Bookshop and from whom he had never bought dope.

He had doubled back around a couple of blocks a couple of times to see if he was being followed and didn't go down any of his usual streets either, just to keep them from springing a trap. He didn't speak, letting his silence do the talking for him, and the Dutchman finally nodded and opened the door.

The tiny second-floor room had a view of the Seine with its concrete banks and the book stands lining it. The water looked oily-gray like the sky. Traffic noises on the one-way street below were muffled by the tall, narrow, closed windows, and the traffic on the opposite bank, next to the marble police station and jail, moved as soundlessly as toy cars.

"I'd like to make a deal," Roger said, turning to face the Dutchman. He knew he was taking a big chance. The Dutchman might inform on him.

"What kind of deal?" the Dutchman said, covering his mouth with his hand. The tip of his bumpy nose hooked over his fingers.

"I've got a half pound of kif with me. I'll trade you for some hash. Good hash. This is good kif."

"Hmmmm," the Dutchman said through his fingers.

"You've got a scale. Let's weigh the kif. It goes for about one-fourth the price of hash, right? The hash goes for five francs a gram on the street. And kif is harder to get and more bubbly fun, right?"

The Dutchman nodded, turned, opened a cabinet and pulled out a small iron scale with round weights. He put the

scale on top of the cabinet and placed a half-pound weight on
the back end. He then hooked the plastic bag of kif Roger gave
him to the beam end and very slowly slid the marker out on
the beam until he reached twelve ounces and four grams.

"That's three ounces and one gram of hash in return,
right?"

The Dutchman nodded again and pulled a plastic bag
filled with slabs of Red Lebanese hashish out of the cabinet
with his long fingers. He hooked up the little iron pan to the
beam again, took off the half-pound weight, put three ounce
weights on the back of the beam, set the marker for one gram,
then began to pile small, rusty-colored slabs of sweet-smelling
hashish on the pan, finally breaking the last portions into
dust until he reached the final gram. He then dumped the
whole panful into a small plastic baggie and twisted the
mouth closed, sealed it with a small rubber band, and handed
it to Roger.

"Want to smoke a pipe?" the Dutchman asked.

Roger nodded, now having to proceed as if the police
might find out from the Dutchman that he had switched from
kif to hash to smuggle it into the United States. He knew they
had followed him and might even know exactly where he was
in the strange hotel at this particular moment. He was risking
his life for dope again, for the creative state of being he used
to write with, something he'd done all his adult life.

The Dutchman sucked on the little pipe and a puff of
smoke came out of the small bowl. He held his breath and
handed the pipe to Roger, who took a quick, deep hit and felt
the solid pull in his lungs, a small hurt that told him the hash
was potent. When he pulled the pipe quickly away to hand it
back without taking another toke, the Dutchman smiled at his
reaction. Roger guessed that if the police had followed him
and the guy didn't cooperate with them, they might think he'd
sold his remaining kif to the guy, which could help protect
him. The Dutchman took another deep toke, then two, then
three, and covered his mouth with his hand to keep it in.

Roger took it from him again and, as he inhaled, narrowed his eyes with the thought that he was clean now, except
for the small packet of hash and the crumblings of kif leaves
that during the year had fallen through the hole in his jacket
pocket into the jacket lining. Penny was carrying the hash in,
and they weren't after her—they only wanted him. They

couldn't bust him for taking in his now-finished book, but they could give him trouble if they got their hands on it, maybe confiscating it and accidentally losing it. Anything. So he'd carry it in on his body, do or die.

2

Roger pulled his hand out of his pants pocket and looked around for anybody that might try to jump him or shadow him in the large, almost empty, tile-floored room. It's walls were lined with baggage lockers. The Paris station had to be for charter buses only, for there was no ticket counter and no crowds of people hanging around. The only employee was a man at the baggage stand in a little alcove.

"Do you have any change for the locker?" Roger asked. Penny took her purse out of her straw bag and opened it, looked in, then shook her head.

"I'll get some change from the guy in the baggage room," he said. "But maybe you ought to come with me just in case he doesn't have any and I have to check the bags there. I don't want to have to watch these bags for three hours until our bus leaves. It's job enough carrying the novel against my back."

He wanted to get away with his book without getting hurt, and carried the thick manuscript in the small of his back, flat against his skin, just above the beltline. It was wrapped in a plastic bag to keep off the sweat.

"All right," she said, and, picking up her bag, followed him the hundred feet to the baggage room where he put down his typewriter and handed the thin man in the gray apron a fifty-franc note.

"Change, please," he said.

"Non," the man said, and handed him back the note, shaking his head.

"What?" Roger asked, suspecting some trick. "Why not?"

"Non!" the man said again, and Roger picked up his typewriter and turned away, angry, but was blocked by a tall man and a woman, both very thin, in dress clothes. Fight! he thought. They're going to jump me with my pack on my back!

"Check it there!" the woman said, pushing against his typewriter with her leg, as if intent on pushing him into doing what she said rather than just helping him to check his baggage.

Roger took a step to go around her, but the tall man blocked him and wouldn't move. He could have been her brother, he looked so much like her. He had the same sharp face and dark hair. Penny was standing on the other side of the woman, blocking him, too, and just for a moment, he suspected something. He wondered if the blond Dutchman had already told. The maid had left the big vacuum cleaner out in front of his room all day, too, like a subtle hint to clean up from Fuzz.

Roger glanced at Penny. She stood right in line with them, completely blocking his way out with the backpack. Yet, she carried all the hashish now, crushed in a plastic bag inside her purse. He was clean. He just didn't want to have to watch the heavy bags for over three hours and have to carry them around while they found someplace to eat. It was a cop trick for sure to search his bags and find out where he was carrying his dope. But if they searched them now, they wouldn't search them at customs in New York, and he didn't want trouble, not when she was carrying the dope, small as it was.

Roger turned back around and put his typewriter and his briefcase on the counter, then slid out of his backpack and swung it on the counter, too. He felt his thick book tighten against his back under the shirt when he straightened his arms and pushed the pack to the guy.

"Check yours, Penny," he said, and took his stubs from the baggage man. He noticed that the tall man and woman stood next to the counter with their small handbags and watched closely. But he had to take the chance. There was no dope in the bags he was checking, and his book was stuffed into the back of his shirt, held in place by his belt. He was clean except for a couple of joints of kif he planned to smoke on the way. And he wasn't worried about Penny now, either.

3

Roger's stomach fluttered like a nest of butterflies and his hands glistened with sweat with the pilot's words over the speaker above him: "...will land in five minutes at Kennedy International Airport."

Penny glanced at him as if she felt the tension, too. They had hardly talked during the long journey, and now again she didn't speak, just looked at him. She got up and, carrying her purse, walked back down the long aisle to the lavatory to transfer the hash from the plastic baggie to her powder box. They already knew it would fit. She had only to dump out the powder in the box and pour the hash in. Once on the other side, he might never see her again.

Roger had watched her sleep all night, the way one spends the last minutes with a dying brother before he passes away, out of sight forever. He had stayed awake the long bus ride to Brussels. He missed her with a huge ache already. He knew how much he loved her, but he knew he could not trust her in the end, like Che and Tania. She would forever be suspect. He would always have to go on alone. It hurt.

He watched her carefully when she returned for any signs of fear on her face, but saw only the long, unsmiling sadness of it. She had already smuggled kif from Morocco into Spain and seemed to have no fear, only sadness at leaving him forever. He had that sadness, but he was scared, too, and he wiped his sweaty hands on his thighs. He was being forced back into a country now under the control of a fascist Republican administration, one which had persecuted him since it had taken control. They had run him to the ground in not quite a year, ending his rebellion in exile. He was approaching the fascist fist of the state on Independence Day!

Roger fastened his seat belt, held his breath and seemed to leave his stomach in the air behind him when the plane dropped down for the landing. He felt so weak he didn't want to get out of his seat when the plane landed and all the students started gathering their bags and moving down the aisle. His stomach was fluttering again, queasy, with just a touch of nausea and nervousness from no sleep the long night. A nightmare world was just beyond the transparent veil in his head. He wouldn't be surprised to see monster cops with guns drawn run down the aisle at him. Just on the edge of reality, between sleep and waking, he could feel the subconscious now like a demon inside his head. Anything could happen, and it would all seem unreal, even his own death. He was on the edge of death now: the separation of two lives forever.

Penny was already standing with her backpack on and her straw bag and briefcase in her hands, her purse in her straw bag. With a shiver of fear, he remembered there was a joint still hidden in the elastic band of his socks at the top of his boots. He reached down and pulled it out and flipped it under the seat in front of him. He felt the plastic covering of the book sticking with sweat against his back. It itched, and his corduroy coat, though it covered the book well, made him sweat and itch even more.

The students seemed to flow in a wide river past him to the custom booths, and he lost sight of Penny. But he didn't worry about it as he got into line. She was okay. He had to watch out for himself now and keep from showing he had something hidden under his pack. His heart pounded in his chest. He must not attract attention. He never did clean the grass leaves out of his coat lining. Maybe that could be a charge? He purposely didn't use the vacuum cleaner in the hall because he didn't want to leave traces of pot in it, though he got Fuzz's hint.

He was going to find out right now if the Dutchman had informed on him. Even if the strange couple in the Paris bus station were cops and found out he had no dope in his bags, they might guess he was carrying it on him! And he didn't want them to confiscate his book!

The middle-aged customs guard skimmed through his passport, stopped briefly at the Morocco stamp and his wrinkled eyes tightened. But he flipped past it, put it down, opened the backpack, glanced at it, then closed it and opened the briefcase. He flipped through the papers, then closed it, stamped the passport and waved Roger through.

Roger heaved his backpack on and walked out onto the sidewalk where the buses were loading to look for Penny. Students were climbing into the buses lined up in front of the customs building, but there was no Penny. He hurried back into the large room, carrying his bags, sweating with his coat and backpack on, and looked around at the counters near him. He couldn't see her there either. He hurried down the counters to his right until he reached the wall, and still couldn't see her.

He went back in the other direction, past the booth he came through, and all the way to the other end of the room, checking each booth carefully as he walked by, barely able to hold onto his bags, his hands were so slippery. Finally, when he reached the last counter, he spotted her standing in front of a young customs guard in a short-sleeved khaki shirt, with very hairy arms. The guard was going very slowly through her backpack, searching into every article of clothing, even unwrapping her socks and sticking his finger into them.

Penny stood on the other side of the counter calmly but very pale.

Hot from heat and fear, sweat ran in streams down his armpits. "Come on, Penny, or we'll miss our bus," he said, and the guard glanced at him from under heavy black brows, but kept searching her backpack.

"I'm going on," Roger said to hurry the guard up. He stepped away, sweat bubbling on his face. Suffocating with heat, smothered by the backpack and his jacket, his novel manuscript a slippery pack of sweat in the small of his back. Trying to give the impression of being in a hurry, he walked all the way back to the bus stop. There, he set his typewriter, briefcase, and his backpack down with a deep breath. Though he was taking a chance of having his bags stolen, he hurried back to Penny again, knowing as he walked through the noisy crowd that this was it! He was walking back to a possible bust! Him, too! This could be a setup, sucking him in to help-ing and then busting him as an accessory. She could be in on it! He had an urge to turn and run, save himself. But her pale face and her narrowed, worried eyes, glancing at him, plead-ing with him for help, like some nightmare vision, kept him walking towards her. Roger worked his way through the huge crowd with swift turns and body movements until he reached the counter again and saw the guard still going through her backpack. He stopped and took a breath, trying to stand as still as possible, then said, "Penny, can't you get a move on? Or we won't get a seat!"

The young, dark-haired guard glanced over at him again, but closed the backpack.

Roger pressed it. "They'll leave without us!" he said, and the guard glanced at him again, but opened her briefcase.

"There's no more time!" Roger said, and made the guard glance over at him again, though he kept going through her briefcase. The muscles on his thick, hairy forearms rippled as he skimmed the books and notes then closed the briefcase. Roger hoped he'd finished.

But the guard said, "Your purse, young lady," and Penny's cheeks went ashen white.

"I better see how the others are!" Roger said, wanting to run and scream to Penny to run, too. But he stayed there, and when the guard pulled out her makeup bag and unzipped it, tremors of fear shot through him.

"Goddamnit, Penny!" he shouted just as the guard picked up the powder box.

Penny's face flushed and the guard looked over at Roger.

"How much longer do we have to wait for you! Is this guy going to keep this up for another half-hour! Everybody's waiting! Don't you understand?"

"I... I..." she said, mouth trembling. "He... He..."

"This is my job, young man!" the guard said. He couldn't have been over thirty.

"It's not your job to make us miss the bus with our group!" Roger said. "It's not your job to pester us until we end up getting lost in New York City! I have rights in this, too! She's my mate!" Roger said, and Penny tilted her head and stared at him, then nodded.

"Don't be telling me what my job is!" the guard said, pointing at Roger, but dropped the box back in the makeup bag.

"I'm sorry for getting upset," Roger said, scared he'd pick up the box again. "But it's been a long, two-day trip. I haven't slept since night before last and I'm a little on edge. Sorry."

The guard looked at her, then back at Roger, stared at him for a moment longer, then said, "Sure," then snapped the makeup bag shut and dropped it back in the purse and snapped it shut, too.

"Thanks," Roger said, and grabbed Penny's pack off the counter and swung it onto his back to hurry him up.

Then when the guard handed her the purse, he said, "Come on, Penny," and turned away.

4

"I'm sorry, Penny," Roger said as the silver quarters clattered down into the metal base of the bus's coin box. His hands were still trembling. He was still afraid that he'd get her busted, that they'd jump on the bus after them and catch her with the hash in her bag. Busted for him. He kept hoping the bus would start moving as he turned away, and, bent over from his backpack and the two bags in his hands, still sweating in the sweltering heat, he led the way down the aisle, through the two rows of shoulders toward the bare back seat.

He put his pack and bags down at the end of the long seat and then helped Penny take her backpack off, slid it down to the end of the seat, then her briefcase, then her big straw bag. He helped her to make up to her for what he'd almost caused her. She could be locked up in a windowless room now, waiting to be interrogated and transferred to a federal jail like a common criminal. When he turned back toward her, he stared at her to convince himself she was really standing next to him.

"You saved me," Penny said. Roger reached out and hugged her, squeezed her really tight, until he felt her arms go around his shoulders and squeeze him back. He sat down, leaving room for her on the long cushion under the rear window in the full flood of the hot sunlight.

"You saved me," she said again, whispering into his ear.

"I risked you. I shouldn't have risked you," he said, whispering, too. He glanced over her shoulder out the window and saw big Fuzz step out from behind the concrete pillar and stare at him with narrowed eyes. He broke out into a hot sweat again.

"Penny!" he whispered, keeping his eyes on Fuzz. He let go of her, jerked his coat off, threw it over the backpack, and reached behind him with both hands. He pulled his shirt up with one hand and felt the book fall into the other. He swung it in front of him. The plastic wrapping was bubbled with sweat, but the pages were dry underneath. He set the book in his lap and looked back out the window at Fuzz, then squeezed the book with a sense of triumph. He had carried it against his body for two full days—the last stage in his battle to write it.

Then wiping the sweat off his palms, he pressed his cheek against Penny's.

"I'm going to let you go like you wanted," he said. "This has convinced me that I can really trust you and I can't risk you over my battles anymore. You're right. There's no reason you have to suffer anymore for me. We can separate tomorrow. You can fly home right away."

"It's not your fault." He felt her hand touch the manuscript on his lap. "You just believe in what you're doing, and not many people do."

"Still, you almost went to jail," he said, leaning away from her and looking into her eyes. The sun streaked across her shoulder. "I would have never forgiven myself if you had. Even right now, Fuzz is..."

"You do love me, don't you, Roger?" she said, reaching up to stroke his cheek, stopping him from speaking.

When he ducked his head to keep the sob down, then nodded, she said, "And I love you, too, but I do have to leave you. I can't be with you anymore as long as I live."

Her last words seemed to reverberate in his chest with the rumble of the bus engine from below the back seat. As long as she lived. There was nothing to say. He raised his voice to be heard and said, "I understand. I expected it. It's ironic that when I finally really trust you, you finally leave me."

"I have to leave you," she said.

"You already said you would," he said.

"I've got to leave you, no matter how brave you were to take a risk for me, and even if you finally trust me."

"I already agree," he said, hearing the peeved whine in his voice.

"When I was standing there—at customs, before you saved me—I saw what you go through. I felt what you go through all the time to do what you believe is your right: smoking and writing."

"Penny," he said, trying to keep the irritation out of his voice as the bus driver ground the gear into low.

"Let me tell you this or I won't be able to live with myself either," she said.

He put his hand on hers and waited for her to finish, trying to keep the pain down.

"I believe you now, Roger, just like you believe in me, finally. But I've got to leave you if I want to live just a normal life. I can't take this constant suffering. It's too hard. Please, understand. Please! Try to see that I love you, but I've got to choose *your* spirituality or *my* survival! Even if you did save me!"

Her lips quivered as if she might cry, and he forgot his own pain for a moment. Then he glanced out the window at Fuzz still staring at him and suddenly understood.

"Let me make it easier for you," he said. "Maybe I didn't save you. The vacuum cleaner was left in the hall for the only time we lived in that building the day we left Paris. That could have been a signal from Fuzz to clean up or get busted. I felt it then, I *believe* it now."

He squeezed her hand hard.

"Fuzz and I communicate on that level. Symbolic symbols. I'm serious," he said when she looked away. He waited for her to look back at him. "That tall couple in the bus station searched my pack when we checked it. They knew there was no dope in it. And they knew from Craig and Ruth that you took dope across the Spanish border before. They guessed that if we had any, you'd take it across. Someone saw you go to that bathroom just before we landed to hide it."

This time she didn't turn away. There was no tightness on her face.

"I think that Fuzz let you get by, not me."

"Do you really think that could be it?" she asked, her eyes widening.

"Yeah. I do. Look! He's standing right there!"

She twisted her head and looked out the window at Fuzz. He stared back. "Oh, my God," she said, and covered her mouth with her hand.

"So you better go," Roger said. When she looked back at him, he said, "Maybe if there's ever a next time, he'll bust you to punish me for not cooperating. You better go so you won't get hurt and I won't die of guilt."

Her mouth twitched again and she looked down at their clasped hands.

"I felt helpless and scared when that customs guard kept searching your bags. I think that was the point. Like I said, Fuzz speaks a secret, symbolic language to me. He knows as a poet and political activist that I pick up on it. So he uses it to communicate with me. I think he staged this to scare us both and break us up. He's standing behind us now to let us know we didn't get away with it."

Pretending he didn't see Fuzz, he lifted his hand from hers, tipped up her chin, then leaned over and kissed her quivering mouth with soft lips and closed lids. He opened

them with the smell of exhaust fumes, saw the fumes billow
out behind the bus, engulfing Fuzz in a stinking black cloud,
and he pulled away from Penny. As the bus jerked into motion
and rolled slowly away from the terminal building, he
watched Fuzz frown, then squint his eyes and turn his back to
the bus.

Roger's mouth stretched in a grim smile, but Fuzz had
still won. He was still running the show. He was driving
Penny away by pain and punishment. This was the price
Roger had to pay if he was going to keep fighting, keep writing. He looked back at Penny. Her eyes were watery with
tears. He pulled her to him and, with the aching sweetness
that kept puffing up into a sob of goodbye in his chest, rocked
her back and forth, back and forth, back and forth.